THE OLYMPIC CHARIOTEER

THE OLYMPIC CHARIOTEER

Helena P. Schrader

iUniverse, Inc.
New York   Bloomington

The Olympic Charioteer

iUniverse books may be ordered through booksellers or by contacting:

iUniverse
1663 Liberty Drive
Bloomington, IN 47403
www.iuniverse.com
1-800-Authors (1-800-288-4677)

ISBN: 978-0-595-36782-5 (pbk)
ISBN: 978-0-595-81197-7 (ebk)

Printed in the United States of America

iUniverse rev. date: 2/19/2010

Cast of Characters

Tegea

Antyllus, a Tegean landowner, politician, and horse breeder
Cobon, his head groom, a slave
Dion and Melissos, stable slaves
Phaedolos, Antyllus' son
Pheronike, Antyllus' wife
Empedokles, Antyllus' nephew, fellow landowner
Philip, a Tegean quarry slave, purchased by Antyllus
Hypathea, Antyllus' former nanny

Harmatides, Chief Strategos and Speaker of the Council of Tegea
Ambelos, his lame son
Casambrus, a priest to Apollo and Minister of Trade
Lampon, the City Treasurer
Onimastros, politician and merchant
Pisirodos, landowner and councilman
Melankomos, landowner and politician
Endoios, senior statesman of Tegea

Kapaneos, best friend of Phaedolos
Phaeax and Polyphom, friends of Kapaneos

Sparta

Teleklos, a Spartan citizen and horse breeder
Lysandridas, his son
Dorothea, his daughter
Derykleides, his son-in-law

Apollonides, Teleklos' father
Hermione, Lysandridas' bride
Zoe, helot housekeeper of Teleklos' home
Cleoetas, helot tenant of Teleklos' kleros (estate)
Chartas and Thorax, their sons
Nikandros, Teleklos' nephew and driver
Agis, Marshal of the Agiad stables, horse breeder
Thessalos, Lysandridas' childhood friend

Zeuxidamas, Teleklos' neighbour, Spartan officer
Leonis, his daughter

Chilon, Teleklos' closest friend, Spartan statesman
Perkalos, his wife
Euxenos, Spartan guardsman
Krantios, Lysandridas' battalion commander
Epicydes, Lysandridas' divisional commander
Orsiphantas, senior member of Lysandridas' Mess
Nicoles, member of the kryptea

Kyniska, Leonis' best friend
Cassandra, elder sister of King Anaxandridas
Polyxena, Spartan maiden

Others

Polycritus, Corinthinan merchant and horse breeder
Damoxenos, Athenian aristocrat and horse breeder

PART I

ANTYLLUS

CHAPTER 1

Antyllus of Tegea would not have won his Olympic victory if it hadn't been for an accident that *almost* happened at the Tegean quarries more than a year before the 56th Games. Antyllus had been Minister of Mines at the time and was inspecting the quarries because certain people had complained about the slow progress on the new theatre. The theatre was being built to celebrate Tegea's victory over Sparta two years earlier, and allegedly construction was falling behind schedule due to insufficient marble.

Antyllus did not believe there was a shortage of marble. He thought, rather, that the *strategos* who had masterminded the victory over Sparta, Harmatides, was simply trying to discredit him. Harmatides and Antyllus had found themselves increasingly at odds in the Tegean Council because Harmatides advocated radical reforms. Antyllus, as a conservative aristocrat in his mid-fifties, mistrusted change in general and opposed Harmatides' proposals specifically because he suspected Harmatides of seeking to dismantle Tegean democracy altogether. Antyllus feared that Harmatides wanted to become the first tyrant of Tegea. So Antyllus decided it would be best to go to the quarries and check on the state of things himself; it could never hurt to have hard evidence to refute any allegations of neglect or incompetence.

Antyllus drove himself over to the quarries in a light chariot on a sunny spring morning. He drove himself because he was a horse breeder and took pleasure in driving. Besides, it had been a cold, rainy winter, so he was happy to give himself and his high-strung horses an outing.

But he had forgotten how miserable the quarries were. First he had to wind his way up a difficult, steep road with many dangerous hairpin turns over sheer drop-offs, which frightened his nervous horses. Then, the closer he got, the more the white dust from the quarries—which looked like a cloud of smoke rising into the air from a distance—started to settle on him. Antyllus soon felt it dry and rough in his nose, mouth, and throat. His eyes started to water and feel gritty.

As he rounded the last turn, he faced a mountainside whose face had been brutally chopped off. The natural slope and cover had been hacked away, exposing the white interior of the mountain. Across this open scar in the landscape, insects appeared to crawl upon the near vertical face of rock. In fact, these were slaves perched on narrow scaffolding and chiselling along the lines of rope stretched across the face of the cliff.

The work of these slaves was both difficult and precarious. With depressing regularity slaves fell from the scaffolding to their deaths or were crushed in landslides. Many lost fingers to careless chisel strokes or—more commonly—to untended infections that spread from cuts. But even those who avoided accidents did not live long breathing in the clouds of stone dust and day out. Most started to go blind from the grit grinding away the surface of their eyes before they died. Only the slaves working in underground mines had more unhealthy and unbearable lives.

At the entrance of the quarries crude shacks provided squalid housing for these miserable slaves. Wooden shelves in the wall allowed them to sleep a score of men in each cubicle, and the stench from the overflowing latrines permeated the entire area. Flies buzzed about in such numbers that the horses started snapping and kicking out in fretful irritation, and Antyllus remembered why he came here so seldom.

A gigantic crane with a block of marble hanging from its hook was being swung slowly to the right by two slaves controlling the drum around which the rope was wound. Antyllus slowed his fractious horses to a walk as the slaves at the crane slowly started to slack away, hand-over-hand, lowering the giant stone gently toward a waiting wagon. Antyllus watched warily, because he knew this manoeuvre required both strength and control.

The near-naked slaves operating the crane shone with sweat, and their muscles stood out sharply—or should have. One of the slaves, however, had little muscle left. Even as Antyllus watched, this living skeleton was seized with a coughing fit. At once the other slave called out in alarm. The sick slave was losing his grip on the ropes as he crumpled onto the ground. The second slave, although a powerfully built Ethiopian, could not take the strain alone. He shouted in alarm as he was dragged forward. Any second he would either have to let go or his hands would be pulled right into the wheel and crushed. Shouting in terror and pain, he started to let the rope slide through his sweating hands.

The stone started to slide downwards, no longer carefully controlled. The ox-cart driver stared upwards in paralysed horror. From somewhere a voice shrieked hysterically.

Antyllus sprang off the back of his chariot, his horses bolting away in terror. He reached the crane simultaneously with the foreman. They both grabbed the rope, while the Ethiopian gazed at them with eyes bulging and hands bleeding. For a second Antyllus and the foreman just stood panting and holding the rope, as the great block of marble swayed in the air only inches above the wagon it would have shattered.

Antyllus felt the sweat of the foreman's body on his own arm and smelled the rank bodies of the men around him. "I can manage, sir," the foreman said as he registered with considerable embarrassment that the Minister of Mines, in his pristine, cotton chiton and stripped himation, was holding the rope with him.

Antyllus nodded and stepped back gladly. The Ethiopian and the foreman brought the stone down to a gentle landing on the back of the wagon. Antyllus turned to see what had become of his team and chariot, and was relieved to find that the drivers of two waiting ox-carts had caught his horses before they had done themselves or anyone else any harm. He went to collect them but was halted by an eruption of cursing.

Antyllus had already forgotten the slave who had caused the incident, but the foreman had not. He was kicking the skeletal young man lying at the foot of the crane and cursing him. "Bring me a whip!" the foreman shouted to the men gawking at him, and then addressed the culprit again furiously, "I'm going to kill you! You miserable, worthless, piece of shit! I'm going to beat the shit out of you, you mother-fucking bastard!"

Another slave put a whip into the foreman's hand and he set to work on the slave who had caused the accident. But the youth at his feet did not cry out or even put his arms up to deflect the blows. Antyllus was close enough to see his face, and what he saw in the youth's eyes chilled him.

"Stop!" Antyllus ordered. The foreman turned to stare at him, his arm still lifted over his head, ready to deliver the next blow. "Can't you see?!" Antyllus demanded. "That boy wants to die. You're only doing him a favour if you continue."

"Huh?" The foreman stared at Antyllus in incomprehension for a minute and then, grasping what Antyllus had said, he flung the whip aside and returned to kicking the slave at his feet.

"Leave him be!" Antyllus urged. The foreman gazed at Antyllus as if he had lost his senses so Antyllus reminded him, "I saw the whole thing.

He didn't let go of the rope intentionally. He was seized with a coughing fit, that's all."

"You don't understand, sir. This one's been nothing but trouble ever since we got him. He had to be taken off the road crew 'cause he tried to run away. You can't trust him with the wagons either—shifty, that's what he is. Sly, unreliable, and now sick, too!"

"Then I'll take him off your hands," Antyllus offered spontaneously. Of course he knew and the foreman knew that all the slaves here at the quarries belonged to the city. The foreman had no more right to sell them than Antyllus was entitled to buy them. But Antyllus and the foreman also both knew that selling state slaves and reporting them "deceased" was a lucrative side business for the foreman of any public works. And Antyllus was the Minister of Mines. If the Minister of Mines was willing to pay for this troublesome, bad slave, the foreman was the last one to protest. "What'll you give me for him, Master?" The foreman was already regretting having declaimed so thoroughly the slave's worthlessness.

"You said he was unreliable and shifty, and he looks half dead already. Add the ribs you've just cracked kicking him, and I'd say he wasn't worth more than fifty drachma."

The foreman looked resignedly at the slave spitting out phlegm at his feet and cursed himself. He knew the city paid as much as three hundred drachma for quarry slaves and sold them for more if they could. But fifty drachma was nothing to sneer at, and he could hardly bargain with the Minister of Mines. He shrugged and said resignedly, "Whatever you think is fair, sir."

"I'll send someone up with the money later. You there," Antyllus pointed to two slaves who were standing around gawking, "bring him over to my chariot —and remove the chains." This sick slave, unlike most of the others, was wearing foot shackles.

Antyllus collected his team while the foreman unlocked the fetters. He led the chariot back toward the crane, and two slaves grabbed the sick man between them and unceremoniously pulled him off the ground. Although the youth's ribs were sticking out and the vertebrae of his spine could be counted, his colleagues seemed to have difficulty carrying him. Then, with an audible grunt, they slung their comrade onto the floor of the chariot like a sack of grain. Antyllus winced as he landed with a thud and a new coughing fit was triggered. The slave rolled forward to spit out what he had coughed up onto the dirt behind the chariot, and then fell onto his back and stared up at Antyllus.

He had grey eyes under dark brows in a face that was fox-like in its sharpness. Antyllus was reminded of the foreman's depiction of the slave as "sly". More startling, he had an ugly scar running from two inches above his left brow to the inside corner of his right eye. It was the kind of scar a man got from brawling. It looked like someone had knocked him out with a rock right between the eyes. Antyllus could well imagine that here in the quarries hand-sized pieces of waste stone were readily at hand when the slaves started fighting among themselves. Or perhaps the foreman had resorted to this method to stop the evidently unruly slave from some act of disobedience. Whoever had delivered the blow had been powerful, however, because they had not only left a scar on the skin, but dented the skull itself. In addition to this old scar, the slave's lips were bleeding and welts from the whip were starting up at the base of his neck and just above his loincloth, where his ribs ended and his belly sank away like a cave.

Antyllus thought he saw the lips move, and he leaned over solicitously, expecting a "thank you" or a request for water. He held his ear close to the bleeding lips, and the slave whispered to him in a rasping, pained voice: "Don't think I'm grateful."

Antyllus drew back, offended, and then he threw back his head and laughed at himself. Hadn't he interceded because he had seen a death wish in the slave's eyes? How foolish then to expect gratitude for saving his life?

He went down on his heels beside the slave and laid his manicured hand on the dust-caked, bony shoulder. "I understand. But you'll get over it." Then he ordered one of the ox-cart drivers to keep an eye on his team—and his new slave—and went in search of the overseer.

When Antyllus had finished talking to the overseer and confiscated the accounts, he returned to his waiting chariot. The slave he had just purchased was lying face down on the floor with his head resting on his arm. As Antyllus approached, another coughing fit seized the slave. He propped himself up on his elbows, and his shoulder blades stood out like thin, brittle slabs under his dusty, sweat-streaked skin. His face grew bright red as he coughed violently. Eventually he finished and spat into the dirt.

"You'd better sit up for the ride down to my estate," Antyllus told him as he stepped over him into the chariot and took up the reins.

The slave obediently pulled himself into a sitting position, his back resting against the inside front of the chariot, his knees bent and his arms wrapped around them. Antyllus turned his team around expertly and with relief drove away from the sinking, dusty, and noisy quarry.

As he drove down the winding road toward the valley floor, Antyllus was at first preoccupied by navigating this difficult stretch without accident and by thoughts of his meeting with the overseer. Although it was hard to put his finger on the source of his suspicion, he was certain that the man was working against him. Since that was dangerous, he must have a very powerful patron—for example, Harmatides, Antyllus concluded.

Gradually the coughing of the slave at his feet, however, intruded more and more on Antyllus' thoughts. Every time the slave finished coughing, he leaned and stretched to spit onto the dirt behind the wagon, thereby jostling Antyllus. Although Antyllus made a mental note of the fact that the young man must have worked in an environment more refined than the quarries, the jostling was annoying. Furthermore, it was dangerous for the youth to hang over the end of the chariot on the rough, winding road. Despite a certain inner revulsion, Antyllus handed the slave his himation and ordered him to use one corner. "It can be washed," he pointed out.

Thereafter the slave buried his face in the himation whenever his coughing fits overcame him. The himation effectively muffled the sound and put an end to the unpleasant jostling, but now Antyllus noticed that the young man was glistening with sweat. As he had not worked for some time, it could only come from fever. Antyllus began to wonder if he wasn't transporting some terrible illness to his home and started to regret his impulsive purchase.

At last the chariot reached the valley floor and shortly afterwards left the main road. Before them Antyllus' estate stretched all the way to the other side of the broad, flat valley where the Parnos range gradually rose up toward the sky. Antyllus drove between the ploughed red earth of recently planted barley fields, until they entered the rich orchards that surrounded the house itself.

By chance, Antyllus glanced down and noticed that his new slave was staring upwards. His expression was unsettling—wide and frightened. "Is something the matter?" Antyllus asked with unease, afraid the man was having fever-induced hallucinations.

The lips moved.

"What was that?" Antyllus leaned his ear closer to the slave at his feet without taking his eyes off his overeager team, which already smelled the barn ahead of them.

"Apple."

"What?"

"Apple trees."

"Yes. Apple trees," Antyllus confirmed, unable to grasp the significance of this simple fact.

They reached Antyllus' spacious villa. It had been built twenty-five years earlier, just before his marriage, on the plans of a famous Delian architect. It was a perfect square around four interior courtyards with a magnificent colonnaded front. There was a much-admired frieze in the pediment on the Western façade, depicting the chariot race of Pelops and Oenomaus. Antyllus drove around to the back of the house, to the slaves' quarters and the stables.

The stables were housed in a separate wooden structure with a tiled roof and porches supported by wooden pillars on the two long sides. Antyllus owned nearly thirty horses including two stud stallions, fourteen brood mares, and his prize-winning racing team. To keep the horses clean, fed, and exercised, he kept three grooms. Too few, he reflected, particularly at this time of year when the mares were foaling, and considering the fact that his most experienced and senior groom, Cobon, was lame and growing old. But slaves were expensive to buy and keep, and slaves who could handle his high-strung horses were rare. He'd had more than one disastrous experience with slaves who had either been terrified of his horses, or thought they could bully them.

Cobon, his head groom, was watering two of the racing team at the trough when Antyllus drew up in the stable yard. Cobon's hip had been shattered 10 years ago in a fall during a horse race in Nemea; on the turn Cobon's mount had shied, tossing Cobon head over heels into the stone seats. For a long time, they had not been sure if he would ever walk again. Eventually the former jockey could get around, but only with an awkward limp, and he stood or sat in a crumpled posture. He had never ridden a horse again, and he was ageing rapidly. His short-cropped, curly hair was almost completely white these days.

Because Cobon was engaged with the race horses, Antyllus called for one of his other slaves, Melissos, but it was Dion who appeared. Dion was a strapping and handsome young man with a shock of straw-like dark-blond hair. Antyllus had purchased him from one of his rivals, Polycritus of Corinth, after a distasteful incident at the last Pythian Games. He was a great asset in the stables and on the whole Antyllus congratulated himself on the purchase—if only he'd been able to shake off the suspicion that his wife, Pheronike, was all too fond of the blond giant....

"Melissos sick, Master," the slave told him in a humble voice as he hastened over, evading direct eye contact as usual.

"Melissos isn't sick!" Antyllus snapped back, exasperated because he knew exactly what the problem was. "He's hung over!" Antyllus told Dion.

Melissos had gone on a binge the night before, drinking far too much wine, and in consequence he had been out cold when Antyllus called for him. This had led to Dion answering when called—just as now. But last night when Antyllus had called for help after returning from a late symposium, Dion had emerged from the *front* of the house. At the time, Antyllus had been too annoyed with Melissos to demand an explanation; but later, after he had gone to bed, the question had kept him awake. What business did a stable slave have in the front of the house in the dark of night?

The mere reminder of last night triggered an unusually harsh tone now, quite out of place in the current situation. Antyllus snapped angrily at Dion, "Don't stand about gawking! I bought this slave from the quarries. He's sick. Take him to Hypathea and tell her to tend to him."

"Yes, Master." Dion obediently came to help the new slave, who had swung his legs over the edge of the chariot floor and was trying to pull himself to his feet. Dion pulled one of the man's wasted arms over his own broad, tanned shoulders and slipped the other around the newcomer's waspish waist. Supporting him, he started for the back entry to the house, but the newcomer stopped in his tracks and stared at the horses. Suddenly, he snapped his head toward Antyllus. The penetrating look that he threw Antyllus from beneath his livid scar made Antyllus' skin crawl.

Discomfited, Antyllus hurried away.

Antyllus kept himself busy with the confiscated documents all afternoon, ordering a light snack brought to his study. At dusk, when the blackbirds called loudly in the cypress trees and the crickets cheeped in the orchards, he remembered his new acquisition, and thought he ought to see what Hypathea had to say about his condition.

Hypathea had been his nanny as a boy, and then nurse to his only child, his beloved son Phaedolos. She was over seventy now, a nearly toothless, arthritic old crone, but she had a lifetime of nursing behind her, and Antyllus swore that she knew more about restoring a person's health than the most expensive doctors.

He walked along the covered colonnade surrounding the garden of this private courtyard to the passage leading to the back of the house. Here the kitchen, storerooms and slaves' quarters were grouped around two courtyards. The kitchen courtyard was planted with herbs and vegetables, and the slaves' court was a cobblestoned yard with a wooden bench surrounding it on which the slaves could sit in the sunlight to do various chores. The laundry was hung out here as well. There were two dormitory halls, one for men and one for women, at opposite sides of a cobbled courtyard, and between the halls in the perpendicular wings a series of individual rooms for the more privileged slaves.

Antyllus found his old nurse sitting on a stool before her little room with a spindle and wool she was working. She was the kind of woman who could not stand idle hands.

"How are you doing, Nan?" Antyllus greeted her as always.

She smiled up at him and nodded.

"How's the patient I sent you?"

She gestured with her head for him to go into her chamber and put her spinning aside to shuffle after him. The room was lit only by the traces of dying light creeping through the doorway. Until his eyes adjusted to the dark, Antyllus heard only the wheezing of the slave coming from the direction of Hypathea's low, rope-and-straw bed. Gradually, he saw that the slave was sitting on the floor with his arms folded on the bed and his head resting on his arms. He drew his head back in astonishment, but before he could even comment Hypathea explained: "His lungs are so congested he can't breathe lying down."

"What disease is it?" Antyllus asked in alarm. "Was I wrong to bring him here? It won't spread to the others, will it?"

"Ach!" Hypathea made a dismissive gesture. "He has nothing but a cold! Untended and weak as he is, it has gone into his chest. It could kill him. It certainly *will* kill him if he gets no rest. But there's no risk to the rest of us."

Antyllus was relieved, and began to feel more benevolent toward his new acquisition again. "Does he need anything? You have only to ask the cook for any herbs or food you want."

"What he needs," Hypathea said with a nod toward the patient, "is a steam bath. It would loosen his air-pipes and make it easier for him to breathe."

"A steam bath?!" Antyllus was shocked. His private steam bath was one of his prides, built specially to please his young bride, Pheronike, two decades ago. Hypathea knew that the slaves were never allowed into it—except to clean it. Hypathea herself had never used it. Antyllus thought he did quite enough for his slaves already without adding such an unheard-of luxury.

"I've washed him up a bit, but we could clean him properly first," Hypathea told her master matter-of-factly, pretending she had not heard the shock in his voice.

"Yes, but—"

The coughing of the patient interrupted them and woke the slave from his dozing. Hypathea had given him a rag of some sort, and he gripped this to his mouth as he coughed into it. It sounded as if he was trying to turn his lungs inside out.

At last the coughing fit was over, and the slave sat audibly hauling air into his lungs. The air whistled loudly at each breath. Antyllus was beginning to think he would indeed die—in which case five obols would have been too high a price for him, much less fifty drachma. Letting the slave use the steam bath was clearly the more rational and economical decision, no matter how distasteful. Yet he couldn't quite overcome his own disgust at the thought of this stinking creature in his marble bath....

He looked at the slave again more carefully. Like all quarry slaves, his head and face were kept crudely shaved. Little cuts with dried blood marked where the barber had been less than careful. A dark shadow of hair was, however, starting to be evident all over his crown and on his chin, cheeks, and upper lip. Antyllus realized that he had underestimated his age before, and guessed now that he was between twenty and twenty-five years old. His eyes were a dark, opaque grey, and the scar with its pronounced dent on his forehead gave him a permanent frown.

"What's your name?" Antyllus asked, to help himself overcome his revulsion and start seeing the slave in more human terms.

"I'm called Philip."

Antyllus noted the careful distinction between his name and what he was called, but that was normal for slaves sold, as opposed to born, into slavery. The unpronounceable, barbaric names of their birth were replaced with names their Greek masters could remember and say easily. Nevertheless the name Philip, Lover of Horses, not only struck the horse breeder but surprised him, as it seemed an odd name for a quarry slave. It was, Antyllus decided, a further indication that this slave had known better times, and had only subsequently been sold to the quarries. He must have done something horrible to a former master—like cuckold him, Antyllus' brain hinted maliciously. He shook his head irritably to try to clear it of the insinuation he was still trying to suppress.

With an act of will, Antyllus concentrated his attention critically on the new slave, deciding that he might once even have been handsome—before he'd acquired the scar on his forehead and become skeletal. The bone structure of Philip's face was very fine, and he had a long, straight nose set between large, well-spaced eyes over a mouth of masculine sparseness. If not for the scar and the fact that the face was now too thin and the eye sockets too deep, he might have been very attractive indeed. And the scar—might it not have been the blow of a jealous husband, smashing his rival to the floor with the next best object that came to hand?

But this speculation was quite irrelevant, Antyllus told himself, irritated with his own thoughts, which were starting to become obsessive. Instead he asked brusquely, "Where are you from?"

The slave glared at him, but did not answer. Antyllus found himself wondering abruptly if the vicious blow to his head had damaged his brains in some way. He might even have amnesia from it.

Meanwhile, the loyal slave-nanny was shocked by such rudeness. "Answer the master!" she ordered the impudent newcomer.

The slave narrowed his eyes at her for a moment and then turned them back on Antyllus himself, and the hate in them surprised the aristocrat. "You bought my body, but not my mind or memory," Philip told him bluntly.

Hypathea had never in her life heard such impudence come out of the mouth of a slave—much less directed at the mild and kindly Antyllus. She was particularly outraged after she had gone to the unprecedented extreme of suggesting this vile creature be allowed into the master's own steam bath. Already she was regretting her advocacy. She slapped the ungrateful wretch on the back of his shaved head, croaking at him as she did so, "How dare you talk to the Master like that!"

Antyllus raised his hand to calm her. "Leave him be, Nan. He's like a horse that was abused as a colt. He flattens his ears and kicks out at anyone who comes near. He needs to learn he can trust us. Clean him very thoroughly, and then have him taken to the steam bath—tonight."

CHAPTER 2

The light of a new day was barely illuminating the sky and the birds were at their most vocal, when an old slave woke Antyllus. "Master, Master? I hate to wake you, but young Ambelos, son of Harmatides, is outside. He says you are expecting him."

The old slave, who had been tending to Antyllus since he was a youth, was torn between outrage at such impudence and distress that this mysterious meeting might be important in a way he could not fathom. Harmatides was so powerful these days....

"What? Oh, for the love of the horse-breeding Poseidon, I forgot," Antyllus groaned as he came to himself.

At a symposium the other night, attended by Harmatides and his teenage son Ambelos, Antyllus had made a foolish promise to teach the boy to ride. Ambelos needed teaching because he had been born with a club foot, and his parents had always been overprotective of him. They thought riding too dangerous; but Ambelos, knowing Antyllus' reputation as a great horseman, had taken Antyllus aside and begged for his help.

In a moment of sentimentality induced by too much wine, Antyllus had agreed to teach the boy to ride because at that moment, in his half-drunken state, he had been reminded of his son Phaedolos. Phaedolos was dead. He had been killed leading a daring cavalry attack against the Spartan Guard. To the amazement of the entire world, the attack had succeeded. The legendary, supposedly invincible Spartan phalanx had shattered under the hooves of Tegea's horsemen. Yet, while the battle had been a great victory for Tegea, it had not been cheap. More than three hundred Tegean youth had died in the battle, and Phaedolos had been one of them—one of the most courageous. Thus when Ambelos asked Antyllus for riding lessons, Antyllus had been reminded of how much Phaedolos loved riding at Ambelos' age, and he had been unable to say "no".

"Has the sun come up?" Antyllus asked his body slave now, squinting toward the window. Then deciding it didn't matter, he ordered, "Give the boy some light refreshment and send him down to the stables. Tell him I'll meet him there in a few moments."

The sun had not yet cleared the mountains and the valley was still in shade when Antyllus joined Ambelos. The youth was dressed very sensibly in a plain chiton with an equally plain chlamys wound about his shoulders against the cold. There was nothing pretentious about the boy, you had to give him that, Antyllus thought, with approval. It was not what he had expected of the son of the flamboyant, popular Harmatides. Indeed, it was a marked contrast to Phaedolos and his circle of friends, who had been wild about extravagant, bright-coloured clothes made of the most expensive imported silks.

Antyllus greeted his rival's son, and at once the boy started thanking him profusely. Antyllus waved the gratitude aside. "First let's see how we get on," he advised. "And we need to find you a suitable mount."

"Ah—would it be possible—I mean—before we do that—might I see your racing team too, sir?" Ambelos asked unable to disguise his eagerness.

Antyllus laughed—surprised by how flattered he was by the boy's interest. Then he nodded, "Of course, come along."

They entered the still dark, cool stables. The horses moved about in their stalls lethargically, only half awake. Antyllus took Ambelos to one box-stall after another, and Ambelos listened attentively to what Antyllus had to say about each horse, asking intelligent questions. He had been at the Games at both Olympia and Delphi, Ambelos told Antyllus with shy pride, adding eagerly that he had cheered Antyllus' team with so much enthusiasm that he had almost broken his ankle jumping up and down at the finish. He glanced down at his deformed foot for a second and then shook the self-pity aside by asking: "Surely they can take the laurels at the 56th Olympiad?"

"I'm not so sure," Antyllus demurred, leading them back outside. His team had come second to the Spartan chariot at the 55th Games, but taken the laurels at the Pythian Games two years later—defeating the very team that had humiliated him at Olympia. But Antyllus did not trust that victory, because the Spartan owner of the team had changed drivers. At the Pythian games his driver had made a series of mistakes.

Ambelos was arguing excitedly, "Tegea has never won the chariot race at Olympia, my father says. It would be wonderful if we could, don't you think?"

"Yes, of course," Antyllus agreed automatically. "But …"

"But what?"

"The team is getting older. Boreas was lame this past winter—though he seems better now. And I don't have the right driver. Besides, sometimes I think the Gods gave Sparta the victory at the Olympic Games in order to give us victory on the field. The latter was more important, surely?"

Ambelos considered the older man long and hard and then asked in a puzzled voice, "Don't you want to compete again at Olympia, sir?"

That was very perceptive, Antyllus noted with an inward start, but he answered evasively, "Of course I want to compete—but only if I have a chance of winning. And why do you want to be a cavalry trooper?"

Ambelos appeared to have expected the question. "I want to serve my city. And I want to prove that I'm not worthless."

"Of course you're not worthless," Antyllus countered, distressed by the boy's evident self-doubt.

"Well, what good am I, if I can't fight for my city?"

Antyllus did not want to get any deeper into this discussion, and so deflected the conversation. "Do you think we are going to have to fight in the near future?"

"My father says the Spartans want revenge for their defeat. They are likely to invade again this summer or the next."

"Is that *really* what your father thinks?" Antyllus asked with raised eyebrows and a piercing look at Ambelos. Antyllus suspected Harmatides intended to use the Spartan threat as an excuse to declare a "state of emergency" and seize dictatorial powers, but he was not so certain the wily strategos really feared an invasion.

When Ambelos insisted, Antyllus wondered if the boy himself were deceived or a tool of his father?

"Technically we're still at war with Sparta," Ambelos was continuing, anxious to show that he understood these things. "There has been neither a truce nor a treaty. They're sure to come back, when they think they can beat us. And when they do, we have to stop them like we did before—with our cavalry. Our hoplites will never be a match for the Spartans."

Antyllus shared Ambelos' (or rather Harmatides') assessment of the Tegean hoplites, but wondered if it was really so certain that Sparta wanted war. Was it impossible that the Spartans wanted peace after such a costly defeat? To be sure, they had not made any overtures towards peace—but they hadn't attacked again, either. Furthermore, third parties, who still traded back and forth across the border, reported that the Spartan kings were at odds and could not agree among themselves—something that was not at all uncommon in Spartan history. More surprising were the reports that the citizens were divided among themselves as well. There was a war faction, observers claimed, reputedly lead by the Eurypontid King Agesikles and some of the younger commanders, but there was a peace faction, too. Unfortunately, this was led by a mere citizen, a certain Chilon.

To be sure, Chilon had a reputation for wisdom that extended far beyond the borders of Lacedaemon. His advice was sought by men throughout the civilised world, and some of his sayings had already been immortalised in stone at Delphi. But the fact remained that he was only one of roughly 6,000 Spartiate citizens and had only one voice in the Spartan Assembly. He wasn't even a member of the Council of Elders. No, there was little point in putting too much faith in such a man or his followers—and certainly no point discussing it with a green boy who was only repeating what his father had said to him. So Antyllus turned his attention to the ageing mares in the paddocks to select a suitable mount for a lame youth and beginner.

Ambelos (as Antyllus had expected) was an over-eager pupil, but unfortunately (also as expected) he had no natural aptitude. He had no developed thigh or back muscles and when frightened he stiffened, became rigid, and easily lost his balance. After he had fallen off the mare at only a trot a half dozen times in almost as many days, Antyllus was relieved when one morning Ambelos sent word that he could not come for his lesson. Hoping the whole futile exercise was over, Antyllus turned his attentions to his racing team instead.

Ambelos' interest in his team and his questions about the Olympic Games had made Antyllus realize he had been neglecting his team. He had fallen into a rare depression after his victory at Delphi. There had been several factors. First, the lingering grief for his dead son seemed to have become worse rather than better with the passage of time. Next, his driver, a freedman, had been lured away by offers of higher pay from his rival Polycritus of Corinth. Finally, Boreas had become lame. Furthermore, it had been winter, not a time for training in any case. Antyllus had resigned himself to the fact that his racing days were over. He'd had a good run, he told himself. He'd almost won the victory crown at Olympia, and he'd worn it at Delphi, but now it was time to quit.

Then Ambelos came along, and for days now he had been asking himself, why shouldn't he make a last try for the crowning glory of an Olympic victory? Boreas seemed perfectly sound now. The other members of the team were younger and just approaching their peak. And they were all fat and lazy simply from the winter of neglect. He owed it to himself, he argued, to at least get them fit again and see how they performed.

Since he hadn't bothered to replace his disloyal driver, Antyllus decided the best thing to do would be to train them himself until he could hire a suitable man. As long as the team was fit, he reasoned, a good driver would be able to get the best out of them with only a little practice.

Optimistically, Antyllus dressed in a short chiton and bound a band around his forehead to keep his wiry grey curls and the sweat out of his eyes. He wore high, well-soled sandals and removed all his rings. With a smile to himself, he realized just how much he was looking forward to this.

As he slipped from his chamber he was startled to encounter his wife, Pheronike, in the shadows of the atrium colonnade. Pheronike, the bride he had brought home a quarter of a century ago, was now on the brink of turning 40. She had been very pretty once, and tried to keep her looks with creams, powders and rouge—something that Antyllus privately thought only made her look older. She also tried to compensate for her fading looks and empty nursery (for the couple had had only the one son), by giving rein to her love of perfumes, jewels, and bright clothes. Antyllus indulged her because he had nothing else to give her. They had no common interests, since Pheronike understood nothing of politics or horses, and they had not shared a couch for almost a decade now. Pheronike had her own chamber on the far side of the atrium, and she was very rarely awake at such an early hour of the day.

"I thought Ambelos wasn't coming today," she greeted him, evidently as surprised to see him as he to see her.

"No, so I'm going to use the cool air of morning to exercise the team."

"Oh. I thought you'd given up that nonsense?" Pheronike remarked.

Antyllus sighed. Why couldn't she, for once, pretend to support his passion? The rest of Tegea did. Even their son, with whom Antyllus had had many differences, had at least been proud of his father's success on the racetrack.

But Pheronike was already moving on. She waved her hand at him limply and turned away as if to say, "What do I care what you do with your day?"

With a slight shock, Antyllus registered that the feeling was, after all, mutual—except that her sudden appearance at this time of day set off that whole chain of suspicions ignited last week when Dion had seemed to come from her chamber....

Again, Antyllus told himself he was being ridiculous. Pheronike had never been one of those women to show a particular interest in sex. She had endured it more than enjoyed it. She had never once sought him out; he had always been forced to go to her. Why would such a cold fish suddenly feel the need for a hot, young, barbaric lover? The idea that Dion might have initiated any relationship with his mistress was even more absurd. The stable slaves had no contact with the mistress at all. No, he was imagining things, he told himself, and focused on the more pleasurable prospect of training his racing team.

Two hours later, Antyllus had to admit to himself that the experiment was not a success. By the time he stepped off the back of the light racing chariot, he was acutely conscious of every one of his fifty-six years. His hands were blistered and his shoulder and calf muscles ached. Worse, he had driven so badly that Cobon had walked away in disgust. No matter how competent he was driving an ordinary chariot, Antyllus had never had the makings of a racing driver. Racing called for a whole set of skills that went beyond the ordinary—above all, the nerves to take terrible risks. In part because he'd bred and raised each member of his team himself, Antyllus just didn't have the nerves to put them at risk. This was the reason he had always paid for professional drivers to train and race his horses.

This morning he had found himself checking them again and again as the horses—eager and full of élan—sought to do what they had been bred for. The only conclusion Antyllus could draw from the frustrating experience was that he had to find a proper driver, sooner rather than later.

But on the other hand, the horses were magnificent! It would be a shame not to let them make another attempt for the ultimate accolade!

So far from discouraged, Antyllus turned the team over to Cobon and retreated to the house to wash and change. As he cut through the slave quarters as usual, the sound of coughing reminded him of his recent purchase. So after breakfast Antyllus sent for Hypathea and asked about Philip.

She shook her head, her careworn face more wrinkled than ever. "I don't know what to say, Master. His breathing is almost normal, and his cough is looser and less frequent, but …" She shook her head.

"What?"

"I don't know, Master. He's not normal."

"What do you mean? Is he crazy in some way?" That blow to his head!

"Oh, no, I don't mean that. But he won't talk unless you make him— and then he only says what he has to and no more."

"Have you found out where he's from?"

"No, Master."

"But surely he's made some reference to where he was or what he did before?"

"No, Master."

Antyllus thought about this a moment, and then decided to try an experiment. "Is he well enough to do light work?"

"Yes, Master, I think so."

"Very well, send him to me in my study in a couple of hours."

Antyllus bathed, changed, and settled himself comfortably in his study. This room opened onto one of the two formal courtyards and had a small window from which he could see through the shade of the peristyle to a bubbling fountain, sparkling in the sunlight. The back wall of the study held ceiling-to-floor wooden pigeonholes for documents, all carefully ordered by topic and date.

Antyllus made himself comfortable in his favourite armchair with a curved back and a seat of sagging plaited leather bands. He spread out the draft of a new bill due to be introduced at the next Assembly on a low table before him and started to read. The bill extended the franchise to all sons of Tegean citizens, regardless of whether the mother of those sons came from a citizen family or not. As the bill was currently drafted, even the sons born to slave women would be entitled to citizenship, as long as their father was prepared to acknowledge them and pay a (hefty) fee for their manumission and registration as citizens—an absurd notion as far as Antyllus was concerned.

Furthermore, the implications were wide-ranging. First, the citizen population would increase dramatically. While Harmatides claimed this would have the positive effect of increasing the number of men eligible for military service, Antyllus feared that the bulk of these new citizens would be poor, uneducated, and unable to outfit themselves with hoplite—much less cavalry—equipment. Yet they would have an equal voice in Assembly. Antyllus feared that once they had the franchise, they would vote any way Harmatides told them to vote.

Antyllus became so caught up in trying to work out his strategy to oppose this bill that he was startled when a low voice near at hand broke into his thoughts. "You sent for me."

He looked up sharply, astonished that he had not heard the slave approach. Then he remembered that the foreman had warned him the slave was "sneaky", and he wondered how long the young man had been standing there watching him. The scar on his forehead, furthermore, lent his look an intensity that made Antyllus uncomfortable. Although Hypathea had given him a slave's short, one-sleeved chiton and an old, narrow belt, his bearing was wrong—too casual, too impudent.

But Antyllus repressed his latent dislike of the youth and tried to act relaxed. "Yes, come nearer." Antyllus sat back in the chair and gestured for the slave to enter the study and stand before him. The slave did so.

Antyllus considered him objectively yet again. His face was clean-shaven, but they were letting his dark hair grow so that he had a fuzz of dark on his skull. He was darkly tanned from the work at the quarries. He was scrupulously clean, but his feet were blackened with ingrained dirt as if he had never worn sandals in his life.

"Hypathea says you are well enough for light work. Do you agree?"

The slave just shrugged.

"What can you do?"

The slave stared at him with narrowed, resentful, hostile eyes.

"I asked you a question," Antyllus reminded him in a firm but not sharp voice.

"I can cut and set stone, work a crane, lug and carry and haul."

"I know. You were a quarry slave. But you weren't that all your life, were you?" This was stating the obvious. A child was not strong enough to be a quarry slave.

The slave did not bother to answer a question that he evidently considered rhetorical.

Antyllus was forced to put the question another way. "What were you before you became a quarry slave, Philip?" He intentionally made use of the name the slave had been given—presumably by a master prior to the quarries—hoping to remind him of a better time.

"I built roads."

The foreman had mentioned that, Antyllus remembered now, but it meant little. The road crews were also state slaves, and Antyllus was absolutely certain that this slave had been trained in a private household at some point. He had been given the name of Philip by someone who thought the name fit him, and he had been taught not to spit in places where it could offend someone of breeding and culture. Antyllus wanted to know about *that* part of Philip's life. "And before that?"

Silence.

"Before that, Philip?" Antyllus insisted.

"I'm not going to tell you."

"I could have you flogged."

"You can kill me, if you like."

They stared at each other, and Antyllus knew he had been trumped. If the young man was prepared to die rather than say anything he did not want to say, than no amount of abuse, much less threats, was going to get answers out of him. So Antyllus asked him, "Is that what you want?"

The slave shrugged.

They stared at one another. Antyllus was intrigued. All his life he had been surrounded by slaves. He had known insolent and rebellious slaves. He had dealt with sullen slaves and lazy slaves, with thieves and drunks. But he had never before found himself stared down by a mere slave. It was as if the young man opposite him did not recognise his own inherent inferiority—despite the quarries.

Antyllus rapped his fingers on the table. His manicured nails were long and made a high, rapid clicking sound, click-click-click, like a horse cantering. He needed an extra hand in the stables, especially if he were going to start training for the 56th Olympics as he was now inspired to do. But if he were to get his team up to peak condition again, it would mean extra work for the stable slaves. He'd considered buying an additional slave for the stables, even before he'd decided to compete again. Now he had a new slave who bore the apparently prophetic name of Philip. Antyllus couldn't resist the temptation: "I'm going to assign you to the stables. Have you ever been near horses before?"

The slave seemed to twitch, but the face was impassive—except for the cold, grey, strangely resentful eyes. Then he shrugged and answered, "Once or twice."

That was not reassuring. Antyllus had hoped he had earned his name by working in the stables of a former master. "Well, we'll give it a try. You know how to get there? Report to the white-haired groom. His name is Cobon. Tell him I have ordered you to help him with light work."

The slave nodded but that was all. He did not say, "Yes, Master," or bow or ask leave, he just nodded and walked out. Antyllus was so taken aback by so much rudeness that he was left sitting with his mouth open. Then he laughed at himself, and returned his attention to the bill.

CHAPTER 3

The following morning Ambelos was back. With resignation, Antyllus took up the hopeless task of trying to teach the handicapped youth to ride. He found it all the more unnerving that Philip watched their awkward lessons with open astonishment. You could not accuse the slave of neglecting his duties. On the contrary, he worked in the stables with an apparent will, and it was immediately obvious that despite what he said, he had indeed worked with horses before. He watered, fed, and then started grooming them with obvious self-confidence and familiarity with each task. Even the temperamental stallions did not intimidate him. He handled them with firm insistence without a hint of undue force, and earned their instant respect. This was all the more notable because Ambelos had not yet convinced the aging brood mare he was learning to ride that he should be taken seriously. The mare grazed quite contentedly—completely ignoring Ambelos' frustrated efforts to coax her to obey his commands.

Philip paid so much attention to the futile riding lesson that he brought Antyllus a lunge line before the latter even asked for it. He simply handed it over to him without a word as Antyllus turned to ask Cobon to bring it to him. "Did Cobon send you over with this?" he asked Philip, slightly irritated.

"No. Don't you want it?"

Antyllus couldn't deny he had wanted it, but it was slightly unnerving —as if Philip could read his mind. It was also further proof he understood more about horses than he was willing to admit. A good buy, Antyllus complimented himself, and then turned his attention back to the hopeless Ambelos.

At the house a messenger was waiting for him. Kapaneos begged the pleasure of his company—"as soon as possible." Kapaneos had been his son's best friend—and a very bad influence. Antyllus blamed Kapaneos for the fact that his son had run up huge gambling debts and spent most of his time at loud, drunken parties—and for the fact that they had been estranged in the year before his son's death.

But Kapaneos had also been the one to bring Phaedolos' body home. Kapaneos had been the one to tell his shocked, disbelieving father how he died—not like the self-indulgent young man Phaedolos had appeared to be in the year before his death, but courageously charging in among the Spartan guardsmen, giving his life for his city.

It had been the discovery that he had misjudged his son so terribly that had really caused Antyllus the most grief. In the first months after his son's death, when his grief had been so intense it had threatened to derange him, Antyllus had turned to Kapaneos. After all, Kapaneos had been grieving, too, and that shared grief had brought them together and temporarily blinded Antyllus to Kapaneos' faults.

In the last year, however, Kapaneos had come increasingly under the influence of a circle of very radical young men led by a certain Phaeax; and Antyllus, recovering his equilibrium, had distanced himself from Kapaneos more and more. He remembered again how Kapaneos had been largely to blame for Phaedolos' dissolute lifestyle, and it was increasingly hard to ignore that Kapaneos was a spendthrift as he pumped Antyllus for more and more "loans". About six months ago, Antyllus had stopped paying out, and for the last month or so rumours had been flying about that Kapaneos was heavily in debt to everyone—including the kind of people who made uncomfortable creditors.

This message from Kapaneos made Antyllus suspicious that Kapaneos wanted money. Very likely, as in the past, he intended to use emotional blackmail to try to get a loan out of his dead friend's wealthy father.

Damn him, Antyllus thought, trying to think of what excuse he could use to evade meeting with the young man. But if he gave excuses, wouldn't Kapaneos just become more importunate? Maybe it would be better to get it over with—to tell the young man once and for all that he did not intend to loan him any more money for any purpose? Besides, he could take the opportunity to stop by and see his nephew Empedokles. Antyllus remembered that he was invited to a symposium at a fellow councilman's home later, so he was going to go into the city anyway. He could stop to see his nephew on the way and discuss this bill calling for an extension of the franchise. The bill was going to go to a vote at the Assembly just before the solstice, and he had to have a strategy for opposing it before it came up for debate.

Antyllus sent one of the house slaves to Kapaneos with a message saying that he would call in the early evening before attending Melankomos' symposium. Then, after bathing, he set out for Empedokles' estate southeast of the city.

Empedokles lived in an old house, built over the generations. It was rambling rather than symmetrical and functional rather than aesthetic. The ground floor was dominated by the wine and oil presses, the cellars and work rooms. Compared to the almost bucolic atmosphere at Antyllus' estate, his nephew's house always seemed to be rather loud, crowded, and hectic. Much of that was the result of his large family, of course. When Antyllus arrived, for example, his two great-nephews were out in front practicing their archery under the tutelage of an old slave. Antyllus stopped to watch for several moments, his thoughts inevitably drifting back to when his son Phaedolos had been the age of his great-nephews. Phaedolos had been an eager archer, but impatient with his own inadequacies. When he didn't do as well as he expected, he angrily gave up and turned his attention to something else. At least the elder of Empedokles' sons seemed more dogged and determined to excel, Antyllus noted.

From the balcony of the house, Empedokles caught sight of Antyllus and called out to him. "Antyllus! What a pleasant surprise! Come join us for lunch!"

Antyllus lifted his hand in greeting and acknowledgement before disappearing into the house to mount the stairs up to the family quarters. Here on the upper floor was the long woman's hall for spinning and weaving, the nursery where the younger children played or had their lessons, and the master bedroom. The long, covered roof-terrace, stretching along the whole side of the house, was where the family gathered.

Empedokles greeted Antyllus as he stepped onto the terrace, leading him by the elbow to his wife, a woman who was now quite plump. She was spinning diligently, but lifted her cheek for Antyllus. Like Antyllus' own wife, Pheronike, she was white with make-up, with rouged cheeks and lips, but unlike Pheronike her smile seemed genuine. "It's been ages since we've seen you, Uncle," she declared. "How are you doing? And how is Pheronike?"

The mention of Pheronike made Antyllus uncomfortable. Instantly an image flashed before his mind's eye of a flushed and sweated Dion emerging from the private quarters of his house in the middle of the night "because the Mistress had sent for him." Damn it, what could she want of the virile young slave in the middle of the night if it wasn't his services? There was no point pretending such things didn't happen. In fact, they were far more common than anyone was willing to admit. Adultery with a freeman was almost impossible for the wife of a wealthy man, simply because she had almost no opportunity to come in contact with any man other than her family and slaves. But slaves were plentiful, and they were not only readily accessible, but bound to both obedience and silence....

Whatever his private suspicions, however, Antyllus assured his nephew's wife that Pheronike was "as well as could be expected", and he was glad of the distraction of his great-nieces. These three girls were sitting together in the far corner, cording and spinning wool. They were also clearly in a dither at the rare intrusion of a man (other than their father and brothers) into their secluded world. Antyllus felt a pang of guilt at the sight of the eldest, Timosa, because she had been intended as Phaedolos' bride. It pained Antyllus to think she had not found another suitor in almost three years since Phaedolos had been killed. That was not good. She must be at least sixteen already, he calculated a little scandalized, as she pulled her himation up over her head and across the lower portion of her face in a gesture of modesty—or embarrassment. The youngest of the girls, in contrast, was still immature and gazed at him with candid curiosity. The middle girl was the one who surprised him, however. She was strikingly attractive with straight dark brows, and she smiled at him with winsome boldness.

"When was the last time you saw my girls?" Empedokles asked as they drifted over to greet them.

"Good heavens," Antyllus tried to think back, "it must have been at Phaedolos' funeral—and I'm afraid I wasn't being very observant."

Empedokles nodded sympathetically. "Timosa," he remarked, indicating the eldest of the three girls, "will turn seventeen at the fall equinox." His expression was grim as he admitted this. Indicating his middle daughter, however, his expression turned to an indulgent smile and he remarked, "Agariste is fourteen and turning into quite a beauty, don't you think?"

"Indeed," Antyllus agreed with a quick glance at Timosa. It must hurt her to hear her father praise her younger sister so.

"Deianeira is only eleven and just learning to weave, aren't you, Dei?" He had a smile for her, too.

They left the girls in their corner and went to the far end of the balcony, where a slave was already waiting with chilled water and wine. Antyllus and Empedokles sat down. "Have you no suitors at all for Timosa?" Antyllus asked anxiously.

Empedokles shook his head, his lips pressed tightly together. "I've talked to Endios about his younger boy and Pisirodos, but—" He shrugged in evident despair. Then with a sigh he added, "Well, you can see for yourself. Anyone looking at my girls naturally prefers Agariste. She'll not want for suitors! So they all waffle about and won't commit themselves, hoping someone else will take Timosa off my hands and then they can bid on Agariste."

"Timosa's not a bad-looking girl, and she seems modest. Surely that should be enough?"

"Should, should. Had you ever laid eyes on Pheronike before your marriage? In our day, our fathers were more concerned about good family ties and modesty. But now everyone wants to give their spoilt sons a beauty with a fortune."

Since Antyllus had no daughters he could neither agree nor disagree, so he decided it was time to change the subject. He asked his nephew what he thought of Harmatides' new bill, and to his distress learned that Empedokles was rather inclined to support it.

"But really! Give the children of slave girls citizenship? Why the next thing, they'll be handing out citizenship to the offspring of prostitutes! What do we need more citizens for? We aren't Athens or Corinth with a fleet to man! I can see that in those cities the citizens of lesser means can make a suitable contribution by manning the oars of their warships, but what good are citizens too poor to outfit themselves with hoplite armour—much less maintain cavalry horses and equipment—to landlocked Tegea?"

"Harmatides would like the city to pay for outfitting the army—just as Sparta does," Empedokles reminded him.

"The city?!" Antyllus asked incredulous. "Where is the city to get the funds for that? Why, it is precisely the Spartan policy of equipping their army which keeps Sparta permanently bankrupt!"

"We can finance the armaments from the taxes we raise from the new citizens," Empedokles answered. "Most of the new citizens will be too old for military service, and they will have to pay based on their income. That's the clever part of the proposal, if you ask me. We can't raise the taxes on the resident aliens because if we did, they could just move away to the next city—maybe even to Lacedaemon, taking their skills with them. But if we give them citizenship, then they'll be committed to Tegea and willing to pay for the prestige of citizenship handsomely. Lampon has calculated that the city will end up with a surplus. He has all the figures. You need only ask him for them."

"I shall indeed," Antyllus declared firmly. If Lampon believed that, Lampon was a fool and a lackey of Harmatides. Antyllus did not believe for a minute that it would be possible to raise the kind of money needed, and he was sorely disappointed to discover that Empedokles had been taken in by the fine-sounding promises of Harmatides and Lampon.

Antyllus left Empedokles in the late afternoon and proceeded to Kapaneos' house in the city, arriving as he had promised when the sun went behind the mountains to the west. Kapaneos' house was relatively small and cramped. It opened onto a narrow street, and faced north. The slave who opened to Antyllus had obviously been told to expect him, and he promised to see to the horses. Because it was still daylight, Antyllus could clearly see that the whole house looked more run-down than he remembered it—and he braced himself inwardly for the appeal for a loan. He wondered just how much Kapaneos would expect, and what remembrance of Phaedolos he would use as emotional coercion. Antyllus noticed that his stomach was tying itself in knots in anticipation. Why couldn't he just let the dead rest in peace?

Kapaneos appeared. He was dressed, as always, in a rather flamboyant chiton with a heavily embroidered himation. He greeted Antyllus as had become their custom in the first year after Phaedolos' death with a kiss on both cheeks. Antyllus noticed with distaste that he was heavily and sweetly scented. His hair, too, was oiled down, and he had used kohl on his eyelids like a woman. But he looked glum. He settled himself on the couch directly opposite and clapped his hands for a slave, who brought them wine, water and light refreshments—but only things that had been bought around the corner at the nearest cook-shop and were greasy and over-salted, not to say rancid.

Antyllus helped himself sparingly. His good breeding induced him to start with the usual pleasantries, asking after Kapaneos' health, and inquiring if he had any successes at the gaming tables.

Kapaneos was pointedly incommunicative. He shrugged, sighed and remarked that his health was indifferent and that he had little "means for pleasure any more." He seemed to expect Antyllus to ask why, but Antyllus was determined not fall into that trap. Unable to keep up the small talk any longer, Antyllus decided he had been polite long enough. He asked directly, "So, why did you send for me, Kapaneos?"

"I have a legacy from Phaedolos that I have been keeping from you. I thought it was time to share."

This was going to be even worse than he had expected, Antyllus registered, his stomach tightening again. He was just starting to get over his grief. He didn't want to reopen the wound with new reminders of his son....

Kapaneos went to a wall cabinet, opened the little wooden doors, and removed a shard of pottery. He brought this over to Antyllus and handed it to him. On the inside of the pottery was scratched:

You are my joy
You are my life
Come to me tonight
No door will be closed
Not to my purse or to my ----
Phaedolos son of Antyllus

Why had he let himself get lured into this cesspool? Antyllus asked himself. Without a word he handed the shard back to Kapaneos.

The young man looked at him questioningly. "Don't you understand?"

"Understand what? That you used my son like a boy—although he was nearly old enough to be a lover himself!" It burst out of Antyllus with a fury he could no longer control. "Did you think I didn't know—or suspect—it all along? Why do you think I was against your whole relationship?"

Kapaneos looked stunned. He stared at Antyllus with large eyes that were swimming in tears. His lips started to tremble. "What is so horrible about loving a young man as beautiful as your son? Why do you want to see something dirty and indecent in it?"

"Phaedolos was almost twenty!"

"I loved him!" Kapaneos insisted. "I still love him!"

Antyllus snorted.

"Don't you understand?!" Kapaneos turned his head away and pulled his himation up over his head in a gesture of grieving. For a short second, Antyllus was almost taken in, but then his instincts got the better of him. Kapaneos' moods were too capricious. An instant latter, Kapaneos turned back on him, his eyes flashing in fury. "I *thought* you loved him, too! But now I see that was wrong. You never really loved him at all, did you? You have only pretended to mourn your son because it is expected of a Tegean gentleman!"

"That is absurd!" Antyllus declared, and swung his legs down from the couch in preparation of leaving.

"No, it's not!" Kapaneos raised his voice and shouted, "You never knew your son! You thought he was just a frivolous, self-indulgent coward. You never saw him as he really was—as I did. He wasn't the spendthrift you think he was. He was generous and self-sacrificing—dying for his city—for your wealth and position—"

"Stop it!" Antyllus retorted, so agitated that he raised his voice. He also slipped his feet into his sandals and tried to leave, but he only made it to the doorway. Kapaneos grabbed him from behind, clinging to him firmly.

"Stop! Don't go! I can't bear it! Antyllus! Why can't you give me a chance?! I loved your son. I could love you, too—if you would just give me a chance! I could be the son you lost!"

"What?!" Antyllus stopped struggling to free himself of the unwanted embrace and stared in shock at Kapaneos.

"Adopt me, Antyllus! It's what Phaedolos would have wanted for both of us! I can be a son to you. I can give you heirs." With each sentence he had lowered his voice until he had, his breath hot in Antyllus ear, "I can make you happier than even you imagine."

Antyllus broke free of his embrace with a single jerk. He faced the younger man angrily. "Don't be ridiculous!" Then he burst out of the andron and started across the courtyard. He had only made it to the far side of the courtyard before Kapaneos again called out. "Stop! Antyllus! Don't do this! Don't drive me into the arms of your enemies." This time his tone of voice was openly threatening.

Antyllus dismissed the threat with an irritated gesture of his hand, but then stopped dead in his tracks. He turned around and went back into the courtyard. Kapaneos was standing in the doorway of the andron watching him with alert eyes in a very strained face. He did not seem to know what expression to put on it at the moment.

"Who *are* my enemies?" Antyllus asked.

Whatever Kapaneos had been expecting, it was not this question. Antyllus could see the surprise in his dark eyes, but then Kapaneos threw back his head and laughed. When he finished laughing, he sneered, "What? The clever Antyllus, the wise Antyllus, the *great* politician Antyllus doesn't even *know* who his enemies are? Ah, what an old fool you are, Antyllus."

Antyllus turned on heel and left the house—he hoped for the last time.

At least the symposium hosted by Melankomos was productive and distracting. Antyllus found that Melankomos was as determined an opponent of the franchise bill as he was, and he had invited three other men who shared his views. All five of them, including Antyllus, were from the oldest and best families of Tegea, and they were all influential. Antyllus began to hope that the bill could be stopped.

Antyllus was particularly encouraged that the others, particularly the down-to-earth Pisirodos, were vehemently opposed to any military adventures as well. Melankomos even suggested that they ought to try to establish contact to Chilon of Sparta directly and see if there was not some way of opening peace talks. "As long as a state of war exists between us, the Spartan kings have the authority to call out their army any time they like without consulting even the Spartan Council of Elders, much less the Assembly. My sources suggest that we have only avoided a renewed outbreak of hostilities because Chilon has the ear and respect of the young Agiad King and—thank the Gods for the Spartans' crazy dual kingship!—the Eurypontid King Agesikles cannot act without the Agiad King Anaxandridas. But, of course, Anaxandridas has other advisors, and the young Spartiates are getting fractious and looking for ways to provoke a new campaign."

"But if things are that bad," Antyllus pointed out, "then Harmatides is not entirely wrong to want to increase the franchise for the sake of building up our own army. We lost almost 300 young men in the last battle! Our citizen body, as it is today, can hardly make good those losses—I certainly have no second son I can send, and my nephews are both too young." (He added "thank the Gods" under his breath.)

"Yes, that's the dilemma," Melankomos admitted.

"Couldn't we introduce a counter-proposal?" Endios suggested. "Something that would expand the franchise without including the more questionable elements—the sons of slave girls and non-Greeks, for example? We could restrict the franchise to the sons of Tegean citizens with Greek women of good birth, and to foreigners who have lived and worked in Tegea for 20 years. Those are the men we really want, you know, the men who have helped build this city with their labour and who have in turn built small fortunes behind the safety of our shields. Their sons should be called upon to protect the wealth their fathers have been allowed to accumulate."

There was general agreement on this line, so the five gentlemen agreed to draft a bill of their own and introduce it as a counter-proposal to that of Harmatides.

It had started to get light before Antyllus returned home. In the stableyard, he decided to leave the chariot out until the morning, but the two geldings had to be returned to their stalls. Rather than call for help and risk the humiliation of Dion emerging from places he should not be, Antyllus decided it see to them himself. He unhitched the first of them, tying the other to a ring. As he entered the barn, he almost collided with a shadow that loomed up blocking the aisle between the stalls. The horse beside him flung back his head in alarm, and tried to spin about on his haunches. Antyllus pulled him back firmly as his eyes adjusted to the deeper darkness in the barn, and he realised that the shape before him was a horse being led by a slave—his new slave, Philip.

"What are you trying to do? Run away?" Antyllus burst out angrily.

The slave looked at him, but didn't bother answering. Instead, he continued walking the horse he had on the halter toward the far end of the barn. "What are you doing? Take this gelding from me and put him away!"

Philip left the mare he was leading at the far end of the barn, came and took the gelding from Antyllus, and did as he was bid while Antyllus fetched the second gelding. After he had put the latter away, Antyllus turned on Philip, who was again leading the mare up and down the aisle, and demanded in an angry voice. "Answer my question! What are you doing?"

"You can see what I'm doing."

For an instant, Antyllus wanted to smack the impudent slave across his face, but he did not want to lower himself to that level. He was a civilised man, he reminded himself. He took a deep breath and got hold of himself. "Why?"

"Because it might help her labour."

The mare Philip was leading was Afra, the last of the pregnant brood mares. She was big with foal and well overdue. "Where did you get a silly idea like that?"

"They make women walk when they have difficulty giving birth."

The answer completely flabbergasted Antyllus. Birth, human birth, was a mystery that only women knew about. Men were not allowed anywhere near a woman in labour. Women in labour were surrounded by their female relatives, neighbours, and slaves. The fact that this young man could make this answer was proof that he could only have come from some barbarian country far beyond the civilized world. Even in Persia and Egypt, women in labour were kept well apart from their men! But that was a topic for another time. At the moment Afra took precedence. She was very young and Antyllus was fond of her. Afra was one of the fleetest horses he had ever owned, but she had proved too easily spooked to enter in competition, much less put before a chariot. He had reluctantly bred her and now put great hopes in her foals.

"What makes you think the mare is in labour?"

"Any idiot could see that."

"Are you calling me an idiot?"

"Can't you see?"

Antyllus made himself concentrate on the mare, and he had to concede the slave was right. "All right. How long has it been going on?"

"Dinner time."

"How long have you been walking her?"

"Midnight."

Antyllus approached Afra and felt along her belly. She threw up her head and thrashed with her tail, but Philip was stroking her neck and soothing her with inarticulate sounds. "The walking doesn't seem to have done any good," Antyllus noted.

"I think the foal's dead."

"Where did you get that idea?"

"It hasn't moved."

Antyllus stroked the belly again. He pressed harder. Afra moved uneasily, in pain. Philip soothed her, stroked her. But the foal did not move. Antyllus rapped with his hand on the distended belly. Only the mare responded. Again he had to concede that the slave was right, but he at once feared for Afra's life. If the foal was dead in her belly but she couldn't abort, she would die.

"It's lying wrong," he remarked out loud, more to himself than to the slave, who could hardly be expected to know how a foal should lie.

"It probably strangled itself as it turned for the birth."

"What makes you think that?!"

"It was moving at dinner time."

A logical answer. "How do you know a foal turns just before birth?"

"Babies do."

That alienating answer again.

"There's only one way to save Afra. I'll have to try to draw the foetus out of her. Do you think you can hold her while I make the attempt?"

When no answer came, Antyllus glanced up, and the expression on the face of the young slave was one of such profound resentment that he would have been angry if he hadn't been so worried about the mare. "Take her back into her stall; she'll be quieter there."

Antyllus had never done what he was about to attempt, but he had seen veterinarians do it more than once. Overcoming his inner revulsion, he stripped off his chiton and flung it over the stall door. He then squatted down and tried to see up into the mare's womb.

"You'd have more light outside," Philip pointed out.

Antyllus glanced over his shoulder. The slave was right, of course, but he hesitated to take the skittish mare outside. "You think you can keep her quiet outside?"

"Yes."

Antyllus doubted it. That was the problem with Afra; she took fright at even a sparrow! But here in the stable he couldn't see a damn thing, and he could hardly hold a torch or an oil lamp under her belly. That would drive her mad. Reluctantly, he stood and nodded for Philip to take Afra back out into the yard.

After the dark of the stables, it seemed almost bright outside. Philip led Afra toward the paddocks and stopped in the lane between them. Antyllus squatted down again and then slowly started to slip his hand inside her. Afra whinnied in surprise or pain, whimpered almost, but Philip somehow managed to keep her calm and still. Antyllus found, as he had expected, the little hooves rather than the head of the foal, and he had to shove his arm deeper and deeper into the womb to find the head and then pull this toward the exit.

It was a messy, stinking, and very unpleasant business, but the trembling little mare was worth it. And when he had succeeded, Antyllus found that he was immensely proud of himself—as if he had just won a race or an election. The foetus was definitely dead, and the umbilical cord was wrapped around the neck twice. Antyllus stared at the foetus with regret; it was full grown and had indeed killed itself during its birth. He glanced up at the slave holding the mare and their eyes met. The slave was watching him warily, waiting to see what he would do or say now that the evidence lay before them.

"How did you know?"

"My grandfather was born like that—but they could revive him."

"You must come from a country with excellent doctors," Antyllus observed, but then felt foolish. Obviously a barbarian country wouldn't have any doctors at all.

Philip shrugged and looked away, his attention on Afra again. "She needs water and feed and to be cleaned." He started leading her away.

"You need some sleep," Antyllus countered. "Take Afra to her stall and wake the others. Tell Dion to come and bury this corpse," Antyllus added with increasing vindictiveness toward the young Slav that came from his festering but unconfirmed suspicions, "and have Cobon tend to Afra."

Philip looked back at him as if trying to decide whether he could accept this gesture.

Antyllus smiled at him. "And thank you. You did more than your duty tonight. You saved her life. I won't forget."

Philip was stroking Afra's neck again and his eyes were on her, but he nodded and then timidly, almost as if he were ashamed of himself for doing it, tossed Antyllus a smile as he turned the mare and led her away.

CHAPTER 4

The incident with Afra reignited Antyllus' curiosity about Philip. He had seen for himself that Philip was good with horses, and Cobon was even mildly enthusiastic about him—something rare for the old slave. "He don't leave 'em around still sweated or without no water, Master—not like that last slave we had. Don't need to explain everything to him ten times neither, like that bone-brained Melissos. He sees something to be done, he does it." That was enough for Antyllus to know his investment had been wise, and that the three or four times the slave had been allowed to use the steam bath had more than paid off.

But Antyllus couldn't help wondering if there wasn't even more in Philip. Since the slave refused to talk about his past, Antyllus started to look for clues about him at every opportunity. Cobon and Hypathea both reported he didn't mix well with the others. The only other person Philip seemed to get on with was Dion—suggesting that the two barbarians gravitated to one another. On the other hand, Antyllus had noticed that Philip had impeccable table manners, and he made up his rough bed as if it had been a fine couch with linens. More significant, however, was his command of the Greek tongue. Antyllus, a man with a sensitive ear, found bad grammar particularly offensive, and had tried to improve Cobon's grammar for years before he eventually despaired. The language learned as a child simply could not be expunged by later efforts, he reasoned with himself. But Philip's Greek was flawless in both diction and grammar, while he had a means of expressing himself that was both concise and precise. He never used a word too many, but the words he did use suggested an extraordinarily large vocabulary from which he drew. All this suggested that Philip had served not just as a stable slave before landing in the quarries, but in a wealthy and refined household, probably at table.

The most important question from Antyllus' point of view, however, was whether Philip had learned about horses before or after his capture. If he had come in contact with horses only after he had been enslaved, than the chances were great that he had served them—but never ridden them. If, on the other hand, his understanding of horses came from the country of his birth, then he might actually be a rider. Light and fragile as he was now from half starving to death in the quarries, he would make the ideal jockey. It was a well-known fact that there were tribes to the north who were natural horsemen. Some people claimed that they were the descendants of (or inspiration for) the Centaurs. At all events, the riders of these tribes seemed to become one with their mounts; neither rearing, nor bucking, nor difficult terrain could dislodge them, and they could coax their mounts to extraordinary deeds.

What if Philip came from one of these tribes?

Antyllus knew that asking Philip directly would produce no useful reply, so he decided on a different stratagem. The next morning when Ambelos arrived, he ordered Philip to join them. Warily the slave came over. "I want you to show Ambelos how to ride this mare," Antyllus ordered.

Their eyes met. Antyllus could sense that the slave's emotions were in turmoil. He seemed to want to rebel—there was anger in his eyes—but then he turned around, placed his left hand on the mare's withers, and flung himself onto her back in a single easy spring. Antyllus hadn't been able to mount like that for thirty years, and poor Ambelos could only catch his breath in humiliation, knowing that with his club foot he would probably never be able to imitate it.

Philip pulled the mare's head up from the grass—and she did not even seem to mind. Now came the moment of truth. Most youths asked to demonstrate their riding skills would bang their heels into the mare's ribs and gallop away in a display of bravado; Antyllus had watched Phaedolos do that with every new horse he'd ever bought.

But Philip turned the mare around and trotted her away from them. He turned her left and right, making her pay attention, then trotted her in circles and in figures of eight. Only after he had ridden her at a trot for five minutes or more did he ask for a canter. Again he cantered her in circles to the left and then the right, getting her to bend properly and tuck her hocks under her. Antyllus now had not the slightest doubt where Philip had come from. He sat as if glued to the back of the mare, and she arched her neck and picked up her feet under him as she had not done in a decade.

"Who is he?" Ambelos asked in an awed and hurt voice, his humiliation and misery all over his face.

"He won't say, but my guess is that he comes from one of the barbarian tribes to the north that are virtually born on horseback. That's his advantage over you: he's probably been riding since he was a very small child. When he is on horseback he becomes one with the horse under him—both physically and mentally."

Ambelos watched miserably as Philip cantered in ever smaller circles, then widened the circles and, with a flying change, bent the mare in the opposite direction. Antyllus was moved to put an arm over Ambelos' shoulder and admit, "I could never ride like that either. I dare say, there are few Tegeans who can—your father being one of the few exceptions, of course."

Philip trotted the mare over towards the waiting Tegeans, and jumped down before she was even halted. He then looked squarely at Antyllus with an expression that was almost defiant, but strangely frightened, too. Antyllus could not imagine what he had to be frightened of after such a flawless display of horsemanship. The slave was more baffling than ever.

"Ambelos here wants to ride as well as you do," Antyllus told him. "From now on, I want you to give him his daily riding lesson. Can you do that?"

"I don't know," Philip answered.

Antyllus had not expected simple assent, much less enthusiasm, from Philip—that would have been out of character—but the answer puzzled him nevertheless. "What don't you know?" Antyllus answered patiently.

"I don't know if I can teach anyone else to ride. I have never taught anyone."

That, of course, made sense. If he had been captured as a young boy—which had to be the case because his Greek was too good for him to have been captured as an adult—then he would in his homeland still have been learning, not teaching. So Antyllus nodded, and told him to try. Then he turned around and walked back to his house, relieved to be out of the difficult obligation of trying to teach the ungifted Ambelos and extremely pleased to have found a natural rider in Philip. It didn't solve his problem of finding a driver for his racing team—the barbarians who rode so well did not even own chariots. But it did give him the option of at least entering in the horse racing. Afra, for example, might under Philip's hand still bring him an Olympic victory. Even if horse racing was less prestigious than the chariot racing, it was something. Philip could clearly take Cobon's place as jockey, and if he could calm Afra—as he seemed able to do—she was the fleetest horse he'd ever seen. They had a very good chance.…

Behind him the two young men were confronting each other awkwardly. Taking riding lessons from an aristocrat and Olympic competitor like Antyllus had been one thing, but it was humiliating to take lessons from a mere slave. On the other hand, Ambelos was also acutely aware that this barbarian slave was vastly superior to him at horsemanship. What use was it to him to be the heir to a huge fortune or the son of Tegea's most powerful and respected citizen, if he could not serve his city? Ambelos wanted to learn to ride more than anything else in the world, and he was far too intelligent to think he would be any closer to his goal of riding well if he shouted or abused the slave in front of him. Because he was too ashamed to be friendly, however, he just stood there staring resentfully at the ground.

Philip was staring at Ambelos, but he said nothing as usual, waiting for the other to take the initiative.

Finally Ambelos raised his head and met his eyes. "Do you know who I am?" He asked.

Philip shook his head.

"I am Ambelos, son of Harmatides, the Speaker of the Council and Chief Strategos of Tegea." Ambelos was intensely proud of his father, and when his words seem to have no effect on the slave, he added, "My father defeated an invading Spartan army more than two years ago." Still the stupid barbarian didn't seem to understand the significance of this remarkable achievement. It occurred to Ambelos that perhaps the barbarian didn't know about the different city-states and was ignorant of Sparta's reputation for invincibility on the battlefield. "Do you know about Sparta?"

Philip flinched as if the question in someway offended him; but then he shrugged, which indicated to Ambelos that he either knew nothing at all or he was indifferent to the differences between the Greek cities. Accepting that he could not impress a barbarian with titles that meant nothing to him, Ambelos asked, "Did I hear Antyllus call you Philip?"

Philip nodded once.

"Shall we start with the lesson then? I don't have all day. My father expects me home by mid-morning. I help him with many things." Ambelos desperately wanted to impress this slave with his importance. Instead, the slave kept glancing at Ambelos' club foot. Ambelos had lived with his hideous foot all his life, and he hated it. But at least in polite society no one drew attention to it, and no one ever, ever stared at it. Only a barbarian could be so rude! His nerves were now so completely shattered, however, that Ambelos lost his temper and demanded in a sharp and too high voice, "What are you staring at? Haven't you ever seen a club foot before?"

"No, I haven't." Philip answered as if the question had not been rhetorical. Ambelos was stunned, and his jaw dropped as Philip continued. "Where I come from, any child born with a deformity is killed at birth."

Ambelos gasped, "How barbaric!"

Philip started and looked him straight in the eye in evident amazement. His answer, after a moment of thought, was even more discomfiting. "I can see why you would think so."

Ambelos felt ice cold and then hot. He was so angered by the slave's refusal to admit that he was a barbarian that he was on the brink of giving up the whole exercise and going home in a rage. But then the slave asked, disingenuously, "Does it hurt to stand or walk on it?"

"No, it doesn't hurt at all," Ambelos answered sharply. "And there's no reason why I can't ride with it, either. It's just that no one was willing to teach me!"

Philip stared at him. "But I thought you said your father was Harmatides, Chief Strategist of Tegea, the man who led the Tegean cavalry against the Spartans?"

"Yes, exactly!" So he had heard about the battle after all, Ambelos noted with satisfaction.

"Why doesn't *he* teach you to ride?"

"Because he—he—doesn't want me to get hurt."

"Riding is very dangerous. You can't learn without getting hurt." Philip told him bluntly, but not unkindly.

"Did you get hurt learning to ride?"

"Many times."

Now Ambelos stared at the scar and dent on his forehead. "Was that from a horse?"

"Yes."

Ambelos swallowed but squared his shoulders. "I am not afraid of pain. I want this more than anything. I want to be able to present myself for muster on my eighteenth birthday. I do not want to be exempt from service."

They gazed at one another; then Philip nodded once and, turning toward the mare, said, "Start by taking hold of the reins and the mane at the withers in your left hand."

A week or so after Philip started giving Ambelos riding lessons, a court case in which Antyllus was involved was due to come before the judge. As a court case could take indefinite hours, Antyllus needed a groom to accompany him into the city and Antyllus had no desire to take Melissos. (He was still punishing him for getting so drunk the last time.) Cobon was too old and lame, and so the choice was between Dion and Philip. Dion was the obvious choice. He was reliable, hard-working, and trustworthy, but Antyllus' suspicion that Dion was Pheronike's lover had become a conviction—one he was not willing to confront. Antyllus was dealing with the situation by trying to avoid both Dion and Pheronike.

Philip was the only alternative, but Antyllus hesitated. To be sure, Philip was an excellent rider and even, from what Antyllus had seen, making progress with Ambelos. Antyllus' hopes that one day he could use the slave as his jockey in competition were growing almost daily, but the fact remained that he had only been in Antyllus' possession less than three cycles of the moon. Furthermore, he was openly insolent and, according to the quarry foreman, had already tried to escape at least once. Nor could Antyllus ignore the fact that if, as he was certain, Philip had been a barbarian, captured as a boy, who had learned his Greek and his manners in the household of a refined, educated, and wealthy man, then Philip must have done something appalling and unforgivable, or his first master would not have sold him to the quarries. Such a sale could only have been an act of anger, even revenge. It might have been something like the seduction of a wife or daughter—or maybe Philip, despite all the kindly treatment he had received from a master, who taught him civilised living, had tried to run away. This explanation seemed the most plausible, and it was what made Antyllus hesitate to take Philip with him on an expedition in which he would, for the bulk of the time, be on his own.

After thinking about it all night, Antyllus approached Philip after Ambelos had left the next morning and announced, "I need someone to accompany me into the city for a court case. Do you think you could manage the team on your own all day? Making sure they're fed and watered, and that no one upsets them?"

"Just," Philip countered sarcastically.

"Can I trust you?"

"That's for you to decide."

"Will you try to run away?"

"No."

"But you have tried in the past, haven't you?"

"No."

"Philip," Antyllus was suddenly very stern and very serious, "I have tolerated your insolence and refusal to answer certain questions, but I will not tolerate lying. If a man lies, he will also cheat, steal, take and give bribes and otherwise behave dishonestly. If you lie to me, I will send you back to the quarries." Antyllus felt quite certain that Philip did not want this. It was too obvious that he liked the work with the horses. He thought that this time he had the trump.

"I am not lying."

"Yes, you are. The foreman at the quarries told me you were taken off the road crew because you tried to escape." Antyllus left no room for doubt that this was a fact.

"That's what he believed."

"And you mean to tell me it wasn't true?"

"I didn't try to escape. I tried to kill myself."

"I don't see how the foreman could confuse the two."

"We came to a bridge over a high gorge. I wanted to throw myself into the gorge from the centre of the bridge, and they naturally assumed I only wanted to get across the bridge into Arcadia. It was an understandable misunderstanding."

Indeed it was—particularly in light of what Antyllus had witnessed that day at the quarries. Philip clearly did have a death wish, even a readiness to suicide. "Do you still want to kill yourself?"

Abruptly Philip's pride and insolence evaporated. He stood looking down at his hands as if he had just discovered that they were covered with ugly, jagged scars—souvenirs from the quarries. Antyllus waited with increasing anticipation. It would have been so easy to say "yes". Since Philip took this long to think about it, something had changed, and Antyllus wanted to hear him admit it.

"No," he answered at last.

"Since you've been working with the horses?" Antyllus pressed him. He could not help celebrating this little victory between them.

"Since I saw the apple blossoms," Philip confessed. Abruptly he looked up and met Antyllus' eyes. Antyllus remembered instantly. It was strangely moving to think that he had witnessed the very moment when a human—even if he was just a barbarian slave—had made a conscious decision away from death and toward life. Now he smiled, "And you like working with the horses, it seems."

Philip shrugged, but it was an affirmative shrug.

"They remind you of your childhood." It was a statement rather than a question and Philip treated it as such.

Antyllus, however, could not resist asking the question: "If you were willing to kill yourself, why not run away—or at least try?"

"Where would I run to? I can't go home, and everywhere else I'd only be a runaway, or at best a stranger of ill-defined status—no profession, no duty, no friends, no family."

That was an intelligent answer, Antyllus conceded to himself. After all, if Philip had been captured as a child, he might not even know how to find his way home. Or perhaps he recognised that he had been changed by civilization so much that he could never again live among the barbarians. In any case, a man who accepted he could not return home would always be an outsider without status on the fringes of an "alien" society. "Surely being an outsider in a strange land would be better than slavery?" Antyllus suggested provocatively.

"Good point. I'll think about it," Philip shot back, and Antyllus could only throw back his head and laugh.

Philip waited tensely for him to stop laughing, apparently expecting anger to follow the surprise. Antyllus felt immensely superior to be able to smile and announce. "I'm going to take you with me. Have the driving chariot out front in one hour."

Philip blinked and parted his lips as if he wanted to speak, but then apparently thought better of it. He closed his lips, shrugged and continued on his way in a gesture of pointed insolence. Antyllus wasn't offended. As he had said to Hypathea at the very beginning, he was convinced more than ever that Philip had been abused at some point and that his present behaviour was nothing but a defensive pose.

An hour later, as ordered, Philip waited before the front portico with the driving team fretting in the traces. Antyllus nodded to him and climbed into the chariot, took up the reins, and then gestured for the slave to join him in the car. Philip came somewhat hesitantly, and it occurred to Antyllus that since chariots were confined to the civilised world—Greece, Persia and Egypt—Philip might never before have set foot in a chariot, aside from that drive home from the quarries when he had been fevered and sat on the floor. He therefore took the trouble to tell Philip to stand well forward and to hold onto the front of the car if he felt unsteady. Then they set off at a brisk trot, cantering now and again as the haze burned off the rapidly warming morning.

When they reached the outskirts of the city, the road became more congested. There were wagons on the way to market, merchants transporting their wares, craftsmen and peddlers in their carts. Then they passed through the eastern gate into the congested, built-up city proper. Antyllus glanced frequently at the young slave beside him, watching for his reactions.

Philip stood immobile and silent throughout the journey, afraid it seemed even to hold onto the car, but very anxious not to unbalance in the well-sprung, light chariot. He seemed hardly to dare to move; only his eyes shifted alertly, taking in much of what went on around him. He did not seem particularly startled or awed, however, confirming Antyllus' theory that his first master had lived in a large city, probably in Tegea itself, or at least visited it frequently enough for tall walls and the bustle of activity not to surprise him.

As they drove closer to the centre of the city, the cobbles turned to quarried pavement, and the narrow, low houses of the craftsmen and small merchants gave way to higher walls, protecting the gardens of wealthier citizens. The horses had to be reined in and kept firmly in hand now. They passed smaller shrines with simple Doric porticoes, and one of the two gymnasiums. At last the theatre, nearly finished, loomed up, and for the first time Philip turned his head and looked at the building with open interest. As well he should, Antyllus thought; many of the stones facing the orchestra in neat rows had passed through his hands—maybe even caused some of the scars on them.

They turned and approached the agora. The council house loomed up on their left, with its dozen steps setting it back and above street level. The courthouse was just beyond, facing a temple to Athena. It was fronted by a long, double stoa in which the clerks, supplicants, and litigants gathered. Antyllus turned the chariot into the alley beside the courthouse and pulled up. Other chariots already waited here, and there were rings set in the walls to tie the horses. He pointed these out to Philip, and also pointed out the fountain house in the northwest corner of the agora. He told Philip to buy a little hay at the market to spread before the geldings. Then he opened his purse and handed Philip a drachma. This was ten times what he had ever given Melissos. "Use that to buy yourself some lunch and a little wine to wash it down with as well. I have no idea how long this could take, but I expect most of the day. You don't have to sit here all day, of course, but check on the horses periodically. If anything happens to them, I'll hold you responsible. Do you understand?"

"I'll do my best," Philip told him, and Antyllus chose to overlook the sarcasm in his voice. It was, after all, one of the most civil answers he'd ever received from Philip.

"I don't ask for more," Antyllus assured him patronizingly, and hastened away. As he reached the corner, he spared his slave one last glance. Philip had already tied the reins around one of the rings in the side of the building, and was unhitching the horses from the chariot itself.

Antyllus stepped under the airy stoa, which fronted the courthouse. The court clerks sat behind tables loaded with documents and wax tablets. They made a harried impression while crowds of citizens demanded information, complained about this or that, or jostled one another to get to the wax tablets with the list of trials scheduled for today.

Then a voice boomed out from the inner propylaeum: "My dear Antyllus!" It was Harmatides.

The Tegean strategos was a tall, well-built man in his early forties. He had a thick dark-blond beard, and a mane of hair bleached a fairer shade by many hours in the sun. He was tanned and his body exuded health and fitness. Harmatides was a great athlete and spent several hours every day in the gymnasium.

Antyllus simply waited warily for him. He was certain Harmatides would want to talk about the three franchise bills submitted to the Assembly. Melankomos had introduced the counter-bill, extending the franchise only moderately several weeks ago. But surprisingly, a third franchise bill had been introduced as well, this last one brought forward by a certain Onimastros.

Onimastros was a man who had made his wealth through trade and manufacturing. Antyllus liked to think of himself as a man without prejudice, and had often told himself that there was nothing wrong with either trade or manufacturing or being a self-made man. Yet Onimastros fit perfectly all the negative clichés about a man who had amassed a fortune by means that were less than transparent. Antyllus instinctively disliked and mistrusted him—just as he distrusted the bill he had introduced. This sought not to extend the franchise, but rather to *disenfranchise* the poorer citizens altogether. Men who could not afford to equip themselves as either cavalrymen or hoplites, Onimastros argued, had no right to vote on the affairs of the city.

Harmatides took Antyllus by the arm and led him through the propylaeum into the inner peristyle around which the judges and officials had their offices. The actual trials took place in a semicircular auditorium to the left. "Didn't you get word that your case has been postponed until after the solstice? I'm so sorry." He didn't sound it, Antyllus noted mentally. Rather it was as if he knew perfectly well that Antyllus wouldn't have had the news. "But since you're here, let me take the opportunity to discuss these three competing franchise bills. You've read them, I presume?"

"Of course, "Antyllus retorted.

"And? Where do you stand? Your son died in defence of Tegea. Surely you see the need for increasing the franchise, and so the men required to fight for the city?"

"Yes, but there is more to the franchise than military service," Antyllus reminded the younger man. "Men who cannot afford hoplite armour or horses are of only limited utility in battle."

"You don't have to remind me that it was our cavalry that broke the Spartan phalanx. It was our cavalry that pierced to the very centre, trampling half of their vaunted Guard and came within a hair's breadth of seizing King Agesikles." Harmatides agreed at once. Ignoring the first half of Antyllus' objection, he continued, "But without the light troops to back them up, the cavalry alone would not have been enough. We need mass as well as an elite."

"In Assembly?" Antyllus challenged him, raising his eyebrows slightly.

To his utter surprise, Harmatides seemed to like his answer. He laughed and clapped him heartily on the back. "I like you, Antyllus. You're a man who says what he thinks." He paused and cocked his head, "Should I take that to mean you support Melankomos' legislation—or Onimastros'?"

"I helped draft Melankomos' bill."

"Um hum," Harmatides answered, and then said with considerable intensity, "I would like you to come to a symposium—an intimate and, shall we say, *working* symposium—the day after tomorrow. Can you make it?" He seemed so intent on Antyllus' answer that his hand tightened on Antyllus' arm.

"The day after tomorrow?" That was the day after the traditional pre-Assembly festival in honour of Orestes (which would be held tomorrow) and the very night before the actual meeting of the Assembly at which the legislation on the franchise would be put to the vote. Only one bill could pass.

"It is very important," Harmatides stressed.

"All right," Antyllus agreed cautiously. It was obvious that Harmatides wanted to use the occasion to bring him into his own faction, but Antyllus was not averse to the meeting. It was always better to know your opponents and to understand their reasoning.

"Excellent, excellent!" Harmatides clapped him heartily on the shoulder, but he was already looking across the peristyle towards a young man who was signalling something at him. "Terribly sorry. I must rush off. An important trial is about to start. Everyone's waiting on me. I'll see you the day after tomorrow." He hurried away.

Antyllus nodded to himself and returned to the front porch. He passed by the harassed clerks and stood in the shade of the stoa looking at the agora. For a moment, he did not know what to do with himself. He had set aside the entire day for the trial. He had been looking forward to seeing what Philip would do with his day of freedom. He had no desire to return home unexpectedly and surprise Pheronike—perhaps with Dion. As for the other aristocrats, there was nothing much they could discuss now until the vote in the Assembly in three days' time. Afterwards, depending on which bill passed, they would have much to discuss, but not today.

The sight of the temple to Poseidon on the far side of the agora, where he had always sacrificed and given thanks for his racing successes, deflected his thoughts to his racing team. He had been training them for two months now, and while his own driving skills were improving, he was not fool enough to kid himself that he could drive them in competition. He really had to start seriously looking for a driver, so they could start training in the hands of someone who had the potential to drive them to victory. But far more worrying was the fact that Boreas wasn't really performing. He hadn't gone lame again, but he lacked the fire and ambition he needed. Antyllus couldn't shake the feeling that if he left Boreas in the team, he would not be able to pull off another victory. He had a four-year-old stallion, Zephyrus, who was wonderful on the two-horse chariot, but he had never put him in the harness of the four-horse chariot. And it was always risky to disrupt a team that had been pulling together for so long....

Lost in thought, Antyllus stood staring at the agora until the sight of Philip drew his attention back to the present. The slave was wandering along the shopfronts looking at the goods offered for sale. Distracted, Antyllus watched in bemusement as the young slave admired the plethora of products. He moved slowly, working his way around the agora systematically. When he had finished the round, he dutifully returned to the alley to check on the horses.

Antyllus became absorbed in watching him. He watched the way he checked the reins, took more hay from the car of the chariot, and spread it before the horses. Next Philip poured water from a goatskin into a shallow bowl and offered it to each horse, neither of which showed particular interest, preferring the hay. Then he left the horses and set off in the opposite direction from the agora. Antyllus could not resist the temptation to follow him.

Melissos, he knew, would have headed straight for the wine shops and brothels, but of course Philip did not know where these lay. All he could do was start looking. No sooner had Antyllus had this thought than he had to discard the theory. Even a stranger does not search for the brothels on the acropolis, and Philip was making straight for the sacred district.

Because Tegea was built upon a flat plain, the acropolis did not tower above the city as it did in Athens. It was not even on a noticeable hill, but it was artificially raised by steps so that it peered over the rooftops. It was thus visible from almost any place in the city. Philip went straight to this central collection of main temples and visited one after the other like any harmless tourist. Antyllus, shadowing him as discreetly as possible, noticed that he bought incense and a small trinket of some kind, which he offered to Zeus. He disappeared into the Temple of Apollo for a long time, and when he re-emerged, he was in a hurry to return to the chariot.

He again offered the team water, and when they showed more thirst, he took them, one at a time, to the trough behind the agora. Finished with the watering, he struck out again, this time towards the theatre. Antyllus was fascinated by the fact that Philip had not yet purchased anything for himself, not even something to eat. At the theatre, Philip mounted to the very top seat and then sat down and gazed back toward the orchestra.

After what seemed like a long time to Antyllus, Philip roused himself. He descended once more to street level and at last sought out a little cook-shop. He bought himself a sausage pie, but no wine. Instead, he took his pastry to the nearest fountain, and there he washed his hands and rinsed off his face before drinking water from his cupped hands. Then he sat, ate, washed his hands, and drank again. Then he returned to the chariot and spread more hay for the horses. His duties finished, he went to the start of the alley and stepped under the stoa of the courthouse. Here he wandered along the tables and looked through the propylaeum, evidently searching for Antyllus. Not finding him, he wandered back toward the chariot, and Antyllus decided it was time to stop playing his game.

He came forward, and Philip, at the sight of him, started to gather up the hay and put it into a sack. "I will have to return at a later date," Antyllus announced, as if he had just emerged from an indecisive court session. "Is everything all right?"

"What should be wrong?" Philip countered, and at once gave him back the change from the drachma.

Antyllus was taken aback. He stared at it. Never in his life had a slave, given money for his own use, returned an obol of it. "You may keep it," he said after the shock had worn off.

Philip looked at the pile of coins in his palm, seemed to consider for a moment, and then closed his palm over them and shoved his closed fist back at Antyllus. "I—don't—want—it," he said slowly, softly and very clearly. In his voice was hostility and anger.

Antyllus frowned in confusion. He was prepared to forgive much, but at the same time he felt good treatment ought to be rewarded. "Why not?"

"That's my business."

"A slave has no business that does not belong to his master."

"My mistake. Not my business; my decision."

Antyllus shook his head ambiguously, but he took the coins back and returned them to his purse. He mounted the chariot and took up the reins as Philip backed the team into the traces and then climbed in beside him. They drove in silence all the way home, but Antyllus was thinking. He had never known a slave to reject a tip, not to mention that Philip's last answer was too clever by half. A decision could not be owned or shared: it simply was. Someone had taught this slave rhetoric and logic, as well as manners and Greek. What was more, nine-tenths of the citizens in the city could not argue with such a precise understanding of the language.

Antyllus turned to Philip. "Who taught you rhetoric?"

"My elders."

"What?"

"As a child, I listened to my elders. Is there any other way to learn?"

"But that was your own tongue; how did you learn Greek rhetoric?"

Philip stared at him for a moment with an unreadable, guarded expression and then he shrugged. "The same way."

Antyllus understood. If he'd served his master at table, he would have heard his master's discussions. Presuming his master had been an educated man, the kind of man who invited philosophers and playwrights to his symposiums, then an intelligent and alert slave would learn all the tricks of rhetoric just by listening.

Although Antyllus left it at that, sensing that he would get nothing more out of the slave, he wondered what kind of young man, given an excess of money and the freedom to do as he liked with it, scorned women, wine, and even trinkets? He had been angry with Melissos for drinking *too much,* but he did not blame him for drinking per se, nor for visiting the brothels. Dion, for reasons he now suspected all too unpleasantly, had been shy of the brothels, but spent all the more money on sweets. And why stop the comparison at the slaves? Phaedolos had gone into debt for his pleasures, whether it was gambling, entertainment, or expensive purchases. Kapaneos indulged himself with gambling and clothes. Pheronike could not get enough of her perfumes and creams. There was something very unusual about Philip, Antyllus decided; but he wasn't sure if the best word to describe him was "unique", "strange", or "abnormal".

CHAPTER 5

The following morning, Antyllus woke with the certainty that Boreas was not up to Olympic competition any longer, and he therefore had to see how the four-year-old Zephyrus would take to the four-horse chariot. The sooner he did so, the better. There was simply no point going to a lot of trouble and expense to find a new driver if Zephyrus was not yet ready for competition. And there was no way to find out except to put him into the traces and see how he responded. Maybe he was ready. It was worth a try.

Antyllus went to the stables directly after breakfast. As usual, Dion was mucking out the stalls, while Melissos tossed fresh straw down from the loft. Cobon was grooming the driving team, and Philip refilling the water troughs in the individual stalls. At the sight of the master, Cobon, Melissos, and Dion nodded respectfully and greeted him with "Morning, Master." Philip nodded but did not greet him.

"Where's Ambelos?" Antyllus asked.

Philip shrugged. "I sent him off on his own."

"With my mare?!" Antyllus asked, incredulous.

Philip stared at him in utter incomprehension. "But he is the son of your Chief Strategos."

"What does that have to do with it?"

"He'll be a citizen."

They were clearly not communicating. Antyllus changed tacks and declared angrily, "But he can't ride! She's sure to throw him!"

Philip shrugged, and seeing that Antyllus was flabbergasted into silence he pointed out. "The mare will find her way home."

"Certainly, but you know enough about horses to know they are most likely to harm themselves when they are off on their own!" By now, Antyllus would have been less surprised if he had discovered Philip had run away; the one thing he had not expected was for Philip to do anything wrong with regard to the horses.

Philip's response only confirmed that instinct. He didn't try to deny there was a risk to the mare, but he frowned and asked, "How am I supposed to teach Ambelos to ride, if I don't let him get a feel for it? He needs to be on his own with a horse."

That made sense, Antyllus admitted to himself, but he still didn't like it. What if Ambelos was seriously injured? Harmatides would blame Antyllus—and Antyllus would blame himself. He felt strongly that Philip had been irresponsible, but the slave seemed to honestly think he was only fulfilling the duty he had been assigned.

Antyllus found himself examining Philip yet again, searching for he did not know what. Philip's face was marred by the scar and dent on his forehead. He had a fuzz of black hair, which was still too short to be attractive. His eyes were a rather chilly grey. He had filled out compared to the skeletal figure he had been on his arrival from the quarries, but he still looked frail. His hands were covered with scars, his fingernails deformed, and his back was covered with the telltale scars of other floggings. But for the first time, Antyllus noticed another ugly scar on the inside of his thigh as well. It looked as though a horse had stepped on his thigh, leaving a dent the shape of a hoof on it, emphasized by thick scar tissue shaped like half a hoof.

"How did you get that?" He pointed to the scar when Philip came out to refill the hydria with water.

"Trampled."

"As a child?"

"A bit older."

"And the scar on your forehead?"

"Same incident."

Antyllus nodded relieved. At least it hadn't been for seducing his mistress…. Then, dismissing the barbarian from his mind, he ordered Melissos to bring out the four-horse racing chariot, and told Cobon to bring the racing team except for Boreas. "What's you up to, Master?" Cobon asked, curious.

"Boreas isn't up to another Olympics, do you think?"

Cobon blew out and kicked at the dirt of the stable yard with his bare foot. "No, Master. I don't reckon he is."

"Well, then, either I forfeit the race or I have to get Zephyrus ready in time. He's got promise."

"Promise? He's as good as his name, Master! But he's young."

"I know, but we have a little more than a year. Let's start today."

Cobon's eyes lit up at that. He loved racing more than anything. He eagerly fetched the other three members of the team one after another: the chestnut mare, Penthesilea, (Penny for short); the bay gelding, Ajax; and the black gelding, Titan. Antyllus himself went into Zephyrus' stall and, after brushing straw from his mane and tail, brought him out.

Zephyrus was a lanky grey colt who had his full height but not yet his breadth. He started and went stock still as soon as he saw his comrades already backing into the traces. He lifted his head, whinnied to them, and got an answer from the mare. It occurred to Antyllus that he might have to castrate him earlier than normal. Penny's position was on the left-hand outer trace, because she was the most supple and responsive of the team. She steadied the others on the curve, like a moving anchor, while the biggest and swiftest of the four, the black gelding Titan, mastered the outside of the curve with his longer stride. The strongest of the team, Ajax and Boreas, were the inner horses, bearing the heaviest burden.

Boreas had been beside Penny, but Antyllus hesitated to put the ungelded colt directly beside the mare, and so he reversed the positions of Ajax and Zephyrus. This rearrangement, the presence of Zephyrus, and the absence of Boreas, who was whinnying from the stable piteously at being forgotten, upset all four horses. Titan started rearing up dangerously, and Cobon, too eager to help, lost his balance and fell down with an audible cry of pain.

Dion instantly dropped his wheelbarrow and rushed forward to pull Cobon out from under the now uncontrolled Titan. Although he succeeded in rescuing the older man, one of Titan's hooves hit his uplifted arm with an audible crack, and the blood drained from Dion's face. Meanwhile, however, the two horses that were already in the traces started to break loose and Zephyrus was backing up with all his strength, his weight on his haunches and his head thrown up so hard that he was dragging Antyllus slowly with him. His hands full with the colt, Antyllus could only shout at Melissos to stop the team before they completely bolted. Melissos, as always, was slow to respond. Philip, fortunately, was already there, catching a horse in each hand. He had them steadied in an instant, so that only Titan was still tearing around the stable yard wildly. As soon as he stopped, confused and uncertain, Melissos risked approaching him and caught his lead.

Zephyrus calmed down almost at once. Although he had broken out into a sweat, he allowed himself to be led up to the chariot. Antyllus carefully backed him into place and then ordered Melissos to hitch up Titan. Philip continued to hold Penny and Ajax calmly.

When all four horses were in the traces, held by Philip on one side and Melissos on the other, Antyllus went over to Cobon and Dion. It was not clear who was supporting whom. Cobon was crumpled over to one side, his hip evidently hurting him, but Dion was holding his left forearm with his right hand in obvious pain. You could not see anything yet, but the pallor of the strong young Slav made Antyllus suspect his arm was broken. "Melissos!" He shouted, "Go fetch Hypathea at once. Have her see to Dion's arm and to Cobon."

"Ain't nothing wrong with me that won't mend," Cobon countered grumpily, straightening up so he no longer leaned on Dion's shoulder.

Antyllus shrugged. "As you wish," he said, and returned to the chariot. This was not an everyday chariot, but a light racing chariot with only a single board to stand on behind a light wicker frame that curved elegantly, and ended just behind the driver. Antyllus took up the reins with inner nervousness. Although he had been practicing his driving diligently ever since that first attempt several months ago, he was acutely aware that trying to deal with this now agitated team might be beyond him. But he was determined to try. He told Philip to let go of the team.

Philip backed off to one side and watched with obvious interest, as did Cobon and Dion (still holding his arm). Philip and Cobon then fell in behind the chariot and escorted it to the training track.

Despite the inauspicious start, the experiment went off surprisingly well. Antyllus circled the track twice at a walk, then twice at a trot before he finally let the team canter. When he had done five rounds, Antyllus brought the team back to a walk and had them circle the course one last time slowly. Very satisfied, he drove back to the stables with the slaves again following behind.

Here Antyllus dismounted, and Philip started to unhitch the team with help from Melissos. Antyllus looked about for Dion, and found him lying down on a bench with Hypathea bending over him and apparently bandaging the arm. That was as it should be. The sight of his wife, however, out here in the stable yard, wiping sweat from Dion's face with one of her own scarves, was a jarring shock. He could not remember Pheronike ever setting foot in the stableyard before—certainly not in one of her beautifully embroidered, multilayered chitons. Her expression of distress would not have disgraced a mother.

I can't deal with this, Antyllus acknowledged mentally, and turned away. It was already time to leave for the Temple of Orestes to sacrifice for the coming Assembly, and he needed to bathe and change. He had no time to think about his adulterous wife or her lover. Instead, angrily, he signalled for Philip, who came still leading Titan. "Give Titan to Melissos to walk out. You have to wash yourself—properly—and change into a clean chiton."

"Why?" For once it wasn't insolence but sheer surprise.

"Because you're coming with me, and I need you to not only tend the horses but serve at table. You can do that, can't you?"

"I was trained as a boy."

"I thought as much. Hurry up; we're late." Antyllus fled toward the house without even acknowledging his wife's presence in the stableyard.

Half an hour later, they stood side by side in the driving chariot, and the sun burned down unpleasantly from the hazy summer sky. During his bath, Antyllus had decided that the only way of dealing with his wife was to ignore her. Anything else would create a scandal that would soon be all over the city. As long as he pretended he did not know what was going on, the household would conspire to "keep the secret". This decided, he felt strong again—as if in some way he was in control of the situation. He was determined not to give her and Dion another thought. He forced himself to focus on other things—such as the success he had just had with Zephyrus.

As he glanced at the slave standing straight and relaxed beside him, he was struck by another thought: this wasn't the third time Philip had stood in a chariot. "Can you drive?"

Philip started visibly. "Sir?"

"'Sir'? Since when do I rate that?" Antyllus challenged him, highly amused by the sudden mark of respect. Philip, however, looked embarrassed, and dropped his eyes to stare at the backs of his scarred hands. Antyllus let it be. "What about driving? Have you done it before?"

"They let me drive the oxen at the quarries once or twice."

"You can't compare oxen to my—" Antyllus broke off his furious reply and shot Philip a sidelong glance. Although he was still looking down at the back of his hands, his eyes shielded by his lids, the corner of his lips seemed to twitch. The slave had been teasing him! Antyllus had to laugh. For just a fraction of a second, Philip smiled as if he wanted to laugh too, but then his face resumed its neutral expression and he fixed his eyes on the road ahead.

"Do you think you can handle this pair?" Antyllus tempted him; his eyes focused on the slave's face as he lifted his hands a little, offering him the reins. There could be no doubt about it. Philip's pulse raced as he glanced at the reins covetously. His hands twitched with desire. He wanted to take them more than he had wanted to die back at the quarries. "Go on. It's a straight stretch." Not without a little apprehension, Antyllus handed the reins over to the eager young man beside him. It gave him pleasure to see how gratified the otherwise sullen and resentful slave looked when he had the reins in his hands. The horses seemed not even to notice the difference—a rare compliment.

Antyllus let him drive for four or five minutes, but then a donkey cart turned onto the road, and at once Antyllus took the reins back. They were getting closer to the city, and traffic would only increase. His little experiment proved, however, that Philip could and would let himself be taught how to drive *good* horses. They had a little more than a year to the Olympics, time enough for training a talented youth. For today it was enough.

As he drove through Tegea, Antyllus mentally praised himself. He told himself that he had taken a difficult decision—to replace Boreas with Zephyrus—well ahead of time, and he told himself that his gesture of kindness in buying Philip had been a gift of the Gods—an indication of their benevolence towards him. Even if Philip didn't prove good enough for competition, it would be an immense cost savings and help if Philip could help train the team up to the point where a professional could take over shortly before the Games themselves.

But after leaving the city by the southern gate, as they drove through thinning outskirts, Antyllus' mood turned melancholy. The image of Pheronike bending over Dion in distressed concern kept coming back to him; and just at the foot of the hills, near the insignificant village of Kamari, was the battlefield on which Phaedolos had so heroically and selflessly given his young life. The images started to get entwined: Pheronike bending over a wounded Dion, weeping over Phaedolos' mutilated corpse ...

In the first year following his death, Antyllus had come here often. He had let Kapaneos show him the exact spot where his son had fallen. He had knelt and taken the soil in his hands, as if he could draw the spilled blood back up out of the earth and the shade back from the underworld. But he had stopped coming at some point, probably as the training for the Pythian Games became too intense. Now there was nothing of Phaedolos here, and even his son's mother had turned her affections to another youth....

Antyllus became aware of Philip's sidelong glances and knew that his abrupt shift in mood had been noticed. He knew that Philip was wondering what had caused the change of mood, and the slave looked about the innocent countryside frowning, looking for something that could have disturbed his master. But the countryside bore no trace of what had transpired here nearly three years ago. The fields that had been torn up and turned first to dust and then to bloody mud had been reploughed, replanted, reharvested. Nothing but a little temple to Nike stood among the waving barley. And Philip was too polite to ask Antyllus what was wrong. For once, Antyllus was grateful for his reticence.

Only after they had passed the former battlefield and started climbing up the steep road to the Temple to Orestes, following in the wake of other chariots and wagons, did Antyllus remark, "That's where we demolished an invading Spartan army. You will have heard of the battle."

Philip looked at him long and hard before he answered simply, "Yes."

He suspects the truth, Antyllus thought to himself. Or he will have heard from the other slaves. They will have talked about Phaedolos.

But then Philip surprised him with a question. "Were you at the battle?"

"Me? No, of course not. I'm too old."

Philip nodded, and looked back over his shoulder at the battlefield for a long time.

The Temple to Orestes was located partway up the hillside that marked the end of the Parnos range. The citizens of Tegea were gathering to offer sacrifices and have the signs read for the impending Assembly. Traditionally, this ceremony had been held at the Temple of Athena in the very heart of the city, but at the last Assembly a silly motion to meet here had surprisingly found a majority. Antyllus did not approve. He did not approve of change just for change's sake, and, more importantly, the Assembly needed the auspices of Athena, the Goddess of Wisdom, not the bloodthirsty, vengeful Orestes. This was just another example of the kind of frivolous things that the Tegean Assembly was prone to these days—and that, even without an expansion of the franchise! The choice of the Temple of Orestes emphasised the aggressive ambitions of the younger members of the Assembly; the originator of this particular nonsense had been one of Kapaneos' new, bosom friends, a certain Phaeax.

Antyllus detested Phaeax, a young man who had inherited an excessive fortune at an early age and seemed to think that wealth alone entitled him to power and, above all, command. He had financed a whole company of cavalry, and he expected to be appointed strategos, despite his youth. (He was only 28.) But another reason Antyllus disliked him was that he was a bachelor despite his wealth and he had a "friend", Polyphom, from who he was apparently inseparable. Polyphom, on the other hand, was reputedly anything but faithful to Phaeax. In fact, it was rumoured that Polyphom sold his favours even to foreigners, while himself indulging in various abnormal, often brutal and bloody practices with slaves that he purchased explicitly for such purposes. More than one of his purchases had later been found dead in the gutter before his house, a broken wreck of humanity. In short, Polyphom was a thoroughly depraved, self-indulgent character, whose influence on Phaeax could only be bad.

His thoughts still with Polyphom, Antyllus manoeuvred the team onto the grass behind the temple, and—as if his thoughts had conjured up the pair—he at once caught sight of Phaeax and Polyphom, arm in arm, and apparently already tipsy. Admittedly, getting very drunk was traditional at this festival—which was why it was held *two* full days before Assembly. It was assumed that everyone would need a day to sleep off the hangover. Nevertheless, it was usual and proper to wait until the sacrifices had been made and above all, the signs read by the priests, before indulging in excesses of wine. Shaking his head in inner disgust, Antyllus ordered Philip to follow him.

There were seven oxen, purchased by the city, that formed the main sacrifice. These had been selected by the priests for their purity and were now garlanded. Because Antyllus was late, the procession was already forming. As this was one festival in which women did not participate (since women did not vote), the procession was about half the usual length. It was headed by the priests, followed by the Ministers and Council, and then the rest of the citizens in more or less order of standing. Antyllus had to take his place near the very front, and he gave orders to Philip to just watch. "You've been at festivals before, I presume?"

"Once or twice."

Antyllus hurried away, annoyed to be late and sweating from all his hurry. He took his place with the other councilmen, headed by Harmatides, immediately behind the priests. The procession escorted the oxen to the altar, where the men who did the actual killing and butchering waited respectfully. The priests gave the usual prayers, the oxen nodded their consent, and then a hefty man knocked them unconscious with a blow to their heads, while a priest slit the throat of each beast expertly. The blood was caught in pottery vessels and then poured over the altar. The lungs and heart of each ox was removed and burned on the altar, accompanied by more prayers. The entrails of the lead oxen were then presented to the Chief Priest, who set about trying to decipher the message they held for Tegea. This was the most serious moment of the entire festival, and so it irritated Antyllus intensely that he could hear whispers and even suppressed laughter coming from somewhere behind him. It was, however, beneath his dignity to turn and see who was causing the commotion.

At last the priest announced with an intense frown that he could see dark times ahead for Tegea. There was much confusion, indications of radical change, and then conflict and bloodshed. Although the priest *sounded* distressed, the prediction fit so perfectly with the hopes of Harmatides—the franchise reform and then war with Sparta—that Antyllus found himself wondering what he had been paid. Antyllus respected the Gods, but priests were mere men, and men were corruptible.

The official ceremonies over, the citizens left the temple enclosure for the trestle tables that had been set up in the shade of the trees behind. Here, slaves were laying out loaves of bread, kraters of water and wine, and trays of dates, raisins, and nuts. They were setting places for the feast that would follow as the meat, now being cut from the sacrificial oxen and cooked in huge pits, was distributed. The Council sat at their own table, and were served by their personal slaves. Antyllus was pleased to see that Philip understood his function well—just as he had suspected, he thought smugly. Without the least instruction, he brought Antyllus water and a towel so he could wash his hands, and then ensured that his kylix was never empty.

Antyllus turned to the other councilmen and asked, "Who was it making all that unseemly noise during the prayers?"

"Polyphom and Kapaneos and that clique; who else?"

"It was their idea to have the festival here in the first place. Have they no respect for the Gods whatever?"

"It seems they heard about Orestes' bones." Casambrus, the Chief Priest, declared with a grimace. Adding defensively, "I tried to keep it quiet—at least until after the festival—but somehow they must have had word of it." He daubed at the sweat on his face with nervous distraction, and then signalled irritably for more wine.

"What bones?" Antyllus asked, looking from Casambrus to the others.

Harmatides and Onimastros exchanged a glance, but the other councilmen, particularly Melankomos, seconded Antyllus, demanding information.

Harmatides drew a deep breath. "A man posing as an exile from Sparta leased a parcel of land from Adrastus, who runs the forge owned by Onimastros here—"

"I had no idea he had done any such thing!" Onimastros declared in his rather high-pitched, whiny voice. Onimastros was a fat, balding man who always seemed to whine, Antyllus thought.

"Of course not, and besides, it was just a lease," Harmatides assured him reasonably, continuing, "but it turns out this was no exile but a Spartiate in good standing, who had heard from Adrastus that under a certain tree there was a huge grave in which were buried gigantic bones. The Spartiate dug them up and took them back with him to Sparta."

"Whatever for?" Pisirodos wanted to know.

"It seems the Spartans had another Oracle from Delphi," Casambrus admitted with a groan.

"What Oracle?"

"Well, obviously we haven't seen it, but it apparently predicted that the bones of Orestes could be found in a forge in Tegea. The grave was located directly behind Adrastus' forge, and I am afraid that our investigations of the grave—after the Spartiate had removed the bones, unfortunately— suggest that it was of ancient origin. Indeed, it could well have been a tomb from the age of Agamemnon. But of course, there is no way of proving that the bones belonged to Orestes."

"No one has to," Melankomos pointed out ominously. "The Oracle is proof enough as far as the gullible masses are concerned."

"How could Adrastus lease such precious land to a Spartiate?" Lampon demanded in an angry voice. "The man should be tried for treason!"

"I questioned him at great length," Casambrus insisted defensively. "He said he was frightened—"

"The damage has been done," Harmatides cut in impatiently. "Not only are the Spartans now encouraged—because the Oracle said they would be able to subdue us if they had the bones of Orestes—but our own youth feels we have been hoodwinked. That is behind the disrespectful behaviour of Polyphom and his friends. They think that we, the elected officials of this city, are weak and cowardly."

"I dare say, they don't think that of you, Harmatides," Lampon hastened to assure the strategos in a flattering tone.

"But of us," Endios, the oldest among them, joined the conversation dourly. "Of us, indeed," he intoned with a look directly at Antyllus and the other aristocrats.

The conversation moved on, but Antyllus' thoughts circled back to one horrible truth: even a reputedly sensible and peace-loving man like Chilon of Sparta would never be able to keep the Spartan hotheads back once they had something as tangible as a hero's bones and a new oracle promising victory. Antyllus was the last man to have blind faith in oracles. They were too often misinterpreted. Look what had happened to the Spartans in this last campaign! But that wasn't the point. The point was that the war faction in Sparta would *use* the Oracle to sway the undecided. Everyone knew the Spartans were particularly devout. A good speaker would convince them that they were now duty bound to seize Tegea because the Gods had given them Orestes' bones—or some such thing. Antyllus began to fear that war was not only inevitable, but near at hand.

While he was lost in these depressing thoughts, the meat was brought. The wine flowed increasingly abundantly. The mixture grew stronger. People started to get increasingly inebriated. From the outer fringes of the orchard, the sound of singing and shouting mounted. Endios and a couple of the elder councilmen excused themselves. Antyllus, too, started to think about leaving, and looked around for Philip. He was nowhere in sight.

Now that he noticed, his kylix was empty, too, and had been for some time. How long? Although his mind suggested that the slave had probably simply gone off to relieve himself somewhere, his instincts were alarmed— and a moment later his worst fears were confirmed. One of Harmatides' slaves ran up to their table and addressed Antyllus directly, "Master! Come quick! Your slave is trying to kill Polyphom. Hurry!"

By the time Antyllus reached the scene, no less than three young men had pinned Philip to the ground, but he had not stopped struggling. He was bleeding from a cut to his forehead and blood was gushing from his nose. Nevertheless, with remarkable agility and tenacity, he continued to fight back—scratching and biting, just as you would expect of a barbarian.

Polyphom himself was standing to the side, watching and holding his throat with both hands. At the sight of Antyllus he burst out with furiously blazing eyes, "Your slave attacked me! He tried to kill me! He seized me by the throat and tried to squeeze the breath out of me!"

Antyllus' first concern was stopping the other three men from breaking Philip's bones. The last thing he wanted was the promising jockey and driver to suffer serious injury. He called angrily for the three young men to desist. "Any damage you do to my property, you'll pay for!" His voice, used to authority, did not lack effect. The three young Tegeans stopped, looked at him in astonishment, and then backed away. He noted that one of them had the beginnings of a black eye and the others were also nursing minor injuries. Philip too responded to Antyllus' voice, at once getting his feet under him. Although his breath was rasping almost as badly as when he had first been purchased and blood gushed from his nose, he managed to stand upright.

"He tried to kill me," Polyphom insisted in high-pitched outrage. "He should be executed. If you won't do it yourself, give to him to me and I'll see he dies in a way he deserves."

"Don't be ridiculous!" Antyllus retorted. "You look very much alive to me. Indeed, you look far less damaged than my slave."

"He attacked me!" Polyphom insisted. "I demand satisfaction for the insult."

"I will see that he is appropriately punished," Antyllus insisted, and though several of the others snorted contemptuously (as if they doubted his word), there was little they could do about it. Antyllus snapped his fingers at Philip as if he were a dog, and headed directly to the waiting chariot. Philip limped after him, trying to staunch the bleeding of his nose with the back of his arm.

Without exchanging a word, they hitched up the team and set off. Antyllus drove away from the temple through the dust of the chariots and wagons that had come and gone all day. They drove across the former battlefield, and it was there that Antyllus noticed Philip was trembling. He looked over and saw something he had never thought to see in this cheeky, suicidal slave: fear. Philip was clutching the front of the chariot car, ghastly pale and trembling from head to foot.

Up to now Antyllus had been intrigued by his secretiveness, bemused by his insolence, and pleased by his skill with horses. He had been angry with him, too—and he was angry now because he had disgraced Antyllus before the likes of Polyphom and Phaeax. But, despite himself, he also felt a surge of sympathy for the young man, blood smearing his lower face and his scar throbbing in his forehead. "Relax, Philip. I'm not going to punish you. Surely you know that? Although I expect an explanation," he added sharply, fearing that he was being too lenient again.

Instead of an explanation, Philip asked, in a tight voice, "Could you stop, please, sir? I'm going to be sick." Almost before Antyllus could draw up, he stepped off the back of the chariot, went down on his knees and vomited into the barley. He vomited a second time. Spat. Wiped his mouth on the inside of his chiton and got unsteadily to his feet.

Antyllus looked at him with genuine sympathy as he climbed with noticeable difficulty back into the chariot. "We'll stop at the next fountain so you can wash your mouth out, and get the blood off your face," Antyllus promised, and the chariot lurched forward again.

On the outskirts of the city was a small fountain house, where many travellers stopped to wash their face and hands before entering the city.

Here Antyllus drew up, and Philip dipped his hands deep into the basin below the spouting brass lion heads. He rubbed the drying blood off his face with it, cupped it in his hands, and swished it around in his mouth before spitting it out. He repeated this several times before he finally drank of it. When he returned to the chariot, however, he still looked weak and shaken. The scar on his forehead seemed to be swelling.

Antyllus decided it was time to get an explanation. "What happened?"

"That—man—the tall, blond one with hair only on his upper lip. He tried to rape me."

The word startled Antyllus so much he jerked the reins and the horses fussed and veered in confusion. Antyllus returned his attention to them for a second, and then he looked back at Philip. The word would never have occurred to Antyllus. Could a man be raped? By another man, yes. But could a *slave* be raped? That depended on the essence of rape. Was rape the use of force to penetrate another sexually, or was it the lack of consent? If force alone were the criteria, than even the use of force within a marriage or between master and slave would be rape—an absurd notion. This meant that consent was the criterion. Consent presupposed the right to deny consent. Since a wife or a slave had no right to deny consent, it was clear that neither a wife could be raped by her husband nor a slave by his or her master—or indeed anyone the master gave permission to. After all, there were men whose major source of income was the prostitution of their slaves.

But did a slave have the right to deny someone *who did not have the consent of his master*? It was an interesting legal question. It was also entirely irrelevant to the case in hand, because Antyllus was not fool enough to think that his consent would have made any difference to Philip. Whatever had happened, Philip had responded not as a good slave, and that was the crux of the matter: Philip did not in his heart accept that he was less a man than Polyphom—or Antyllus.

They returned to the chariot and drove into the city in silence. Although Philip's trembling had ceased, it was evident he was still badly shaken. There was nothing of his usual insolence or even any interest in the horses. Antyllus noticed to his own surprise that he did not like this docile, beaten Philip as much as the cheeky one that had stood beside him on the outward journey.

On the far side of the city, after they had driven out of the gates and onto the road leading directly to his estate, he could stand it no longer and asked, "What is it Philip? You say yourself he 'tried' to rape you, and it is evident you defended yourself—rather more than was your right, I might add. If you had killed Polyphom, I would indeed have had no choice but to have had you killed as well."

Philip turned and stared at him, and his grey eyes were dark and molten. "There is dignity in death. Soldiers die. Even heroes die. But rape ... is worse than death. It is a violation of more than the body. It is a violation of one's being." Antyllus met his eyes, not so much understanding what he said as respecting the fact that he felt this way. Philip looked away, staring at the road ahead, his face still pale and his expression one of defeat.

It was disheartening to see this spirited creature broken. Antyllus wanted to restore him to his self-respect, but didn't know what to say. So after a moment he offered, "Do you want to drive?"

Philip jumped. He had been lost in thought. He looked at Antyllus questioningly, then at the horses, the reins, back to Antyllus. "If I may, sir?"

Antyllus smiled and handed the reins over to him.

CHAPTER 6

There was no question that Philip would accompany Antyllus into the city for the symposium at Harmatides'—even though Melissos looked sullen and grumbled about it being "unfair" that Philip got to go to town "yet again".

Philip had cleaned himself up as best as possible, but the cut on his forehead was very obvious and his nose and lips were still swollen, so anyone could see he had been in some kind of a fight. No doubt Harmatides' slaves would ask him what had happened, and Antyllus wished them luck trying to get an answer out of him. They climbed aboard the chariot and set off in the first cool breaths of early evening.

There were six other guests already assembled, and a harpist was playing light, unobtrusive music from a corner. Harmatides set his kylix aside on the table before him and rose at once to greet Antyllus. "What a pleasure to welcome you to my home at last, Antyllus." Harmatides indicated a vacant couch with silk cushions directly beside his own. Antyllus sat, removed his sandals, and then stretched out. He nodded to the other guests in greeting. Ambelos, Antyllus noticed, was not present at this meeting, and nor were the other strategoi or any of the young, radical, and aggressive faction that usually surrounded Harmatides in public. Instead, these men were almost all wealthy merchants and parvenus like Lampon and Onimastros. The presence of Onimastros particularly surprised and disquieted Antyllus. Onimastros' father had worked his way up from travelling peddler to a wholesale merchant of nearly everything. While Onimastros himself was the first in his family to own an estate and live like a gentleman, he still earned the bulk of his income from provisioning the army and quarries and, increasingly, from land speculation and building. Onimastros purchased raw materials such as wood, limestone, marble, and tiles, and built under contract. Antyllus guessed that he employed several hundred skilled workers and owned nearly a hundred slaves. In public, Harmatides and Onimastros were barely civil to one another. With a shudder as if something had run down his spine, Antyllus started to suspect something that the Assembly thought impossible: that Harmatides was not the "man of the people" he appeared to be in his speeches.

The wine offered was a very light mix, far more water than wine, and on the tables were nuts and dried fruits, but nothing heavy or excessively sweet. This was evidently indeed intended to be a "working symposium".

The conversation was at first focused on the unfortunate incident with Orestes' bones, and again Harmatides cut the discussion short in a sharp voice that ended all the idle chatter and got to the heart of things.

"Ultimately, the issue is not whose bones they are or how the bones got to Sparta, but what Sparta will do with them?" The question was rhetorical and he answered it himself. "They have an Oracle from Delphi which promises them victory over Tegea if they capture the bones of Orestes," he explained. "Now they believe they have the bones. In short, we can be certain that even now they are planning to attack. *This* is the reason, gentlemen, that we can delay no longer. We must act!" He spoke as if he were in assembly, or at least council.

"What do you mean, Harmatides?" Lampon asked, as the slaves brought the first course of smoked eels and cabbage soup.

"It is clear that the Assembly is going to vote for an increase in the franchise—whether for my version or Melankomos'." He nodded in Antyllus' direction as he said this, then turned back to the others. "This means that by the next Assembly we will have between two and three thousand new citizens—according the estimates of my clerks. That's an increase of twenty to thirty per cent over the present Assembly."

Antyllus was surprised to hear that Harmatides didn't particularly care if his own bill or Melankomos' passed. Apparently, either suited his purposes well enough. Harmatides meanwhile expounded on the need to re-equip the entire army before the next confrontation with the Lacedaemonians.

"I'm sure Antyllus here would agree that our army, particularly our cavalry, needs better equipment, don't you?"

"Every cavalryman brings his own equipment," Antyllus countered.

"But that's the point! Everyone brings what he can—or is willing to—afford, and the quality varies from first-rate modern breastplates to leather jerkins and from true javelins to crooked staffs with a point carved on one end! We *must* standardise the equipment, and we must pay for the equipment from the public purse."

"But if we start paying for cavalry equipment from public funds, why not hoplite and other equipment?"

"Absolutely! We need a professional army—like the Spartans have! The funds would be much better spent equipping every new citizen properly, than idlers and drunks for doing nothing!" Harmatides retorted in exasperation.

"My son had a fancy, modern cuirass," Antyllus pointed out, "and it didn't stop him from getting killed." Rather to his surprise, he instantly had the attention of the others, and felt compelled to continue: "Equipment alone brings nothing but expense. What would the Spartans be without their interminable drill? Training more than equipment is the key to a professional military, and—" Antyllus had wanted to point out that the young men of Tegea—most especially the young men who clustered around Phaeax and Kapaneos—were far too lazy to put in even one day of drill as the Spartans did it, day in and day out.

But Harmatides did not let him finish. Exuberantly, he agreed, "Excellent point, my dear Antyllus! In Sparta they train their young men practically from birth and then require them to serve ten years on active duty and thirty years in the reserves...."

"And we beat the shit out of them!" Lampon countered smugly.

"You seem to forget it was a very near thing," Harmatides countered. "We fielded three men to every two of theirs, and still our casualties were higher. It was our cavalry that was decisive."

"What is it you propose exactly?" Antyllus wanted to know.

"Let's turn the increase in franchise to our double advantage by taking a leaf from the book of our enemies! Just as their kings can rule without consent of the Assembly during war, we should use the impending invasion to declare an emergency, suspend the Assembly, and put the city on a war footing immediately. Then we can call up the eligible citizens and start training them at once. We could even pay a daily wage," Harmatides suggested, "but only to those under arms—not the lame and the lazy!"

There was stunned silence for a moment, and then two of the others started congratulating Harmatides and praising the idea effusively.

Antyllus felt another chill run down his spine. Suspend the Assembly? If they suspended the Assembly for an emergency, who was to say when the emergency ended? Who was to restore power to the citizens? Surely not the same men who had a free hand as long as there was no Assembly?

Around him, however, the lively discussion took no objection to the proposal itself but rather focused on the *tactics* that should be pursued in implementing it. "Wait," Antyllus tried to stop the flow of the discussion, but they were already too passionately involved in their plans. Did they have to send an embassy to Lacedaemon first? Surely it was obvious that the Spartans would lie. Even if the Spartans were planning a new invasion, they would never admit it. There was no point in trying to negotiate at all, not with an aggressive power like Lacedaemon. But the danger would have to *appear* acute, someone was arguing, if they were going to convince the Assembly to give up powers even on a temporary basis.

"That is why this whole incident with Orestes' bones is so propitious," Harmatides remarked with evident enthusiasm and the dynamism so characteristic of him. "It is the common masses who are most riled up and unnerved by the loss of the bones."

"Yes, but mostly because they interpret it as an indication that Apollo sides with Lacedaemon, rather than Tegea. They are saying the Gods have chosen Lacedaemon," Lampon pointed out, frowning.

"They may say that, but I don't think they are prepared to just let themselves be helotized like the Messenians!" Harmatides countered energetically. "Give me a half hour in the Assembly, and they'll be screaming for Lacedaemonian blood. They'll *demand* war. They'll *beg* me to seize power!"

Antyllus feared that he was right. Phaeax and his friends had been baying for Lacedaemonian blood for at least a year. The only comfort was that they were a minority—if a vocal one.

Onimastros entered the discussion for the first time, declaring in his high-pitched voice, "You'll never get a majority unless you appear to be opposed by the oligarchs. That is what will truly get the new citizens lined up behind you."

Antyllus had forgotten about them, the new citizens. As the franchise would already have been increased before the debate about the emergency powers was put to the Assembly, the new citizens would be voting. Antyllus was not so sure, however, that they would side with the emergency powers. Why would they been ready to give up a privilege they had just won? Before he could think things through, however, Onimastros went on to suggest, "I think it would be best if I urge an embassy to Lacedaemon, even hint that it might be sacrilegious to oppose a new invasion—since obviously the

Gods are on the side of Lacedaemon. If I go to the Assembly urging peace and submission to the Spartans, then surely you will support me, won't you, Antyllus?"—he smiled at Antyllus with open contempt—"You and your whole, aristocratic faction would support a peace mission to Sparta, surely?"

Antyllus opened his mouth to say yes, indeed; but he didn't get a chance because Onimastros continued, pointedly turning away and announcing smugly, "You will find it much easier, Harmatides, to arouse the mob to belligerence if the wealthy citizens oppose you."

Antyllus looked from Onimastros to Harmatides and his alarm grew exponentially. Not only did these two men work together, Onimastros called the tune. Harmatides was nothing but his popular and energetic puppet.

"Oh, and another thing:" Onimastros decided, "I think I should threaten to stop you—promise to stop you. We must make the mob believe that the democratic process works *against* their interests."

Antyllus was too shocked to speak. They were discussing nothing less than a coup d'état against the democratic constitution of Tegea. These seven men—and ipso facto, himself—were discussing the best way of tricking the Assembly into suspending itself—permanently. Antyllus did not believe for a moment that Onimastros intended to restore power to the Assembly at a later date.

Indeed, he reflected as he watched the others interact, once Onimastros had "emergency" powers conferred on Harmatides, he would clearly use them to entrench himself. Harmatides was only the figurehead—the popular, charismatic leader he was using to gain power. Once he had enough power, once there was no longer an Assembly to manipulate or a mob to charm, he would probably get rid of Harmatides, too. He was seeking absolute power. He—not Harmatides—wanted to be Tyrant of Tegea.

Didn't the others see that?

"You're very quiet, Antyllus," Onimastros took notice of him with ill-disguised suspicion.

"I am surprised by what is being discussed here."

"Surprised? Or disapproving?" Onimastros pressed him, with an almost threatening edge to his voice.

"Both. We are discussing the ancient constitution of Tegea. Don't you think we should be very cautious before we consciously do violence to the legacy of our ancestors?"

"Antyllus, much as I respect your intellect, I must stress that we have no time for long debate." Harmatides' tone was exasperated. "We must act quickly, or it will be too late."

"What do you mean too late?"

"The Assembly will have voted themselves even more power, and all at our expense! The radicals—soon to be supported by many new citizens— have all sorts of mad ideas for enriching themselves at our expense." Harmatides explained impatiently.

"Haven't you heard the latest?" Onimastros sneered. "They want the city to pay out a minimum wage to citizens who have an income less than one hundred drachma a year—for doing nothing!" His contempt was as great as his indignation.

"And they want the landowners to donate wine free of charge for civic celebrations." Lampon added indignantly. At once the others chimed in with news of various other proposals or rumours of proposals attributed to the Radicals.

Antyllus had heard many of these rumours himself, but dismissed them as mere parliamentary gossip. Much of what was being said now was sheer nonsense, and Antyllus was inclined not to take any of it too seriously. Harmatides and Onimastros, however, were determined to make him do so.

With an ominous tone in his voice, Onimastros leaned toward Antyllus and said slowly, "Do you know what your *friend* Kapaneos wants now? He wants public officials to be selected by lottery rather than election."

Antyllus started visibly. He didn't like to hear Kapaneos referred to as his "friend" —especially not in that tone of voice—and the idea of public office being distributed by lottery was an absurd—no, childish—idea.

"He said," Onimastros continued in his low, sneering voice, "that such a procedure would be gambling for real stakes—and for a professional like himself, it would be child's play to control the results."

Antyllus felt his blood rising. "The idea of a lottery is absolute nonsense! I don't care who suggested it. Kapaneos does not speak for me."

"We never thought he did," Harmatides assured him, breaking into the conversation in a friendly tone with a smile to Antyllus and with a frown toward Onimastros.

The conversation took new turns. They started discussing the appropriate time for their coup. They discussed the various measures they would introduce first. Antyllus was in turmoil. How could they be so sure he wouldn't betray them?

Betray them to whom? To the radicals that he detested as much as they did? To his aristocratic friends who were as helpless as he was? To the strategoi who worshiped Harmatides? Who could stop them?

Although the wine was heavily watered, Antyllus felt as if he were drunk. When he went to the latrines for the umpteenth time, he noticed that the sky was already greying beyond the tiles of the roof. He returned to the andron, and rather than taking his place again, announced that it was time to depart. "I have to get up early to train my racing team," he said, excusing himself, although all he really wanted was to get away from this company and the disturbing discussion. He needed time and peace and fresh air to think.

Harmatides expressed regret that he should depart so early, but made no serious attempt to stop him. Antyllus buckled on his sandals, said a polite good night to all the others, and Harmatides escorted him back to the courtyard. "I hope you weren't too shocked," Harmatides remarked in an almost teasing tone.

"It is treason," Antyllus responded sternly.

"You didn't say that in there," Harmatides gestured with his head toward the inner parts of the house. "Don't be a fool, Antyllus. Onimastros very nearly succeeded in getting you impeached for incompetence as Minister of Mines, but I managed to convince Onimastros that you would be more useful on our side than working against us. He was most reluctant. For some reason, which I do not understand, he doesn't like you. Besides, you stand to gain if we seize power. We will reward and rely on men of circumspection, wisdom, and honesty. I can't believe you want to see the fate of our city turned over to the rabble."

"I don't! *You* are the one who has agitated consistently for an increase in the franchise!" Antyllus protested. "I was very happy the way things were."

"Antyllus, nothing can stay the same for ever. Surely you know that? I had to demand an increase in the franchise because I need more men for the army—not the Assembly. That has been the dilemma all along, Antyllus. There may be fools in this city who think that we are stronger than the Spartans because we won one battle, but you and I know better. We were lucky last time. Very, very lucky. Next time—and there will be a next time—we may not be so lucky, unless we can replace our losses and more. If we want to avoid the fate of Messenia—and I do!—then we *must* have a larger, better equipped and better trained army. That can only be assured by increasing the franchise. But the last thing any thinking man wants is for the government of this city to be in the hands of a mob! Surely you see the sense of what we are planning?" He seemed almost to be pleading with the older man, adding in a confidential, brotherly tone, "That's why I invited you here: to make you start seeing things *realistically*. Things can't—and won't—go on the way they were."

He paused, but when Antyllus said nothing, he took up the argument again, returning to his more vigorous, argumentative voice: "Tegea is in acute danger, noble Antyllus. The Spartans will come again, and they will come in force, with thoughts of revenge and the confidence of being favoured by the Gods. We must oppose them. The alternative is utter and abject submission. Do you know what that would mean? To have our lands divided up among the victors while we are turned into helots bound to till our own fields for Spartan masters. You don't want that any more than I do!"

"Of course not!" Antyllus agreed angrily. "But I am not willing to concede there is no way of negotiating. I admit this incident with Orestes' bones complicates—"

Harmatides was shaking his head. "You don't really believe the Spartans would retreat any more than I do. War is coming, and the question is who will guide this city through the crisis? Not you and your friends, Antyllus. You no longer have the rudder in your hands. Either the city will be governed by a mob led by young and foolish radicals like Phaeax and your son's old friend Kapaneos, or it will be led by the men in my andron. You can—and must—choose between responsible, mature men of substance—even if they are not your old friends, Antyllus—or the rabble and their irresponsible, young leaders. And you must choose soon. The time for indecision is running out. Good night." He gave Antyllus his hand and then disappeared back into his house with firm, military strides. He was not the least bit drunk or even weary, Antyllus noted with wonder.

Still in shock from all he had learned this evening, Antyllus crossed the cobbled yard and entered the strange stables. Horses stirred and nickered slightly. Snoring came from the loft. He found Philip curled up on the clean straw of an empty stall and shook him awake.

Philip had been in a deep asleep and was disoriented. He stared up at Antyllus as if he did not even recognise him. Then he remembered. He dropped his eyelids to shield his thoughts, scrambled to his feet, and started seeing to the horses wordlessly.

Antyllus paced about in the yard uneasily. Was Harmatides right? Did he and his friends have no chance of guiding the course of the city any more?

As they clambered into the wagon, Antyllus tired and distracted, Philip refreshed and wide awake, Antyllus gave him the reins. "You can manage, can't you? There will be no traffic. I'll give you directions here in the city, and after we exit the east gate it's a straight road almost the whole way. Just take us home at an easy trot."

"Yes, sir."

They set out through the darkened and abandoned streets. From the factory opposite, not a single light glowed any longer. They skirted the central part of town and once they'd exited by the gate and were on the main Argive road, Antyllus paid no more attention to the drive and sank into his thoughts.

His thoughts were disordered. He felt besmirched by the way—with that slight sneer in his voice—Onimastros had referred to Kapaneos as "his friend", as if they were lovers! The idea of public offices being assigned by lottery roused his indignation more violently the more he thought about it. How typical of Kapaneos and his irresponsible friends to want to introduce gambling even into serious civic affairs! And suddenly it seemed obvious that Onimastros had been behind the intrigue to disgrace him as Minister of Mines, because Onimastros—with all his building activities—would, of course, have used the mines for his own enrichment. He would have cheated the city blind!

And that was the crux of the matter: Onimastros wasn't interested in what was good for Tegea. Even with regard to Lacedaemon, Onimastros wanted war because as principal wholesaler to the army, he stood to *profit* from war. He saw war as a means to enrich himself, indifferent to the cost in blood. He had no sons, after all, and was too old and fat to fight.

And very soon, if someone didn't stop him, he would have more power than ever....

But that was the vicious circle! If Harmatides was right, and the aristocratic faction around Melankomos was too weak to sway the Assembly—old or new—then indeed he had a choice only between irresponsible hotheads like Phaeax, Kapaneos, and the rabble that followed them, or cold-blooded, power-hungry Onimastros and his faction.

And where did Harmatides himself fit in? He was neither a fool nor a greedy tyrant-in-the-making. Antyllus' head was spinning.

They turned off the main road onto the secondary road leading to Antyllus' estate. The horses knew they were nearly home. They started fretting. They tried to break into a canter and when Philip held them back, they snapped at one another, even kicked out with their heels and bucked. Philip glanced sidelong at Antyllus, but the older man was lost in thought. He eased the reins and let the horses canter.

Antyllus didn't notice until it was too late. The turn-off into the drive was only a half-dozen paces away, and they were tearing forward headlong at much too fast a pace. He called out, "Slow down, you fool! I said a trot! What the—" The slave beside him was smiling.

In that horrible instant, Antyllus realised that Philip was mad. He was suicidal. He was driving them both intentionally to an accident. He wanted to pitch them both out of the chariot as it turned over. He wanted to kill them both.

Instinctively, Antyllus dropped down onto the floor of the chariot, his arms up over his head, his weight flung onto the outside wheel in a desperate attempt to keep the chariot from turning over. He felt the outside wheel lift off the ground for half a heartbeat, and then it clumped back down again and they rolled forward at a slowing pace.

Antyllus slowly pulled himself back onto his feet and looked at Philip's smiling face, and he had never in his life been so furious. This impudent piece of property had just tried to kill him and now grinned contemptuously at him for having taken cover in the bottom of the carriage. "You bastard," he told the young slave in fury too great for screaming. "You'll pay for this! You can't try to kill me and mock me! I'll give you a lesson you never forget!"

Philip looked at him as if he didn't understand, but then his face hardened into impassivity and he pulled the horses to a neat halt just inside the stable yard.

"Put them away and then go into the slaves' courtyard."

Philip jumped down and unhitched the horses, while Antyllus stormed into the house and took down from over the door of the entryway a whip that had hung there since his father's day. He had trouble getting it down and it was cobwebbed, but he wasn't going to let anyone get away with mocking him like that. "They are all mocking me," a part of his brain said; "mocking me for not knowing who my enemies are, mocking me for letting them plot against the Assembly, mocking me for letting a slave sleep with my wife...."

He shouted into the slave's hall, "Melissos! Dion! All of you! Get out here! You think you can do whatever you like with me, don't you? You think I'm an impotent old fool, who you can hoodwink and mock! I'll show you what I can do!"

They came stumbling out of their beds bewildered, while in the courtyard Philip just stood waiting. "Cobon! Melissos! Strip him and tie him to the pillory! I'll show you what insolence will earn you. GO ON! Tie him to the pillory!"

Cobon and Melissos, though dazed, each grabbed one of Philip's arms, and led him to the pillory in the corner of the courtyard. The pillory was almost obscured from view by a chestnut tree that had grown up in the last decades. They pulled his chiton down to expose his back, faced him to the pillory, and would have fit his hands into the rusting handcuffs that hung from it, but suddenly he thrust them aside so violently and unexpectedly that he nearly knocked Cobon over and was free of them. He spun around to face Antyllus, screaming loud enough to wake the dead: "I'm not a beast!" He made no move to run away. "You don't *chain* me! I can stand!" He faced the pillory again, and gripped it just above his head with both hands, offering his shoulders to the whip like a sacrifice. The scars of other floggings stood out sharply on his naked back.

In that instant, Antyllus felt the first qualm of guilt. But he had made too much of a scene to stop now. He reminded himself of the smile on Philip's face as he—in blatant disobedience—let the horses gallop toward the curve. He reminded himself that they would both be dead—or at least seriously injured—if he hadn't crouched down and managed to weight the outside wheel enough to prevent the chariot from overturning. He reminded himself of Philip's smile of triumph as he saw he had frightened his master, and it merged with Dion's red and sweated face as he rushed from the front of the house in the middle of the night—Dion, who was now standing and gaping with open mouth as he cradled his splinted arm. Antyllus brought the whip down on Philip's exposed back with all the strength he had in him.

Philip's back—frail and bony—flinched, but not a sound came from the slave. Antyllus felt humiliated. Was he so weak and old that he couldn't even hurt the skinny, little barbarian? He gathered his strength again, and moved in closer. He brought the whip down and the sound of it made him wince, but there was nothing audible from Philip. He started beating faster and more furiously. The skin finally burst. Blood started to seep up out of the crevices torn in the flesh. It collected and ran down the gullies of flesh like rain in the furrows of a field. From behind him, Antyllus could hear the gasping and mutterings of the others.

Suddenly he saw himself from the outside. A brutal man, no better than the foreman at the quarries or the contemptible Polycritus of Corinth. He too was flaying a slave who was neither defending himself nor trying to evade the punishment. In horror Antyllus flung the whip away as if it was burning him and rushed for the house, shouting to cover his own humiliation. "Just remember you could be next, Dion!" It felt good to say that. Dion deserved a flogging!

So why had he been beating Philip? What was it about the young slave that apparently drove his masters to abuse him?

Antyllus stopped dead in his tracks in the darkened corridor. Behind him he heard Cobon ask in horror, "What did you do? What did you do to provoke the Master like that?!" He sounded as if he couldn't imagine anything on earth that could have produced this brutal reaction from the mild Antyllus.

Philip barked out between what had to be gritted teeth, "Ask *him*!" and it sounded like an accusation. It *was* an accusation.

Antyllus turned and looked back. The courtyard was well lit by the dawn and he could see how all the slaves had rushed forward, their jealousy forgotten in the horror of what they had witnessed. He saw Philip move stiffly, his face a grim mask of denied pain. He saw him gesture for Dion to help him to the slaves' washbasin. There Philip turned and eased himself into the water back first, while Dion—despite his own splinted and bandaged left arm—held him with his right hand and arm so he wouldn't drown. Hypathea had already sent one of the younger girls to fetch linens and as Philip emerged from the basin, she stretched a broad napkin across his back and pressed it against his wounds firmly and steadily. Philip gripped Dion so hard that the latter screwed up his face, but stifled any protest. The cook came out with a cup full of wine, which he helped Philip drink.

"What was *that* all about?" Pheronike asked her husband, standing in the darkness of the passage with a wide, woollen shawl around her shoulders over a loose nightgown. Her hair was in disarray and her make-up smeared below her eyes.

"Just a warning to your friend Dion!" Antyllus flung at her vindictively and fled from the scene of the crime.

CHAPTER 7

When he woke up hours later, Antyllus lay in bed staring at his panelled ceiling, asking himself if it had all been a nightmare. He couldn't really have beaten a young man bloody? Why? For trying to kill him? Where had he gotten that silly idea? It was absurd. There were far easier and surer ways of killing him than driving a chariot around a corner too fast.

What was more, the punishment might have been appropriate if the chariot had turned over and someone—man or horse—had been injured, but it hadn't. So what had Philip been guilty of?

Of disobedience, yes. He'd been told to keep to a trot. But he was a young and inexperienced driver with a hot, fresh team within scent of their own barn.

Maybe he hadn't been able to stop them?

No, he had been enjoying it.

What young man with the blood of a horseman in his veins didn't enjoy driving a fast team?

So he had exceeded his instructions. What slave didn't, when given the chance? There wasn't a slave alive that *always* obeyed his master. It was no reason for beating any of them bloody!

Philip had misjudged the curve and overestimated his own skill. Was that a reason for beating him? Of course not.

Antyllus could only conclude that he had himself gone mad. He sat up and stared across the room at the window. A gentle breeze was lifting the curtains and bringing the scent of roses from his garden.

What had come over him? He had been tormented by thoughts of Pheronike and Dion for months now—and he had been lying to himself to think he could just ignore it. He had been upset too by the incident with Orestes' bones—not because he necessarily believed they were the bones of the Homeric hero, but because it put an end of any hope for peace. War with Sparta was inevitable now, and like Harmatides, he was far from confident that Tegea would win the next round. A year from now he might—as Harmatides had put it last night—find himself tilling his own fields under a Spartan master. What was more, it might be a master who not only harvested his crops but also abused his horses. But mostly he was upset by the evening at Harmatides'. It was a shock to realize that he and his entire faction of reasonable, well-educated, and responsible men were dismissed as completely irrelevant and politically impotent. It was equally distressing to realize he had a choice between two equally appalling alternatives: the rule of the mindless mob, or the rule of the voracious and corrupt parvenus. Last night he had felt as if he were not only physically but morally impotent. He let *every*body do with him what they wanted, whether it was Onimastros, Pheronike and Dion, or even an ex-quarry slave like Philip. Everyone walked over him and mocked him behind his back.

Was that any reason for acting like an uneducated foreman or Persian despot? If he was impotent and politically powerless, at least before last night he had still had his dignity and civilisation. Now he was not only a fool, but a petty tyrant as well. Antyllus ran his fingers through his wiry grey hair. He was ashamed of himself.

A knock at the door made him sit up straight and call out warily. "Who's there?"

"Your wife," came Pheronike's timid voice.

"Come in."

She was dressed and her hair had been combed and put up, but she wore no make-up, no jewels, no perfume. She had bags under her eyes and her skin sagged. She came into the room and went down onto her knees before him. She wrapped her arms around his legs. "Antyllus. Husband. Don't be angry with me. Please. Forgive me." Tears were brimming in her eyes. Her lips were trembling. "Please, Antyllus. I—I only did it because you never come to me any more. I thought—but I was wrong. Oh, please, forgive me, husband."

Part of him thought she was only putting on a good show, but he stroked the back of her head and then patted her shoulder. "You can get up off your knees, my dear. I'm not going to divorce you."

She hesitated a moment more, and then gratefully (with an unconscious grunt) dragged herself upright. She sat down beside him on the bed and took his hand in hers. "We had some good years, Antyllus. It was long ago, but we did have our good times."

"I know. I remember."

"If only Phaedolos—" she dissolved into sobs, and he put his arm around her shoulders and held her until she'd calmed herself. "Dion—" she sobbed and he stiffened. "Please! Hear me out! Dion just reminded me of Phaedolos" (it was not plausible; Dion was oversized, blond, and blue-eyed, while Phaedolos had been short and plump with brown eyes and hair). "He only did what I asked him to do," Pheronike continued more convincingly. "You won't really do to him what you did to your new slave, will you?"

The gesture surprised him. Pheronike had always been indifferent to the fate of slaves before. She must really care for Dion, he thought, remembering the way she had washed his face yesterday morning. This thought almost hurt him more than the fact that she had used the Slav to satisfy a sexual hunger he had not even realized she had. But what was the point of punishing her—or Dion—for hurting him? No doubt she hadn't wanted or expected to *like* the slave. Very probably she had only intended to use him. If Dion had won her affection, it was to his credit. Antyllus shook his head and sighed. "No, I won't beat him."

"What did the other slave do to make you so angry?"

"Nothing," Antyllus admitted. "Nothing at all," and Pheronike looked at him strangely—as if she was now truly afraid of him because he must have gone mad.

It was days before he had the courage to face Philip. It was easy to avoid him at first because there was the Assembly to attend. Antyllus took Melissos with him to look after the horses, and the vote went for Harmatides' own bill and the maximum extension of the franchise. After that, things only got worse.

With a sense of déjà vu, Antyllus watched as Onimastros urged the Assembly to send an embassy to Lacedaemon and the Assembly shouted him down. He watched helplessly, too demoralised to even speak up, as the Assembly voted for war and then for "emergency powers", and so for its own destruction.

Utterly discouraged, Antyllus turned his back on politics, refusing the invitation of Harmatides to join his "government". He also avoided personal contact with Harmatides and his faction, preferring to withdraw to his estate, pretending he wanted nothing but to train his racing team. But how could he do that without facing Philip?

To avoid facing him, he avoided the stables, neglected his team, and when he went anywhere he had Melissos bring the chariot around to the front of the house. He had Hypathea report to him on Philip's progress, and his old nurse begged him to say what on earth the young man had done. But Antyllus had no good answer, so he gave none.

When the moon had waned from full to new, however, it was time to go into the city for his postponed lawsuit, and at last Antyllus sent for Philip.

In the library he paced nervously, trying to decide what he should say. Suddenly the young man darkened the doorway, and they just stood staring at one another. "How are you doing?" Antyllus asked.

"Fine."

"How's your back."

"I've been flogged before. It won't kill me."

"Do you feel up to driving?"

"Do you want me to?"

"I want you to come to town with me. I have to spend the day in court. I want you to tend the horses."

"Your wish is my command, master," he sneered.

"Don't do that," Antyllus requested wearily.

Philip dropped his eyes.

"Go get the chariot ready."

Philip turned on his heel and was gone.

They stood side by side in silence, Antyllus driving. A half-dozen times Antyllus found himself wanting to speak, to explain himself. Once he was even on the brink of apologising. He was sorry, but a master does not apologise to his slave.

At the courthouse, Antyllus dismounted and remarked wearily, "You know what to do." He took a drachma from his purse and held it out. Philip just stared at it. He put it on the top of the chariot rail.

"It'll get stolen there," Philip warned. "I can't guard it and see to the horses at the same time."

"You'll need to buy yourself something to eat and drink."

"There's water at the fountain house."

"And to eat?"

"I can fast all day."

"Why won't you take it?"

"I don't take bribes."

"Bribes?" Antyllus asked in genuine surprise. "Bribes are given in exchange for some illegal service. Whatever I want from you is my right to demand."

"I told you once before that you bought my body, not my soul. But that's what you're trying to buy. That's a bribe." He nodded contemptuously toward the drachma.

"That wasn't my intent, but since you see it that way ..." Antyllus replaced the drachma in his purse and went into the courthouse.

It was a long, tedious trial that took, as he had feared, all day. In the end a "settlement" was reached which required Antyllus to pay his opponent a fee in exchange for letting his sheep and goats graze in pastures that he felt were legally his in the first place. It was a completely unsatisfactory result, but one designed to remind him of the growing power of the rabble. He could all but hear Harmatides lecturing in his deep, melodic baritone: "Things would only be worse, dear Antyllus, if we hadn't managed our little coup."

Outside it was oppressively hot. The air was heavy with haze and there was no breeze. The stench of refuse came from the now closed market: fish guts, rancid olive oil, rotting vegetables, sour wine. The city sewers stank particularly noticeably today as well, and the smell offended Antyllus. He was anxious to get away from the sordid city, back to his orderly, clean estate.

In the alley beside the courthouse the manure was thick and flies swarmed. Strays slunk along the side of the buildings, adding their excrement to that of the horses. Antyllus picked his way forward in his sandals with distaste, and was relieved to find Philip waiting patiently in the chariot. He at once jumped down from the car, untied the reins, and handed these to Antyllus before rehitching the horses.

They did not exchange a word until they had left the city behind. Then as the horses trotted happily between the near ripe fields, Philip managed to say, "I'm sorry, sir."

Antyllus turned and stared at the young slave beside him, not sure he had heard correctly. "What did you say?"

"I'm sorry, sir. I didn't realise how your son died. The others talked about the 'young master' sometimes and it was clear that he was dead, but they never mentioned how."

"So who told you now?" Antyllus asked more confused than ever.

Philip was looking straight ahead, apparently still too ashamed to face him. "No one. I visited the necropolis. I found his grave. Phaedolos, son of Antyllus. It said he was killed in victorious battle against Sparta."

"You can read?" Antyllus asked in amazement.

"Of course," Philip replied with a frown and a flash of his old impudence.

There were many citizens who now voted at Assembly who could not read, Antyllus reflected, and while an intelligent slave boy might learn good Greek and even rhetoric just by listening to an educated master and his guests, learning to read was impossible without a teacher. He didn't get the chance to ask further questions, however, because Philip was remarking, "He was in the cavalry. He must have been a good driver."

"Not nearly as good as he thought he was," Antyllus replied honestly, attracting a surprised glance from Philip.

Philip was silent for a long time, thinking, and then he asked, very cautiously, "Is that why you were so angry the other night? Did I remind you of him by taking unnecessary chances?"

Antyllus hadn't thought of it. He considered the suggestion, but then dismissed it with a shake of his head and a sigh. There was nothing about this lean, taciturn slave that reminded him of his spoilt, plump son.

They did not speak again until they reached the turn off into the drive. Here Philip said again, "I'm sorry, sir." Adding, "I didn't mean to frighten you the other night. I—I thought you'd be pleased I could take the turn at that pace."

Antyllus glanced at the slave standing still and sad beside him, and inwardly gasped at his own idiocy. How could he have been so blind? Such a stupid fool? But the only answer he gave was: "You start training the team tomorrow."

Antyllus was up before dawn to take advantage of the coolest time of day. Dressed only in a short chiton, he breakfasted light, and then made his way to the stables as the birds started to whistle and trill. Philip was already up, his eagerness so patent and unfamiliar that it lifted Antyllus' spirits further. But Philip's first question was, "What about Ambelos? He'll be here soon. Should I give him his lesson first?"

Antyllus had forgotten all about Ambelos. "Has Ambelos come here every day?" Antyllus answered in surprise. "Was he here even the day after …"

"Of course, sir."

Antyllus was shamed to the marrow of his bones. Given the state Philip had been in, Ambelos couldn't have helped but notice. He would have asked what happened, and the answer would have been the same as to Cobon: that Antyllus had beat him bloody for nothing. He cringed at the mere thought of it.

"I said you beat me for attacking Polyphom, sir." Philip soothed his unspoken agitation.

Antyllus opened his mouth twice, but no sensible answer emerged. How could he thank the young man he had so unfairly flogged for protecting his reputation as well? It was more than Antyllus could bear, so he changed the subject. "I'm sure Ambelos will be happy to watch first and ride after. We'll take the two-horse racing cart and hitch up the driving team. You know them, so it's just a matter of getting familiar with the lighter racing chariot."

Philip nodded and went at once to fetch the chariot. He hauled it into the yard and then fetched the normal driving team. Cobon came out of the loft yawning and stared at his master and young colleague. "What you up to now, master?" he asked at last.

"I'm training Philip to drive."

Cobon looked sceptical but he gave Philip a hand with the horses nevertheless, brushing the stable stains from their coats and quickly picking out their hooves. Then he hobbled along beside the chariot as Philip drove it out to the training track.

By now Ambelos had arrived and been told what was happening. He joined Cobon and Antyllus on the rail, while Philip took the light chariot onto the track and pointed it toward the distant curve.

"Take them around the track once at a walk and then a trot. Do NOT canter them until I tell you."

"Yes, sir." Philip's face was serious and there was nothing insolent about him this morning. He did exactly as he was told. Cobon and Antyllus noticed how he moved about on the thin boards, trying to find the right place to stand, and how he fussed several times with the reins, trying different holds. At the end of the trotting round, the horses, remembering the routine from their own racing days, wanted to break into a canter on their own and Antyllus watched carefully, his eyes narrowed to see how Philip responded. He used his whole body to brace against the pulling of the horses, but he brought them to a prancing, fretting halt right at the start. He glanced over at Antyllus.

"Well done. Ease up on the reins gradually, but whatever you do, don't give them their heads. Check them constantly. Do you know what I mean? Don't pull back at the same time. Alternate hands. Work them against each other. Pull and release. Pull and release. Don't just tug on them. They're stronger than you are. Now go on and do another round."

Philip nodded and they could see him lick his lips in concentration as he eased up on the reins and the two geldings realised they were free to move forward again. They gathered speed slowly at first, but then the sheer joy of movement took over and they started racing forward. Cobon caught his breath, and Antyllus gripped the railing, hardly breathing. Ambelos was biting his lower lip with tension. Antyllus could see his horses fighting the reins, trying to throw their heads up to evade the bit. The off-gelding flattened his ears and tried his old trick of edging outwards. And all the time the distance to the turn was narrowing rapidly.

They went into the turn not fully collected and the chariot swung far too wide for a good turn, but it did not actually go off the track or turn over; and as he came back toward them, Philip seemed to be getting a better grip of things. Antyllus lifted his hand and waved him on to a second round, remarking to Cobon, "There's only one way to learn. Do it." He cast Ambelos a guilty look as he said this, remembering that Philip had used exactly that argument to let him ride about on his own—and the young man had been making notable progress ever since.

By the third round, Cobon was gripping the railing in amazement. "He's a natural, master! He's got them exactly where they should be. Look at that!"

At the end of seven rounds, the old team was panting loudly and the sun was now up over the mountains, bright and burning. Antyllus signalled Philip to slow, calling out: "Trot one round and then walk one round, and bring them back to the stables." Philip was grinning from ear to ear, and for once his scar did not seem the least bit gloomy or ominous. Antyllus felt as happy as the young slave looked. Ambelos turned to the older man and remarked, "There's something special about him, isn't there?"

"Yes," Antyllus conceded, comforted that he wasn't the only one who had come under Philip's strange spell.

By the time Kapaneos' letter arrived, high summer was past and the autumn equinox approaching. It was a dangerous time of year because, with the worst heat gone out of the sun and the harvest in, it was an ideal season for a quick military campaign. If Sparta was as aggressive as Harmatides claimed, then now was the time for a Lacedaemonian army to darken the passes over the Parnos. Antyllus avoided the city as much as possible, concentrating fanatically on improving Philip's driving. He could now handle any pair of horses, even intentionally mismatched ones, and Antyllus thought he was nearly ready for a full four-horse chariot.

The arrival of a slave boy carrying a letter from Kapaneos interrupted the routine like a siren call from his past. Antyllus could not imagine what Kapaneos could have to say to him now. After all, Phaeax was enjoying ever-increasing influence and had been appointed strategos. Kapaneos was hanging on to his coat-tails, and reportedly was heavily in debt to both Phaeax and Polyphom—but they weren't calling in his debts as long as he danced to their tune.

Antyllus sent the messenger around to the kitchens to get something to eat and drink, and retired apprehensively to his study to read the letter in peace. He sat down, made himself comfortable, and broke the seal.

"*Honoured Antyllus.*

"*You need not fear that I have designs upon your purse. You were always grudging with it anyway—even to poor Phaedolos, who had every right to his father's largess.*

"*Nor need you fear I will beg your favours ever again. I have seen the direction of your affections, and can only warn you that you make yourself the laughing stock of all Tegea. Am I—the son of a Tegean nobleman—truly supposed to compete with a barbarian slave from the quarries? Never would I sink so low.*

"*There is one thing, however, that I must say to you. Something I cannot say in public because I would not want to disgrace the memory of Phaedolos. He was not the man you are, perhaps, but his love was real. He loved me, Antyllus.*

"*No, I do not want to besmirch Phaedolos' memory by saying this in public, but I think you ought to know how he really died. You see, I lied to you when I said Phaedolos led the spearhead of the cavalry attack that broke the Lacedaemonian phalanx. He was not at the forefront except by accident. His stallion—the beautiful white stallion he bought in Thebes—bolted and ran away with him. He dropped his javelin to cling onto the mane and when the stallion reached the line of Spartan Guardsmen it shied sharply, rearing up on his haunches so abruptly that he was flung off—right among the enemy—and they stabbed him to death.*

"Now I think I've said all there is to say. You need not worry that I will ever bother you again for any reason.

"Kapaneos"

For over three years, Antyllus had believed that his son had died as Kapaneos had told him the day he brought his body home. It had been such a heroic image—so at odds with the way Phaedolos had lived—that it had made Antyllus certain he had misjudged his son. For three years, he had cursed himself again and again for not seeing his son more clearly while he lived. He had cursed himself for being so critical—seeing only his gambling debts, his too frequent hangovers, and his ineptitude at sport, his irresponsible handling of horses. This image of Phaedolos being thrown by a stallion he had never really mastered fit so perfectly with the Phaedolos Antyllus remembered, that he did not doubt it for a moment. He was certain that this was indeed how Phaedolos had died.

What Antyllus could not fathom was why Kapaneos felt the need to send this message. Why did he want to hurt him? Why did Kapaneos hate him? Why send this message *now*? Were there now new intrigues in which Kapaneos was involved? But what could he possibly gain with this hateful letter? And why the nonsensical insinuations about Philip? No one could seriously think Antyllus would sink so low as take a full-grown slave as his lover, could they? Or was there a disguised warning—or threat—in this message that he was too dense to comprehend?

Antyllus sent word to Kapaneos' slave boy that there would be no return message, and then closed himself in his study. Here he tried for the thousandth time to understand his relationship to his dead son. Gradually the sun slipped down the sky. The courtyard was cast in shadow. A light breeze stirred. His body slave timidly peered into the room. "Do you want dinner, Master?"

"Dinner?" He looked up bewildered that it was so late already, but then waved the slave away. "No, no; I'm not hungry."

It grew dark. Antyllus stood, stiff from having sat immobile for so long. By the light of the moon he went through the passage between the formal and the kitchen courtyard. Light and laughter spilled out of the kitchen. He lifted up his long chiton and picked his way across the rows of parsley, cumin, and coriander to the entry. He peered inside. The cook was sitting with his feet up and a jug of wine in his hand. He was laughing heartily at some joke he had probably told himself. The kitchen boys were finished with the washing up, and putting the pottery back onto the shelves. The sight of the master in the doorway startled them all. They looked at him wide-eyed and—something inconceivable before the flogging of Philip—frightened.

The cook recovered first; quickly if awkwardly swinging his feet down and getting to his feet, he asked: "Master? Can I get you anything?"

"Prepare a snack for me with plenty of wine and ask Philip to serve it to me in my study."

Antyllus retraced his steps in the dark, but rather than going into his study, he sat down on the edge of the fountain in the centre of the courtyard. His mind was empty.

Philip emerged with a tray and was about to turn into the study when he saw Antyllus at the fountain. "Sir?"

"Bring it over here," Antyllus gestured.

Philip brought the tray, setting it down carefully on the well-tended grass. He picked up the water pitcher and poured water over Antyllus' hands. Next he held out a linen towel. When Antyllus handed this back, he poured wine for Antyllus in a kylix and handed it to him. Then he squatted down beside the tray and started to slice the bread. He offered it up to Antyllus in a basket. Antyllus took a slice and started nibbling at it.

"We talked once before of how my son died."

"Yes, sir. He was killed in battle against the Spartans."

"Today I learned the details. He was thrown from a stallion—a beautiful white stallion—that he couldn't control properly. He lost his javelin before he could use it and was thrown in among the Spartan Guard. They stabbed him 8 times. I saw the corpse."

Philip didn't move. He didn't even seem to breathe. He waited for Antyllus to continue.

"And all because he insisted on riding a horse he couldn't handle. I told him to get rid of that stallion. But he was infatuated with it because it was huge and muscular and pure white. It was a beautiful stallion, but it had a wild streak in it. It was unpredictable." He handed his empty kylix to Philip, who filled it again.

"I'm going to get drunk tonight, Philip. Would you go and fetch more wine and bring a second kylix."

"Sir?"

"I don't want to drink alone."

Philip disappeared in the dark passageway to the kitchen courtyard and returned with a squat pelike and a tall amphora, one with wine and the other with water, and a krater to mix in. He sat down on the grass at Antyllus' feet and refilled the kylix Antyllus handed him.

"Do you remember your father?" Antyllus asked.

Philip looked up sharply, and Antyllus sighed, knowing he would now get one of those curt, angry refusals.

Philip looked away and helped himself to some wine. "My mother died giving me birth."

Antyllus was so surprised to hear Philip talk about himself that he almost dropped his kylix. Then he held his breath, hoping for more.

"When I was about four or maybe five, my sister told me that. She told me it was my fault we didn't have a mother any more. 'You killed her! And I hate you!' she shouted at me. I went running to my nanny and demanded to hear that it wasn't true. But my nanny was an honest woman, and she admitted that in a way I had killed my mother, but tried to explain that it wasn't my fault. I didn't like that answer, and so I ran away as far as I dared at that age—which was out to the fountain house on the banks of the stream that cut through our property. Of course all the slaves knew I was there, but they let me be. My father came looking for me. He asked me what I was doing crouching in a corner of the fountain house when I could be having a nice dinner at the house. I said I didn't feel like eating because I'd killed my mother. So he sat down on the floor beside me and explained that I had had an elder brother. He explained that at the birth of this elder brother, my mother had been very ill and nearly died. He said the doctors told my mother that if she gave birth to another child it would kill her. But when my brother died three years later of a fever, she had been miserable and begged to have another child. 'So you see,' he said, 'your mother loved you so much that she was willing to die for you.' 'But that's horrible!' I protested. But my father answered: 'Only if you don't grow up to be the brave young man your mother died for.' That's my earliest memory of him." Philip finished in a bland tone.

Antyllus was so upset he didn't know what to say. But he was beginning to understand that wherever Philip had been born, he had been born into a wealthy, landowning family with slaves and nannies and family honour. With memories like that to carry around with him, it was no wonder he still resented his enslavement. Worse still, he evidently believed he had betrayed his mother by not growing up to be a warrior.

Finally Antyllus managed to ask, "Is your father still alive?"

"I don't know. I hope not."

That was understandable. He did not want to think of his father in slavery.

"Your father was a wealthy man?"

"Not really. We were poor relations with just the one farm—and the horses, of course. But they were more an expense than an asset."

"But he was an aristocrat," Antyllus pressed him.

"No. He was a peer. And proud of it."

The term meant nothing to Antyllus in this context, but Philip's tone had become harsh and defensive again—so he left it at that, and simply handed his kylix back for refilling.

As he did so, Philip remarked in a pensive tone, "We had apple orchards at home. That's why the sight of them here made me want to live after all. And not just apple. We had pear, quince, plum, fig—and, of course, the almonds up by the house. My grandmother had planted the almonds because she liked the blossoms so much. My grandmother didn't die until I was ten. She was a formidable old woman."

They were silent together, and then Antyllus risked asking, "Tell me. Did you ever quarrel with your father?"

"My father?" Philip looked up at Antyllus in surprise. "Not very often. I was more apt to quarrel with my grandfather and my sister. My father was my best friend."

"I quarrelled with my son constantly," Antyllus admitted, swishing the wine about in his kylix. "I would have liked to be his friend. I don't think there is anything else in the world—not even an Olympic victory—that I would have liked more."

"He died a hero—and I'm a slave."

"He's dead."

"He has a gravestone." Slaves did not get tombstones. They were buried in unmarked pits just like animals.

"And I'm sitting here talking to you as I never did with him."

"Did he never serve you wine?"

"Did you serve your father?"

"Until I—" Philip stopped himself so sharply, Antyllus could hear the intake of breath.

"Until you were captured," Antyllus finished for him gently.

Philip nodded and drank from his own kylix until it was empty.

Antyllus stood. His bones creaked. "I think it's time to go to bed. Tomorrow take out the four-horse and put the old team—Boreas rather than Zephyrus—in the traces."

"Yes, sir. Good night, sir." Philip was already collecting the things onto a tray. Antyllus left him to it and made his way to the domestic courtyard on silent sandals.

CHAPTER 8

When they saw Philip take out the four-horse racing chariot, the others left their chores and collected in the yard to watch. Dion helped Philip get all four horses ready, while Cobon fussed with the harness and Melissos gazed in wonder. "Can he drive that?" he asked, disbelieving.

"We'll soon see," Cobon retorted; but you could see he was nervous and anxious. As always, word spread throughout the household, and by the time they had driven out to the training track, even the kitchen boys, laundry maids, and body slaves had come out to line the track and watch. Ambelos, too, was there as always—and more openly excited than anybody else.

Antyllus was on the board beside Philip. He placed the reins in the young man's hands, showing him exactly how to hold them. With his hands over the younger man's, he showed Philip how to pull each of the four heads individually. Dion was holding the team during this explanation, and Cobon was standing just behind, listening to every word.

Philip listened attentively, nodding occasionally to indicate he understood. At last Antyllus could think of nothing more to add. "Do you think you're ready?"

Philip looked at the reins in his hands. "I hope so."

"Do you want me to ride the first round with you?" Antyllus asked nervously.

"Would that make you happier, sir?"

Their eyes met. Antyllus caught that slight glisten of mirth lurking behind Philip's impassive mask, and at once stepped down from the chariot.

"Just—"

"Start at a walk, then trot, and then stop. I know, sir."

Antyllus sighed and looked at Cobon in exasperation. Cobon grinned. "He'd be an idiot if he didn't know the routine by now."

Antyllus nodded and signalled to Philip that he could start. Dion let go of the horses, and they were in Philip's hands. Dion moved to the side, frowning. The chariot moved away decorously. The laundry maids were gossiping and a scuffle of some sort broke out among the kitchen boys. As Philip passed the starting point and picked up a trot, the others gradually turned their attention back to the track. "Boreas is overexcited to be back at the traces," Cobon remarked.

"He's on the inside," Antyllus countered. "If Philip has any difficulties it will be with Titan or Penny."

Cobon wasn't so sure, but he was not a slave who openly contradicted his master.

Bringing all four eager horses to a halt after the second round was more difficult than with just two. Philip didn't manage until he was a quarter of the way beyond the line, and then they started backing up. Antyllus ducked under the rail and went out onto the track to hold them himself while he talked to Philip again, giving him more advice. Cobon kept scratching his greying beard. Antyllus moved out of the way, and Philip had the team pick up a trot again. He trotted a second round, and then a third and a fourth. The horses stopped, expecting a canter. And that was when he asked it of them—not at the start, but after the turn on the backstretch. Then he kept them going for another three rounds before pulling up at the finish with a broad grin of triumph. Despite the scar on his forehead, at the moment he was a handsome young man. "All right?" he asked Antyllus.

"It'll do for a first try," Antyllus answered, and then burst out laughing, unable to suppress his good spirits. Ambelos joined him, sharing in the excitement and the triumph quite without self-interest. Antyllus flung his arm around Harmatides' son without thinking. Philip might have a lot to learn, but he had never before seen a man who learned so fast and so easily.

The fall equinox was past, and still the Spartan invasion failed to materialise. The first voices of protest against the emergency powers granted to Harmatides were raised—and as quickly suppressed. Antyllus kept out of the city as much as possible. By the time he put Zephyrus back into the team, Philip was so adept at driving that it seemed to make no difference at all which horses were in the traces. Antyllus could all but smell the olive crown of Olympia. With this team and this driver, he told himself, he had a real chance of being the best. Of course, one never knew what other teams were being trained all across Greece; but in his bones he believed that this time he had it.

The sun was approaching the winter solstice and there was sometimes frost in the night when he ordered not only the four-horse chariot harnessed, but the two-horse as well. Antyllus announced he would drive the two-horse on track at the same time as Philip drove the four-horse, to simulate racing conditions. It was time Philip learned how to overtake other chariots.

To his utter astonishment, Philip balked. "I won't do that."

"What?" Antyllus asked, baffled.

"You don't expect me to drive this team in competition, do you?" Philip countered.

"Of course. What do you think we've been training for?"

Philip did not have a ready answer to that; but after a moment, he said, "We're training your team for Olympia, but you'll have a hired driver for the competition."

"Why should I have a hired driver when I can have you?"

"Because I won't drive your team at Olympia." The insolence was back in his voice for the first time in months—for the first time since he'd started training.

"What's the matter with you?" Antyllus stared at Philip, flabbergasted. It was not his tone of voice alone that astonished Antyllus, but that the gifted driver would refuse the most coveted athletic prize—a chance to compete at Olympia.

"I won't drive your team at Olympia or in any competition," Philip insisted stubbornly.

"I'm offering you an honour that no Greek would dream of turning down! Do you know how many young men throughout Hellas dream of nothing else but an opportunity like this? It is an honour, Philip!"

"I know it's an honour."

"Then what *is* it?!" Antyllus was getting exasperated. The days were short now, and the horses were getting very fractious in the chill. The other slaves had collected as usual and were openly eavesdropping. Ambelos, fortunately, was absent. He no longer took riding lessons, having purchased one of Antyllus' younger mares in preparation for presenting himself for muster at the spring equinox, but he usually rode over to watch Philip train.

"I can't." Philip declared definitively.

"Of course you can!" Antyllus countered. He had never imagined that this insolent, self-assured young man would have self-doubts. It seemed utterly out of character, but he tried to reassure him. "We have a good eight months to train still. By the time you go to Olympia you'll be the finest driver in all Hellas."

Philip's lips twitched. "Maybe, but that doesn't change things."

"Have you gone mad?! I'm offering you the chance to drive in an Olympic event! By all the Gods, I'm offering you more than that! I'm offering you the chance to *win* an Olympic event! Not even the Gods would turn down such a chance!"

"The victory in equestrian events goes to the owner, not the rider or driver," Philip observed dryly.

"So what? You're the one who'll have the thrill of the race itself." Antyllus told him, suddenly aware of how much he envied the young man. "You're the one who will see the finish line ahead of you—and no other chariot between you and it. You're the one they'll cheer." With open envy, Antyllus told him, "You have no idea what an ecstatic sensation that is—galloping down the home stretch past thousands of shouting, waving, cheering men with an Olympic victory coming nearer with each thundering hoofbeat!"

"YES I DO!" Philip shouted at him.

Stunned silence. They stared at each other.

Philip was so flushed, he looked as if he'd just run the course on foot. "You were there," he whispered.

"When?"

"At the last Olympics."

"Yes. So what? I lost."

"Don't you remember who won?"

"How could I forget! Teleklos, son of Apollonides."

"Who was driving his team?"

"His son, Ly- Ly- Lysander."

"Lysandridas."

"Yes, that's right, Lysandridas, who was killed just afterwards. That's why Teleklos' team lost at the Pythian Games. He had a different driver, I think it was his nephew—"

"Teleklos was at the Pythian games?" Philip asked, and his face was now drained of blood, and the anger and arrogance of just a moment ago was gone so abruptly that Antyllus was beginning to think he had imagined it.

"Yes, as I said, with the same team but a different driver. Lysandridas had got his wish and been selected for the Spartan Guard. He was killed defending his King against our cavalry."

Philip was shaking his head, his eyes opaque and blind, the colour of molten lead under the livid scar.

"What is it?" Antyllus demanded, vaguely alarmed. Things were happening too fast. First the slave was stubborn and arrogant, then he was angry, now he looked as if he would be sick any second.

"Not killed—wounded, captured, enslaved."

Antyllus stared at him. "But—Sparta ransomed all the captives."

"No. The families ransomed the captives. My family didn't."

"That can't be." Antyllus stared at the slave, but suddenly felt dizzy. He turned and stumbled back toward the house. He could picture the end of that Olympic race all too clearly: his own team trailing by two lengths despite the whip cracking over their heads. His heart had fallen gently but steadily, with each thundering stride, as he realised it was absolutely hopeless. They were defeated. Fairly and soundly. And then he had been utterly alone as he stood among the cheering crowds gone wild for a charioteer who had scorned 1000 drachma for this moment. He remembered, too, the victory celebration: Teleklos pulling his son into the circle of revellers, placing his arm over his shoulders, crowning him with the victor's wreath, saying again and again it was *his son's* victory, Lysandridas' victory, not his own. He remembered Polycritus sneering at the young man with a contemptuous wave at his crown of olives and his ribbons. "They won't even buy you a pair of sandals when you're old and crippled. What good is an Olympic victory to the likes of you!?"

"It means I'll stand *in front* of my King in battle," Lysandridas had tossed back.

Antyllus walked blindly across the slaves' courtyard, tripping on the cobbles, stumbling over his own feet. The images were clear—so clear that he could not grasp how he had failed to recognise him despite his scars. Then again, Antyllus pictured the slave he had purchased, his head shaved and his body wasted away to practically nothing. He had nothing in common with the Olympic charioteer in peak physical condition. The winning charioteers' muscles were toned not only from the hours in the chariot, but from his daily drill with shield and sword. He had been magnificent. There had been no scars on him anywhere. Certainly not the ugly scars marring his forehead or mutilating his thigh.

Trampled! He had been trampled! When the Tegean cavalry broke the Spartan phalanx, they had trampled down half the Guard. The Spartan Guard had flung themselves forward against the horses to give their King a chance to escape! They had killed Phaedolos. They had stabbed him 8 times.

And Lysandridas' father had not ransomed him. No wonder Lysandridas had tried to kill himself! But how could his father have left the son who had given him an Olympic victory in slavery? Antyllus couldn't grasp it. He couldn't imagine it. How could *any* father let a son—no matter how disobedient or apparently worthless—languish in slavery? It couldn't be.

He remembered Teleklos at the Pythian Games. He had been a broken man. He had hardly seemed to care if he won or not, and when someone asked why he didn't have the same driver as before, he had said in a toneless voice full of bottomless grief: "My son is dead."

Maybe he really thought his son was dead?

Antyllus turned about and started running. He burst into the stableyard where the slaves were collected in a horde, all chattering at once. "Is it true, Master? He's *Spartan*?!"

"He's an Olympic charioteer, you fools! Where is he?"

"He's in the stables."

Antyllus lifted his long chiton and ran. In the doorway he stopped and stared. There was no one in sight except the horses. They looked curiously over the doors of their stalls. One or two nickered at him in greeting. Titan, as always, kicked at his stall door in a perpetual demand for more food. But Afra had always been Philip's favourite. She was not looking over her stall door. Antyllus walked into the barn slowly and deliberately. He did not even need to look over the stall door. He opened it without delay, following the sound of the sobbing.

The mare was nuzzling her keeper in confusion, but looked over at Antyllus questioningly. Antyllus sank down on the straw and pulled Philip/Lysandridas into his arms.

"I thought—he—was dead," Lysandridas sobbed without need for introduction. "I always thought he was dead. I was sure—it was my brother-in-law—who had refused to pay. He's related to the Eurypontids—is in the kryptea. I knew he—would say it was a—disgrace for a Guardsman to survive. But that my father—" He was choking on his tears, unable to get enough breath.

Antyllus felt tears on his own face. "Phil—Lysandridas, maybe your father doesn't know. I heard him say you were dead."

Lysandridas shook his head. "Dead to him. A Guardsman shouldn't—survive a defeat."

Antyllus couldn't believe it, but he couldn't prove the contrary, either. All he could do was hold Lysandridas in his arms until he had cried himself out. Then he washed his face down with cold water and let him lay back in the straw.

"I can't face the others," Lysandridas declared bluntly.

"Not yet," Antyllus corrected.

"Do you understand now why I won't drive your team in competition?"

"Of course."

"Someone might recognise me—Polycritus, for example. Think how he'd crow and dance to see me in chains! 'A thousand drachma would have bought your freedom,' he'd chortle."

"You aren't in chains," Antyllus reminded him gently, but Lysandridas didn't seem to hear him.

"Now I know I might have to face my father, too." The voice was tight again, but he managed to bite back the sobs and the tears. He was getting used to the pain. Making himself get used to it.

"It might do him good," Antyllus suggested softly.

Lysandridas shifted his head so he was no longer staring upwards at the cobwebbed rafters of the barn, but at Antyllus. "What do you mean?"

"Either your father really thinks you're dead, and then he would be overjoyed to see you, or he is a cold-hearted bastard who deserves—"

"Please. Don't talk about my father like that. I still love him. Even if I don't—understand—how he could do this to me." Philip closed his eyes and the tears oozed out from under his black lashes.

Antyllus put a hand on his shoulder and sighed. Afra contentedly munched on her hay, not at all put out to share her stall with the two humans who had rescued her from the horrible thing in her belly.

Antyllus began trying to think what he should do with this Spartiate Guardsman and Olympic charioteer. He could hardly have him mucking out stalls any longer. The reaction of the other slaves indicated that they would not want him in their midst, either. He ought to set him free, but the young man had said he could not go home, and Antyllus could now understand. "You recognised me right from the start, didn't you?"

"Not at the quarries; only when I got here and saw Titan and Ajax in the yard."

Antyllus nodded, wincing inwardly at how he'd asked an Olympic charioteer if he knew anything about horses; how he'd shown him how to stand in a chariot and how to hold the reins; etc., etc., etc. Was it any wonder the slave had sometimes responded with acidic bitterness? Sarcasm? Or more recently, with ill-disguised amusement?

The other "mysteries" of his past all started to make sense too: his flawless Greek and command of rhetoric, his excellent table manners and skills serving at table. These were all things Spartiate youth learned as boys serving as mess boys to their elders in the famous Spartan syssitia, or messes. His speech, in retrospect, was so "laconic" it should have given him away in itself! His old flogging wounds—not to mention the way he had endured Antyllus' flogging defiantly!—were also clearly the products of his harsh Spartan upbringing—something infamous throughout Greece. Even his apparent familiarity with childbirth made sense in a society where girls attended public school, where maidens were allowed to engage in sports under the eyes of the entire city, and where even married women went about unveiled in public.

In retrospect, Antyllus was ashamed he had not guessed Philip/ Lysandridas' nationality—if not his identity—at least on the day he learned from Kapaneos how Phaedolos had been killed. That night Philip/ Lysandridas had pointedly denied that his father was an aristocrat, despite being a landowner, calling him a "peer" instead. At the time of the 25th Olympics, Sparta had been torn apart by revolution, and only a massive land reform and the introduction of a new constitution under Lycurgus had restored peace to the city. Since then, the Spartiates considered themselves "equals", or peers, because the Land Reform had divided up the great estates and distributed them equally among the citizens so that each citizen had an equal land allotment. Other laws prohibited the hoarding of precious metals and the pursuit of trade, thereby reducing inequality of other forms of wealth.

"We didn't mean to stab your son eight times," Lysandridas said without opening his eyes. "As he fell amongst us, we all stabbed out of instinct. None of us could be sure the other had already killed him. It wasn't intentional disrespect."

"That's all right.... Phil—Lysandridas, from now on I want you to move into one of the individual chambers, the one next to Hypathea. You are relieved of all duties—except training, of course.

Lysandridas lay very still. "You don't have to do that. I can't go home—now less than ever. I might as well—"

Antyllus patted his shoulder. "There is no way I can treat you like a slave now that I know who you are. You will have your own chamber, I will provide you with proper clothes, and you will share your meals with me."

"I don't want everyone to know."

"Believe me, the whole city will know by nightfall. I don't know how, but slaves with gossip seem to be able to communicate it to the very sparrows."

Lysandridas' face was stony. "It doesn't make things easier."

"Then it's true?!" A breathless and excited voice broke in on them, and they both looked up, startled, to see Ambelos leaning on the stall door, his face flushed with excitement. "What the slaves are saying? That Philip is really the Spartan who drove Teleklos' chariot to victory at the 55th Games?"

Antyllus just looked at Philip/Lysandridas, who sat up, resting his arms on his knees and met Ambelos' gaze. "Yes."

"But that's wonderful!" Ambelos declared opening the stall door and lurching in, his awkward gait exaggerated in his great hurry. "Didn't I always say there was something special about him?" Ambelos flung at Antyllus without awaiting an answer. He pulled a still somewhat stunned Lysandridas to his feet and embraced him. "Now we can truly be friends!" Ambelos declared with obvious enthusiasm.

"I'm still a slave," Lysandridas parried rather stiffly.

Ambelos cast a disbelieving look at Antyllus and then declared forcefully. "If Antyllus doesn't set you free, my father will buy your freedom. You can come and live with us!" With each sentence his eagerness increased. "We can ride together every day—and you can teach me everything you know about war. Philip—no!—what is your *real* name?"

"Lysandridas son of Teleklos."

"Lysandridas! Of course! How could I forget? But don't you see? This is the work of the Gods—bringing you here, giving you to us. I can't wait to tell my father!"

Antyllus, sensing Lysandridas' discomfort, intervened gently. "Let's take things one step at a time, young man. Of course I will free Lysandridas, but he will stay here. He must continue to train my team—get them ready for the next Olympic Games. Surely you see the sense in that?"

"Oh, yes, of course," Ambelos said dutifully, deferring to the senior statesman, "but afternoons Lysandridas can come into town. I can show him our city as he has never seen it before. We can go to the theatre together and he can attend my father's symposia. You'll learn to love Tegea, Lysandridas, I'm sure of it. And then you can drive Antyllus' team—Tegea's team—to victory at the next Games. And my father and I will be there to cheer you as never before!"

Lysandridas looked helplessly at Antyllus.

"Not so fast, Ambelos. Lysandridas was just explaining to me that he did not want to drive in competition ever again."

"But—" Ambelos started to protest. Antyllus silenced him with a hand gesture.

"He has his reasons, and I'm sure he'll explain them to you in good time. For now, he has agreed to help me train this team, and that is enough."

"And there are always new colts," Lysandridas suggested with just the ghost of an attempted smile.

Antyllus smiled back. "That's right. There's the breeding season and more brood mares to worry about, and new foals and the yearling sales and the two-year-olds to be backed and trained to the traces, and then new teams—always better than the last—to train and drive." It was, for him, a pleasant prospect rolling into old age. But the look of puzzled disbelief on Ambelos' face reminded him that it was not really enough for a young man. He took a deep breath and suggested, "Now, why don't the two of you go for a long ride before the weather gets any worse? The team can have a day of rest." He clapped Philip/Lysandridas once on the shoulder and gave him a smile, saying, "We can discuss the rest of what must be done when you get back." Then he nodded to Ambelos and left the stables.

How capricious the Gods were, Antyllus thought. They took away his worthless son and gave him a youth who was a hundred times his superior. If he had been my son, Antyllus thought, I would have sold myself before I let him suffer slavery. The father who would reject this youth did not deserve him.

PART II

TELEKLOS

CHAPTER 9

The summer of the 55th Olympic Games had been the most hectic Teleklos could remember in his fifty-six years. After thirty years of horse breeding and training, he had finally raised a quartet of colts he thought worthy of Olympia. He had spent two years preparing the team for competition, and he left for Olympia two months before the 55th Games were scheduled to take place. He and his twenty-two-year-old son Lysandridas led his team across mountainous Arcadia on foot with the racing chariot dismantled and loaded on pack mules. He was one of the first participants to arrive at Elis, and had concentrated on the final training in an atmosphere of religious devotion. The arrival of the spectators—loud, irreverent, frequently drunk and rowdy—had irritated him in the extreme. He would have preferred the competition to take place in the presence of the judges and the Gods alone.

But the Olympic Games had become a festival over the last two hundred years; and over time, more and more spectators travelled from ever further away to attend them, taking advantage of the Olympic peace to cross the territory of even their worst enemies unmolested. There was a large contingent of Spartan spectators, as always. Many of Lysandridas' friends and age-cohort had come to see him drive; and King Leon, ailing though he was, had insisted on attending with his still immature grandson and heir Anaxandridas. Teleklos' son-in-law, Derykleides, was there, too, with a group of friends from the kryptea; and Chilon, his own best friend through all the trials of life, came to give him moral support in the greatest competition he had ever faced. Chilon was the only one of them Teleklos was actually glad to see, though he was glad for Lysandridas' sake that so many of his friends and rivals had come to support him.

The night before the chariot race, Lysandridas burst in on him in a state of youthful outrage. Shocked and insulted, he reported that their rival from Corinth, Polycritus, had just offered him a bribe of 1,000 drachma if he would ensure that his father's team did *not* win the race the next day.

Lysandridas had taken it as a personal insult and affront to his honour. He kept asking: "Where did he get the idea I could be bought? What have I done to earn such a reputation? How can I wash myself clean of this disgrace?"

He had been far too upset to keep his voice down, and since all the athletes slept together in the spacious but nevertheless crowded "guest house" by the river Kladeos, soon other athletes were crowding in the doorway and asking what had happened. Lysandridas explained, shaking with fury.

The Hellanodikai were called in. Lysandridas was made to swear an oath that he spoke the truth in the sacred Altis itself, and then Polycritus had been called to testify. He had made some kind of weak defence, claiming it was a misunderstanding and the 1000 drachma had been a future salary if Lysandridas would drive for him. It was not a credible story; Lysandridas was already a Spartan citizen, and everyone knew Sparta's laws prohibited her citizens from pursuing any profession except that of arms. Polycritus had been duly disqualified from the race.

The race itself had been almost more than Teleklos could bear. After so many years of preparing for this moment, and two months training against the very teams that lined up that morning on the arrow-shaped starting gate, he realised he didn't have the nerves for the sport after all. His team had drawn a bad position: directly beside the starter. This meant that the four young horses were first distracted by the golden eagle which shot up to mark the opening of the race and, almost as bad, all but one of the other seven teams were already in motion before the ropes across their own starting stall dropped. Even from his seat behind the judges' tribune, Teleklos could see that Lysandridas had his hands full trying to keep the team from bolting too soon and disqualifying themselves. And when they came out of the gate, they were sheering to the right, still distressed by all the mechanical gadgets that marked the start of the race.

It had taken more than a lap for Lysandridas to calm them enough to concentrate on overtaking the other chariots, all but two of which were leading him by that point. But when he started to pass the other chariots one at a time, trying to cut them off at the curves, Teleklos suddenly realised that he was risking his only son's life for the sake of a worthless crown of olive leaves. He had driven in his youth and trained Lysandridas in the sport ever since he'd been taught to drive the donkey cart at the age of eight. But it was only during that decisive race at Olympia that the dangers of the sport really penetrated Teleklos' brain.

There was no question that his team was the best in the hippodrome that day; but the Tegean entry was only marginally less strong, and the Theban team was very experienced and steady, even if a little past their prime. It would not have taken much—only a small miscalculation on Lysandridas' part—and either of these teams could have snatched the victory away from him. Lysandridas made no mistake.

The Theban team had taken an early lead after breaking from a good starting position. More important, they appeared supremely at ease with both the mechanics of the start and the cheering of the crowds, giving them a significant advantage over the younger, inexperienced teams that were unnerved, shying, and sweating in the unfamiliar atmosphere. The Tegean team, however, steadily gained on the Theban until they were pacing one another. The Tegean inched his team up on the inside, waiting for an opportunity to slip past the Thebans, but the Theban driver, a grey-bearded freedman with numerous scars, made sure that the opportunity never arose. He took each turn just close enough to the post to prevent the Tegean from cutting him off.

Lysandridas took his team up on the outside of the Theban, and challenged him on the stretch rather than the turns. He had sufficient speed to move ahead of the Thebans on the straight, and although he twice lost ground on the curve, he always caught up again on the stretch. In this way, the Theban was forced to ask too much of his horses too soon. Lysandridas trusted that his younger team had the endurance to keep up a pace that the Thebans could not match for long. At last, two laps short of the finish, the Thebans started to lag. The whip was out, but the team was spent.

Lysandridas then slipped in front of them elegantly on the stretch and had only the Tegean team to cope with. This team pulled up beside him on the inside, and it was a stronger, younger team than the Theban. Lysandridas could not hope to catch it on the stretch if he lost too much ground on the curve. On the very last turn before the finish, he drew his chariot off the rail before the turn, raising a moan of disappointment from the Spartans. When the Tegean swung out to get around the curve safely, however, he was in a position to cut sharply between the Tegean and the inside post in a manoeuvre that brought all the screaming spectators to their feet. The Tegean team was so upset by the unexpected appearance of another chariot on their left that they veered sharply right. The driver took precious seconds getting them back on course, and crossed the finish almost two lengths behind the Spartan team.

Teleklos couldn't remember what happened next. He had nearly died when Lysandridas cut the corner, and hadn't entirely recovered when everyone started congratulating him. King Leon was there and Prince Anaxandridas was beside himself with triumph. Derykleides was (for once) full of praise for his brother-in-law, and the younger men had stormed onto the hippodrome, against all the rules, to surround Lysandridas, take him from the chariot, and carry him on their shoulders around the course.

At the celebrations that followed, Teleklos was embarrassed by the crown of olives and the speeches praising him to the heavens. He had bred and trained a fine team, but without Lysandridas' skill, there was no question in his mind that the Tegean team would have won. He said as much to anyone who would listen. He pulled Lysandridas into the winner's circle. He removed his own olive wreath and placed it on Lysandridas' head, but of course his son insisted on giving it back. Lysandridas had no need of his father's recognition; his peers were giving him enough adulation.

Only for a brief moment had the atmosphere of euphoric, mindless triumph been interrupted. Polycritus had come up as if to congratulate the victor and his driver, and Lysandridas had sobered so quickly that Teleklos realised he wasn't drunk at all, not even with emotion. Polycritus had sneered at him, "So you've got your crown of olives; what good is it to you? It won't even buy you pair of sandals when you're old and crippled!"

"It means I can stand *in front* of my King in battle!" Lysandridas bragged back, and Teleklos winced and quickly glanced to King Leon. On a yearly basis, the Council of Elders, which was composed of both kings and twenty-eight other elected citizens over the age of sixty, selected the best 300 citizens between the ages of twenty-one and thirty for the Guard. Any citizen on active service who distinguished himself was eligible for the Guard, and any Guardsman who failed to live up to the standards of excellence (or simply failed to impress as much as another citizen) could be expelled. Only Olympic victors were automatically granted a position in the Guard for as long as they were on active service, but Lysandridas was technically not the victor. Teleklos was.

Lysandridas, however, had once again gambled and won. His answer earned a thunderous cheer of approval from the Spartans surrounding them. King Leon threw his arm around the young citizen and declared, "There is no one I'd rather have between me and the enemy—unless it was no one at all!" And Chilon had winked at Teleklos to indicate it was all right; Sparta might not approve of its citizens bragging among themselves, but when it came to a Spartan putting a Corinthian in his place, then he could be assured of the approval of his fellow citizens.

It was only the next day, when Teleklos woke still a little dazed by the realisation that it was over and he had indeed won, that Chilon took Teleklos aside and informed him that while he was away, King Agesikles had convinced the Assembly to invade Tegea. Without the knowledge of the Council of Elders or the Assembly, King Agesikles had sent to Delphi, asking if it would be "propitious" for Lacedaemon to seize Arcadia. The Oracle had replied:

> You asked me for Arcadia. You asked me for much. I will not give it to you. There are many men who eat acorns in Arcadia who will stop you. But I am not grudging to you. I will give you Tegea to dance upon with stamping feet, and a fair plain to measure out with the rod.

"As soon as the Olympic peace is over, we will march," Chilon explained to his friend. "That's why King Agesikles, the polymarchs, and the lochagoi are all missing—if you haven't noticed." Teleklos hadn't noticed; he'd been too concerned about his horses, the weather, the track conditions, the competition, his son.

Now he was a little bewildered. "War?"

"As soon as we're back in Sparta."

His next thought was for his son. "Lysandridas—will he be in the Guard?"

"You can't doubt it. They think it is an omen to have an Olympic victory—and so pointedly over Tegea! Lysandridas now symbolises that victory and the promise of the next."

"You don't sound convinced," Teleklos observed.

Chilon sighed. Although they had been friends ever since, at the age of seven, they had gone to the agoge together, Chilon had always been more active in civic affairs. While Teleklos had devoted himself to his motherless children, his estate, and his horses, Chilon had been elected to one civic office after another. He had served at various times as magistrate, judge, and headmaster of the agoge. He had been sent as an envoy on various occasions to Athens, Argos, Elis, and Corinth. He had been elected priest of Apollo and Athena and Zeus, one after the other. He had earned a reputation for divination, although he insisted he was not trained in it and only reluctantly read the omens if requested.

The two friends were walking along the banks of the Kladeos, and they could hear on the breeze the cheering of the crowds at the stadium watching the final day of events. "You know I would never call a Delphic

Oracle into question," Chilon reminded his friend seriously—but with a slight glint of mockery in his eye as he spoke—"but King Agesikles' priest was the only one present when the Oracle was delivered. Agesikles has been agitating for this war too long."

"But why Tegea? We have had friendly relations with Tegea for as long as I can remember. They didn't even side with Argos in the last war, did they?"

"No," Chilon confirmed. "Tegea is tempting to Agesikles only because it is a neighbour with rich land and he—and incidentally Anaxandridas—feel that Sparta's kings are too poor. You know as well as I do that the Eurypontids have never really accepted the Lycurgan Land Reform. The annexation of Messenia in our grandfather's time only whetted their appetite for more land rather than sating them. The precedent was set after the Second Messenia War of dividing *conquered* territory not equally among the peers, as the original Lacedaemon land was divided in the Reforms, but on the basis of "contribution". What's more, our Lacedaemon kleroi are inalienable and cannot be divided up amongst heirs, given to daughters, or sold. The conquered territories are not under the same strict control. In consequence, Messenian land is already very inequitably distributed among the peers."

Teleklos did not need to be reminded of this last fact. His grandfather, Agesandros, had been one of the heroes of the Second Messenian War. Agesandros had captured the city of Phigalia with only a single company. He had rescued four captive Spartiate youths from slavery at the hands of the infamous Messenian leader Aristomenes. He had commanded a unit which fought a guerrilla war against the elusive Aristomenes, bringing the only successes in the early years of the long, bloody conflict. Agesandros had been accordingly rewarded with vast estates in Messenia, but in just three generations these had become concentrated in the other branch of the family, the descendants of the "elder" of the twins born to Agesandros, Areas.

Teleklos' father, Apollonides, had been the younger twin, nearly strangled by his own umbilical cord at birth, and thus almost condemned to death by the Council of Elders that guarded over Sparta's sparse resources by insisting that only healthy children likely to become or breed effective hoplites be reared to adulthood. He had inherited the "lesser" half of his father's Messenian lands, and divided these among his three children. The eldest two of these children had then been married to their first cousins, thereby re-consolidating the estates somewhat. Teleklos, however, had married a girl who did not stand to inherit anything in Messenia, and to finance his expensive investments in racehorses, he had sold off his own

Messenian portion to his cousin. Since then, Teleklos lived exclusively from his Lacedaemonian kleros, and this was all that Lysandridas would inherit from him.

"King Agesikles thinks he can enrich himself in Tegea without arousing resentment among the Peers?" Teleklos tried to summarise what Chilon had told him.

"He's had his head turned by the extravagance of tyrants like Aeschines of Sicyon or Symmachus of Thasos. You need only look at the way they dress themselves and entertain here to understand that Agesikles and Anaxandridas feel they look shabby in comparison. The fact that Aeschines and Symmachus are mere tyrants without the blood of Heracles in their veins or fourteen generations of kingship behind them rankles. They are parvenus, whose claim to power is dubious at best. Is it any wonder, really, that our kings feel slighted and humiliated by the way these tyrants strut about in so much excess luxury?"

"Surely you don't support a war against Tegea so our kings can compete with the extravagance of tyrants!?" Teleklos was shocked.

Chilon laughed. "Of course not—but I try to understand the motives of others at all times. Especially my opponents and my kings."

"Particularly when they are one and the same?"

"No." Chilon was decisive and serious. "I do not consider my kings my opponents, but it does bother me that our kings have the right to muster the army and go to war without the approval of the Assembly or indeed any man on earth. Agesikles presented this alleged Oracle to the Assembly to increase the support for his planned aggression—but he didn't have to. He could have simply mustered the army and marched it out on his own authority, without telling a living soul where he was heading. I consider it a serious weakness in our Constitution that our laws allow that."

Teleklos was silent. He knew of no other Spartan citizen who would dare question the wisdom of Sparta's laws. Since the Time of Troubles following the First Messenian War when there had been widespread lawlessness, insurrection and a smouldering civil war, the Spartans abhorred disorder more than anything. They had accepted Lycurgus' radical and revolutionary laws because these had put an end to the lawlessness. The Lycurgan Reforms had brought Sparta prosperity and internal peace for 100 years. While other Greek city-states, including Argos and Corinth, went from crisis to crisis, and when even Athens was ruled by a wild and fickle mob, Sparta's democracy had proved remarkably stable. Teleklos felt a chill of discomfort at the mere thought of questioning any part of the Lycurgan Laws.

Chilon was a more courageous man than Teleklos, and he did not believe anything was perfect. Seeing his friend's discomfort, however, he dropped the subject. "Enough of this talk. You should be enjoying your victory, not listening to me grumble about things I can't change. Let's go back and see the final race. We have two entries and stand a good chance of winning."

"Lysandridas has entered, too, you know."

"Pressing his luck a little, isn't he?"

"It bothers him that he doesn't really have the right to be in the Guard on the basis of yesterday's victory."

Chilon could understand that and he nodded; but he could not help adding in a concerned voice, "Still, he should not ask too much of the Gods; they punish us if we are too greedy."

CHAPTER 10

At fifty-six, Teleklos was still in the reserves and subject in time of war to a call-up; but, as was to be expected, the senior age-cohorts were assigned garrison duty, while the active units and the first ten age-cohorts of reserves took the offensive. Drawn up with his unit near the bridge over the Eurotas, Teleklos watched the army march out of the city in its best parade-ground form.

It was impossible not to be proud of his son as he marched by in the elite company of the 300 Guardsmen, sometimes still referred to as "knights" because in some forgotten past they had been mounted. Now the Guard was made up of Sparta's universally admired hoplites. They wore scarlet chitons under their polished breastplates and groin-flaps, polished greaves of bronze but no sandals, and they wore their crested helmets shoved back on their necks so their faces were exposed.

The day the army marched out was always a festival day in Sparta. It was a truism that Sparta was the only city-state where war was a welcome relief from the tedium of training for war. During war, rations were more generous, drill less onerous, and various other rules and regulations relaxed. With the auspicious Oracle from Delphi, no one seemed to even consider the possibility of defeat, and hardly anyone present could remember the long and wearisome Second Messenian War.

Even Teleklos' father, Apollonides, who was now over eighty, had been a young boy not yet in the *agoge* when the Second Messenian War had been brought to a successful conclusion. In private, Apollonides had been very critical of the present war, recalling all the tales he had been told of the brutality of the Messenian War and the horrible price Sparta had paid for ultimate victory. His mother, particularly, had raised him on stories of the horrible Massacre of the Children, which had taken place when the Messenian leader Aristomenes crossed into Lacedaemon while the entire Spartan Army was deployed in Messenia. Aristomenes had slaughtered the little boys and girls attending the public school, the agoge, in the city itself. An entire class of eirenes, the 20-year-old instructors at the agoge, had been slaughtered while futilely defending their charges against the Messenians. But during the actual march-out, Apollonides was as exuberant in his cheering as all the other spectators.

The boys of the agoge lined up by unit, and the youngest of them had never seen the army deploy before. Teleklos could see how excited they were by the difficulty their eirenes had keeping them in line. The senior classes were almost visibly green with envy as they watched their elder brothers march out to the sound of flutes and pipes and the singing of rousing songs.

Even the women were in high spirits, Teleklos noted. It was unthinkable that a Spartan wife or mother would weep or otherwise show grief when her husband or sons went to war, but he had witnessed more than one occasion when the mood among the women spectators had been sober and even apprehensive. Today there was none of it. The women waved their scarves to their men, who cheerfully waved back. The younger girls were dancing and singing, clapping their hands, and swaying back and forth to cheer their brothers and fathers as they passed, and the maidens were garlanded and blowing kisses at their sweethearts, sometimes running along beside the column to drape flowers over their favourites.

Hermione honoured Lysandridas in this manner, and Teleklos was glad for him. Hermione was the kind of blonde-haired, blue-eyed, well-formed maiden who reminded the world that Helen "of Troy" had been Spartan. Hermione was the daughter of Persandros, a well-respected citizen, and had just turned seventeen. Lysandridas had not even left Olympia before he announced to his father that now that he had the victory in the chariot race and had been assured a position in the Guard, he intended to ask for her. He had then (Teleklos smiled at the memory) spent the rest of the journey home talking his father into going to Persandros on his behalf, his self-confidence not quite as great as he would have liked the world to believe.

Lysandridas, knowing it was only a matter of days before the deployment, had given his father no peace until Teleklos kept his word and approached Persandros. Hermione's father knew of his daughter's popularity. It had not escaped his notice that when his daughter took part in girls' races, half the bachelors of Sparta turned out to watch. The fact that she invariably lost did not discourage either her from participating or the young men from watching. Lysandridas had never missed a race in which Hermione took part.

Not so long ago, the elders had "suggested" it was time he prohibit his daughter from participating in the races because she was becoming "disruptive". At seventeen, Hermione was still considered rather young for marriage by Spartan standards. In other Greek cities, maidens were married by their male relatives as soon as they were old enough to breed—usually at thirteen or fourteen—but in Sparta, Lycurgus had ruled that no girl should be married until she was old enough to enjoy sex. He had been explicit in saying that forcing shy young girls into marriage and the resulting use of force produced lasting damage to a woman's health, which made it difficult for her to survive childbed. In the years since Lycurgus' reforms had been introduced, it had become increasingly customary not to marry girls before they reached the age of twenty-one—i.e., the age at which youths became citizens and so "young men".

But that was custom rather than law, and Hermione was the type of maiden who had clearly matured early. There was little shyness about her and equally little doubt that she was ready for the marriage bed. Her father admitted that she was quite interested in marriage, and not averse to the idea of marrying an Olympic victor and Guardsman. Teleklos got the impression that Lysandridas had not been her first choice before the Olympic victory, but that this extraordinary achievement had made her revise her opinion of this particular suitor.

Teleklos didn't like that. He thought Lysandridas would be far happier with a woman who loved him for himself and not for his success or fame. But it was too late to make the young man change his mind. Teleklos knew that a young man in love was not about to listen to his father's advice. Or rather, in Sparta, he would listen very politely with his hands at his sides and say, "Yes, father," just as he been taught to do at the agoge—and then he would go out and do exactly as he pleased. Emotions and affections could not be commanded, not even in the most disciplined society in Greece.

Thus any attempt to dissuade Lysandridas from his choice would only have resulted in a breach between them. Teleklos had long ago made the decision that he wanted to be his son's confidant and friend rather than his teacher. Spartan law required the sons of citizens to attend public school from age seven through twenty, and Spartan custom encouraged all full citizens—but especially those in the reserves—to take an active role in training, teaching, and disciplining the boys and youths in the agoge. Boys were required to address all young men as "sir" and all men out of active service as "father". Teleklos felt that with roughly nine thousand citizens watching over his son's behaviour, making sure he learned his manners and showed respect for his elders, that Lysandridas needed at least one mature friend to whom he could turn for advice without risking a lecture.

This had been the basis of their relationship ever since Lysandridas had—with evident trepidation—left his parental kleros to attend the agoge seven miles away in the city of Sparta. To have tried to exert pressure on Lysandridas at this stage or to stand on parental authority that he had let lapse would have been foolish and futile. Rather, Teleklos inwardly criticised himself for not having taught his son what he should look for in a bride at an earlier age, before it was relevant and so when he would have been willing to listen. Once a youth was confused by sexual desires and primeval attraction, he was no longer open to reason.

If only his wife had been alive, Teleklos thought for the thousandth time. If only Lysandridas had grown up with a good marriage to observe and to imitate. Lysandridas' mother had been no mouth-watering beauty like Hermione. She had been, even as a girl, somewhat plain, with the curly, black hair Lysandridas had inherited from her. She had married late, at twenty-three, because she had not been coveted by dozens of bachelors, but she had by no means taken Teleklos in despair. She had been running her father's kleros quite capably and happily when they started to take an interest in each other. Teleklos had asked her, not her father, if she would marry him, and she had taken almost three days to decide. But once she decided, she had never wavered in her loyalty and commitment. He had received her father's permission the day afterward, and they had celebrated the wedding within the fortnight. Teleklos had never regretted his decision until the day she died. Then he had cursed her bitterly for preferring another baby, at the risk of her own life, to a lifetime into old age with him.

With time he had learned to forgive her, but he had never wanted to give so much of himself to any woman again. He had never risked the pain of loss again. He had never even considered remarriage. All the love he had in him, he lavished quite uninhibitedly and without the least shame on his two children, his little girl Dorothea and his surviving son, Lysandridas.

But the memories of what his marriage had been made Teleklos uncomfortable when he signed the marriage agreement with Persandros. The fathers agreed that the details would be left to the two young people, and an actual removal of the bride to Teleklos' home was planned only tentatively for the following spring, presumably after the army was back from Tegea. By then Hermione would be eighteen, a more suitable age if still somewhat young, and Lysandridas twenty-three. Both fathers were in agreement that they should postpone the wedding even longer if the young people would allow it. Both fathers were fairly certain that this would not prove possible—unless the war got in the way.

On that day when the army marched out so blithely, Teleklos had not consciously wanted the war to get in the way of his son's marriage. It did occur to him, however, that it might not be a bad thing if it proved just a little bit more difficult to conquer Tegea than the laughing maidens and cheering youths seemed to expect. Nothing warned him of what would come.

The first news of the defeat came by runner and reached King Leon in the middle of the night. He at once roused the entire Council of Elders, and by dawn the word was out across the city. Teleklos himself was informed at morning muster, when his battalion commander announced simply that Lacedaemon had suffered a severe defeat on entering Tegean territory and the army was in retreat. The defeat had been so quick and so complete that it left everyone stunned.

At noon, word spread that the first units of the returning army had been sighted coming out of the Parnon range. Everyone not actually on duty dropped what they were doing and made for the bridge. The agoge training broke down entirely and the gymnasiums, palaestra, and baths emptied. The shops of the agora closed, and merchants and shoppers alike flocked toward the river. Even women from the surrounding countryside turned up, and Apollonides came the seven miles from Teleklos' kleros on foot despite his age.

The first units across the bridge were perioikoi auxiliaries. These units were composed of the free, non-Doric citizens of the other towns and cities of Lacedaemon. They were good fighters and valuable allies, but they did not interest the citizens of Sparta at a time like this. The damaged equipment, dented and scratched shields and helmets, and bloody bandages of the wounded were noted but did not cause distress. But then the first of the Spartan units came down from the pass, and the crowd grew tense. It had been too short a time since they had marched out so confidently. No one really grasped what had happened. How could they have been defeated? Already? What of the Oracle? "I will give you Tegea," it had said....

A murmur went through the crowd when King Agesikles and Prince Anaxandridas were sighted. Anaxandridas was only 19, too young for active service if he had been an ordinary citizen; but because his father had pre-deceased him and his grandfather was too old and fragile to represent the Agiads on the battlefield, he had been allowed to march out. He returned looking dazed, although he had suffered no apparent injury. Agesikles was also unharmed, but looked as if he'd aged a decade; his skin was grey, his eyes sunken, and his lips chapped and thin. They were surrounded by what appeared to be a depleted company of the Guard, but Teleklos did not immediately grasp the implications. He assumed the remaining two companies were forming the rearguard, as was traditional in a withdrawal. One company, the first, always remained with the Kings, while the remaining two stiffened the rearguard.

Thus it was only when the last of the Spartan units—lacking any baggage, supplies, and support—had crossed the Eurotas that Teleklos began to worry. Now there was nothing at all moving down from the Parnon range—not even helot stragglers—and Teleklos turned in bewilderment to the remnants of the crowd still standing with him by the bridge over the Eurotas and asked, "But where is the Guard?"

The question went unanswered.

Bewildered but not yet willing to believe that the rest of the Guard was dead, Teleklos went with his father to the Eurypontid palace, where a large crowd was gathered. King Agesikles kept them waiting, but eventually he did face them: still in his armour, unwashed, his long hair crusted with salt from sweating inside his helmet. His voice was hoarse, his message terse. "We were defeated."

"We can see that!" someone called from the crowd rudely; and the others muttered uneasily, some angry with the catcaller, some agreeing with him.

"Nearly 500 men did not return! Where are they?" Another voice demanded.

"They broke our phalanx with a cavalry attack," Agesikles announced.

Cavalry? Cavalrymen couldn't wear heavy armour, carry shields, or use an eight-footer. Cavalry usually came no nearer than a bowshot, or at best the range of a thrown javelin. Cavalry had always shattered on the Spartan phalanx in the past. What could have gone wrong this time?

"The casualties will be posted tomorrow in the stoa." The King turned and returned inside his palace.

By nightfall, the news spread through the city that the defeat had been too much for King Leon. He had died of heart-failure shortly after his grandson reported what had happened. The city, already in mourning for as yet unnamed casualties numbering in the hundreds, was plunged deeper into mourning for one of her kings. Anaxandridas, at nineteen, was now a ruling monarch.

Chilon, who like Teleklos had been too old to deploy, was summoned to the Agiad royal palace. Afterwards, although it was the middle of the night, he walked the seven miles to Teleklos' kleros, northwest of the city. He did not even try the front door with the formal porch and portico. Instead, he climbed up the stone steps leading to the back terrace from the stables on the banks of a little tributary to the Eurotas.

The terrace was paved with local terracotta tiles and rimmed with potted palms. Wooden benches were set up next to the house on which the helots spent much of their day spinning and darning, peeling and chopping, cleaning household articles, or sharpening farm implements. As long as he had been coming here—since he was a little boy visiting his best friend's house—this had been the heart of the kleros. From here one had a magnificent view over the surrounding orchards sloping down to the valley of the Eurotas below. Chilon sat down on one of the benches and waited. The crickets cheeped and a nightingale called. The potted palms rustled gently.

He dozed on and off until the helot woman, who had run the kleros since Apollonides' wife had died twelve years ago, emerged from the kitchen wing of the house with a hydria to fetch water. She started in surprise at the sight of someone on the terrace, and then she seemed to collapse onto the nearest bench. The hydria she was carrying clunked on the paving tiles. She stared at him, her eyes getting wider and darker until the tears overflowed and started running down her face. She understood.

Zoë had raised Lysandridas almost from the day he was born. She had come to the kleros only shortly after Lysandridas was born, when she married the helot overseer of the estate, Cleoetas. Helots were state slaves. They were tied to the land and could not leave it without the permission of the Spartiates to whom the land had been allotted. They were required to work the land and give half the produce to their Spartiate masters, but they could do what they liked with the remainder. In no sense were they chattels. Their "masters" did not own them, and could neither buy nor sell them. Nor could their masters dispose of them in marriage. Helots, unlike slaves, had fathers, wives, graves—and pride.

When Zoë arrived at this kleros, a happy young bride, she had found a house in mourning for the dead mistress, a baby neglected by an adolescent wet-nurse, and a bewildered little eight-year-old girl who had started to suck her thumb and wet her bed again in distress. Zoë had taken control of the household with an instinctive practicality that had earned her the respect of everyone who knew her. Apollonides' wife, already well past sixty by then, had gradually and contentedly turned over the daily management of the estate to the competent young helot woman; but most important, Zoë had brought laughter back into the house. Zoë was a woman who always saw the sunny side of things and seemed to bring sunshine with her wherever she went; but this morning she was defeated.

"Is it certain?" she asked Chilon as she wiped at her tears.

He sighed. "No. The corpse was not recovered. We retreated. We left all our dead on the field—except those who died of their wounds during the withdrawal. Almost five hundred men have been lost in this debacle. Some may have been taken alive, but the chances for Lysandridas are almost nil. He was in the Guard, Zoë."

From the kitchen someone called, asking where Zoë had got to, and then the greying head of her husband peered out of the door. When he saw Chilon sitting on the terrace, his face creased into a puzzled frown; and then he saw his wife's tears and came out and laid his hand on her shoulder. "The young master?"

Chilon nodded.

"Should I go wake Teleklos?" Zoë asked, pulling herself together.

"No, let him sleep as long as he can. I can wait."

"I'll bring you some fresh milk," Zoë offered and went to fetch it. Her husband took up the hydria and disappeared in the direction of the fountain house.

Apollonides came out first. Old men sleep lightly, and he had heard voices coming from the terrace. He came down the outside steps from the balcony that ran around the outside of the main house. His long white hair was neatly braided from forehead to waist, as was the custom with Spartan citizens. His beard was neatly trimmed. He wore a simple chiton and went barefoot, but a himation had been wound about his torso to ward off the autumn chill. "Are you the bearer of bad news, Chilon?" he asked, his face stiff.

Chilon nodded.

Apollonides' lip seemed almost to tremble. "That wretched boy!" he burst out angrily. "What a fool! I told him he wasn't good enough for the

Guard!" He turned around and dragged himself back up the stairs as if he were angry, but Chilon had seen the tears glistening in his cloudy grey eyes.

Chilon waited what seemed like a long time. The sun came up and shone brightly across the valley. Teleklos finally emerged, not from the house but coming up the stairs from the stables beside the stream below. He was not surprised to see his friend. "I was down at the stables," he explained.

"All night?"

Teleklos just smiled faintly.

"Anaxandridas told me some details of the battle," Chilon started. Teleklos nodded and sat down beside his friend. Chilon continued, "When the Tegean cavalry charged our phalanx, the perioikoi units broke and fled. No, I'm lying. Not *just* the perioikoi. No one had trained for something like that; everyone had been so confident of success. The younger hoplites lost their nerve. The Tegean cavalry was within a hundred feet of Anaxandridas and Agesikles. Agesikles was paralysed with indecision, giving no orders despite repeated requests from the polymarchs. Poor Anaxandridas didn't know what to do and gave no answers either. Finally, Euryleon" (the commander of the Guard, as they both knew) "ordered the 2nd and 3rd Companies to attack the cavalry, and the 1st Company shepherded Agesikles and Anaxandridas off the field."

"They counter-attacked the Tegean cavalry?"

"On foot."

"How many survived?"

"None rejoined the main body of our army during the retreat."

"Euryleon?"

"Anaxandridas says he personally saw Euryleon go down under the Tegean hooves as he led the Guard forward."

Teleklos' eyes were dry, his face still. "I don't believe they all died. Not all of them. Not unless the Tegeans were barbarous enough to slaughter them afterwards. Horses always try *not* to step on a human, if they can help themselves."

"Teleklos, even if the *horses* were not trying to kill them, their *riders* were. The Tegean cavalry was spearing them with javelins like they were hunting boar—or fish in a barrel."

"Not all of them—not 200 men without exception."

Chilon took a deep breath. "All right. We'll wait and see if the Tegeans send us word of any prisoners."

"We'll ask, won't we?" A touch of alarm was clearly audible in Teleklos' question. Sparta did not approve of men surrendering.

"If I have anything to say about it, yes," Chilon assured him.

Teleklos allowed himself to be comforted by that and walked his friend back down to the road. They didn't speak until they parted. "I don't believe he's dead, Chilon. I can't."

"All right," Chilon accepted, and made his way back to the city feeling wearier than he could remember in his whole life.

CHAPTER 11

The autumn rains came and the peaks of Taygetos were white with snow before Tegea triumphantly sent a list of captives. The Tegean ambassador had also been the commander at the battle itself, a certain Harmatides. He had extremely polished manners, but he left no doubt about the fact that the captives were now slaves. Harmatides had heard of the Spartan oracle, and he pointed out that it had been quite accurate: Spartans were indeed measuring out Tegea's plain—namely, ploughing it under the watchful eyes of their Tegean masters and sowing the winter wheat, which their Tegean masters would harvest. And as for the dancing feet, the Spartan slaves had to "dance" to their masters' tune now—unless, of course, Sparta was willing to buy them back at a price of 350 drachma apiece.

The young Agiad king, Anaxandridas, left the council chamber in rage before he said aloud what he was thinking. King Agesikles heard the Tegean ambassador in stony silence, and then said the decision would be taken by the Council and Assembly and the Tegeans informed in due course.

The Council session that followed was stormy. Sparta had two serious problems with the ransoming of the captives. First, there was a strong traditional bias against surrender. The ethos of the Spartan army was that one fought to the death. One returned "with one's shield or upon it". But for all that, they were talking about nearly 200 men, more than half of whom were bachelors, who had not had the chance to sire offspring. Since Spartan citizenship was restricted to the children of full citizens, there was always a risk of the citizen body shrinking if casualties were too high among young men who were not yet fathers. There were many in the Council who argued that they simply could not afford to sacrifice another 200 young men after losing roughly that number in the battle itself.

But although this argument won over the majority, the next problem proved insurmountable. Where was Sparta to come up with nearly 70,000 drachma? Sparta did not tax her citizens. The citizens were required to pay monthly contributions to the messes, to the syssitia, and, if they had children of school age, to the agoge. Sparta's only state funds came from the taxes paid by the free perioikoi cities of Lacedaemon and a tithe from the conquered territories of Messenia. These revenues went to supplying the army, which in contrast to that of other Greek city-states, was fully equipped and maintained at state expense. The remaining funds went to maintaining the temples and monuments; the public buildings of the Council, Assembly, army, and agoge; the baths, fountains, and gymnasiums; etc. Sparta, as a state, was notoriously poor. There were no silver mines in Lacedaemon to keep the city-state swimming in liquidity. The Spartan treasury quite simply did not have 70,000 drachma available for the ransom of captured citizens.

The Council therefore came to the only conclusion it could come to under the circumstances. They would have to levy a special tax of ten drachma per citizen for the purpose of purchasing the captives. Such a tax had to be approved by the Assembly, however, and so an emergency Assembly was convened.

The resulting debate in the Assembly was one of the ugliest Teleklos had ever witnessed. The council had wisely refused to release the list of survivors before the debate, so that none of the families of missing men could know if they were voting for the ransom of their own relatives or of others. Even so, the minority faction that called the survivors "cowards" was both vocal and vociferous. These citizens argued that the nearly 200 young men who had allowed themselves to be captured alive had disgraced the city. In consequence, they were the very last men on earth who deserved assistance from the city they had "betrayed" and "abandoned". Some of the speakers implied that the entire battle would not have been lost if "these weaklings" hadn't lost their nerve. Others claimed that the survivors deserved slavery, because they were already slaves at heart the minute they surrendered.

Teleklos was so certain that Lysandridas was on the list that he took every insult to the survivors personally. He tried to respond once or twice, but was shouted down by men sneering that he, of all people, ought to keep his mouth shut. If his son—a Guardsman—had let himself be taken, he deserved slavery.

Shaking with emotion, Teleklos shouted back: "This is madness! It is better to survive and serve Sparta in the future!"

"Serve? By running away at the next battle? Causing a new defeat? Better they were all dead!"

"He gave you an Olympic victory!" Teleklos reminded them, his voice hoarse with raw emotion.

"He was nothing but a driver—something suitable for slaves!"

Stunned by such an attitude, Teleklos just stood with his mouth open, and Chilon gripped his arm for a moment, offering sympathy and support without words. Then Chilon addressed the assembly.

When Chilon spoke, the others quieted down noticeably. "You, who call the captives cowards, should remember that just last month you called these same men "comrade" and considered them your peers. Now, you call them names and try to blame them for something you do not understand: a defeat you thought impossible. But the unfortunates, who are captives, are no more responsible for our defeat than any of us! Less responsible than our kings and polymarchs, who led us to this debacle."

"If they had fought like brave men rather than surrendering, it might not have been a debacle!" an older man shouted out.

"You talk as if you'd never been in battle in your life," Chilon scoffed back so contemptuously that Chilon's challenger audibly caught his breath in outrage. Chilon gave him no chance to reply but continued in a confident, self-assured voice, "I, for one, know that a wounded man can be captured without his consent. I know, too, that a man can be overwhelmed before he has had a chance to turn his weapons upon himself. I have known battles where the confusion was so great, that no one could be sure where the lines ran and who was friend or foe. You, who would have us believe that each and every one of these 197 captives is a coward, sound like little children trying to blame someone else for your own failings."

There was a roar of protest from the most vocal critics of the captives, even though Teleklos had the impression that Chilon had shamed the majority into silence. The protests of the rabid minority, however, only became more bitter. "It would be better to spend 70,000 drachma to buy Sicilian mercenaries, than to buy freedom for these worthless warriors," one man shouted.

Teleklos couldn't bear it and shouted back, "You are only jealous of those of us who have produced sons!"

Chilon tried to calm his friend down, because he felt such a slur on a man because he had failed to sire children was beneath Teleklos' dignity.

"Better none at all than one who would prefer to grovel at the feet of Tegean masters!" came the inevitable reply.

Chilon interceded again. "Enough! Have we all gone mad?! Hasn't Sparta bled enough without inflicting new wounds on herself?" he asked his fellow citizens. There was shamed silence. Into this silence he suggested in a resigned, tired voice, "Let the families of the captives raise the ransoms of their sons and bring them home! These so-called citizens, who are more concerned about their purses than preserving the ranks of our army, should keep their drachma for themselves! By hoarding their wealth rather than aiding their comrades, they have shown they are less Spartan than the men who risked slavery for the sake of their retreating comrades!"

It was against Sparta's laws for amendments to proposals to be accepted from the floor of the Assembly. The Council alone had the right to submit any proposals for debate; but this suggestion clearly appealed to the Assembly, and the original proposal was consequently soundly defeated in the vote. The Council closed the Assembly by announcing that the families of the captives were free to secure their freedom at their own cost, and that the list would be available in the council chamber.

Teleklos was among the crowd pressing in to see the list. He would have liked to elbow his way past all the others, and it took a great deal of self-restraint to simply wait his turn in the rough line that formed. He was already turning over the means of raising 350 drachma. He didn't have it, of course; but his elder brother Lycurgus, who had married their cousin Agistrata, held fully one-half of the original Messenian lands granted to their grandfather Agesandros. If Lycurgus didn't have the cash readily available, he could raise a loan on his Messenian estates; or Teleklos could approach his sister Agiates, married to their cousin, Agesandros the Younger. One way or another, he was certain the family would be able to scrape together the ransom payment.

At last he was at the table with the wax tablet lying open. The names were scratched in the wax neatly by some Tegean clerk. Teleklos was in much too much of a hurry to read each name; he simply skimmed down the list looking at each name starting with lambda. When he got to the end of the list and had not found Lysandridas, he was annoyed with himself for having skimmed too rapidly. He went back to the start and read the list more carefully, one name at a time. But he still did not find Lysandridas. He was starting to get nervous, and around him the others that had not got to the list yet were getting noticeably impatient. "It can't be," he said out loud, to make them understand his dilemma. "I must be going blind. Can you read for me?" he asked a younger man who was trying to read over his shoulder.

"Of course, father. What name are you looking for?"

"Lysandridas, son of Teleklos."

"But wasn't he in the Guard?"

"Yes, but there must have been survivors, even in the Guard."

The young man looked sceptical, but dutifully read the list from the top again. "You're right, there are several Guardsmen here: Celeas son of Damonon, Antalkidas son of Cleodacus, Euxenos son of Ramphias; but I'm sorry, father," he sounded sincere, "Lysandridas is not on the list."

"He has to be!" Teleklos protested and then, seeing pity in the eyes around him, he pushed his way out of the council chamber. Outside, he tried to collect his thoughts, but they got away from him. He realised it was raining and pulled his himation up over his head. He started back for his kleros and then remembered that it was too late. It was nearly dinnertime. Time to go to his syssitia. But how could he go to his syssitia and have dinner as if everything were normal? He stood indecisively in the pouring rain. Nothing was normal. The list of captives had finally arrived, and Lysandridas wasn't on it. And if he wasn't a prisoner and he wasn't back in Sparta, then he could only be dead. But Lysandridas couldn't be dead. He was too young. Too full of life. Too full of promise. Lysandridas couldn't be dead.

Teleklos arrived at his syssitia soaking wet. The others exclaimed in concern and called for towels from the kitchen. They made him strip off his wet clothes, and one of the younger members wrapped him in his own himation. The mess boys, young sons of Spartiates between the ages of seven and fourteen, were sent running to fill a brazier with hot coals. The cook brought Teleklos a mug of hot black broth, and he held it in his trembling hands, letting the steam warm his face. No one needed to ask what was wrong. They knew him too well. A man was required to join a syssitia as soon as he attained citizen status. A young citizen applied to the syssitia of his choice, and, provided all existing members approved, he was admitted for life. These men therefore knew how proud Teleklos was of his only surviving son. They knew that Lysandridas had not returned with the army. They could guess what had happened.

When the next day Teleklos sent one of his helots to report that he was sick, they were not surprised. He had clearly caught a dangerous chill the day before. After four days, the eldest member of the syssitia walked out to Teleklos' kleros to check up on him. They found that he was in bed with a fever. His daughter Dorothea had come from her own home to look after him.

Dorothea was thirty-one years old and had been married for the last nine. She had two little girls and an infant son by her husband Derykleides. Like Lysandridas, she had her mother's dark curly hair, which she wore tied back from her face. She had been born and raised as a little girl on her father's kleros, but at seven she had gone into the city to the girls' agoge. When she left the agoge at fourteen, she had gone to live with her Aunt Agiates to learn her duties as future wife of a Spartiate citizen, something she could not learn in her father's wifeless household. She did not entirely approve of the status Zoë, a mere helot, enjoyed in her father's house since her grandmother had died. She made it very clear to the helot that *she* was mistress for as long as she attended her father.

Zoë was too wise to protest, and retreated into the wing of the house where the helots lived, leaving the care of Teleklos entirely in Dorothea's hands. Dorothea ordered roots of coltsfoot mixed with milk and honey and fed this to her father three times a day. She also kept a brazier burning in his chamber—although her grandfather grumbled that this was a "luxury" that would only "soften" his son into a "weakling". For all her care, Teleklos showed little improvement.

"He doesn't want to live any more," Apollonides told his granddaughter as they sat together over a sparse breakfast.

"But that's ridiculous!" Dorothea replied indignantly.

Apollonides shrugged; he understood his son even if he didn't approve of such weakness.

"It's time we thought about putting up a stone to Lysandridas," Dorothea added, her thoughts moving on.

"I don't think Teleklos will agree to that," Apollonides warned her.

"We'll see," Dorothea said determinedly and took her mixture of warm milk, honey, and coltsfoot into her father on a tray.

"How are we doing this morning?" she asked brightly, setting down the tray and opening the shutters to let in the morning sunlight. It was one of those suddenly warm days the Peloponnese got throughout the autumn.

Teleklos coughed in answer. Then he struggled to get himself into a sitting position as his daughter handed him a one-handed mug typical in Sparta but known nowhere else in Hellas. He sipped the cough mixture dutifully.

Dorothea considered him as he drank and did not like what she saw. He had not washed, combed, or braided his hair since he had fallen ill, so his long, curly locks were a rat's nest of greyish brown hanging about his shoulders. Nor had he trimmed his beard in days, and it was beginning to look shaggy. He looked, in short, like some wild barbarian. There were circles under his running eyes and his nose was red, swollen, and chapped. Dorothea decided this had been going on long enough.

"Father, it's time we put up a stone to Lysandridas."

Teleklos started sharply and spilled milk down his shaggy beard. He looked up at his daughter with bloodshot, accusatory eyes.

Dorothea ignored the look, and proceeded resolutely, "He deserves it, if anyone does." Spartan law prohibited marked graves for everyone except men who died in battle and women who died in childbed. Dorothea used this fact now to suggest, "We could put a stone up beside mother's—"

"NO!"

"But, Father—"

"NO! Your mother died giving him birth. Do you want to mock her sacrifice by putting his stone beside hers?!"

"Father, you always said her sacrifice wasn't futile as long as Lysandridas grew up to be a brave citizen. He did just that! He died fighting for his city. He was a Guardsman. *He* didn't surrender and let himself be enslaved like those worthless 197! We owe it to him to put up a stone commemorating his sacrifice in battle, when others were less noble."

"And his Olympic victory?"

Dorothea sighed. "It wasn't really his, but if you want to mention that he guided your winning chariot, I suppose we could make some mention of it."

"I dreamt of him last night, or maybe it was the night before. I was out hunting on Taygetos and heard him calling to me. He was trapped in a cave and I could hear his voice, but I couldn't find the entry to the cave. I looked more and more feverishly and he kept calling, 'Help me, Teleklos, help me!' At last I found the entrance to the cave, but inside it was so dark, I couldn't see where I was going. He was still calling, 'Teleklos, I'm here. Help me! Get me out!' I tried to go to the voice, but I fell off into a bottomless pit—and that woke me up."

Dorothea was still for a long time. She pitied her father. His grieving was so intense. She had loved her brother, of course, and she had wept for him in the privacy of her home, but she did not understand her father's refusal to accept the facts. She sat down on his couch and took his hand. "I don't have to be Chilon to interpret that dream, Father. Lysandridas is trapped in the underworld, and the only way you can go to him is to die. But you aren't ready to die yet, Father. You're still in your prime, not even old enough for the Council, and perfectly fit. You have three little grandchildren you can give so much to. You have to accept the facts: Lysandridas is dead."

Dorothea returned to her own home, and Teleklos let them put up the stone near the temple to Castor and Polydeukes, because Lysandridas had always been close to the Dioskouroi. But he refused to go and look at it. Whenever he was in the city, he avoided the street with the little monument that stated simply: "Lysandridas son of Teleklos, Guardsman, in battle against Tegea."

When the captives started to trickle home from Tegea, Teleklos sought out one of the surviving Guardsmen, Euxenos. The man had an ugly scar running down his cheek, chin, and throat—a javelin thrust that had slipped along the opening in his helmet. He was blind in one eye, and his right leg had been so badly mangled that it was now stiff and the knee could not bend.

"Tell me about my son, Lysandridas," Teleklos urged him as they sat before his fireplace, his wife at the loom behind them.

"He fought well, as well as any of us," Euxenos assured the grieving father.

"How was he killed?"

"I—I didn't see. In the end, we were just a handful. As the Tegeans surrounded us, some of my colleagues turned their swords on themselves."

"Lysandridas?!" Teleklos asked in horror.

"No. No, I'm trying to remember. He wasn't there. He was already down. At the end there were just a dozen of us. Half killed themselves and we others were taken alive. But Lysandridas was already down. He must have been dead already."

"Can't you remember anything?" Teleklos begged so piteously that the half-blinded Guardsman strained his memory yet again, forcing himself to conjure up images he would have preferred to forget. "I remember a Tegean charging us on a white stallion that was rearing up and flailing its hooves above our heads. The stallion threw his rider, and we all lunged to be sure he could do us no harm. Your son, however, tried to catch the stallion's reins, to keep him off us. He shoved his helmet back, because it seemed to be terrifying the horse even more. One of the hooves hit him squarely between the eyes; he went out cold, toppling over backward; but then the rest of the Tegean cavalry was upon us. They rode right over your son. He—was trampled to death."

Teleklos stared at the Guardsman and the disfigured man stared back with his good eye unflinching. Teleklos nodded. "Thank you for telling me. If there is ever anything I can do for you, you need only ask." He rose, thanked the man's wife for her hospitality, and started for the door. Euxenos stood to see him out, but Teleklos waved him down.

At the door, Teleklos stopped and turned back. "You were right not to kill yourself. Your sons need you." Teleklos nodded to the crib beside the loom and a little head that was peeking around the corner of the door from the inner chamber, waiting impatiently for the guest to go.

Euxenos and his wife exchanged a quick glance, and he said, "Thank you. Not all citizens agree. I have been thrown out of the Guard."

"With your leg, you cannot serve except in garrison anyway," Teleklos pointed out reasonably.

"But all six surviving Guardsmen have been disgraced."

"People will forget with time. Long ago, in the Second Messenian War, my grandfather seized Phigalia when we were technically at peace with the city. He did so because Phigalia was openly aiding the Messenians and had murdered an unarmed Spartan officer. The Phigalians went to Delphi, and we were ordered to restore the city to its citizens. In consequence, my grandfather was 'disgraced' and 'demoted'. He was prohibited from fighting with the army. Instead, with a handful of volunteers, he lived like an outlaw in Taygetos, attacking the Messenians at night and by stealth. For years he was the only one inflicting any notable defeats upon the Messenians. His disgrace turned to honour. More and more young men clamoured to join his unconventional unit. It became an elite unit. It came to be called the kryptea. Now it is regarded almost as highly as the Guard itself. As long as you know that what you did was right, as my grandfather knew, you need not feel shamed. Look back at those who would scorn you with contempt for their stupidity. Walk with pride! You were right to come home."

Euxenos was too overcome with gratitude to find any words, but his wife left her loom and crossed the room to take Teleklos' hands in hers. She bent and kissed them. "Thank you, Father! Thank you!"

Teleklos went home and cut off all his hair, one long braid at a time.

CHAPTER 12

The winter was bad enough; but it seemed to pass in a fog of gloom. When spring came, the pain grew more intense. In later years, Teleklos found he could remember absolutely nothing about that first winter after Lysandridas' death—nothing except that meeting with Euxenos. But the spring that followed remained with him always as the most painful of his long life—worse even than the season following his wife's death.

It started when the crocuses began to bud around the house. Lysandridas had always rejoiced at the sight of the first crocus. Teleklos found himself remembering how as a little boy of five or six he had come running inside one early morning breathless with excitement, "The crocuses, Teleklos! The crocuses have *popped* up overnight!"

Lysandridas had never once called him "Father" or "Dad" or "Daddy"— only Teleklos. It must have come from the fact that Zoë and the other household helots had taught him to speak, because Teleklos himself was utterly uninterested in the infant that had murdered his wife. Among themselves, the helots of his kleros always referred to him by name rather than as "master", because they were not his property.

The first time Teleklos had taken any notice of his son had been the day he "ran away". Coming back from visiting Chilon on one of the festival days, he noticed that his son wasn't at the kitchen table eating with the helots as usual. "Where's the boy?" he'd asked the room at large.

"He's in the fountain house," Zoë told him, a disapproving look on her face.

"What's he doing there?"

"Crying."

"Why?"

"His sister told him he killed his mother," Zoë answered with a stern look at Dorothea. (Because of the holidays she was home from school and eating in the kitchen, too.) She was only eleven at the time.

Teleklos turned and stared at Dorothea, who was fussing with her food and kicking at the table leg sullenly. "Did you tell your brother that?"

"It's true! You said it yourself!" Dorothea defended herself.

She was right, so he turned and went out to the fountain house on the side of the hill. The water gurgled and splashed from the mountainside into the basin and flowed away again to the washhouse beside it. He didn't hear his son's sobbing, but he saw the bare knees clutched in skinny arms and the patch of black, curly hair like a patch of black sheep's fleece tipped on top of the knees.

Teleklos went down on his heels before the little bundle of misery and asked, "What are you doing out here when there's a nice hot dinner waiting for you in the kitchen?"

Lysandridas had looked up with a red, tear-streaked face and wide, astonished eyes. He was completely confused to have the awesome, distant, silent Teleklos suddenly paying attention to him. Teleklos discovered that he couldn't blame the little boy any longer. After explaining how his wife had died and why, he stood again to go back up the house. Lysandridas put his little hand in his in a gesture of trust and acceptance that shamed Teleklos. After ignoring and neglecting the boy for the first years of his life, he did not deserve the little boy's trust. But from that moment on the bond was sealed.

Lysandridas took to following his father about wherever he went on the kleros. At first Teleklos was annoyed to have a silent, but somewhat unsteady and inept, shadow with him everywhere. The little boy could not keep up with his father's long strides, so he would fall behind and then fall down and scrape his knees when he tried to run to catch up. Teleklos learned to pace himself to the little boy's speed, or lift him onto his shoulders if he were in a hurry. If he was trying to do the accounts, on the other hand, Lysandridas was impatient and fractious, but could not be persuaded to "go out and play". He would sit down and try to be still—and that a dozen times in an hour. And he had always wanted to come with his father to the stables.

That was where Teleklos drew the line. The horses were just too dangerous, and he told Lysandridas that he was not to cross the stream at the foot of the hill. When Teleklos went to check on his horses, to ride or drive them, Lysandridas followed him down to the foot of the hill but had to wait on the near side of the stream, while his father waded across to the paddocks and stables. No matter how long he was gone, Teleklos always found Lysandridas waiting for him when he came back.

When Lysandridas was six, Teleklos finally relented and took Lysandridas across the stream—but only on the condition he be "good" and did *exactly* what he was told. Lysandridas had hardly dared breathe for fear of doing something wrong and being banished back to the other side of the stream. Yet he had taken to horses like a duck to water. Teleklos soon knew he could be trusted around them, while the horses all doted on him as if he were a foal.

From that day forward, their relationship had been cemented by the shared love of the beautiful four-legged beasts. But Lysandridas' love of flowers had hardly been less impressive. When the iris and narcissus started blooming among the trees of the orchard, Teleklos was reminded of the way Lysandridas had gathered them up and put them on his mother's grave, year after year. Teleklos had watched from his window as the boy/youth/young man squatted down in front of the simple stone marking his mother's grave and arranged the iris and narcissus in a terracotta vase he had dug into the ground before the stone. He took great care with the arrangement, so that white and blue iris and yellow narcissus always harmonised perfectly. And Teleklos never found a dead flower in the vase; the flowers were always fresh—or there were none at all.

When the orchard started blooming in sequence—almond, apple, quince or plum—Teleklos was reminded of the way Lysandridas would come home with petals clinging to his hair. He loved climbing trees, and he found endless games in their branches. When the fruit harvests came, one after another, he liked to climb up and shake the ripe fruits down to the waiting helots—or he had until at fourteen he'd broken a branch in his exuberance and come down with it. He'd broken his arm in the incident, and his eirene at the agoge had flogged him for having been so careless and injuring himself "pointlessly" so he could not take part in drill and training for more than a month. But it had been a symbolic flogging rather than a serious one, and left no scars.

The only other time Lysandridas had been flogged was when he was seventeen and a citizen had mishandled one of their horses. To get into town for dinner at the mess, Teleklos often rode one or the other of their horses and left it tied in front of the mess. Spartan law, however, gave any citizen the right to ride another citizen's horse whenever needed. A certain Akrotates, seeing Teleklos' horse waiting for him, had decided he "needed" it for some reason. Teleklos couldn't remember what his excuse had been any more, but he took the horse and started riding it through the streets with a heavy hand and flapping heels. Unfortunately, he crossed the path of Lysandridas' agoge unit as they returned from the drill fields on the far side of the Eurotas. Lysandridas had recognised his father's horse instantly, and in a blind rage at what he considered "maltreatment", he leapt up and dragged the citizen off the horse.

In so doing, he'd broken the law twice over. Not only did the citizen have a right to ride the horse any way he wanted, but as a mere youth still in the agoge, Lysandridas owed every full citizen obedience and respect. Pulling him off a moving horse, throwing him to the ground, and pinning him there while the horse got clear away did not exactly fit the Spartan ideal of obedient and respectful youth. Lysandridas got soundly flogged for that and Teleklos made a point of being there to watch, emphasising by his presence his approval of the punishment ordered by Lysandridas' eirene.

It had been one of the few times they'd quarrelled. Lysandridas insisted that the law was wrong to let anyone use a horse even if they were a "bear-fisted baboon". He'd pointed out that he'd saved one of their precious race horses from serious injury by getting rid of the rider before he could do more damage to his back and mouth. He raged at his father that age alone didn't make a man worth anything, and this citizen was certainly not a man otherwise respected or known for any virtues. Quite the contrary, he was often used as a bad example because he was considered lazy and greedy.

Lysandridas' rage had smouldered in his eyes even as he went into the sandpits where the public floggings took place, and it had been so intense that he had refused to ask for mercy. They'd had to beat him unconscious, which was his way of proving he was in the right. *That* flogging had left scars.

Eventually, Lysandridas had forgiven his father, or at least put aside the incident. They had started training together the four colts that were eventually to take them to the laurels at Olympia. That was why Teleklos could not bear to go near the horses now. Instead, he went to the Marshal of the Agiad royal stables, who was the only other trainer of note in Sparta at the time, and offered to give him the team.

Marshal Agis, the great-uncle of King Anaxandridas and so himself of royal blood, listened patiently to Teleklos but replied, "I won't take advantage of your grief to enrich myself." With a nod of his head he indicated Teleklos' cropped-off hair. Despite Zoë's efforts to style it, Teleklos' hair still shocked in a society where adult males wore their hair long and only women cut their hair in mourning. "If you still want to sell your team a year from now, we can talk again," Agis concluded the interview.

Teleklos had no choice but to return to his kleros, but he avoided the horses.

Not long after that, when the poppies had turned his fields red, Persandros came all the way out to the kleros to visit him. Teleklos had been helping Cleoetas and Chartas shore up the terracing of the olive orchard on the eastern face of the Taygetos behind the house. When Zoë sent her youngest child, her fourteen-year-old daughter Doris, to fetch him, he had been soaked in sweat, dusty, and barefoot. He told Doris to have her mother serve the guest chilled wine and a light snack in the hall, while he hastened over to the fountain house. He stripped down, washed himself vigorously in the icy water, and pulled on a still-damp chiton which had been hanging out to dry on the porch of the wash house. He entered the cool of the house with his hair and beard still wet from washing. "Persandros! What a pleasure."

Persandros rose from the couch and greeted his host with an unconvincing smile. Teleklos waved him down, checking that he had enough wine in his kylix and that the krater was well filled with the light mixture of one-third wine, two-thirds water. "What can I do for you?" Teleklos asked.

"Nothing, nothing at all. I—just wanted to tell you myself. I don't want you to hear it from someone else."

"What then?" Teleklos asked, although in his bones he already knew.

"Thessalos came to me not long ago. He asked for Hermione, and I agreed. You know there is no one I would rather have had as a son-in-law than your Lysandridas, but since that is not to be ..."

Teleklos was stunned. Of course Hermione would have to marry someone else. Of course she couldn't be expected to stay unmarried just because Lysandridas was dead. But so soon? She was only eighteen, after all. She could easily have waited a couple of years. It would not have been too much to expect of a girl who had just lost the young man she loved. And Thessalos? Thessalos had been Lysandridas' best friend.

Lysandridas had always been a bit of a loner, preferring to come home to his own kleros and the horses than to hunt, fish, or hang about the gymnasiums in gangs as most boys and youths did. Rather than a gang of friends, he had had only one: Thessalos. Thessalos was Marshal Agis' grandson, and so they shared the love of horses, riding, and driving. Thessalos had been at Olympia and had been one of the men to carry Lysandridas on his shoulders in a victory lap. He'd encouraged Lysandridas to ask for Hermione. He had also been one of the few young men to distinguish himself on the last campaign. Teleklos hadn't listened carefully, but he knew that some story about his courage had made the rounds. In any case, he'd been selected for the Guard. It was as if he had taken Lysandridas' place in every way.

"And Hermione?" he found himself asking stupidly.

Persander looked embarrassed, "She—she grieved sincerely, but she's young and she wants a husband. Indeed, she needs one."

"When?"

"Very shortly. That's why I wanted to come." Persander repeated.

Dazed, Teleklos nodded. "Thank you." It didn't really matter, he told himself, as he politely saw his guest out by the front porch. He only hoped that Lysandridas could not see her from Hades, see that in less than a six-month she was eagerly going to another man's bed. He'd always thought the girl was unworthy of Lysandridas, but this was an insult that rankled badly, and he brooded for days.

His father took him to task for it. "You aren't going to bring Lysandridas back by sulking all the time! It's time you got on with your life. You're acting worse than when your wife died!"

"Am I?" Teleklos replied in surprise. "But then I had the children to live for."

"You have three fine grandchildren! It's time you took more interest in them. Why don't you go visit Dorothea. She's asked more than once. You could stay there a month or two and pull yourself together. The way you mope around is a disgrace!"

Teleklos took his father's advice and went to live with his daughter and son-in-law on their kleros, half-way to Gytheion. It was a rambling house built over the generations bit by bit. It had a large front terrace looking out toward the Eurotas as it meandered through the fertile plain some 200 yards away.

The banks of the Eurotas were sandy and shallow, so that even the little girls could go wading in the cooling waters. Day after day, Teleklos took his granddaughters down to the riverbank and sat in the shade of the plane trees, watching them splash and play in the shallows. Evenings, however, he and Derykleides drove into the city to attend their respective syssitia, and Derykleides took the opportunity to lecture his father-in-law on the need to "pull himself together". He was too polite to say that Teleklos was disgracing them, but Teleklos understood his feelings nevertheless.

His sister and brother-in-law also visited him while he was with Dorothea. They asked if it wasn't time to start training his victorious team for the Pythian games at Delphi.

"Who's to drive them?" Teleklos answered listlessly.

"Well, I mean, Nikandros isn't a bad driver for a start, or Derykleides, if you prefer."

Nikandros was his sister's younger son, a youth of nineteen, who was indeed more than competent at the reins. Teleklos asked disinterestedly, "Would Nikandros like to enter the team? I'll give it to him."

"He can't do that! He's not even a citizen yet! When should he have time to train a team!" Teleklos' brother-in-law responded in open disapproval.

Agiates laid her hand on her husband's arm to calm him, and then leaned and touched the back of Teleklos' hand. "The point isn't to give the team away; the point is to take an interest in them again."

"I can't stand the sight of them," Teleklos answered sharply and honestly.

"Oh, Teleklos! You can't go on like this!" his sister cried out in despair.

"You're right. I can't," Teleklos agreed, but that didn't change anything.

It was high summer, and the blooming oleander reminded Teleklos of the way Lysandridas always garlanded the horses in wreaths of it for the Feast of Apollo at the summer solstice. Lysandridas had always spent the night before the feast weaving the pink and white blooms together and then laid the flowers in the basin of the wash house overnight so they'd still be fresh in the morning. At dawn he'd be up to groom the two horses honoured for the day, and only at the last minute before departing would he bring out the wreaths and lay them over the withers of the horses.

The festival had always been one of the most important in their little family, because Apollonides had a special affinity for Apollo. Although Apollonides had been so weakened at birth that he really shouldn't have been allowed to live, the Gods had compensated by giving him a beautiful voice. As a youth and young man well into his prime, he had been a favourite soloist at all the festivals. Apollonides had even competed at Delphi in the singing contests, and he had won the laurels three times. Apollonides revered his patron God sincerely, and no one in his family dared miss the summer solstice festival in honour of him.

This year was no exception, and so Teleklos dutifully went with his daughter and her family to Amyclae, where a great, forty-foot statue to Apollo loomed up from the sanctuary atop a little rise in the middle of the valley. From all over Lacedaemon the families came in their carts or chariots with offerings of flowers, wine, oil, cheese and baked goods, chickens and—if there were something special to thank the God for—lambs, kids or pigs.

But music was the heart of the festival. Ever since the Athenian schoolmaster Tyrtaios had helped Sparta to victory over the Messenians in the Second War with his inspiring marching hymns, Sparta's traditional love for music had gradually been transformed into a sacred duty. The fame of Tyrtaios had attracted other poets and musicians to Sparta. As a result, the already rich musical heritage of the city had been greatly enriched over the last eighty years. Now, throughout Hellas, Sparta had a reputation for musical talent and accomplishment. The poet Alkman, particularly, had a pan-Hellenic reputation, and he wrote mostly for festivals and for girls' choruses rather than for the army as Tyrtaios had done. Not surprisingly, therefore, there were choral competitions at this festival.

Dorothea took her father's hand and laid her head on his shoulder. "Do you remember the year my chorus won?"

He smiled for her, remembering it very well. She had been a nubile maiden of fifteen in a bright pink peplos and oleanders in her hair. Lysandridas had picked the blossoms for her specially. Teleklos told his daughter how beautiful she'd been, but did not dare to mention Lysandridas' contribution.

But then in the crowds he caught sight of Hermione. She was clinging to Thessalos' arm and he held her to his side possessively. They looked unbearably happy, whispering and giggling like young lovers, and kissing each other on the mouth when they thought no one could see. Her belly was already round with child, and in outrage Teleklos registered she looked more like she was six months pregnant than three! Her father's words, "Indeed she needs a husband," came back with new meaning. She'd taken Thessalos to her bed *before* she had her father's blessing. The realisation that she transferred her affections in three months or less after Lysandridas' death took away all Teleklos' budding joy that day.

There was dancing late into the night; the rounds of garlanded girls gave way to the faster, more acrobatic dancing of the youths from the agoge. At sunset the young men came out and did a sword dance to the whining of the pipes and flutes.

At sunrise the following day, King Agesikles made the official sacrifice of oxen for the city. He took the opportunity to announce that he had sent again to Delphi and received a new Oracle. This said that Sparta would gain the upper hand against Tegea when Agamemnon's son was brought home to Sparta. That left everybody more confused than ever, and Chilon was not alone in murmuring that King Agesikles had done enough damage to the city with his "oracles". Teleklos agreed with them, but what was the point in grumbling? The damage was already done. They could do no worse to him. Lysandridas was dead.

CHAPTER 13

After the festival, Teleklos returned to his own kleros. Although everything here reminded him of Lysandridas, still it was somehow good to be home. Zoë smiled and waved from the terrace when she saw him coming. By the time he reached the front porch, she was waiting for him with a broad kylix brimming with watered wine in which orchids were floating.

Cleotas and Chartas emerged from around the side of the house, drying their hands, and behind them came the other six helots who worked the estate for him. They all welcomed him home as if he'd been away for years—or at war. As the dusk settled over the valley, he went round to the back terrace where the helots sat laughing and yarning as the air cooled to a comfortable temperature. He took his usual seat on a bench below the stairs, and asked what had been happening while he was away.

They gave him the news and the gossip of the estate and the neighbourhood. Zoë and Cleoetas' second boy, Thorax, had got into a fight over a girl from a kleros beyond the Eurotas. The kryptea had arrested all those involved and put them in the stocks for two days. Teleklos was shocked to hear this and asked why they hadn't sent him word. Zoë and Cleoetas just looked at each other. Thorax himself shrugged and said he was none the worse for it. But Teleklos knew Zoë and Cleoetas worried about Thorax because he was hot-tempered and dissatisfied with his lot in life. When his father died, his elder brother would take over running the estate, and Thorax could hope for nothing better than to be his brother's labourer as he was his father's. Thorax himself sometimes talked of "joining the army": every hoplite had one to two helot servants to help keep his equipment and to aid him on campaign, but Zoë and Cleoetas didn't want their son to be part of such rough company. They had explicitly asked Lysandridas not to take him. It had saved his life, but Thorax remained restless.

They changed the subject, talking about the fox that had been lurking around the estate and which they had failed to trap. They discussed the weather and the various crops and the rumours that a bear had been sighted by one of the neighbours when he was out hunting in Taygetos. "Oh, and Leonis has been exercising the horses while you were away." It was added so "innocently" that Teleklos knew they'd been afraid of telling him all evening.

Leonis was his neighbour Zeuxidamas' daughter. She had lost her mother and brother in a horrible accident when she was four. Her brother, two years older than she, had either jumped or fallen into the stream beside their estate during the autumn torrents. His mother had plunged into the stream to save him, only to find the current was too strong for her as well. They were swept together to their deaths, their bodies not recovered until they were washed up south of the city in the reeds of the Eurotas.

Zeuxidamas never remarried, preferring to devote himself to his duties. He was an officer in the army and so could live in barracks even after he turned thirty-one. This he did. Without any ado, Zoë had included Leonis in her family of "motherless orphans", and Teleklos had not objected. Leonis was two years younger than Lysandridas and ten years younger than Dorothea. Dorothea had mothered her, treating her like a living doll, and Lysandridas had always treated her like a younger sister—fighting with her, often annoyed with her tagging along, but protective. He'd picked flowers for her, too, and cheered her at the maiden races.

Given her parental neglect, it was hardly surprising that she grew up rather wild. She'd always tried to match herself to Lysandridas, running, climbing trees, and riding with him. As a young girl in the agoge, she'd even enjoyed a degree of fame because she was so fleet that she could beat even the boys of her own age-cohort. She won all the maiden foot races, and Teleklos had been talked into letting her ride one of his horses at the horse race of the Gymnopaedia—to Lysandridas' outrage, because she had beaten him.

As she grew up, however, her excellence at sports no longer redounded to her credit. She still won the races at fifteen and sixteen, but the young men came to see Hermione lose rather than to see her win. While other girls matured and became coy and flirtatious, Leonis seemed locked in childhood. She was flat-chested and overly thin, with light brown hair she kept cut short like a youth, and freckles. As far as Teleklos knew, she had no suitors, although—he calculated—she must be twenty-one or so now. It was time she married.

"You don't mind, do you?" Zoë asked, bringing Teleklos back to the present.

"No, why should I? She can handle them. Has she been riding or driving them?" Sparta was the scandal of the Greek world for letting maidens race, ride, and drive at all; but even in Sparta a young woman, as Leonis now was, did not normally ride—at least not in public. Driving two-horse chariots, in contrast, was a sport that was encouraged, and there were even "ladies' races" at the major festivals.

"She started by just lunging them. Then she rode them. She started driving half a month ago."

Teleklos nodded his approval. That was the sensible way to go about it. His high-strung racehorses had been completely neglected since Olympia. It would have been madness to try to put them straight into the traces after six months of freedom. "When does she come?"

"At dawn, when it's still cool, and then again after dinner time."

Again Teleklos nodded, and then changed the subject.

The next morning Teleklos got up at dawn and went down through the dewy, long grass to the river. He waded across on the "ford" he had built himself a quarter of a century earlier, and entered his little stables. This was built of wood with just eight stalls, one of which was empty and used to store hay. The horses nickered and stirred uneasily at his unexpected appearance, one after another sticking their heads out over their stall doors to look at him.

Nearest the door was his oldest horse, a big dapple-grey stallion. He had called him Taygetos for the mountains behind the kleros because his withers were white as if with snow, but he got darker and darker from shoulder to belly and feet. Teleklos had bought him as a yearling. Lysandridas had just been seven at the time and was having a hard time adjusting to the rigours of life in the agoge. Teleklos had taken him along to the yearling sales as a treat to help cheer him up. Because of his unusual colouring, Taygetos had not found favour with the royal stables and had been rather cheap. Lysandridas had insisted, however, that he was the "best" colt there. As much to indulge his seven-year-old son as because he saw anything in the colt himself, Teleklos bought him. He had never regretted it.

They won the horse race with him at Nemea when Lysandridas was ten, and repeated the success at Delphi and Isthmia, but just missed the Olympic victory by a head to a Thessallian colt entered by an Athenian. Then Taygetos injured himself in their own pasture, and Teleklos had put him to stud, buying two mares especially for him.

In due time, Taygetos had sired all but one of Teleklos' future Olympic team, three greys like himself. The eldest was Agamemnon, who occupied the stall directly beside his sire and greeted Teleklos by laying back his ears and trying to snap at him. Agamemnon had always been bad-tempered. His year-younger full brother, Menelaus, was by contrast always friendly, and nickered with his ears forward as Teleklos approached. Beyond was their half-brother Achilles, the same age as Menelaus, but out of the other of the two mares. Menelaus and Achilles were both now seven. The last member of the team was Hector. He was black except for a star on his forehead and one white pastern on his off-fore. He had been sired by one of the royal stallions, in a deal Teleklos had made with Marshal Agis. On account of another injury, Teleklos had not wanted to risk breeding Taygetos the year after Menelaus and Achilles were born, but he wanted a fourth colt. He therefore arranged to take both his mares to the royal stables and turn over one of the foals sired by the royal stallion to Agis in exchange. The royal stables got the pick of the foals, and Hector was the rejected colt.

From the day he was rejected by the royal stables as too small, however, Hector had been Lysandridas' favourite. He had lavished more attention on the foal than any of the others. He'd walked him through a severe colic, risking a beating for being away from the agoge all night (but in this case his eirene turned a blind eye). He'd spent literally months getting the overly sensitive colt used to the traces. He had one very bad accident, when the colt spooked while pulling the two-horse, bolting off the road and breaking an axle. Lysandridas had had a badly wrenched shoulder and numerous bruises from that. Any other trainer would have lost his patience. Teleklos certainly did. He kept telling his son they'd made a bad deal with Agis, and they just had to wait another year for a new foal from Taygetos. But Lysandridas insisted that Hector had the potential once he gained confidence in himself.

Teleklos accused his son of being "sentimental", but Lysandridas shrugged off the insult and carried on with his intensive training. When his father insisted on castrating Hector, Lysandridas had done it himself, rather than let anyone else "do a hatchet job". In the end, Lysandridas had been proved right; placed on the far left hand, Hector acted as the pivot for the whole team and had contributed to victory no less than any of the other three.

Teleklos stopped in front of Hector's stall and stared at the somewhat undersized gelding. The horse looked back at him with large, unhappy eyes. He had lost weight and looked listless.

"He misses Lysandridas," a woman's voice said from the doorway, and Teleklos spun around. He had been expecting her, but he was surprised nevertheless. Leonis was dressed in a simple Doric peplos, slit well up the thigh for freedom of movement. The peplos was of unbleached, natural linen, with green stripes woven into it lengthwise. She was wearing sturdy sandals that came up over the feet—a good precaution in a stables. Her limbs were slender and tanned. Her light brown hair was kept back from her face by a narrow scarf tied at the back of her head, leaving long curls tumbling down her back. So she'd stopped cropping her hair, Teleklos noted. She was also wearing earrings: miniature bronze hoplite shields dangled from her ears, and brooches in the same motif held her peplos at her shoulders. She was still slender, but there was a touch of femininity to her as well. She was no longer the wild tomboy Teleklos remembered, but a young woman. She was no beauty like Hermione, but she was, Teleklos registered with approval, attractive in the same way a healthy young filly is attractive: she was naturally graceful and full of vitality.

She came to stand beside him and looked at him with hazel brown eyes set under chestnut lashes. Teleklos was not tall. He was stocky and slightly bow-legged. The slender young woman was as tall as he was.

"They told you I've been exercising them?"

"Yes. Thank you."

She reached over the stall door and stroked Hector's neck. "They've all missed you," she corrected her earlier statement.

"What had you planned for today?" Teleklos asked her.

"I wanted to take Hector and Menelaus out in the two-horse. I had Agamemnon and Achilles out yesterday. Evenings I lunge or ride the two I haven't driven."

"A lot of hard work for a young woman."

"I enjoy it. You know that."

"We can do it together," Teleklos suggested.

She looked up and smiled—a real, surprised, heartfelt smile that warmed Teleklos' heart as he had not thought possible any more.

Throughout the summer they kept to the same routine. They met in the stables early in the morning and again after dinner, when Teleklos returned from his syssitia. Leonis couldn't handle the four-horse chariot, and so every third day Teleklos took it out himself with the full team. Otherwise he let Leonis alternate teams on the two-horse. Evenings they would ride together around their neighbouring kleroi so that Leonis was not riding "in public". That way the mares and old Taygetos got the exercise they needed, too.

Eventually Leonis had the courage to ask, "Are you going to take them to Delphi next year?"

"Who'd drive them?" Teleklos answered gloomily and rhetorically. Leonis didn't press him.

It was fall when Zeuxidamas intercepted Teleklos as he left his syssitia one evening. Zeuxidamus was a tall, lean man with a receding hairline; his long, thin braids started in the middle of his skull. He greeted Teleklos politely and asked if he could walk him home. Teleklos agreed a little apprehensively. Zeuxidamas had never walked home with him before, although they had been neighbours all their lives.

They walked at first in silence. Zeuxidamas was evidently having difficulty finding the right words. In the end, he decided for laconic directness. "My daughter is twenty-one. It is time she was married."

"Of course," Teleklos agreed sadly. So he was going to lose this last little ray of sunshine, too.

"She's a good girl. She's run my kleros practically since she left the agoge. She works hard, and it yields more than ever it did in my mother's time." He did not mention his wife, and Teleklos understood that. "I know people call her 'wild' and 'rude', but she has a good heart and a good mind. Nor is she immodest; she just …" Zeuxidamas didn't seem to know how to word it.

Teleklos assured him, "You don't have to defend her to me. I think highly of your daughter."

"Have you never thought of remarriage?" Zeuxidamas was clearly ashamed to raise the issue himself, and he kept his eyes on the road ahead of them as it wound along the foot of Taygetos with the playing fields to their right.

Teleklos was thunderstruck. Marry again? Marry Leonis? She was thirty-six years younger than he was! "What does Leonis think of marrying an old man?" Teleklos asked cautiously, afraid of becoming fond of the idea.

"What should Leonis think? I can hardly ask her if I don't know your feelings on the subject!" There was anger in that, anger because Zeuxidamas resented having to ask another man to take his daughter. It should have been the other way around.

Teleklos touched his neighbour's elbow to calm him. "I didn't mean that. I—I just wouldn't want to force her into something she finds distasteful. I'm old enough to be her father. Indeed, she's looked on me like a kind of uncle all her life."

"But what do *you* think?"

"I think your daughter is one of the kindest, most sensible, most attractive young women I have ever met. I think it would be an honour to call her my wife." A wife could give him sons. No one could ever replace Lysandridas, but it would be a pleasure having young children in the house again. It would be healthy to have a woman in the house after all these years. It would be wonderful to have a wife who shared his love of horses. The idea was enchanting.

Zeuxidamas looked over at him sharply, waiting for the "but". It didn't come. "Are you saying you would like to take my daughter to wife?"

"Yes, I am."

Zeuxidamas smiled with relief. "Then let us meet again to discuss the details. Would the day after the equinox suit you?" At the equinox there was another festival and the army would have leave, so Zeuxidamas would be home. Teleklos nodded, his heart already beating faster. They parted, Zeuxidamas hurrying back toward the city with a light, relieved stride and Teleklos in a bit of a daze.

In the stables he found Leonis grooming Hector. She smiled over her shoulder at him as he entered. "I'm almost finished." With the shorter days, they had less time to ride, and she now tried to have everything ready for him. Agamemnon waited for him, already tacked up.

Teleklos moved over to her and stood beside her rather than leading Agamemnon out into the yard. She looked up surprised. "Is something wrong?"

"Not at all. Your father and I just had a talk."

"What about?"

"You."

She went dead still and her eyes widened in alarm. She dropped her eye-lids a fraction of a second too late. He had seen the expression clearly, and the little dream of marital bliss and a new beginning was shattered. She did not want to marry an old man. He turned away from her, his shoulders sagging. "Never mind. I won't force you."

"Oh, Teleklos!" Her voice was anguished. "Please don't be angry! I was just taken by surprise."

"I'm not angry." He did not dare face her. He was sure his face would betray that he was hurt. He started to collect Agamemnon's reins.

"Teleklos! Give me a chance. I—I just need to get used to the idea. I never thought—"

"Of course not; why should you? It was a foolish idea. I'm sorry I mentioned it. Forget it." He led Agamemnon beside the mounting block and flung himself onto the broad back. He then turned and looked at Leonis.

She still had not moved. She was standing facing Hector as if she was paralysed.

"Come on. We're losing the light."

Leonis turned to look at him, her face strained. "I will marry you, Teleklos, if you'll have me." There was something odd about her voice, as if she was going to cough. "That way no one else can take me away from all that's left of him."

"Him?"

"Ly—" she broke down.

How could he have been so blind? He jumped down and shoved Agamemnon back into his stall. Then he rushed over and took the girl in his arms. She didn't resist, though she was clearly unused to physical comfort. She hadn't been held by anyone except Zoë as long as she could remember. Embarrassed, she tried to apologise, and he silenced her. "There's nothing to be sorry for! He deserved your love! It honours him!"

"He didn't care. He never even noticed," she sobbed.

That, unfortunately, was true. "He loved you like a sister—more than his own sister."

She pulled away from him, wiping away her tears with her bare hands and leaving streaks of dirt on her cheeks. She started fussing with Hector to try to overcome her embarrassment at such a disgraceful display of emotions. "I never wanted to marry anyone else. I couldn't bear the thought of marrying anyone else. But I never thought about you—"

"Of course not. I'm an old man. Forget it. It was a stupid idea. I'm too old to marry anyone. Too set in my ways. Come on." He laid his hand on her shoulder again. "Don't give it another thought. What we're going to do instead is get this team ready for Delphi. Don't you think that's what he would have wanted?"

She looked over at him, her eyes wide with confusion. "But if you've talked to my father—"

"Let me handle your father. You get yourself mounted before we have no light left at all, all right? Come on. We have less than a year, and I have to get Nikandros trained to drive the team in that time." He went and took Agamemnon out of his stall again.

CHAPTER 14

When Teleklos left for the Pythian games, Apollonides, despite his age, insisted on travelling with him. Nikandros, now an eirene, was given special leave from his duties as instructor at the agoge to take part in the Games, and it seemed like half his age-cohort was there in a loud, cheerful gaggle to see him off. His father promised to come for the Games themselves, as did Derykleides. The other family members and Chilon came out to wish Teleklos success, and Marshal Agis, who was not competing, also wished Teleklos well.

"I knew you didn't really want to be rid of your team," he reminded Teleklos of their conversation of eighteen months earlier. "But at the 56th Olympic Games you'll have my new team to contend with. Hector's brothers," he stroked the fidgeting black gelding affectionately, "are going to put him in the shadow at the next Olympics."

Teleklos smiled and nodded. He could never face another Olympics. It was bad enough going to Delphi without Lysandridas. He would be content to let Agis represent Lacedaemon at Olympia in two years. Indeed, a part of him was not up to even this competition. He had only done it for Leonis, and now she stood off to one side, clutching her green shawl about her as if she were cold.

Teleklos left the crowd of well-wishers and went over to her. "It's unfair that you can't come with me—at least to watch." He remembered how she had made an unseemly fuss when they'd set off for Olympia two years ago. She'd raged about it being unfair that women couldn't even set foot on the sacred premises or watch the games, much less compete.

At the time Lysandridas had teased her, insensitive to how deeply hurt she really was. "There's no point in letting women compete at the Games," he'd laughed, "because only the Spartans would come anyway. None of the other cities let their girls out of their houses—much less run around half-naked like you do! And you know you can beat the other Spartan girls; you don't have to go to Olympia for that!" Lysandridas had been too excited and full of himself to notice Leonis' tears of frustration. Even at the time, Teleklos had felt sorry for her.

Today, when she more than anyone was responsible for his team being fit enough to compete, she made no fuss. She smiled at him sadly and shrugged. "It's the way it is. Do you have Lysandridas' charm?" Lysandridas had never entered a race without a small bronze charm depicting the Dioskouroi on a chain around his neck.

Teleklos' face fell. "He was wearing it when he marched out."

"I'm sorry! I didn't—" She could have kicked herself.

Teleklos leaned forward and kissed her on the forehead. "How could you know? It's all right. Take care of the mares and Taygetos. They'll be lonely."

To avoid Tegea, they travelled by way of Messenia and then up the west coast of the Peloponnese to Rhion. There they were ferried across the Gulf of Corinth to Antirhion, and then followed the steep coastal road to Delphi. They timed it so that the horses would have several days to rest before they started the final month of training, but Teleklos did not want to stay a day longer than he thought absolutely necessary. He did not look forward to facing all the competitors he had defeated at Olympia. He dreaded having to tell them—particularly the Tegean—that his son had died in that foolish invasion attempt.

During the journey, Nikandros provided some distraction from his memories. He was a very different youth from Lysandridas, and if sometimes that awakened painful memories by virtue of the contrast, on the whole Teleklos enjoyed watching the gregarious youth on his first trip outside of Lacedaemon.

Nikandros at twenty was excited by everything new, and he had no shyness whatsoever. He'd talk to anyone, ask questions without the least inhibitions, and remark loudly on anything that struck him. At times it was embarrassing—like the first time he saw a hetaera being carried through the streets by two slave boys in a litter. "Can't she walk with all that gold on her, or what?" he asked in a voice that seemed to carry to the far side of the agora. Apollonides had angrily told him to shut up, but Teleklos had laughed with all the others in the marketplace.

Apollonides started giving his grandson lectures on why Sparta's laws discouraged travel. He told Nikandros he was being corrupted by all the strange and immoral people he came in contact with, and hissed at him not to talk to strangers. Nikandros respectfully listened to his grandfather, said "yes, father" like a good Spartiate youth, and then waited only until the old man dozed off before setting out to explore the worst parts of the cities they passed through.

Teleklos was on Nikandros' side. He'd made his own discoveries the first year he'd travelled to pan-Hellenic games, in his case to Isthmia, and he'd let Lysandridas gather his own experiences as well. Teleklos felt that a young man had to suffer a frightful hangover before he could appreciate the wisdom of Spartan temperance. He had to get robbed, cheated, and lose his chiton at a gambling table before he would learn to be wary of certain types of men and promises. And it was better for a young man to learn the sordidness of brothels before he married, than to think he had missed out on something when he settled down.

Once they reached Delphi, however, the time for experimentation and self-discovery was over. Teleklos expected, and Apollonides insisted, that Nikandros settle down and concentrate exclusively on training. For his stay at Delphi, Nikandros was on "bread and water", Apollonides informed him—and his grandfather slept on a mat in the doorway of the room he shared with his uncle to ensure he did not go anywhere without Apollonides knowing.

The day after they arrived and had settled into the guest house, they set out to pay their respects to Apollo. The guest house was located near the gymnasium and baths, between the Temple to Athena and the sacred spring. They went first to the spring and washed themselves thoroughly. They then proceeded up the sacred way past the little, mostly wooden treasuries in which the gifts of various cities to Apollo were housed. Only the Corinthians and Athenians were wealthy enough to have built treasuries in stone. At the Temple to Apollo, Teleklos and Nikandros made the sacrifices they had brought with them.

It was then nearly mid-morning, and the face of the steep hillside was alive with activity. Priests were going in and out of the temples; athletes and trainers were, like themselves, taking in the sights or coming to make sacrifices. Visitors to the oracle were likewise congregating before the full moon when the oracle could be consulted. They were sightseeing and socialising with one another as they waited. Apollonides was tired and irritable, so they left him sitting in the theatre reminiscing about his musical triumphs while Teleklos took Nikandros up to see the stadium. The hippodrome they had inspected the evening before.

It was extremely hot and they were thirsty when they started weaving their way back down the sacred way towards the athletic district. As they passed the Tegean treasury, a brightly painted wooden building with a portico supported on four Doric columns, Apollonides got it into his head that he wanted to visit it. "All tarted up and expanded since I was last here," he proclaimed in a loud irritable voice.

"They can afford it," Teleklos murmured, trying to gently pull his father down the slope, and thinking of the nearly 70,000 drachma they had charged for the Spartiate captives.

"Let go of me!" Apollonides yanked his arm free. "I want to see what they did with our ransom money." He was attracting attention. Other athletes and pilgrims were turning to see what was going on, and it was all too easy to see that Apollonides was a Spartiate. Although Teleklos himself had been careful to dress in a simple green chiton, Apollonides had insisted on wearing Spartan scarlet. And whereas Teleklos' short-cropped hair made him look like all the other Greeks, his father's long, braided hair was no longer fashionable anywhere outside of Lacedaemon. Nikandros and Teleklos exchanged an uneasy glance and then followed Apollonides into the little treasury.

It seemed very dark after the glaring sunlight outside, and it took a minute or two for their eyes to adjust. The chamber was full of "clutter"— tripods, statues in stone, bronze and wood, amphorae and krater. But stacked up against the back wall were hundreds of eight-footers behind a heap of helmets and shields. It took a half minute to realise what these were, and then—even as Teleklos went to take his father's arm and pull him out—the old man saw it: his own shield. It was the shield he had given his grandson to carry, the shield with the Dioskouroi on it.

Apollonides let out a growl, and with a sharp spring that Teleklos would not have thought the old man had in him, he lunged forward. In an instant, he had snatched up the shield, knocking several others over in the process. The shields he knocked down hit the base of the spears, and these soon came clattering down on his head and shoulders as he backed away, now clutching his shield like a hoplite in battle. The clatter of falling shields and spears brought the watchman rushing out from the back of the treasury.

The position of watchman at a Delphic treasury was always an honorary post for worthy but impoverished citizens. No one expected anyone to try to steal the gifts given to Apollo. This man was no exception. He was short, fat, and lame. "What's going on here?!" he demanded in an alarmed voice.

"I'm taking back my shield! You've no right—"

"Father, in the Name of Zeus, put it down! It's not yours any more!" Teleklos was trying to yank the shield out of his father's hands, but his father was gripping it with a tenacity and strength that completely astonished Teleklos.

"Leave me be! By the Twins, I carried it in more battles than—"

Nikandros came to his uncle's assistance and together they tried to wrestle the shield away from Apollonides, while the Tegean watchman was shouting at the top of his lungs, "THIEF! THIEF! HELP!"

A half-dozen men stormed into the treasury and at once rushed to the assistance of the white-haired old man, who was apparently being assaulted by two younger men. The Tegean watchman, however, shouted hysterically. "No! NO! He's the thief!"

At that moment, when everyone was confused, Apollonides almost got out the door with his shield, but Teleklos shouted to Nikandros to stop him. With a helpless, shocked look over his shoulder the eirene asked, "You mean tackle him, sir?"

"YES!"

Nikandros did as ordered, wincing as he brought down his own grandfather with a flying tackle. The shield was knocked out of the old man's hands as he crashed to the ground and rolled onto the porch.

One of the other visitors, now putting things together, rushed out after the shield and brought it back into the treasury, while Nikandros, apologising profusely to his grandfather, tried to help him up. Apollonides had cut his cheek and his forehead in the fall, and he was dazed enough to have stopped shouting and struggling.

"Take him down to the guest house," Teleklos told his nephew in a low, urgent voice. "At once."

The eirene helped his grandfather to his feet and, supporting him with an arm around his waist, carefully led him out onto the porch and away.

The crowd burst into exclamations and a loud chatter of excitement. Everyone seemed to be asking everyone else what had happened and who the old man was. Teleklos had the opportunity to take the shield away from the man who'd brought it inside and carry it back to the heap of other spoils on display. He lingered, brushing his fingers over the caved-in front of the shield where a heavy object had landed and then slid off, tearing deep scratches in the surface and wrenching one of the bronze twins half off the face. He couldn't help wondering what part of Lysandridas it had been covering when the hoof crashed down on it and half-slid off again.

"What was that all about?" the crowd was asking. The watchman, still shaken by what had happened, was shouting at Teleklos as if he had been the offender, "How dare you come in here and try to steal something from Apollo?"

"Forgive him; he's an old man," Teleklos begged, as he started standing up the eight-footers again, and replacing the other shields that had been knocked over.

"Who was he? What made him think he could steal something from Apollo?" a priest asked indignantly.

"He is my father. It was his shield. He forgot where he was. Believe me, he meant no disrespect to Apollo. He just lost his head when he saw his shield," Teleklos tried to explain wearily.

"But he must have known it was here! He must have brought it here himself!" someone else suggested in a tone of open scepticism.

"He gave it to his grandson. His grandson carried it into battle two years ago and never came back. How was he to know it had been brought here? He was not prepared to find his own shield of forty years here. It unhinged him briefly. Forgive him. No damage was done."

The crowd was starting to disperse.

"Aren't you Teleklos of Sparta?" a well-dressed man asked as he started out.

Teleklos stopped and looked at the questioner. He was a handsome, blond man with an aquiline nose and penetrating blue eyes. He wore a long white chiton over which he had wrapped a maroon himation with casual elegance around his waist and then over his shoulders. He had good sandals on his feet and smelled of bay leaves. Something about him was vaguely familiar, but for the moment Teleklos could not place him. "Yes," Teleklos answered the question.

"I'm Damoxenos of Athens. I entered a team at Olympia, but they were soon left in the dust by yours." He smiled as he said this, not because he was happy about it but to show he wasn't angry, either. "They've improved since then, however. You may have more trouble here."

Teleklos nodded. "I'm sure it will be a hard-run race—as always."

The man was looking at him very curiously, as if he were looking for something, but Teleklos could not think what.

"Was the young slave that just helped the old man out your new driver?"

"No—that is, he *is* my driver but he is no slave! He's a Spartan eirene, if you know what that is." Teleklos was overreacting to the slight, but he did not want any mistake about Nikandros' status. Because eirenes were not yet citizens, they did not yet have the right to wear Spartan scarlet. They wore unbleached chitons and coarse black himations. There were many slaves of rich masters who went about better dressed, and this made it all the more imperative to clarify things. If Nikandros were treated like a slave, he would be hurt, and if his feelings were hurt he wouldn't concentrate on driving as he should.

"I'm sorry. I meant no offence," the Athenian bowed graciously. "He is a relation of yours?"

"He is my nephew," Teleklos told him.

"I see. Shall we walk back to the Pyntaneion together? I presume that is where you are headed?" This was the large communal dinning hall for the athletes located behind the gymnasium.

Teleklos felt he didn't have a polite way of declining and nodded.

"Polycritus is here again, you know. And Antyllus of Tegea."

"How many teams altogether?"

"Less than at Olympia, unless there are some surprise late entries. We are just five at this time: you, I, Polycritus, Antyllus, and a team from Plataea. I've seen them and don't think they're quite up to the competition—at least not yet."

Teleklos nodded. The other teams were formidable enough, even if he'd beaten them once—even if *Lysandridas* had beaten them once, he corrected himself.

Throughout the next month as they prepared for the Games, Teleklos tried to convince himself that he had a chance of winning. The Plataean team really was weak, and the entry said more about the owner's vanity than his sense. The Corinthian had the team which had been disqualified at Olympia; they were good, but the driver was a slave who did what his master ordered rather than driving on his own instincts and skill. The Athenian team was not only much improved, it had an Egyptian professional at the reins who, as far as Teleklos could see, never made mistakes. Still, the real competition was the Tegean team. This team, like his own, was at its peak, young but with some experience behind it, and it had been entrusted to a professional driver who was canny and ambitious.

Day after day the owners stood beside one another, making polite conversation while their teams warmed up and prepared for the race itself. Apollonides sat wrapped sullenly in his himation watching the training, never talking to the others, leaving Teleklos to socialize with the savvy, rich men who treated him with the respect due an Olympic victor—but without real collegiality.

The others shared more than just horse racing. The Plataean, Athenian, and Corinthian were all merchants, men who owned fleets of merchant ships or factories or mines and held hordes of slaves. The Tegean was poor by comparison, but his stable was five times as large as Teleklos' and his estate at least ten times the size of the state-allotted kleros from which Teleklos lived. All the others were also citizens who held public office of one kind or another. They were patrons of the arts. They were well travelled.

Teleklos felt provincial, poor, and uneducated by comparison. He kept himself apart as much as possible, particularly avoiding Antyllus of Tegea. He knew that the elegant, gracious landowner was not personally responsible for Lysandridas' death, but he was the enemy. For all Teleklos knew, he had fought in the battle on the winning side.

The day of the race brought a surprise rain shower, as if Apollo wanted to ensure ideal track conditions. The countryside was refreshed and washed. The air smelled clean. The birds rejoiced. Wild gladiolus, bellflowers, and marguerites peeked out from the rock faces. The participants first sacrificed to Apollo and then returned to the stables where the teams were groomed and readied by the slaves: in Teleklos' case, by Thorax.

Nikandros was nervous. He kept fussing with the bandages Teleklos had bound around his hands, complaining that they were too tight. He had slept poorly. Teleklos offered to rebandage his hands, but Nikandros irritably shook his head and pointed out that the other drivers didn't have anything on their hands. "The Egyptian wears leather gloves," Teleklos pointed out. But scowling, Nikandros insisted he didn't need the bandages. He tore them off, flung them aside, and climbed onto the chariot.

Teleklos went from horse to horse, stroking and patting them. They could sense the difference to training. Agamemnon was stamping and snapping with unusual vehemence, making Menelaus snap back, which was not like him at all. Achilles started balking—something he otherwise never did—and Nikandros cursed him and smacked his rump irritably. This wasn't like Nikandros, either. Only Hector was in good spirits, dancing about with his eyes alert and his ears straining forward. He could hear the flutes and pipes of the opening ceremonies and whinnied in delight.

The spectators collected well before the start of the race, bringing snacks and wine with them. Merchants moved up and down the stone steps hawking fresh-baked pastries, bread, and sweets. The priests and judges entered the stadium. Sacrifices were made at the altar at the top of the curve. The judges took their places. Music signalled the start of the procession, and one chariot after the other rolled out of the stableyard along the narrow road to the hippodrome. Teleklos let the others go first. Only when all were gone did he and Apollonides follow behind in the dust.

By the time they reached the hippodrome, the lots had already been drawn. At Delphi there was not an elaborate starting gate as at Olympia, only a rope drawn across the start. Nikandros had drawn the second inside slot—an ideal starting position, particularly since the weak Plataean team was on his inside.

A place was reserved for Teleklos behind the judges' tribune, but Apollonides had to find a vacant seat. He was clearly offended to discover that the other spectators, who had claimed the good seats around the judges' tribune very early, were not about to give one up to him. He moved around the hippodrome rather forlornly, drawing snickers and even a few catcalls from the spectators. Fortunately he came upon a group of Spartan spectators, all of whom at once stood to offer the old man their seats. Apollonides sank down with relief, and the younger men squeezed in closer together.

Antyllus remarked, "Your young men shame the rest of us."

Teleklos looked over, unsure what to make of the remark.

Antyllus answered his look, "In all Hellas we teach our children to show respect for age, but only your youth do it. Why is that?"

"I don't know," Teleklos answered honestly. But they had no time or nerves for further discussion. The teams were all in place and with a blast of a trumpet, the rope dropped and the race began.

From the start, Nikandros made one mistake after another. Despite his good starting position, he asked too much of the team too soon. He took an early lead and then clung too close to the inside of the track. He was so close to the inside that he had to slow the team down on the turn, and then would whip them up again to their top speed on the stretch. This confused the team, which was used to a steady pace and Lysandridas' wide, elegant turns—which Teleklos *thought* he had taught Nikandros to imitate. The strong teams only had to wait for his team to tire, and then almost at leisure they started to overtake him. First the Corinthian, then the Athenian, and last the Tegean, who then just kept going and passed the other two teams as well. In the final lap, Teleklos stood up and shouted at Nikandros to stop trying. The team was exhausted. He was doing them more harm than good to shout and curse and crack the whip. All he managed was to overtake the Corinthian at the last minute and place third in the field of five.

Teleklos was the first to turn to Antyllus and congratulate him. "A splendid victory. Well deserved. Your team is a joy to watch."

Antyllus was grinning, but had no chance to answer. Others were surrounding him to congratulate him. Teleklos recognised the Tegean ambassador, the man who had bragged about Spartiates "dancing to the tune of their Tegean masters". Teleklos couldn't stand the sight of him. He turned abruptly and squeezed out of the winner's circle.

Shoving and squirming his way through the crowds, he made his way down to the track where the teams were trotting their last, "cooling", lap. His brother-in-law and Derykleides managed to reach his side. "What happened? What was wrong with the team?" Derykleides asked.

"There was nothing wrong with the team," Teleklos told him emotionlessly.

"You aren't going to blame my Nikandros for that defeat," his brother-in-law started to defend his son at once.

"I'm not blaming anyone. We were outclassed, that's all."

Nikandros drew the chariot up in front of his uncle, father, and cousin's husband. He was white in the face, his hands bloody. "I'm sorry, sir—"

"It's all right. You did your best," Teleklos told him, not looking him in the eye.

Nikandros knew he'd made mistakes. "Sir, I—I—"

"You were too nervous, that's all. Next time, when you can see it's hopeless, don't keep driving the team like that. Ease up on them." Teleklos was running his hand down the backs of the legs of each horse in turn, feeling for heat, swelling, or injury. The horses were swaying with their breathing and dripping sweat onto the churned dirt of the track. He finished his inspection and straightened. "Drive them a couple of rounds at a walk—no, I'll do it. Go clean up your hands."

Nikandros, trembling with shame and exhaustion, stepped down from the chariot and turned over the blood-sticky reins to his uncle. As he withdrew, Teleklos heard his brother-in-law start to praise him, and Nikandros cut his father off. "No, Dad, it was my fault. It was all my fault."

Teleklos didn't hear any more. He heard only the creaking of the wheels, the dull patter of hooves, the subdued and inarticulate murmur of the dispersing crowds. He felt nothing. Not disappointment nor anger nor shame. Nothing. He drove back to the stable where Thorax already knew what had happened. The young helot looked more disappointed than Teleklos, who was moved to clap him on the shoulder and remark, "Maybe next time." But in his heart he knew there wasn't going to be a next time.

He helped the helot unhitch the horses and then pour water over them and scrape it off with sweat scrapers. They worked together, Teleklos' best chiton getting soaked with horse sweat and dirty water. They had just finished with Menelaus and started washing down Achilles when Polycritus arrived at the stables.

His face was bright red. Teleklos assumed that he was already drunk, and then the Corinthian opened his mouth and started screaming. Astonished, Teleklos realised he was red with sheer rage. Polycritus' team had ended up crossing the finish fourth, behind Teleklos' team. They too had been spent at the end, their heads bobbing with strain and the whip cracking over their heads furiously. Now the Corinthian stormed into the stables, leaving Teleklos and Thorax gaping after him in astonishment. They could hear him shouting and screaming, presumably at his four grooms; and then the next thing they knew, he was out again, but two of his slaves were holding a third between them.

Teleklos couldn't believe what he was seeing. The Corinthian, still raging like a mad dog, ordered the exceptionally large Nordic slave chained up against the side of the stables and started laying into him with a racing whip. Teleklos was horrified. "What are you doing?! This is sacred soil! You—"

Polycritus turned on him, his eyes bulging out of his face, and screamed at Teleklos to mind his own affairs. "I can do what I like with my own property! I can sacrifice it to Apollo if I like!"

Teleklos was stunned into silence. Around him the grooms of the other participants collected in mute outrage. None of them dared protest, but Teleklos could smell their horror on their sweat.

Thorax asked him in shocked disbelief, "Can he do that, Teleklos? Does he have the *right* to do that?" Teleklos did not have the right to flog his helots; only the Spartan authorities had that right, and then only for specific crimes. Teleklos could only shake his head and mutter, "Apparently."

As the other teams returned from the track, the drivers called for their grooms and then, seeing what was happening, they were stunned into silence.

The victim went from gasping to moaning to crying out in agony. He started begging for mercy. He hung on the chains, no longer able to stand, and his head rolled back and forth as he tried to evade the agony. "Please, Master! Please!"

Teleklos had been flogged as a youth in the agoge. He had even flogged youths himself when serving his year as an eirene instructor. He had watched Lysandridas and all his nephews get flogged at one time or another. But they used canes in Sparta, not horsewhips. More important: the boys were never chained. They stood grasping a wooden bar and when they didn't want to take any more, they let go of it and fell into the sand pit, signifying the end of their endurance. Of course any boy who gave in too soon was scoffed and ridiculed by his peers as being "weak" and "slavish". But never had Teleklos seen a man beaten after he was "finished"; he'd never seen a man beaten while he begged for mercy. The blood was splattering with each new lash, and Teleklos shuddered. This couldn't go on. He opened his mouth and took a step forward, but he was too late.

Antyllus was between him and Polycritus, and it was Antyllus who reached up his elegant beringed hand and caught Polycritus' arm. "How dare you besmirch my victory with this?"

Polycritus turned his red face, drenched in sweat from his exertions, and came face to face with the taller, leaner Antyllus wearing the crown of laurels. Although Teleklos would not have thought it possible, Polycritus actually got redder. His eyes protruded more than ever. His flabby cheeks trembled with indignation. He yanked his arm free of Antyllus and, flinging the whip away, stormed out of the yard.

Antyllus turned to the slaves around them. "For Apollo's sake, cut him down! Someone fetch a physician. Cobon, what was this all about?"

A grey-haired slave limped forward out of the crowd. "The Corinthian blamed Dion for not hot-walking his team properly last night, Master. He says the team was stiff this morning, and that's why they lost. That's what his driver told him."

Teleklos glanced sharply at the driver of the Corinthian team, who was slinking away into the stables; but he was a slave, too. He had only saved his own skin by coming up with an excuse that put the blame on someone else—someone Polycritus could vent his anger on.

"Is that true?" Antyllus was demanding.

"No, Master. Dion walked his team even longer than I walked yours. He was very careful with them, Master. He did nothing wrong. He's one of the best grooms here."

They unchained the victim, who sank onto the ground with a moan. A huge crowd collected around him. Teleklos turned to Thorax and told him to soak his himation in fresh cold water and then bring it over to him. He went down on his knees next to the slave with the cool, dripping himation, and he pressed it gently onto the wounds, carefully and methodically. Only after he'd been at it for a few minutes did he realise that Antyllus was on the victim's other side, and he was helping hold him steady. Their eyes met, and in that instant Teleklos felt a strange bond. Then the physician arrived and the two amateurs made way for him.

"You will join me after the official banquet for an intimate symposium, I hope?" Antyllus remarked in his gracious, aristocratic way.

Teleklos wanted to decline, but he couldn't. It would have been rude, and Antyllus didn't deserve a rebuff. He had won fairly. He wasn't to blame for the fact that King Agesikles had decided to invade Tegea two years ago—and lost half a thousand men trying. So Teleklos forced himself to smile and nod. "I'd be honoured."

The private symposium was held in one of the smaller rooms specially provided for such events. There were just eight couches. All the other owners—except Polycritus, of course—were invited, along with two other men who had racehorses rather than chariots in the competition, and another Tegean, a spectator in some way related to Antyllus. Teleklos was the last to arrive, because he had not attended the official banquet and misjudged the time.

Antyllus greeted him warmly, rising to come and embrace him. "You'll be interested to know that I purchased that poor groom from Polycritus. It's not easy to find slaves who can handle racehorses, and my own head groom swore the man was talented."

"Will he be all right?" Teleklos asked with sincere concern, as he settled onto the waiting couch. He could still not understand beating a man who begged for mercy.

"He will have scars the rest of his life, but he seems otherwise in excellent health. An ox of a man, really. Slavic origin."

Teleklos nodded politely. Because Sparta relied for agricultural labour upon the natives of Lacedaemon and Messenia, which had been conquered 500 and 100 years previously respectively, Sparta had virtually no chattel slaves and no slave trade. He did not know, as the other men in the room seemed to know, what "Slavic" meant or how this was relevant to a slave's worth.

A small black boy was offering to pour wine for him, and Teleklos noted just in time that it was unmixed. He held up his hand and shook his head.

"Is something wrong?" Antyllus asked anxiously.

"No, of course not—I'm just not used to neat wine. May I have it mixed?"

"But of course." The boy was sent scurrying to the kitchens for water.

"Teleklos, we were talking about your new driver," Antyllus remarked in a kindly tone, as if he had no idea that his words were lacerating Teleklos. "I mean, I'm perfectly certain that my team would not have won so easily— if at all—if your new driver hadn't—"

"He's very young. He was overwrought. It was his first competition ever. He made mistakes." Teleklos was looking into the broad, shallow bowl of his kylix, staring at the magnificent patterns painted in brown and cream and highlighted with red—and seeing only Lysandridas.

He did not see the other owners exchange surprised looks. "But why did you replace your son after he drove so magnificently at Olympia?" The question was raised innocently, in a tone of genuine bewilderment, by Antyllus.

Teleklos started so sharply, wine slopped over the edge of the kylix and spilt onto the floor. He stared at the elegant Tegean in disbelief. How could he torture him like this? But then he realised that the Tegean honestly didn't know. He took a breath and forced himself to say it out loud. "Lysandridas is dead."

"Dead? But he—" Antyllus' eyes understood. His lips parted. He swallowed. "I'm sorry. I'm so sorry. I didn't realise...."

Teleklos looked down into his kylix again and then took a deep, long gulp.

Damoxenos leaned forward. "Dead? Are you sure?"

"Of course I'm sure!" Teleklos snapped rudely, and then got hold of himself again. "He was in the Guard. He was killed in the battle against Tegea almost two years ago."

Damoxenos was frowning at him oddly, but Antyllus broke the tension. "My son, too, was killed in that same battle, Teleklos. My only son: Phaedolos."

Teleklos turned back to his host, and saw his own grief reflected on Antyllus' face. So that was the bond between them, he thought. A blood bond.

Someone managed to change the topic. Everyone made an effort to restore an atmosphere appropriate to a victory celebration. Teleklos, too, made an effort not to grieve in public or be resentful. How could he be resentful when Antyllus had paid the same price? They parted cordially, Teleklos again congratulating Antyllus, and Antyllus assuring him that his team was still a match any day. They left it at that.

The sky was starting to grey with dawn. Teleklos felt stiff and tired. "You don't mind if I join you?" It was Damoxenos again, who had apparently slipped out of the symposium right behind him.

"I'm afraid I'm too tired to be much company."

"It's only a short walk back. I just wanted to ask you something."

"Yes?"

"You said your son was dead."

"Yes." His tone was sharp and defensive again. Why did this man persist in tormenting him?

"Is that really what you believe—or do you mean it figuratively—because he surrendered, he is dead *to you*?"

"What makes you think he surrendered?!" Teleklos was raw with anger. "He was killed. If he'd surrendered, I would have been able to ransom him like the others."

Damoxenos stopped and forced Teleklos to stop. Teleklos stared at the Athenian, frowning with fury at this unnecessary interrogation, but the other man met his eyes steadily.

"I was travelling through Tegea on the way to Argos. I saw your son driving an ox cart from the Tegean quarries."

Teleklos didn't move, didn't breathe.

"I'm sure it was he. I called to him by name three or four times and he turned away, refused to answer. If it had been anyone else, they would at least have looked over out of curiosity." Still Teleklos couldn't move. He felt as if his heart and the blood in his veins had frozen. "It was that pride that convinced me it was *really* Lysandridas."

"How—" The moment he opened his mouth, the air rushed into his starved lungs. He had to catch his breath and then try again. "How—long ago was that?"

"I shipped from Argos for Piraeus and then came straight here. It was a month ago at the most."

Teleklos was still paralysed. Damoxenos realised that he was in shock. "That's all I wanted to say. In case you didn't know ..." He backed away, leaving Teleklos alone. When he was almost out of hearing, Teleklos whispered after him, "Thank you."

CHAPTER 15

Teleklos didn't dare mention to his companions what Damoxenos had said. He was certain they would dismiss the claim as absurd. A part of him didn't dare believe it himself. He had read the list twice. He had had another man read the list for him. Lysandridas was not on it.

Damoxenos must have been mistaken. After all, he hadn't known Lysandridas very well. He had not seen him in more than two years. He had seen a man who reminded him of Lysandridas and drawn the wrong conclusion.

But Teleklos could not sleep at night for thinking: what if? What if Lysandridas were alive? What if he were a slave? He remembered again his dream of Lysandridas calling to him for help. And Damoxenos was right. Why would another slave turn away when a rich man called out to him—even by the wrong name? Another man would have looked over out of curiosity, or even pretended to be who he was not in hopes of some tip or reward. Or just ignored what did not concern him. Why look away except in shame?

Teleklos consulted the Oracle before departing, but could not make heads or tails of the answer he received. More confused than ever, he set off for home. His companions assumed his distracted, morose mood was caused by the loss at the Games and tried to cheer him up. Nikandros was promising he'd do better next time. "Lysandridas didn't win his first race, either," he reminded his uncle defensively.

"Of course not. It was my fault. I should have given you more explicit directions." That was true, Teleklos told himself. He had not given Nikandros enough guidance. He had treated him like Lysandridas. But Lysandridas had raised the team from when they were colts. He had backed them and trained them personally. He knew their moods, could read a problem from the flick of an ear or the set of the tail, feel a weakness through the reins in his hands. It had been unfair to expect that of Nikandros, who had been driving a mature team less than a year.

"We can go to Isthmia next year, can't we?"

"We'll see."

They left him alone after that and talked among themselves. Nikandros had recovered his good spirits by the time they were back in Lacedaemon.

The first thing Teleklos did on the morning after their return was to seek out Chilon. Because Chilon's kleros was almost on the coast, too far away for walking or even riding to the syssitia every evening, he maintained a town-house. This was located on one of the back alleys, squeezed in behind the Agiad gymnasium and the barracks of one of the active units. A high wall shielded it from the street. Through a wooden door in the wall (that was half unhinged and never locked), one entered a cobbled courtyard with a fig and chestnut tree struggling to survive. The house itself surrounded the courtyard on three sides, two stories high. On the ground floor a colonnade fronted the house with whitewashed Doric pillars shading a terracotta walkway. On the upper floor, the pillars and floors were of unpainted wood. Between the pillars on both floors, potted pinks and impatiens hung in terracotta bowls.

When Teleklos arrived, he was greeted by two cats trotting out with their tails in the air to greet him. They rubbed themselves up against his bare legs, purring loudly. Then a voice called from the open door at the right, and a middle-aged woman emerged in a homespun peplos, wiping her hands dry on a cloth. "Master Teleklos," she greeted him with a smile. "The master's at the gymnasium. I'll send my boy to fetch him."

Meanwhile, from the balcony above, Chilon's wife waved and called, "I'll be right down."

Perkalos was a woman in her early fifties who wore her greying, dark hair pinned up on the back of her head. She wore a turquoise-coloured peplos with an embroidered border, but was barefoot in her own home. She led her husband's oldest friend into the hall and offered him a snack. Teleklos declined, asking for water only, which she brought him herself.

From the courtyard came some childish shouting, and she excused herself to see what was going on. Chilon had a son and three daughters, all of whom were married and had young children of their own. It was years since Teleklos had visited his friend's house without finding it full of grandchildren. He could hear Perkalos admonishing her offspring to quiet down. When she returned, the noise in the background was more subdued. They had hardly had time to discuss the race at Delphi, however, before the noise in the courtyard reached new heights, and squeals of "Grand-dad!" announced Chilon's arrival.

Smiling, with one little girl on his arm and a boy riding his shoulders, Chilon entered the hall. He was still flushed from whatever sport he had been pursuing in the gymnasium, and his long, braided hair was damp at the roots. He smelled of oil and sand and sweat. He went down on his heels and set his granddaughter on her feet, while his grandson clambered off his shoulders on his own. Then he sent them both forward to greet Teleklos like well-mannered Spartan children, with a "Good day, father!", before he sent them out of the hall.

Perkalos rose and withdrew with a murmured, "You'll stay for the midday meal, I hope, Teleklos?"

Chilon's expression was concerned as he studied his friend. "What's happened? This defeat can't mean that much to you. It's something else, isn't it?"

"Damoxenos—do you remember him? The Athenian contestant at Olympia?"

"A rich merchant of oil and almonds, as I remember."

"Yes, and owner of a pottery factory. He—he took me aside and said he had seen Lysandridas—alive—in Tegea just last month."

Chilon leaned against the nearest pillar, but he didn't answer immediately.

"He wasn't lying. I'm sure of that." Teleklos insisted with conviction. "He meant well. He asked me if I *really* thought my son was dead, or only said that because I had disowned him for surrendering. When he realised I thought he was dead, he told me about seeing him. But how is that possible?

I mean, *is* it possible? Or did he just mistake someone who looked like Lysandridas?"

"Both explanations are possible."

"You mean that Lysandridas might still be alive? But he wasn't on the list. Do you mean the Tegeans might not have reported all the survivors to us?" Clearly Teleklos wanted to believe this, and Chilon wanted to be careful.

"No, I don't think the Tegeans had any reason to intentionally conceal prisoners from us. They asked a high enough price per head for it to be worth reporting every single one—even near-corpses. You know that in—what was it? —three or four cases at least, the captives died before their families could get them home. One man died on the journey, leaving his wife bereft of both his ransom and himself. They put everyone on the list."

"But how, then ...?"

"I was just thinking that the battle took place only a month after the 55th Olympic Games. Lysandridas' name had been on everyone's lips. Even people who had never seen him would have heard of him. He might not have wanted to give the Tegeans the satisfaction of knowing the charioteer of the winning wagon at the last Olympic Games had fallen into their hands. He might have feared they would ask a higher price for him, or he might just have been ashamed. In short, he might have given a false name."

"By all the Gods," Teleklos whispered in horror at the implications. "But how do we find out?"

"We start by going through the list again."

"But weren't all the men on it bought back?"

"Who knows? From the minute it was a private affair, the city stopped keeping track. As I said, some men died before their families could pay the ransom, and others died on the journey or after they returned. At all events, they came back in ones and twos. No one counted."

Teleklos looked pale. "Lysandridas might not be the only one who lied. There might have been others—Guardsmen particularly—who lied about their identity."

"First let's see if we can find a name that might fit Lysandridas. Then we can inquire of Tegea if the named individual is still in their hands or has been returned or died—"

"But Damoxenos said he'd seen him last month—"

Chilon raised his hand. "He saw a slave in Tegea that looked like Lysandridas. We don't know that the man he saw really was Lysandridas; and even if he did see him, it could be a month or more before we hear from Tegea. A slave could have a dozen fatal accidents in that space of time. Didn't you consult the Oracle while you were there?"

"Of course," Teleklos answered in an agitated tone of voice. "It gave out the usual gobbledygook which no one can rightly understand!"

Chilon laughed at his honesty, but sobered quickly because this was no laughing matter. "What exactly did it say?"

"I asked if my son was still alive—something that should have produced a clear 'yes' or 'no' answer—and it came back with: 'Part with that you love and accept another man's son.' What do I want with adoption at this stage in my life!? I don't want another man's son. I want Lysandridas back!"

Chilon smiled indulgently at his friend's outburst, and then remarked softly, "But don't you see? If he used a pseudonym, he will have a different patronymic as well?"

Teleklos stared at his friend a moment and then hit his hand on his forehead. "Why do you put up with such an idiot for a friend?"

Chilon laughed again. "Come on, let's take a look at that list—but try not to get your hopes up too high."

It was pointless advice.

Chilon took Teleklos to the council house and requested that the clerk take out of the archives the infamous list of Tegean captives. It took the clerk almost an hour to find it, but eventually he laid it before them. Teleklos was so worked up by now that he could hardly focus. "What sort of pseudonym do you think he'd use?" he asked Chilon helplessly.

"In his shoes, I would have given my father's name—but you, too, were famous at the time, so perhaps his grandfather or great-grandfather, Agesandros son of Medon?" Agesandros was Lysandridas' most famous and successful ancestor. "He would have chosen something that he hoped *would* be recognised by *you* but *not* by the Tegeans."

But there was no Agesandros on the list. "All right," Chilon said, although his stomach was growling and he would have preferred to go home for a lunch with his wife and grandchildren. "I'll read each name on this list aloud to you, and let's see if between the two of us we can find a name that *doesn't* match a citizen we know. I'll have the clerk join us."

They went down the list one name at a time. In three cases, none of the three men present could remember ever hearing of a citizen by that name. And then toward the very end, Chilon read: "Philip son of Philippos."

Teleklos let out a little cry. "That's it! That's him! I'm sure of it! Oh, Demeter, how could I have missed it? How could I have failed him like this? Two years of slavery—"

"Calm down. We can't be sure yet. But it's a lead worth following. Let me finish the list."

But Teleklos wasn't listening any more. He held his head in his hands, thinking that he had failed his son. What had his son suffered in the last two years? It dawned on him that Lysandridas must think he had not been *willing* to pay the ransom for him. But he was alive! He could be brought home. "How do we get word to Tegea?"

"First we go and have a nice lunch," Chilon told him, thanking the clerk and taking his friend by the arm, "and then this afternoon we can discuss ways of getting word to Tegea."

"Can I go there myself?"

"Teleklos, you know you can't. You're a Spartan citizen still subject to military service. You can't just go off and approach a hostile government."

"Why not?"

"Who's to say you'd ever come back?" Chilon tried to calm him. "We can draft a letter this afternoon, and I will make inquiries among the foreign merchants. We're sure to find one who would be willing to either deliver the message himself or arrange for its delivery. These merchants often have very efficient courier services."

It was well past the equinox before the merchant entrusted with the mission reported back to Teleklos. The merchant Chilon had selected to act as Teleklos' agent was a certain Euthynus. He traded mostly in luxury goods, which he imported from Egypt, Persia, and Phoenicia for trade throughout the Peloponnese. The arrival of a richly-dressed man at the old kleros created a minor sensation. While Zoë tried to make sure he was made comfortable in the hall, Thorax was sent to fetch Teleklos from the stables.

Teleklos had no nerves for pleasantries. Rushing in to his hall dripping wet with rain, he burst out at once, "You bring me news from Tegea?"

"Indeed. You asked about a certain Philip son of Philippos."

"Yes."

"According to the Tegean registrar, he is working at the state quarries and can be purchased for 350 drachma."

Teleklos' legs gave out and he sank onto the nearest couch. He did not know what he would have done if the news had been that this "Philip" was dead, or sold, or purchased by someone else; but although this was the news he had prayed for, he still couldn't entirely believe it. "Did you see him?"

"Who?"

"This Philip."

Euthynus looked somewhat confused. Chilon had explained that Teleklos suspected the slave might be his son. He found it odd that he was called "this Philip," odd that Teleklos did not rejoice at what should have been good news. "No, I didn't ask to. Is there some reason why I should have?"

"No. But if you had seen him, I would have asked you how he looked, if he was well. But it is enough. It is—wonderful." He smiled tentatively. Then suddenly he had to throw his arms around the utter stranger and started saying over and over, "He's alive. He's really alive. I can bring him home!"

The trouble began almost at once. Apollonides was the first to tell Teleklos he was "mad". The old man told his son that he was more foolish than an old woman, if he believed that this "Philip son of Philippos" was Lysandridas. "For all we know he is some Thracian or a Macedonian—with a name like that. Why should it be Lysandridas?" Nothing Teleklos could say could convince his father that it was—or might be—Lysandridas.

"You saw his shield—my shield!—at Delphi!" Apollonides shouted at him furiously, "Are you saying he let someone *take* it from his *living* hands? If he did that, I don't ever want to see him again! Do you hear me!? Never! I gave him *my* shield to carry. My shield with Castor and Polydeukes! If he dishonoured it, then he deserves slavery!" Apollonides was shaking with emotion and his face was bright red under his white hair. "How can you think such things of your own son? How can you believe he would grovel at Tegean feet? How can you dishonour him by suggesting he was alive, when they took his shield from him!?"

Teleklos didn't argue with his father. He let him rage and shout and repeat himself again and again until he was hoarse and stomped off to his own room. Then Teleklos just sat with his head in his hands, until Zoë came in and sat down beside him. "Is it true? Is Lysandridas alive?"

"Yes." Teleklos lifted his head and met her eyes.

Her face was brown and the crow's feet around her dark eyes were deep. Her face was lined across her forehead and from her nose to the corners of her mouth. And all the lines deepened as her face lit up and she grasped his hands in her wiry, callused ones and declared, "But that's wonderful! That's wonderful! We must celebrate! Oh, Teleklos, that's the most wonderful news I've ever heard."

"Yes," Teleklos agreed, cheered already by her joy. "We now know where he is—in hell. And we have to free him."

Apollonides' attitude hurt Teleklos, but it was not the worst he faced in the months to come. His brother and cousins flatly refused to support him in what they termed "this nonsense". His cousins insisted that there was no reason to believe "this Philip" was Lysandridas, and were not prepared to take out loans or sell off precious assets for the sake of "some barbarian slave the Tegeans wanted to get rid of". Teleklos pointed out that he would not pay a drachma until he had seen Lysandridas. Since none of his relatives had the price in coin (as this was against Spartan laws against "hoarding"), they would have to first raise the silver by selling something. In short, as they put it, "the damage would be done" before he could prove that "this Philip" was Lysandridas. His sister did, however, open her own "secret" chest and handed over twenty-six drachma. It was all she'd put away in recent years.

Teleklos' brother, named Lycurgus for the reformer and lawgiver, was worse. He argued, "Even if it *is* Lysandridas, it is too late. It would have been one thing," he insisted in a patronising tone to his younger brother, "if he'd come home with the other captives. With 197 of them, it wasn't such dishonour then, but now? He's been a slave for more than two years. You can't expect people to look at him as a peer any more."

"Why not?" Teleklos asked, uncomprehending.

His brother threw up his hands in exasperation. "By all the Gods, Teleklos, he's learned slavery. How can he be a peer?"

"The others have been restored to their status."

"But they were only in slavery a few months. Six at the most. If Lysandridas has endured it this long, than he has learned to adapt—"

"What are you saying? Those two years of slavery have made him a different man? That he is less educated, less intelligent, less talented, less kind-hearted, less good, less brave?"

"How do you know what two years of slavery have done to him?" his brother shot back. "Have you ever seen a chattel slave that didn't grovel, lie, cheat, flatter? If he's alive, he'll have learned to be like the others."

"You don't know that! And even if he has adapted, what choice did he have?"

"Do you really have to ask that question?" his brother snapped back disdainfully.

"Are you saying that he should have killed himself?"

"Yes. It would have been better for everyone."

"Not for me! Not for him! He was twenty-two years old when he was captured! He's only twenty-four now! He's got his whole life ahead of him! He can marry. He can have children. He can train and drive new teams to Olympic victories! He can earn his way back into the Guard."

His brother rolled his eyes in disbelief and declared, "You are blinded by your own fantasies. You are making a fool of yourself and all of us. Have done with this!"

"I am not going to abandon my own son!"

"Well, find the 350 drachma on your own then! You'll get not an obol from me."

But no one hurt Teleklos as much as Dorothea. It wasn't that she and Derykleides had much money or the opportunity to raise it. He hadn't expected a major monetary contribution from her, but he had expected her moral support. Instead, she dutifully handed over all her jewellery and told her father that if he insisted on going through with this, she would "not stand in his way", but she made it equally clear that she did not want him to go to Tegea.

"Father, I can't bear to see what you're doing to yourself," she told him as they walked beside the Eurotas in the chill of a winter morning. His granddaughters frolicked out in front of them, squealing with delight as they found remnants of snow among the tall stalks of the straw-coloured reeds. "You grieved so piteously and had only just started to get back to normal, and now this comes along!"

The sun was weak behind heavy cloud cover, and the Taygetos were white with snow deep into the treeline. The lower slopes were grey and dark from the leafless forests.

"You've got yourself all worked up again!" Dorothea continued. "From the start, you didn't want to believe Lysandridas was dead, and now some snake-tongued Athenian has poisoned your mind with false hopes and you've gone quite mad. If Lysandridas had been alive, his name would have been on the list."

"Chilon agrees with me," Teleklos reminded his daughter stiffly. "He even gave me fifty drachma—which you know he can ill afford with his large family."

"Chilon *pretends* to agree with you," Dorothea countered, pulling her thick, rust-coloured shawl more tightly around her shoulders. "I have lost much respect for Chilon in this whole affair."

"Just because he doesn't agree with *you*?"

"No, because he is not being *honest*. He is far too wise to believe the fairy tales this Athenian fed you—"

"Why do you assume that just because he is Athenian, he must be telling lies?"

"Don't let's start arguing about that! You know the Athenians can't be trusted."

"Why not?"

"Father, don't try to distract me. I'm trying to get you to see sense for your own good."

"The worst that can happen to me is I raise 350 drachma, go to Tegea, see this 'Philip son of Philippos', and he is not Lysandridas."

"Yes. Exactly." Dorothea stopped and turned to face her father directly. "That is exactly what could happen. And then? What then?"

"Then I come home." Teleklos told her softly.

"Really? Just like that? After working yourself up into expecting Lysandridas? After begging all over Lacedaemon and making yourself a laughing stock? What do you think is going to happen to you, when you come face to face with a complete stranger? When you come face to face with the fact that Lysandridas *really is dead*? Don't you see, Father? It will kill you! I don't want you to go through that!" Her voice was full of genuine anguish. Part of Teleklos registered that, but he still could not forgive her for trying to stop him—by whatever means.

"I would rather kill myself than live with the knowledge that there is just one chance in a thousand that Lysandridas lives—and I did nothing to bring him home." He turned on his heel, and left his daughter standing among the reeds.

He had got no more than five paces when she screamed after him, tears in her voice, "I wonder if you would have done so much if it had been *me*?!"

Teleklos spun about. She was standing with her fists clenched and her arms crossed over her breast, her shawl over her head like a woman in mourning—and tears running down her face. A little voice in his brain said: "She's jealous. She's always been jealous of your love for Lysandridas."

Teleklos walked slowly back and stood looking her in the eye. "I don't know." He told her slowly, watching the words hurt one at a time. "But one thing I *do* know: your brother would not have slept a single night until he brought *you* home. I think he would have sold himself, rather than let you live in slavery." Then he turned his back on her and went home.

The stables were warm and pungent with the smell of manure, hay, wet wood, and leather. He was greeted by one of the cats, who sprang off the bales of hay in the near stall and came to him meowing. Farther away, the horses stirred to see who had come, and nickered at the sight of Teleklos. Thorax, who was mucking out one of the far stalls, paused in his work to see what the commotion was and nodded to Teleklos. Leonis was grooming one of the mares in the narrow aisle between the stalls, and she smiled over her shoulder at him.

Teleklos bent to stroke the cat at his feet unconsciously. He let his eyes slowly move along the line of stalls with his team. Agamemnon had already swung his rump at him, and the crack of his hoof against the door came a second later. Menelaus nodded his head. Achilles resumed chewing at the wood on the top of the door. Hector pointed his nose out and seemed to sniff for something. Teleklos went to each one of them in turn, his heart heavy with grief.

"You make your own life miserable," he told Agamemnon. He put his shoulder under Menelaus' head and clapped him on his withers. "You're all right," he told him. Achilles knew that he would get smacked for chewing wood and drew sharply back into the stall. Teleklos held out his hand. "Come here, you old woodworm!" Achilles tentatively came forward to lick his hand. Last but not least, Teleklos let Hector nuzzle at his neck and chest.

Leonis was watching him, and he could feel her intelligent eyes on his back. He was dreading this moment. Dreading telling her. But there was no point putting it off. He took a deep breath and turned to face her. "I don't have any choice. Even the Oracle said I must part with that I loved." Her face was solemn but not puzzled. She knew what he was going to say. "I'm going to sell the team."

"All of them?"

"What good would it do to break them up? Besides, they're worth more as a team."

"350 drachma?"

"I hope more. I'll ask 500."

"Five hundred drachma?" It was an unimaginable sum to the Lacedaemonian girl, who had never seen even ten drachma at one time. "Would Marshal Agis—"

He was shaking his head. "Agis doesn't have that kind of money, and he has a new team he believes in. He's not interested in these old veterans." Teleklos affectionately pushed Achilles' head away as the horse tried to nibble at him from behind.

"Who, then?"

"Polycritus of Corinth."

"A Corinthian?" Leonis was shocked. "But he might win the 56th Olympic Games with them!"

"Without Lysandridas? Not a chance! But I hope he'll think so. How else can I convince him to pay me 500 drachma for them?"

She laughed at that, and Teleklos realised that she was not protesting or pleading with him not to sell the team, as he had expected. "You don't mind?"

"How can I mind? The faster you raise 350 drachma, the better. Every night I go to bed thinking: it's another night for Lysandridas in slavery. It's almost three months since we first found out, and he doesn't even know—"

"Don't remind me." The thought of Lysandridas enslaved and believing he had been abandoned tormented Teleklos. He tried not to remember. "I will write to Polycritus tonight and find someone to take my letter to Corinth at the first opportunity. If he shows interest, I can take the team to Corinth by ship; that's faster than overland. I should have the 350 drachma by the spring equinox and can travel direct from Corinth to Tegea."

"Will you get leave?" Leonis asked with concern. As a Spartan citizen still subject to military service, Teleklos needed permission from his commander to leave Lacedaemon.

"Why shouldn't I?"

CHAPTER 16

Teleklos' divisional, or lochos, commander responded to his request for leave with unease. "I don't know about this, Teleklos," he said, frowning.

"What do you mean? I have reason to believe my son is still alive and still held captive in Tegea. You can't seriously mean you want to prevent me from finding out?" Teleklos drew a breath to deliver the speech of outrage he had prepared in the event of opposition, but his Commander waved him silent.

"I understand your desire to bring your son home, and I would personally welcome the return of Lysandridas. He was a fine young man. I haven't forgotten what an excellent instructor he was as an eirene—or how much he helped my son through a difficult period. Nor have I forgotten the way he drove your chariot at Olympia. That's not the point. There are reasons, however, which I cannot disclose at this time, that make it impossible for me to give you leave to travel to Tegea. Take your team to Corinth, raise the ransom money, and then return here immediately."

"But—"

"Teleklos!" he warned with his look. "That's an order. If you are not back in Sparta by the Feast of Artemis Orthea, you will be viewed as a deserter and automatically exiled."

"What good does the ransom money do me if I can't use it to secure Lysandridas' freedom?" Teleklos protested helplessly.

"I didn't say you couldn't use it; I said there were reasons why it is not propitious for you to set foot on Tegean soil in the coming months. More I cannot say."

There was nothing for it but to do as he had been ordered. Teleklos had received word from Polycritus that he was interested in purchasing the team. Teleklos enquired about transport and learned that no ships were sailing north yet. The winds were still too strong and unfavourable. He made arrangements for word to be sent to him as soon as the weather changed.

The spring equinox passed before he received word that he could hope for passage north in a suitable vessel. Teleklos took Thorax along to help him with the horses during the journey, and Leonis travelled with him as far as Gytheion to see him off. There, Teleklos went aboard a sturdy merchant galley bound for Kenchreai, the eastern harbour for Corinth.

In Corinth, Teleklos did not seek out Polycritus at once, but rather took lodgings in a guest house. He wanted the give the horses a day or two to recover from the sea travel before he presented them for sale. Only on the next day did he go in search of Polycritus.

At the merchant's house, Teleklos was admitted to a small walled garden with a fountain dribbling water into a trough and a foot bath. Rosemary, thyme, sage, lavender, parsley, asparagus, and other kitchen plants grew around the edge of the paved yard. An elderly slave led him down a corridor to an atrium with sculpture and a spouting fountain among blooming lilac, lilies, and daisies. They walked around two sides of the atrium and passed through a narrow colonnade into to a large room paved with mosaics and lit by tall doors opening onto a terrace with a view down to the Gulf of Corinth. The breeze off the water lifted the embroidered linen curtains framing the tall doors and gave the room a refreshing coolness. The walls themselves were plastered, whitewashed, and decorated with a delicate floral pattern. The mosaics on the floor were cream-coloured with a border of blue and green in a wave pattern. A merchant vessel under sail and oar was depicted in rich brown stones in the centre of the room. Scattered symmetrically across the rest of the floor were mosaic seahorses and shells.

Polycritus came towards Teleklos on sandals sewn with gold and lapis beads. His long, salmon-coloured silk chiton fluttered about his legs, and his lime-coloured silk himation hung off his shoulders elegantly. The hand he extended to Teleklos had a ring on every finger. Despite that, he failed to cut the impressive figure he aspired to: his hands were stubby, his face round, his chin double, his hair thinning. Polycritus was past fifty, and in recent years he had pursued his business less vigorously and his pleasures more. Horse racing was only one of his pleasures—the healthiest of them.

He greeted Teleklos with the pseudo-cordiality that Teleklos expected from him. He offered him a seat and clapped his hands for a slave boy, who entered with a tray of refreshments: pomegranates, figs, cashews and almonds, little pastries with liver, cheesecakes, sesame cookies. Teleklos took only a fig. Wine was also offered, but Teleklos took water instead.

"What's this I hear that you have stolen the bones of Orestes from Tegea?" Polycritus opened the conversation when the pleasantries were concluded.

"I've never stolen anything in my life!" Teleklos answered indignantly.

Polycritus threw back his head and laughed. When he could stop, he remarked, still chuckling, "Not you personally. Sparta. Surely you know?" Polycritus could see that Teleklos hadn't the faintest idea what he was talking about. "One of my couriers brought the news up from Tegea just last night. Some Spartan managed to locate Orestes' bones, dig them up in secret, and spirit them back to Sparta."

Teleklos felt ice cold. Now he understood the second oracle that Agesikles had announced. Teleklos was certain this had all been arranged and the new oracle merely invented to justify a second invasion of Tegea. However, he also instantly understood why he had been prohibited from setting foot in Tegea and why he was required to return to Sparta no later than the Feast of Artemis Orthea. For a brief second he thought, "If we win this time, Lysandridas will be freed without a ransom. I don't have to sell the team." But then he reminded himself that Sparta might lose a second time. There'd be new prisoners, new ransom demands. It was better to have the money.

Because Teleklos stubbornly refused to comment on the sensational news about Orestes' bones, Polycritus was forced to change the subject. "So you want to sell your team?"

"I have decided to." Teleklos stated firmly.

"Because they lost at the Pythian Games?"

"No. They could have won. My driver was at fault."

"Ah." Polycritus looked at him through narrowed eyes that measured him. "Why, then?"

"I have decided to give up racing."

Polycritus looked sceptical. "But why?"

"I find no pleasure in it any more."

Polycritus looked more sceptical than ever, but it was hardly an answer he could argue with. A man had to decide for himself where he found his pleasures. "And what do you want for them?"

"Five hundred drachma."

"Five hundred?!" Polycritus made it sound like an outrageous price.

"You offered my son 1000 just to stop them once," Teleklos pointed out coolly.

"That was at Olympia! Besides, that was nearly three years ago. They're older now."

"Yes. Better. Less nervous."

"But they were soundly beaten at Delphi. *Some* of the problem may have been your driver, but not all."

"They beat your team, even so."

"That was because of the neglect of one of my slaves!"

Teleklos didn't answer, and Polycritus fussed with his himation and twisted his rings around his fat fingers.

"I'll give you 400 drachma. One hundred apiece."

Part of Teleklos knew that he should bargain. That was what the merchant expected. Too late, he realised that he should have asked a price of 1000 drachma if he wanted 500, but Teleklos didn't have the temperament for haggling. He just wanted to get the whole unhappy business over with and go home. Four hundred drachma still covered Lysandridas' price, and left him money to get home. The armour he had wanted to buy for Lysandridas would have to wait—or he'd sell his mares to Agis. He nodded, and Polycritus smiled uncertainly, surprised by his easy success.

The next day they brought the horses to Polycritus' stables. It was a small comfort to know they would henceforth live in greater luxury than they had ever known before. Polycritus had a slave for every two horses. He had large box stalls with running water directed to a shallow trough that ran the length of the stables. The hay was sweet and the finest quality. There were bins of wheat and barley, and barrels of carrots and apples. Polycritus' horses ate better than the poor of Corinth, Teleklos reflected, as he took his leave of each of his team, one at a time. The horses were distracted by their new surroundings. They could not know they would never see him again. They paid him no particular attention, except Hector. Hector nuzzled him, slobbering all over his expensive new chiton, and he could hardly tear himself away.

At home in Sparta, the city was in an uproar. Orestes' bones were duly displayed, and it was quickly resolved to build a temple to house the hero's bones; but the sentiment in favour of a new war was entirely lacking. Worse than that, a substantial faction of citizens, led by Chilon, openly accused King Agesikles of trying to manipulate the city into a new war that it could not afford.

Agesikles responded by saying he had a right to take them into war wherever and whenever he pleased. Chilon openly challenged the King, saying that if he tried to take the army to war against the will of the Assembly, he was risking more than defeat. He did not specify what this "more" was—but the citizens were saying in their syssitia and to their wives, and the boys of the agoge were whispering, and the young men on active service were declaring in their barracks, that what Chilon *meant* was civil war. Chilon, they said, had the backing of three of the five lochagoi: three of the divisional commanders.

Teleklos was frightened for his friend—and for Sparta. He could imagine nothing worse than civil war. He sought Chilon out, and his friend asked him to join him for a walk. Together they made their way through the crooked streets of the city, past various agoge and divisional barracks, past the Temple of Artemis and the Monument to Lycurgus, past the baths which were reserved for the women at this time of day, past the gymnasiums and stadium filled with youths and boys at sport.

They passed the busy workshops and sheds of the craftsmen, assaulted by the smells of wood, leather, bronze, and glass being worked. They walked beside the lumber yards on the Eurotas, where whole trees were sawed down into planks with so much noise they could not hear themselves think. They passed the kilns of the pottery factories producing simple cream-coloured tiles and terracotta pipes.

As they progressed, Chilon commented on what they saw. "Lacedaemonian sculptors are commissioned by Delphi and Delos, by Elis, and even by Athens. We export our bronze works to the entire world; they command a high price in Syria and Egypt and have been admired by the Shah of Persia. Our hounds are the most coveted in the world. Our horses are prized. The game and timber of our forests are famous. Our poets are honoured, their works recited far beyond our borders. Our music carries the laurels at Delphi more often than that of any other city—and we don't even send our maidens there, who are by far our best performers." He indicated with a smile the strains of a girl's chorus coming from one of the girls' schools they were passing. "Our dances earn the applause of every visitor that chances to see our festivals. And for a city of our size—one-third the number of citizens of Corinth, a fifth of Athens! —we have also taken the crown of olives at Olympia more often than our numbers alone warrant. We even have a world-famous cuisine!" They both laughed at this, because Spartan cuisine was famous for being inedible unless a man was raised on it.

They had reached the arching stone bridge that crossed the Eurotas north-east of the city. On the floodplain beyond the river a number of active units were at drill. It was something that could be seen every morning, all morning, on any non-festival day. The occasional shouts of command came to them on the morning breeze. Bronze shields caught the morning sunlight as they were swung on command to high-port, right, left, down. The men were in training armour, their helmets crestless, and their breastplates and greaves were made of leather rather than bronze. There were no scarlet chitons or himations to provide splashes of colour. And yet it was a beautiful sight. The units turned and wheeled, performing one complicated manoeuvre after another to the sound of pipes.

Chilon indicated the training troops. "Yet for all our many virtues and accomplishments, *that* is our pride." Chilon pointed again to the men sweating under a cloud of dust as they lunged in formation and then fell back on command. "Why?"

Teleklos was baffled. He'd never thought about it. It was just the way it was.

"I'll tell you why." Chilon continued. "Because it is the guarantee of our democracy. When Lycurgus gave us our laws in the generation of our great-grandfathers, there was no other city-state in all Hellas that gave equal rights to all citizens. To this day, no other city-state guarantees a minimum standard of living to each citizen by giving every citizen on coming of age an estate large enough to support him and his family. I know that inequalities of wealth exist because of acquired land; but none of our citizens has to fear hunger or homelessness, none has to earn his living at another man's bidding. And our laws make the display of wealth difficult, so that those of our citizens with only modest means—like you and me," he pointed out with a smile, "do not have to be ashamed.

"I know that some cities have given their Assembly more powers than ours," he continued, "and these newer democracies look down on us for still voting aloud. I know that many cities have eliminated councils with life members, requiring all persons in public functions to be subject to the censure of the vote. I know that some cities have gone so far as to appoint men to public office by lottery rather than election, allegedly to assure equality of opportunity—as if such lotteries could not be manipulated!

"As is so often the case, the innovator of new ideas—in this case Sparta—has been overtaken by the improvements of our imitators. But in my opinion—and in this I am a 'conservative oligarch', according to our Athenian cousins—it remains to be seen if these innovations are truly more just and more conducive to good government than our laws."

"I'm sure they're not," Teleklos assured him passionately, relieved that his friend was not the critic of Sparta's Constitution that some people whispered he was. Teleklos firmly believed that even if things weren't perfect, they were better off the way they were. "Look at Corinth," he hastened to reinforce Chilon's scepticism of other cities. "It is so rich—and never have I seen so much poverty. There are beggars everywhere—they only keep them out of the agora by force! And you see no honest women on the streets; they hide behind their walls or the curtains of the litters, if they must go out. Instead, one is accosted everywhere—even on the steps of the temples—by prostitutes with their faces painted on. And boys not old enough for the agoge sell their 'services' in every guesthouse. All in the name of free trade and democracy!"

Chilon let his friend express his outrage, listening patiently. He, too, had travelled throughout Hellas. He was familiar with the shadow side of all the glittering glory of Greek democracies.

When Teleklos had said his piece, Chilon continued calmly, "But the best laws of mankind are of no use if they cannot be enforced—or if they can be corrupted, undermined, or overturned. That is what tyrants have done in too many Greek cities already. They come to power through the democratic process—only to then dismantle the system of government that spawned them. Sparta has remained true to her Constitution because our army and agoge defend it."

"But surely the greatest threats to our democracy come from inside, not outside. I don't see …"

Chilon smiled. "I don't mean they defend our democracy with their arms. I mean simply by binding us to one another and to our laws. It is because we all go through the rigours of the agoge, wear the same homespun chitons, and go barefoot through our boyhood. It is because we have all gone to the pits at least once and bear the scars of it on our backs. It is because we all serve in the army, wearing identical red chitons and himations. It is because we have all had to steal our brides in the dark of night—and report to the barracks again before dawn. These common experiences do not make us homogeneous; but they prevent the deep contradictions and conflicts of interest that you find in other Greek cities."

Teleklos wasn't so sure, but he held his tongue, waiting for Chilon to finish what he was saying.

"But this war with Tegea could threaten all that, and that is the reason I oppose it. Indeed, I am willing to risk an open confrontation with the kings and an internal conflict that could shake the foundations of our city."

Teleklos looked up, horrified.

"It threatens all we have gained in a hundred years, because Sparta can only lose. What I mean is that even if we win—especially if we win—we lose."

"I don't understand," Teleklos admitted.

"If we lose, we will have sacrificed more young lives for nothing. Other families—or even the same families—will be forced to pay huge ransom sums they can ill afford. Our reputation throughout Greece will decline. The Argives certainly, and very likely the Messenians, will be encouraged to challenge us. Argos could well attack and the Messenians revolt in a coordinated effort, causing us to fight on two fronts. If Argos, Messenia, and Tegea join forces, we could be crushed completely."

Teleklos was horrified. "You seriously think Tegea is that powerful?"

"No. I don't. I simply think no city should go to war without considering the consequences of defeat. But the far more likely scenario is that we will conquer Tegea. And then? Consider what we will have done. We will have conquered yet another free-minded Hellenic people that will oppose us at least as vehemently as the Messenians." Chilon let this sink in and then continued. "What did we gain by the conquest of Messenia? Our territory doubled; our natural produce, trade, and material prosperity increased in every respect. And our security? How do you keep twice as much territory and twice as many helots under control with the same number of citizens?

"Consider the fact that in Lacedaemon we have perioikoi who support us and share the burden of our defence. In Messenia we are an occupation power. In Tegea it would be no different. How do you think we can spread a citizen body of at most 9,000 men across an ever greater territory? Isn't it bad enough that we constantly fear a Messenian revolt? Do we want to live in fear of a Tegean revolt as well?"

Teleklos shook his head sadly. It would be a nightmare.

Chilon continued, "A city—no less than an individual—has to know the limits of its power. 'Know thyself' is the most important lesson any boy—or man—can learn. Sparta cannot expand without endangering its own ethos and integrity. That is why I believe a victory in Tegea would be even worse than a defeat."

Teleklos was still. He had no arguments against his friend's logic. But precisely because he had never been very concerned with politics, he now asked anxiously, "But what does it mean? Agesikles wants to invade. He has the right to call up the army and lead it. What can you do to stop him?"

"Teleklos, there are enough men who agree with me to make Agesikles frightened that his orders won't be obeyed. If he tries to force the issue, he risks being deposed altogether—and he knows that."

"You have that much support?" Teleklos was amazed.

"I'm not sure—but nor is he. And, thanks to wise Athena, neither of us wants to risk an open conflict."

"But that means the war is pending. It hasn't been called off as long as Agesikles wants it, and it won't start as long as he's afraid you'll stop him."

"That's a fair assessment."

"But when can I go to Tegea?"

Chilon heard the anguish in Teleklos' voice and he understood it, but he did not have the power to help him. He was happy to keep the present stalemate, to prevent hostilities without risking outright civil war or revolution. The only comfort he could offer was: "When you turn sixty, you are no longer subject to military service. Thereafter, no one can call you a deserter for going anywhere you please."

"I won't turn sixty until next year!" Teleklos protested.

But Chilon couldn't change that.

CHAPTER 17

Teleklos waited through the summer and fall and winter. The waiting was far harder for him than mourning or even uncertainty had been. Now that he had the means to free Lysandridas, his inability to do so ate away at his heart. He did not sleep well at nights for thinking of Lysandridas in slavery, picturing him working in a quarry, sick, abused, hopeless. Or he tortured himself with images of all the ways a slave might die in a quarry: falling from the precarious scaffolding, crushed under a falling stone, torn down a mountainside by a wagon out of control. He thought of the bad food, the floggings, and the stone dust clogging his lungs. He tried again and again to mentally find words to explain himself to his son.

By the end of the summer, he had lost fifteen pounds. Dorothea was so distressed, she insisted that Teleklos come and live with her again so she could "feed him properly"—as if Zoë weren't a better cook than her own housekeeper. It did no good. By the autumn equinox, Teleklos had lost another five to seven pounds, and his hair started to fall out. The once stocky man, whom people had liked to compare to a badger, had no muscle left at all.

By the winter he had turned into a fragile old man, exceptionally sensitive to cold. He caught a cold early on and never seemed to shake it off entirely. Throughout the darkest part of the year, he was coughing and his nose ran continually. He was excused from going to the syssitia every evening.

Then shortly after the winter solstice, the kryptea crossed into Tegean territory and clashed with Tegean troops. Whatever the kryptea's intention, the results were ambiguous. The Spartans again suffered a dozen casualties—although they inflicted twice that number on the Tegeans—and they proved that the Tegean cavalry was more alert and active than ever.

When the actions of the kryptea came up for debate, Teleklos dragged himself to the first Assembly he'd attended in months. The debate was bitter, King Agesikles and the minority vehemently defending the actions of the kryptea, while the majority (led by Chilon) condemned them for trying to provoke new hostilities. Teleklos tried to speak up, to add his voice of criticism against his own son-in-law, but his voice gave out on him and he had to be led away coughing.

As soon as the pass over the Parnon range was open, he started making his preparations. There was still snow on the peaks and the north flank of the mountains. The trees were barren and the grass grey. The nights were bitterly cold, but Dorothea did not think of trying to stop him. She realised that the waiting and mourning were killing him slowly. Confronting reality could be no worse than what he was going through. She argued only that he should not go alone, but even here she failed. She was eight months pregnant and not fit to travel such a distance, even if Derykleides had been willing to let her go, which he was not. Teleklos would not hear of anyone else going with him, anyway. Not even Thorax. It was as if, Dorothea told her husband, in his heart he already knew he would not find Lysandridas, and did not want anyone around to say, "I told you so."

"But he'll have to admit that when he comes back," Derykleides pointed out.

"I don't think he's coming back," Dorothea replied, trying not to cry. "He—he really doesn't want to live any more. The team is gone, and none of us mean anything to him—not even the children. The only thing he cares about any more is Lysandridas."

"Now, that's not fair," Derykleides told his wife to comfort her, rather than from conviction. "He's obsessed with the idea that Lysandridas is alive, but if he faces the fact that he is not, I think he'll come to his senses. I think he will come home, relieved of this horrible sense of guilt. We have to let him go."

"I know," Dorothea admitted, but she was crying all the same.

Teleklos insisted on travelling on foot. He would carry his sword and a dagger to protect himself against thieves, he said. Although he was far too weak to wield them effectively, no one dared point this out to him. He sewed three hundred fifty drachma into the inside of his belt, and carried the remaining twenty-one he had left in a purse. He took a T-shaped walking stick, a broad-brimmed straw hat, and a backpack. In the latter he carried the chiton he'd bought in Corinth, the blue himation he always wore abroad, a pair of sandals, his comb, a towel, and rations for a week. He also had one goatskin for wine and a larger one for water.

It was forty miles to Tegea through the Parnon range. The army could cover the distance in a long day, and runners took it in half that time, but Teleklos was sixty, and he was not completely oblivious to his own decline. He planned three days for the journey each way. He set out at dawn on a brittle day that promised the first kiss of warmth and cut right across the Eurotas valley north of the city and joined the main road well beyond. Partway up the road he noticed the first sprouts of crocus.

The road wound its way up to the border where two hostile stone fortresses confronted each other. By chance, the young men on garrison duty were from Lysandridas' old unit, the one he'd belonged to before he'd joined the Guard. The platoon leader came running out when Teleklos was reported. "Teleklos! What are you doing here? You aren't going to Tegea?" In his eyes was reflected the horror everyone felt when they saw how Teleklos had wasted away in the last year.

"I'm sixty, and no one can stop me any more. I'm going to Tegea to bring home my son," he told the young officer belligerently, daring him to challenge his right to leave Lacedaemon.

"Is there any way I can help?" The answer took Teleklos completely by surprise and he looked at the young man, confused. "I wish I could send an escort." The young Spartiate continued, "After this last incident with the kryptea, I fear they may enslave you or hold you for ransom. We're still at war."

"That is a chance I have to take," Teleklos told him. "But what good is an old man like me?"

The young Spartan officer looked distressed, but he chose not to voice his fears that Teleklos might be tortured for information or simply murdered out of hatred. He was sure that Teleklos must have thought of this, and decided to take his chances anyway. All he said was, "Can't I lend you a mule at least? Do you have enough food and drink?"

"Thank you, I'm well provisioned. And a mule just needs to be fed and looked after."

"At least spend the night here! It's already getting cold and there's no shelter for the next half-dozen miles. Stay the night here and set off refreshed in the morning."

Teleklos did not need to be urged a second time. He was tired, and the wind was bitterly cold up here in the mountains. He was glad to warm himself at the fire and spend the night sleeping in the garrison barracks. But he did not sleep for thinking of the coming confrontation with Lysandridas. Lysandridas had a right to be angry with him. He would ask why it had taken so long, and Teleklos was ashamed that he had been too stupid to see through the pseudonym.

The next morning, the officer told him, "If you aren't back in ten days, I'll report you missing. We can make inquiries. Make a diplomatic protest. It might help." The officer was clearly doubtful about the efficacy of diplomatic protests in the present state of hostilities.

"Thank you. I hope to be back sooner."

"And not alone," the commander added earnestly.

"And not alone," Teleklos seconded, nodding. Neither smiled. They both knew there were many reasons why Teleklos might well return alone. It was now roughly fifteen months since he'd had word that Philip son of Philippos was still alive. He might have died since then. And there was no guarantee that he was indeed Lysandridas. The closer he came to confronting the mysterious slave, the more Teleklos feared it was all a terrible mistake.

The Tegean sentries were less respectful and made fun of him. "What? You've waited nearly four years to come after your son? Not exactly a favourite boy, was he?" Teleklos did not feel he owed these ruffians an explanation, and just stood grimly waiting for them to stamp his papers. After a long time, he was made to understand that if he wanted to proceed it would be "helpful" if he could tip the clerk responsible for documentation. Without further ado, he took a drachma from his purse and laid it on the table with a loud clack. The insult made the Tegean clerk flush with anger, and for a moment he considered sending Teleklos back into Lacedaemon, just to demonstrate his power. But the drachma was already on the table, and the sentry at the door was pretending not to have noticed anything. The Tegean clerk snatched up the drachma and shoved Teleklos' papers back at him.

By late afternoon of the second day, Teleklos was stiff and lame from so much walking, and he started looking for a suitable place to spend the night. The countryside was rugged and forested only with pine and scrub-brush. It was cold here as well, with patches of snow on the north flanks of the hills and in among the trees. He was relieved to find a shepherd's hut and took shelter there for the night. He had no fire with him or means of lighting one, but there were some old sheepskins, so he lay down on one of these and used the other to cover himself. He rested more than slept until it was light enough to continue the next morning.

Despite the bad night, Teleklos made better progress the next day. He was now walking downhill and nearing his goal with each step. The latter realization kept him going even as he wearied. With luck, he told himself, he would see Lysandridas before sunset.

But as he started down the last stretch of winding road to the flat, fertile valley, his stomach became nervous. He remembered that Euxenos had said Lysandridas had been kicked in the forehead. What if he'd suffered damage to his eyes, skull, or brain? Teleklos had heard rumours of men who lost their memories after a blow to the head, and no longer knew who they were or recognised their loved ones. What if Lysandridas had given a false name because he couldn't remember his proper one? He remembered, too, that Euxenos had said Lysandridas had been trampled after he fell. Might he not have other injuries? If he worked in the quarries, then surely he was not crippled, he comforted himself. A cripple was of no use in the quarries, unless, of course, he worked in the kitchens. Or—what had Demoxenos said? He had been driving an ox cart. That was a job that might be performed by a one-legged man.

He reached the valley floor and Tegea was clearly visible ahead of him, tall walls rising above the low houses and orchards of the outlying farms. Just before the gate there was a small fountain house, and Teleklos stopped here to wash himself thoroughly. He stripped down to nothing and washed his feet, hands, and face vigorously. The things he had been wearing disappeared into the backpack. He combed out his now very thin hair. Although he had started to let it grow again when he'd had the news that this "Philip son of Philippos" was alive, it was still not shoulder length. He could just bind it up at the back of his head, which he now did. Finally, he dressed in his best blue chiton and blue himation and put sandals on his feet. He thought he looked like a respectable craftsman in his new guise.

Nothing fancy, and nothing gave him away as Spartan. In fact, he looked like a dying old man.

He entered the city and at once asked the way to the city registrar's office. He was directed to the courthouse where all city records were kept. By the time he arrived, however, the clerks were already clearing the tables, and he was told he would have to return again the next day. Teleklos tried to argue, but they hardly paid him any attention.

"You're here about a slave, old man?" one of the men asked. "That can wait till tomorrow! All the records are locked up now."

Teleklos stood in the broad shady stoa overlooking the agora and didn't know what to do. He hadn't expected to spend the night here—not on his own. He sank down on the steps and just sat for a long time, too weary for sightseeing and too restless to rest. But at last he realised he had to find someplace to spend the night and asked after "respectable" lodgings.

The man he stopped considered his clothes, his worn face, and his skin hanging loose on his shrunken body, and took him for a man who had once been well off but had now fallen on hard times. He directed him to a small guest house in a back alley. There was only one large communal room with benches along the wall for each man to roll out his own bedding, but it was clean and there was a cook-shop next door. Teleklos slept even more poorly here than he had in the shepherd's hut.

The next morning he was waiting under the stoa before the first clerks arrived and started to set up their tables. Of course, he wasn't alone. Other supplicants and litigants were also collecting, waiting to pounce upon the clerks when they appeared. Teleklos was sent from one table to another, and had to stand in line again and again. Eventually, however, he found himself inside the courthouse at the office of the overworked registrar of state property. For what seemed like the thousandth time, he stated his interest in purchasing from the city of Tegea a certain slave called Philip son of Philippos, who had been captured almost three and a half years earlier in the battle with Lacedaemon.

The registrar gave him a piercing look from under his bushy brows and then without another word, disappeared into his archives. After what seemed like a long time, he re-emerged and dropped a scroll of parchment on the table. He then reseated himself, unrolled the parchment, and started reading. He grunted, and looked up from under his brows again. "Here he is. Philip son of Philippos, Spartiate captive, Guardsman." He gave Teleklos a piercing look as if this must be some mistake. He had thought Teleklos was perioikoi.

Teleklos' heart started pumping overtime.

The registrar looked down at the parchment again. "He was assigned to the road crew and then—after an escape attempt—" he looked reproachfully at Teleklos as if this reflected badly on him in some way, "he was assigned to the quarries."

Teleklos was already fingering his belt to remove the drachma; he wasn't watching the clerk as he read: "Died of fever."

Teleklos' heart stopped. He couldn't move. "What?"

"I'm sorry. The slave is deceased. Died of fever, eleven months ago."

Teleklos looked at him. "But ..." But what?

The registrar was already rerolling the parchment and retying the ribbon around it. "These things happen, you know."

Eleven months ago. That was *after* he'd sold the team. After he had raised the ransom money. "No," he said out loud, but very softly.

The registrar gave him a sharp look, as if he were calling his work or his honesty into question.

Teleklos turned and stumbled out of the office. He pushed his way past men in fine, long chitons and out into the stoa again. In his mind, he kept saying "no", but he didn't know what he was saying "no" to. There wasn't any hope left. He started out from under the shade of the stoa, down the steps to the agora. The sun blinded him, and his mind was numbed by the news. He was not watching his footing. His left foot landed only on the edge of a step, and the next thing he knew he was falling forward. He tried to reach out a hand to stop his fall, but the steps were steep and fell away. His knee cracked onto the marble, sending a jarring pain up his leg, and then he found himself rolling down the remainder of the steps with bone-jarring, bruising speed until he landed on his back at the foot of the stairs.

Even as people crowded around him and tried to offer him help, he could tell that his right knee was shattered. "I can't," he told the people who would have helped him up.

Someone officious was asking, "Where does it hurt? Where are you injured?"

"My knee; my right knee."

The others moved back to let the well-dressed and knowledgeable man get a better look. He ran his hands down his leg, very gently turning it left and right. Teleklos gasped and broke into a sweat. "That's all right. Just stay still for a moment."

"Are you a physician?"

"Yes. Just relax."

Teleklos had no choice. He was sweating and nauseous. He closed his eyes against the bright sun burning down on him. Around him, a crowd had collected and he could hear them saying, "Who is it?" "Was he pushed?" "Just slipped," "Foot went out from under him."

The physician broke through the chatter in his calm, commanding voice. "Are you a stranger to Tegea?"

"Yes."

"Do you have any friends here? Someplace you can stay a month or more?"

"A month?"

"I don't think you'll be able to walk on that knee before that. Do you know anyone here?"

"In Tegea?" Teleklos asked stupidly. And at once he felt a flight of panic. He was in enemy territory. He knew no one in Tegea! Then he remembered, "Antyllus. The horse breeder."

"Antyllus? You know Antyllus? A good man to know. I'll send someone to him at once. Who should I say requests his hospitality?"

"Teleklos, son of Apollonides."

PART III

LYSANDRIDAS

CHAPTER 18

Penny was acting up, and Lysandridas suspected she would soon be in season. They would have to confine her until her time was past, but he decided to drive her today. It was such a beautiful spring morning that he couldn't resist spending it on the track with the full team.

Antyllus emerged from the house with his himation wound tightly around him, expecting the usual morning chill. Feeling the warmth of the sun, he glanced up and loosened his himation as he came over to Lysandridas. "Beautiful morning," he remarked, automatically stroking his team.

"Have you seen the crocuses?" Lysandridas pointed as he swung himself up onto the chariot, and Antyllus looked toward the paddocks and smiled. "Beautiful. Almost a shame to send the mares out into them, isn't it?"

They laughed and set out for the training track.

When driving, Lysandridas could think of nothing else. All other thoughts were driven from his head as he focused his attention exclusively on the four horses and the track. Today, with Penny acting silly, he had to concentrate harder than ever. Rather than acting as a good anchor on the inside, the mare kept fighting the reins and drifting right. The more Lysandridas tried to get her to bend to the left, the more she stiffened, laid her ears back, and swung her haunches against Ajax. Although the gelding was a tolerant veteran, this unfair treatment gradually began to upset him.

With the two inside horses fussing at each other and Penny refusing to bend, Lysandridas could not take the curves as neatly as usual; as he finished ten laps, he called to Antyllus that he was going to do another couple of rounds. Penny was finally starting to give up her resistance, and he wanted her to do at least one lap properly before he put her away. He had been careful not to ask for maximum speed the whole morning and so felt an extra two laps would do no harm. He ended up doing three, but on the last turn Penny had finally settled down and was supple again. Satisfied with the day's work, he walked the team for two laps before pulling up before Antyllus.

Antyllus looked at him very strangely.

"I think Penny is going into season. We'll have to train without her for a bit," Lysandidridas explained himself. But Antyllus still looked at him so earnestly that he was compelled to ask, "You think I shouldn't have done the extra laps?"

"What? Did you do extra laps?"

Lysandridas gaped at the horse breeder. He had been here the whole time. He couldn't possibly have missed that Lysandridas had done three extra laps.

"I was distracted," Antyllus explained; "a messenger from the city."

Lysandridas' first thought was that the hostilities had flared up again. His heart protested. How could war start on such a beautiful day? But it had been a beautiful day when they'd marched out last time, too, Lysandridas reminded himself. It had been a beautiful day, and he had thought war was something splendid—last time. He had not found the fine weather incongruous. "What is it?" Lysandridas demanded.

"There was a minor accident. A man slipped on the steps to the courthouse and has torn the ligaments in his knee." Lysandridas did not know what was so tragic about this, and could only gaze at Antyllus blankly. "It was a stranger. The only person in Tegea he knows is me. The doctor sent me word that he needs my hospitality for a month or so."

"Do you want me to move back into the slave quarters?" Lysandridas asked, not so much offended as baffled that Antyllus should treat such a simple development like a catastrophe.

"No. No, you will probably want to share your chamber with this guest."

Lysandridas had spent most of his life living in barracks: as a boy in the agoge, as a Spartan citizen on active service, as a slave. He shrugged, "You know I don't mind. Why are you so upset?"

"The guest is Teleklos, son of Apollonides."

Lysandridas stopped breathing. He stopped seeing or hearing. He stopped being altogether for a few moments. Then gradually his senses returned and he was still standing beside the restless, sweating team at the entrance to the training track. The sun was shining. There was a light breeze. The crocuses waved at him from across the paddocks all the way to the stables.

"The courthouse is where we keep records of state property," Antyllus was saying. "Your father must have come for you after all."

"Three years too late," Lysandridas whispered bitterly.

"I will take the chariot to collect him. Do you want to come with me or wait here?"

Lysandridas did not know what he wanted. But the thought of "waiting" was intolerable. "I'll ride Afra, so you'll have room for him in the chariot."

Lysandridas rode beside the chariot as they cantered easily over the straight, flat roads. Although Lysandridas could feel Antyllus looking over at him frequently, he was far too confused to face Antyllus' gaze.

After they passed through the city gates, Lysandridas finally broke the silence. "I'll ride ahead, if you don't mind."

Antyllus nodded sadly. What was he supposed to say: "No, you can't go to your father without me"?

Afra sprinted away, leaving the chariot in her dust. Lysandridas was aware that he was nervous, and that the mare was taking advantage of that to gallop far too fast. He sensed that he was being irresponsible to let her run headlong down the cobbled streets. More than once a pedestrian had to spring aside, and he vaguely heard curses shouted after him. As he turned the corner into the agora, Afra's hooves slipped on the cobbles, but he paid no attention. He spotted the crowd at the foot of the steps to the courthouse.

Lysandridas jumped down easily and started forward, his eyes fixed on the cluster of gawkers around an old man propped up against the steps. This man, clearly the centre of attention, had a thin mane of white hair— not the long, neat braids of a Spartiate. Although he had the pale-greenish colouring of a man in pain, he seemed too frail and old to be Teleklos. Only as Lysandridas came nearer did he start to recognise his father's features in the aged face.

Teleklos was staring at him from sunken eyes in a bony face covered by sagging, wrinkled skin. The brow rose high and hairless to his receding hair-line. His neck was scrawny, with folds of wrinkled flesh hanging to prominent collarbones. This was a very old man with a frightened, disbelieving face. And then he reached out claw-like hands that had once, Lysandridas remembered, been strong enough to control four galloping racehorses, and a ruined voice croaked out: "Lysandridas? Is it you, Lysandridas? But—I thought you were dead. They told me you were dead. I thought you were dead."

The last words he said into Lysandridas' chest, because Lysandridas had pulled the old man into his arms. How could he possibly be angry with this ruined old man?

He held Teleklos, feeling acutely how thin he was and how frail he had become, but his eyes had gone back to Antyllus slowly dismounting from the chariot and coming towards them cautiously. Antyllus' face was carefully composed. He had even managed to put on a smile of welcome for his rival and guest, but his eyes were infinitely sad.

Teleklos pulled back from Lysandridas' embrace and started trying to explain everything at once. "Your name wasn't on the list. I looked for your name. I asked others if you were on the list. Everyone said I had to accept that you were dead." He was holding Lysandridas by his arms, gazing up into his face earnestly as the speech tumbled out. "It wasn't until the Pythian Games—do you remember Damoxenos of Athens? He told me he'd seen you here in Tegea. I couldn't believe it, but Chilon suggested you might have used a pseudonym. When we found 'Philip son of Philippos' on the list, I thought it might be you, but we couldn't be sure. We sent a merchant to inquire if this Philip still lived, and when he said 'yes' I had to raise the ransom. And then they wouldn't let me travel to Tegea. This damned war! I had to wait until I was out of the reserves, and for the pass to open. And when I got here they said you died of fever! Eleven months ago! They said you were in the quarries, but—"

"It's all right." Lysandridas calmed him, aware of Antyllus behind him. "Here's Antyllus."

"Teleklos." Antyllus held out his hand. "What a pleasure to see you again—even if the circumstances are somewhat awkward. I've brought the chariot to take you to my estate. Do you have many slaves travelling with you?"

"I came alone. My things are in a lodging house."

"I'll send someone to collect them later. Come; let us help you to the chariot." Although Antyllus offered his arm, Teleklos clung to his son, who with his arm around his father's waist helped him to hop on his good leg over to the waiting chariot. He helped his father get comfortable on the floor of the chariot, and then collected Afra from the boy who was holding her reins and mounted to ride back behind the chariot.

The whole ride, Teleklos stared at him, as if he still could not believe what he saw. Not for a moment did he take his eyes off his son, riding easily on a fine mare. At the end of the journey, after driving up the long drive flanked by cypress trees, Antyllus drew up before the elegant marble portico of his grand house.

The porch of Antyllus' house was supported by four Ionic columns. The triangular pediment formed by the tiled roof held a scene from the chariot race of Peplos. The four horses of the leading chariot turned and half leapt from the pediment, and the spectators were crowded into the triangular ends, kneeling as they cheered or covered their eyes in horror.

Lysandridas jumped down to help his father out of the chariot; Teleklos gazed up at the magnificent frieze framed over the porch and then glanced back at the tree-lined drive. His eyes sought his son's in confusion. "I don't understand," he admitted softly. "I was told you were sold to the quarries. That you died of fever there."

"I nearly did. Antyllus bought me from the foreman when I was sick with fever and restored me to health."

"So you belong to Antyllus now?"

"I've been helping him train his team." Lysandridas evaded the question of ownership.

Teleklos seemed to notice his simple but quality chiton, his sandals, and his confusion only increased. Antyllus was suggesting Lysandridas take Teleklos to his chamber, offering the hospitality of his baths, playing the perfect host. Lysandridas helped his father out of the chariot and up the steps into the entry hall.

Teleklos let his eyes sweep over the elegant frescoes and then hopped forward into the formal atrium. He noted the marble columns, the mosaic walkways, the flower beds where the first crocuses bloomed and the daffodils were sprouting tall shoots. He let himself be guided into a well-appointed room with a mosaic floor, plastered walls, and elegant furnishings. As he sank onto the couch he looked up earnestly at Lysandridas. "I don't understand," he repeated. "How did you come to be here?"

Lysandridas was acutely ashamed, and he did not dare meet his father's eyes. Defensively, he blurted out, "I didn't surrender! I was knocked out by a Tegean stallion." Unconsciously his hand went to the wound in the middle of his forehead. "And when I came to again, I was a prisoner." He kept his eyes averted as he continued. "I was naked but for the bandages on my head and thigh. When I was well enough to stand, I was assigned to a road crew—*in chains*. There were half a hundred of us there. They tried to keep us apart, housing us in different sheds and putting us in different work teams, but we caught sight of one another at meals or in the infirmary or the like. We would pass on news of who we'd seen or ask about friends. Somehow someone heard that we were to be ransomed. We even heard the price. And then one by one the others started disappearing. Sometimes they had a chance to say, 'My ransom's come,' or 'See you back in Sparta.' More often they were just gone."

Teleklos let out a little cry and grabbed his son's shoulder, forcing him to look at him. "But you weren't on the list of captives! It almost killed me when your name wasn't there! I couldn't believe it! I refused to believe it! But what could I do? How could I ransom someone that wasn't on the list? Oh, Lysandridas, try to understand! I know I was a fool—an idiot. I know that now, but it wasn't what I wanted!"

Their eyes met for a moment, and then Lysandridas looked away and continued, "Even when there was no one else left, I didn't give up hope. I thought you were having trouble raising the ransom. I told myself that my uncles were being obstinate, that you had to find someone who would buy the team; but when the second autumn came, I started to realise that the ransom wasn't ever going to come.

"Still I didn't blame you. I told myself that you were dead. I was so certain you would not have abandoned me that I told myself you must have died of some accident or illness. I told myself it was Derykleides or Grandfather or my uncles who had refused to pay the ransom. I even hoped for a while that Hermione would talk her father into paying it. With the passes closed, I put my hopes in the spring, thinking that by then surely Hermione and Dorothea would have prevailed. But when the passes cleared and still no ransom came, I faced the fact that no one was ever going to pay my ransom. That's when I started trying to kill myself."

"No," Teleklos moaned, grabbing his son's hands, making him look at him again. "Not that. You couldn't have wanted to destroy your own life! Not then! Not after surviving the battle itself!"

"What would you have done?" Lysandridas snapped back. Despite all the pity he felt for the aged man before him, he could not just forget what he had suffered. "If my family was not willing to pay my ransom, then I had only a lifetime of slavery ahead of me. Do you have any idea what that is like? Chains on your ankles—"

"I've tortured myself with thoughts of it ever since Damoxenos said he'd seen you! I haven't slept for months for the thought of you in chains—but you aren't ..."

"I was! Believe me, I was! I was on a road crew, cutting a road out of the side of the mountain, dragging the stones into place, sleeping chained together with barbarians in the open much of the time. During the actual work we weren't chained to each other, because the risk of one slave dragging others with him to their deaths if he slipped or got caught in a landslide was considered too great. So one day I tried to run for a bridge over a gorge to throw myself off, but they caught me. Later I planned to drive a whole quarry wagon over the edge of the road, but the other driver betrayed me. Then I stopped eating, trying to starve to death. They were clever, though: suddenly, rather than the usual salted pork and sour barley meal, they started offering me fresh grilled meats, fruits, and wheat rolls. I broke down and ate. When I was halfway well again, they put me on the crane in the quarries. I caught a fever and got so weak I collapsed at work—nearly causing a dangerous accident that might have killed someone. The foreman would have flogged me to death—which I hoped for—but Antyllus happened to be there. He was Minister of Mines and was on an inspection. When they started to flog me, he stopped them and brought me here. He didn't know who I was at first, but when he found out, he—he refused to treat me like a slave any more. In return, I have been helping him train his team for the 56th Games."

"And that was eleven months ago—that he bought you?"

"Yes."

"But the records listed you as dead."

"Of course. The foreman pocketed the price Antyllus paid, rather than passing it on to the city. It happens all the time here. That's how men like that make a little extra on the side."

Teleklos looked shocked, and Lysandridas had to smile faintly and shake his head. His father had always been naively honest. But Teleklos recovered quickly, and he looked about the room again. He seemed to grasp the significance of what Antyllus had done only now. Slowly he stated, "We have much to thank Antyllus for."

"Yes," Lysandridas admitted, feeling guilty already. He owed Antyllus his life. He owed him respect, obedience—and love. Antyllus asked only one thing: that he stay and be the son he'd lost. And Teleklos, unknowingly and innocently, was going to take that away from him.

"Can you forgive me, Lysandridas?!" Teleklos broke into his thoughts with sudden urgency. Reaching out to his son again, he grabbed his arms and made Lysandridas look him in the eye yet again. "Can you forgive me for being so stupid? For putting you through hell? For taking away almost four years of your life unnecessarily?"

What could Lysandridas say to that? He put his arms around Teleklos and held him, resting his head on his father's balding skull. "Of course I can forgive you. It doesn't matter any more. It's over."

"I—I've brought the ransom money!" Teleklos drew back again, already starting to recover now that Lysandridas had spoken the words of forgiveness. "I'll buy your freedom today, at once. I couldn't stand to have the money on me a minute longer. Send for Antyllus. I want it over with. Even if I stay here another month or more, I want you to be his guest, not his slave. Send for him." He was fumbling with his belt, working to free the 350 drachma hidden inside.

Lysandridas hesitated a moment, started to speak, but could not find the courage to admit to his father that he had been free for several months already. If he admitted that, he would have to explain why he was still in Tegea, why he hadn't gone home. Worse still, he would have to admit he had allowed himself to be adopted. How could he possibly tell Teleklos that he had taken Antyllus as his father knowing that Teleklos was still alive? The words seemed to jam in his throat, all but choking him. Teleklos was still urging him to go fetch Antyllus, so he fled into the atrium.

Here Lysandridas paused and tried to think what he should do. He was acutely aware that if he didn't tell his father the truth, he was doing Antyllus an injustice. It was wrong to let his father think he was still a slave, when Antyllus had been so generous. When he was about to hurt Antyllus to the quick by abandoning him, surely the least he could do was tell the truth about the magnitude of his generosity? But it would hurt Teleklos nearly as much or more to hear that Lysandridas had chosen to stay in Tegea after he was free to leave. Furthermore, with each moment Lysandridas was becoming more afraid of Spartan law. The consequences of all his actions here in Tegea might cost him his Spartan citizenship. The fact that he had remained, had allowed himself to be adopted, and had—at Ambelos' pleading—agreed to help train the Tegean cavalry could all be construed as treason. Lysandridas began to fear that he would face humiliation, disgrace, and possibly even exile or death if he returned to Sparta with his father. But how could he refuse to return? It would kill Teleklos!

Gradually Lysandridas became aware that Antyllus was standing in the doorway to his study watching him. He turned to him. "Sir, I—"

"Come in here where we can talk." Antyllus retreated into his study, and Lysandridas followed him. He paused inside the door and stared at Antyllus' back. The older man was standing beside his desk, fingering the inlay absently. Finally Antyllus turned and faced Lysandridas. A sad smile played at his lips. "Your father's aged a decade since I saw him last. He looks a half-century older than at the time of his victory. He must have suffered these last years. Why didn't he come sooner?"

"A mistake," Lysandridas answered, only registering the full import of it for the first time himself. He explained, "Sometime while I was still in the hospital, I was asked my name. I was ashamed to admit who I really was—at the time I was so full of myself that I thought everyone knew my name—so I made up a name. It never occurred to me that they wanted my name to report the list of captives. Even when I heard about the ransom payments, I assumed the Lacedaemonian government knew who had been captured." He shook his head at his own stupidity. "I was too wrapped up in my own troubles to think through the fact that if our army hadn't retrieved our dead, the kings had no way of knowing who was dead and who was captured—except by what the Tegeans reported." Lysandridas paused, and then with a sour smile summarised what had happened: "My own vanity is the reason my slavery lasted so long."

Antyllus took a moment digesting this information. It couldn't have been worse from a personal perspective. Until this moment, he had hoped that Lysandridas would not be able to forgive his father. He had said so clearly, "Three years too late!" But if Teleklos had wanted to ransom Lysandridas from the start, then Lysandridas could not deny him forgiveness. He felt his throat tightening and turned his face away again. A part of his brain was screaming in fury at the Gods. How could they do this to him? How could they take a son from him a second time? What had he done to deserve this?

"Antyllus." Lysandridas' voice was weak. "I'm sorry. I know I owe you my life. Not just physically. I've been happy here. I don't just *owe* you, I respect you and I honour you—"

"Let it be. You aren't to blame." Antyllus cut him short briskly. He could not face him. He was not strong enough yet. He kept his back turned to this son he had chosen, not merely sired.

"Teleklos asked me to fetch you. He—he wants to pay you my ransom."

Antyllus made a vague gesture of dismissal and then, pulling himself together, said firmly: "Tell him I'll come shortly."

"May I bring you both wine?"

"Yes. Do that." He still had his back to Lysandridas and gestured impatiently. "Go fetch us wine and something light to eat."

Lysandridas retreated quickly, hastening toward the kitchens. His emotions were more unsettled than ever. It was as if he had only now realised how very much he *liked* Antyllus. Of all the people in the world, Teleklos and Antyllus were probably the two men he loved best. Now he was not only being forced to choose between them—he could not please one without cruelly hurting the other. He wanted to scream, but he had been raised to believe that it was as shameful to scream for emotional pain as for physical pain. His upbringing forbade it. He could only go to the kitchen and start preparing a tray with refreshments for his two fathers.

Antyllus wiped his face with his hands, took a deep breath, put a smile on his face, and strode briskly to the room in which his unwanted guest waited. "Teleklos, are you comfortable? Lysandridas is fetching you something to eat and drink. Is there anything else I can do for you? Wouldn't you like a bath? I'll have my body slave—"

"No, there is something else we must settle first," Teleklos burst in somewhat rudely. Antyllus' gracious good manners got on his nerves. He was in pain and he was still reeling from the unexpected encounter with his son. He wanted to finish what he had come here for—even if the circumstances were so very different from what he had expected. "Lysandridas tells me you bought him from the city of Tegea. He says you saved his life by purchasing him from the quarries, when he was near death. I can't ever thank you enough for that, but here—" he shoved a little canvas purse at Antyllus—"here is the ransom. I want it paid. I can't stand for Lysandridas to be a slave a day longer—no matter how well treated. I appreciate how good you've been to him, but I want him freed!"

"Lysandridas is free," Antyllus said softly. "You need not pay me."

Teleklos thought Antyllus meant that he was prepared to free Lysandridas now without payment, and he shook his head vigorously. "You have done so much for him already. You have a right to the ransom! Take it! It's no good to me! I'm not allowed to have so much money in Sparta anyway, and the team is sold."

"You sold your team to raise the ransom?" Antyllus exclaimed, his own pain audible in his voice. He understood what it meant for Teleklos. He could remember how Teleklos, even at Olympia, had helped tend his own team. He remembered Teleklos rushing down onto the hippodrome to stop his foolish nephew from doing harm to them after his inept driving at Delphi. He remembered Teleklos rubbing down his horses after the race. Teleklos wasn't a man like Polycritus, who *invested* in horses. He loved them. To have sold the team that had brought him an Olympic victory must have broken his heart.

"Wouldn't you have sold your team for your son's freedom?" Teleklos asked back.

"Of course," Antyllus answered, and Teleklos remembered—too late—that Antyllus' son was dead. He was instantly ashamed of his own rudeness.

"Forgive me! I—I didn't mean it like that. I know you *wish* you could buy back *your* son! I understand you utterly—I've been there. Please, don't be angry with me! But take this ransom. I hate it. I want to be rid of it. I want this behind me!"

Antyllus reached out and took the offered purse from Teleklos' trembling hand without another word.

Later, when Teleklos had fallen asleep exhausted from his journey, injury, and all the emotional turmoil, Lysandridas took Boreas and rode into the city to find Ambelos. In the few months since Antyllus had freed and adopted him, Lysandridas and Ambelos had become friends. In a way, Ambelos had become the first real friend Lysandridas had ever had. At home in Sparta, he had only had one close friend, Thessalos, but they had been as much rivals as friends. Because Ambelos could never be Lysandridas' equal in sport, there was no rivalry between them; but because Ambelos was the only one—except Antyllus himself—who had accepted Lysandridas completely and without reservations, Lysandridas had come to trust and depend him as he had no one else.

To be sure, Lysandridas had been introduced into Tegean society. He was Antyllus' adopted son, and it was a measure of how well-respected Antyllus was that a former enemy and slave was nominally "accepted" at all. Antyllus had even talked his nephew into betrothing his eldest daughter to Lysandridas. But for all the official acceptance by Antyllus' generation (out of respect for their own friend), the younger men had made it very clear that for them Lysandridas was still "a slave"—and a hated Spartan one at that.

But Ambelos had been different from the start. Even when Lysandridas was still a slave, teaching the youth to ride, Ambelos had started to talk to him as a human being. With the passing months, Ambelos had confided in him more and more—and far from the sight of Antyllus, his father, and the other slaves, the two young men had sometimes laughed and talked about Ambelos' hopes and dreams. Lysandridas had realized even then that Ambelos was a very lonely young man. Because of his club foot he had always been somewhat of an outsider, pitied more than accepted by the youth of his own city and class.

But after his father seized "emergency" powers, Ambelos had become more isolated than ever. Some youths and young men then hated him for what his father had done, while others became sycophants and flatterers who sought to use him in order to gain access to his father. Lysandridas had been impressed by how sensitively Ambelos could distinguish between the motives of them all—and flattered in his own way that Ambelos never once suspected Lysandridas of anything but candid honesty. Ambelos expected Lysandridas' honest friendship so guilelessly that Lysandridas had had no choice but to give it.

And it was from Ambelos, more than from Antyllus, that Lysandridas had learned about Tegea. Antyllus claimed that he had "withdrawn" from politics altogether and wanted nothing to do with the present regime. In consequence, he refused to discuss "public affairs" with Lysandridas at all. But Ambelos loved to talk about what was happening in his city. He even joked self-consciously that he was repaying Lysandridas' lessons about horses and war with lessons on Tegean politics.

"You see," Ambelos had explained with a little diffident smile, "Antyllus isn't really retired from politics at all—he is plotting against my father. But please don't tell him we know!" Ambelos had added earnestly.

Via Ambelos, Lysandridas had come to know Harmatides, too. The charismatic "dictator" had welcomed Lysandridas into his home as his son's friend—and insisted that Lysandridas could come to him anytime with any request. "I am honoured that such an outstanding young athlete should be my son's mentor—and not a little amused to think a Spartiate guardsman is teaching my son the skills of war."

Amused Harmatides might have been, but not condescending. On the contrary, he had taken Lysandridas aside and begged him to drill Ambelos to the limits of his endurance. "He is a strong young man," Harmatides said proudly of his son. "His *heart* is strong—but his body must be toughened. I was wrong to give in to my wife on that, and Ambelos was right to go behind my back. Press him to his outer limits, and I will thank you in ways you cannot even imagine. You can be sure that when you ask a favour of me, I will be generous. What you have given my son is a debt I will always honour."

Now, as he rode toward Tegea, Lysandridas knew that he would have to call in that "debt"—and would soon see how good the dictator's word really was. It was a task made all the more difficult by feeling that he was about to ask for a reward disproportionate to his services. What had he really done for Ambelos? He had taught him to ride and throw a javelin. They had wrestled some, swam, and competed at archery, but it had been very little by Lysandridas' own standards. The long marches and running, much less the drill with sword and spear that were so much a part of Spartan training, were impossible for the handicapped Ambelos.

And now Lysandridas must ask of Harmatides the one favour he did not want to grant: that Lysandridas be relieved of service.

Harmatides' house was well guarded, but Lysandridas was granted immediate and unquestioned admittance. Harmatides himself was in the city, he was told, but Ambelos hobbled out to greet Lysandridas gladly. "Lysandridas! I wasn't expecting you before—what's happened?" Ambelos was very sensitive to the moods of others and easily read the strain on Lysandridas' face.

"Could we go for a ride?"

"I'll get a chlamys." Ambelos left Lysandridas for only a few minutes and then returned dressed for riding. As they started out of the stables, however, one of Harmatides' guards—one of the many Tegean cavalry troopers fanatically loyal to Harmatides—stopped them. "Your father does not want you riding out alone, my lord. Wait while I arrange an escort."

So it had come to this, Lysandridas registered with surprise: Harmatides was now so unpopular that he feared for his son's safety.

"But I won't be alone. The brave Lysandridas is with me," Ambelos answered the cavalryman evenly.

The Tegean nobleman's son gazed sceptically at Lysandridas. He did not seem to think the former Spartan slave a suitable or adequate escort for his commander's son and heir. "My orders are not to let you ride out without an escort," he insisted stubbornly.

Ambelos looked helplessly at Lysandridas, who sighed and asked if they could talk in private somewhere in the house. Ambelos at once led him to a walled garden in which a small house temple stood behind a bubbling fountain. "We will be undisturbed here," Ambelos assured his friend.

Lysandridas looked towards the altar and then to the bubbling fountain, and tried to find the words to tell this innocent young man who had become so dependent upon him that he was leaving. Only now did he realise *how much* he had come to like Ambelos—a youth who would have been killed at birth in Sparta! To his horror, he realised that he, too, now found that barbaric. How could he go back to Sparta, seeing it as he did now, as a partially barbaric place?

Ambelos could bear the suspense no longer. "What is it?" he asked again anxiously. "Has my father been accused of another atrocity?" Not long ago an outspoken critic of Harmatides had been found poisoned in his house. Although the slave cook confessed to the crime under torture, Ambelos knew that many—including Antyllus—thought his father was behind it. Ambelos had insisted indignantly that his father would never stoop so low as to poison his opponents, but Ambelos wasn't sure the Spartan was entirely convinced. Ambelos also recognised that the actions of his father's loyal troopers suggested that some kind of crisis was brewing.

But Lysandridas shook his head. "I am here on a personal mission."

Ambelos waited, more puzzled than ever, but no less tense.

With a glance toward the altar, Lysandridas took a deep breath and asked, "Do you believe we have a purpose in our lives?"

"Yes, of course."

"Why do you think the Gods let me drive the winning chariot at Olympia only to make me a slave less than a month later?"

"Maybe it was so you could come here and help us...." Ambelos suggested timidly. He felt sure of this, even if he was a little embarrassed to suggest it out loud to his friend.

Lysandridas turned around and faced Ambelos at last. "I was afraid you'd say that. But you do not know what they have done now.... They have sent my father, my real father, here."

"Your *Spartan* father?" Ambelos asked, unbelieving.

"Yes. The man who sired me. The man who nursed me through childhood colds, when other boys had mothers. The man who taught me my letters, the names of the flowers, and the constellations in the night sky. The man who taught me everything I know about horses. The man who let me drive his chariot at Olympia, and who set his own crown of olives upon my head.... He's here in Tegea. He's come to take me back to Sparta."

"But I thought he abandoned you?" Ambelos protested, resisting the implications of what Lysandridas said.

"So did I. But it seems it was all a mistake. My father thought I was dead. When he learned the truth, he sold the team to free me from a slavery he still believes I suffer."

"But you don't have to go," Ambelos protested. "You can tell him that you're free and adopted and betrothed here. You can stay if you *want*."

"Could you do that to *your* father, if you were in my shoes?"

Ambelos caught his breath, and Lysandridas saw that his words had struck him where he lived, because Ambelos adored his father. For a second his eyes recognised the truth of what Lysandridas said and he empathised, but then the dictator's son had a second thought. "By Zeus and Ares, Lysandridas! *My* father won't understand! He won't let you go! Oh, Zeus the Saviour, *listen* to me!" he cried out in genuine distress. "My father will call you traitor and have you detained, arrested!" Much as he loved his father, Ambelos knew that he could be ruthless when he thought it was necessary.

"Arrested?" Lysandridas had never considered this complication. He gazed at Ambelos in alarm, and his stomach knotted itself tighter. "Would your father truly be so unjust?"

"Is it unjust?" Ambelos shot back, suddenly angry. "You know all about our cavalry!" he pointed out. "You know our strengths and weaknesses. You know our commanders—and their horses—by name. You know our tactics! If you return to Sparta, you can betray all you know to our worst enemies. How can we let you return to Sparta? We must keep you here. If not willingly, then as a prisoner—"

"Or a corpse, you mean," Lysandridas added with a sour smile.

"No. Not that."

"Why not? It would be kinder." Lysandridas' voice cut through Ambelos' selfish anger.

Ambelos was so shocked it took his breath away. He stared at his friend with new intensity, and he saw something that Antyllus once had seen. "Lysandridas? Are you asking us to kill you?"

Lysandridas was so confused, it was as if his thoughts were making him dizzy. He understood Ambelos, and even Harmatides, all too well. He understood Antyllus. He did not dare to think of poor little Timosa, the bride they had picked for him. She was just seventeen—but in Tegea, he had been told, she was already considered "old" for a bride. She would feel rejected and utterly abandoned. Yet all these ties were like silk threads beside the chains of iron that bound him to Teleklos—and Sparta. He could not get around it. No matter how hard he tried, he could not image himself telling Teleklos he had chosen his adopted father and city over the father and city of his blood and birth.

Ambelos' anger was gone. He went over and gently touched Lysandridas' arm. "It's all right, Lysandridas. I'll talk my father 'round. I'll—I don't know—but I promise you he'll let you go free. Will you do one thing for me in return?"

Lysandridas waited in silence to hear the price of his freedom.

"Will you promise *not* to betray us when you are back in Sparta?"

Lysandridas drew his sword and laid it on the altar. With his hand on the hilt, he intoned: "By Zeus and the Twins, I swear that I will not betray anything I know about the Tegean cavalry or army to Sparta. I swear I will strike this sword into my own heart before I tell a single soul in Sparta anything which might help Sparta attack or harm Tegea. Zeus and the Twins are my witnesses!"

CHAPTER 19

The apple trees were starting to bloom when the little party set out for Sparta. The sight of them made Lysandridas' heart heavier than ever. He could remember seeing them from the floor of Antyllus' chariot. In retrospect it was as if Persephone herself had spoken to him, whispering through the blossoms that life could be sweet again. But if the quarries had been hell and Antyllus' fine estate earth, then Sparta was something else again. Lysandridas was not sure what. He only knew he was reluctant to leave Tegea and apprehensive about what he would encounter beyond the mountains in Lacedaemon.

Teleklos, by contrast, could hardly wait to be gone. The month he had been forced to stay under Antyllus' roof at the doctor's orders had been increasingly difficult for him. He had never eaten so well in his life, never been better treated or entertained; but how could he help noticing the affection that Antyllus bore Lysandridas? Or the fact that Lysandridas returned it? He knew his son had suffered. He could see it in the mutilation of his hands and the new flogging scars, which Lysandridas explained he had received at the quarries the day Antyllus bought him. Teleklos could well imagine it; he had witnessed Antyllus' purchase of Dion under similar circumstances. He understood that his son was grateful to Antyllus. He ought to be. But it hurt him to see how well they understood each other. Teleklos had never had to be jealous of his son's affections before. Even his son's infatuation with Hermione had not had the slightest impact on their relationship. With Antyllus it was different.

And then there was the Tegean tyrant's son who'd come daily to see Lysandridas. Lysandridas said he had taught the young man, who had a club foot, to ride. That was something a slave might do. And perhaps it was not so surprising that after Lysandridas' true identity had been revealed, even the son of a tyrant treated him with respect. But here, too, Teleklos sensed there was more to their relationship. They laughed easily together and seemed to communicate with just a glance. It was unsettling.

Equally disturbing were vague references to a girl. Once or twice Teleklos had heard something that suggested that a marriage had been arranged for Lysandridas that now had to be broken off. But slaves didn't marry. Lysandridas assured Teleklos that he had misunderstood. He claimed he had become fond of a certain prostitute. That was all. Certainly he had taken the news that Hermione had married Thessalos and was now the mother of two small children very hard. He had gone off for a long ride and not come back until after dark. Teleklos had worried about him—and so had Antyllus.

Yes, Teleklos was anxious to return home and to take Lysandridas with him—away from this strange world of luxury and back to the familiar and ordered world of Sparta. Teleklos told himself it was not good for a young man to live as Lysandridas had done this past month, with no duties other than the driving he loved. It was better for a young man to serve his city, living in barracks, drilling at arms, and training his body in sport and competition.

Because Teleklos' knee was still swollen and he could only limp, it was unthinkable that he walk the forty miles back to Sparta. Antyllus therefore gave Teleklos a mule. He also insisted that Lysandridas keep Afra so they could both ride back to Lacedaemon. And then, the night before their scheduled departure, Antyllus came to Lysandridas and asked him to take Dion with them as well.

Lysandridas protested. He could take care of Teleklos and the two animals for the two- to three-day journey himself, and once they were home they had a house full of helots to serve them. But Antyllus insisted. He could not fully forgive Dion, he admitted. The mere sight of him reminded him daily that his wife had been unfaithful to him. He could sell Dion, of course, Antyllus explained, but he preferred to think of him in good hands.

"Spartiates don't generally keep slaves," Lysandridas demurred uncertainly.

"Then free him, if you prefer, but take him with you."

"But you'll be more short-handed than ever in the stables."

"I will buy two new slaves. Your father gave me your full ransom, remember? Afra and Dion represent roughly that value."

Lysandridas looked down in shame.

Antyllus laid his hand on his shoulder briefly; and when Lysandridas looked up questioningly, Antyllus gave him a sad smile. "Don't feel guilty. You really have no choice—although, I admit, it comforts me to see how difficult it is for you. If you had frolicked home without a backward glance, it would have hurt me more. As it is, all I can do is wish you the best and hope we'll meet again from time to time in the future. This summer at Olympia, for a start."

"My father sold the team."

"I know. But that doesn't stop you from coming as a spectator—and cheering for my team—does it?"

"I'll be there," Lysandridas promised, with earnestness inappropriate to the event. What he really meant was that he wanted to see Antyllus again—and he wanted his team, the team he had spent months training, to win.

"Good." Antyllus clapped him on the shoulder and would have left it at that, but Lysandridas flung his arms around him and held him for a moment in silence. Then he let him go as abruptly as he had embraced him, and turned away.

Antyllus nodded to himself and left him alone.

So it was a party of three that left Tegea on a bright spring morning, with the apple trees budding in the valley and the bees humming everywhere. They skirted the city, crossed the unrecognisable battlefield, and wound up the steep road into the mountains that separated Tegea from Lacedaemon. They spent the night in one of the shepherds' huts and reached the border at mid-morning the following day.

Lysandridas was very nervous. All night he had slept fitfully, thinking of the fact that the sentries of either side might arrest him: the Tegeans because Harmatides might have sent orders to prevent him from returning to Sparta, and the Lacedaemonians for failing to return sooner. The Tegeans treated him with disdain, waving the little party through the gates with a sneer. One of the men even called after them, "Go back where you came from, slime! We know how to deal with the likes of you, if you ever try to enter Tegea again!"

At the Lacedaemonian border post they were met by a Spartiate officer neither Lysandridas nor Teleklos knew personally. Teleklos had sent word back to Lacedaemon shortly after his arrival, explaining that he had injured himself and would be staying in Tegea longer than expected *and* that he had found Lysandridas. Thus their arrival caused no particular sensation. The Spartiate officer greeted Teleklos as respectfully as a young man was supposed to treat a man over sixty, offered him refreshments and a rest, and turned on Lysandridas a bland face to remark, "Lysandridas son of Teleklos, you have been reassigned to the Amyclae Lochos, 2ⁿᵈ Battalion, 4ᵗʰ Company, 2ⁿᵈ Platoon. You should report to Krantios son of Cleomenes."

"Yes, sir." Lysandridas kept his face as neutral as possible. The internal relief, however, was immense. Apparently the kings, council, and assembly had not seen fit to take away his citizenship. There wasn't even any mention of a trial or inquiry. After convincing himself that he might even face death for what he had done in Tegea, it was almost anticlimatic to find that the official reaction of the Lacedaemonian government was this practical reassignment of a man still on active duty to a military unit—and nothing more.

When they came around the curve that gave them the first glimpse into the Eurotas Valley, Lysandridas actually smiled for the first time since setting out on this journey. He jumped down from Afra and led her forward to the edge of the steep slope. Shading his eyes, he gazed in apparent wonder at the hazy valley before them until he at last found the contours of the hill on which Teleklos' kleros sat.

Twisting around and smiling at the others, he called Dion forward. "Come see your new home! See that cleft in the Taygetos foothills?" Lysandridas asked Dion anxiously. The Slav nodded. "In this haze you can't make out the little stream that formed it, but there is a small tributary that comes down the mountains there. And to the right, see that hill stretching like a finger into the valley?"

"The one that's whitish?" Dion asked hesitantly.

"Yes! Exactly! Those are our orchards. They're blooming, too." Lysandridas turned to throw a smile to his father, and Teleklos sighed with relief. Everything was going to be all right. Lysandridas was clearly overjoyed to be home.

They descended to the valley by the steep, occasionally winding road that ended at the head of the drill fields. These were given over to the younger classes of the agoge at this time of day, and Lysandridas stopped to watch the boys. Teleklos indulged him gladly, more and more of his cares and worry falling away from him with every moment. Lysandridas explained to the bewildered Dion that the boys were the sons of Spartan citizens, attending the public school and learning their future profession.

Lysandridas was lost in memories as he gazed at the imperfect ranks and files of the young boys. Their ineptitude with the wooden swords and light wicker shields was so obvious that it brought a smile even to Dion's face. These were little boys of nine or ten at most, and their efforts to carry out the instructions of their evidently exasperated eirenes were marked by confusion, trips, and even falls. A trumpet call that meant "left about" to every Spartiate alive resulted in such complete chaos that Lysandridas laughed aloud, and glanced over at his grinning father.

They continued over the wide stone bridge leading into the city itself. The river was rushing cold and strong with melting snow. It hissed and gurgled under their feet, and even the air was cooler on the bridge. Beyond the bridge the city began in a leisurely manner. There was no wall, but without any particular warning a couple of civic buildings had been built, seemingly at random, notably the ancient monument to Ares opposite a Temple to Asklepios. Slightly back from the road and higher up was an imposing Temple to Zeus. Then came the barracks of the 1st Battalion of the Pitanate Lochos, and a gymnasium.

"I'll report to Krantios at once," Lysandridas decided abruptly.

Teleklos had not expected so much devotion to duty, and he was obviously disappointed. "But couldn't you let that wait till tomorrow?" he pleaded. "Your grandfather and Zoë and—" he stopped short, not sure how Lysandridas felt about Leonis— "everyone is so anxious to see you."

Lysandridas was too afraid of being accused of treason to risk any act that might be imputed as negligence of duty. He did not even want to ride any longer, for fear it would be interpreted as arrogance. "I expect Krantios will let me go home for the night. But I want to report. We can meet after dinner." He vaulted off and turned Afra over to Dion, hurrying away before his father could try to dissuade him.

Making his way through the twisted streets, he ran into many people who knew him. Most simply looked surprised and then greeted him. Some of the helots and perioikoi, who did not know him except by sight, stared at his scar. Once or twice someone came over to take his hand and welcome him back. Once or twice he also thought he saw men turn away as if they wanted nothing to do with him. He tried to tell himself he was mistaken or that it didn't matter.

At his battalion barracks, Lysandridas was told that Krantios was at home. This was not surprising at this time of day; men on active service drilled in the mornings and had the afternoons to themselves. Krantios was married and had several children. It was only logical that he would spend the afternoons with his family before reporting to his mess for dinner. The sentry on duty, however, sent a helot attendant to Krantios' house to tell him Lysandridas was back, and the battalion commander interrupted his afternoon to come greet the latest member of his unit.

Krantios had commanded the company Lysandridas had served in before he was selected for the Guard. His promotion to Battalion Commander had apparently come after the battle with Tegea. Lysandridas had not had close contact with him before, but he remembered him as a fair and intelligent officer.

At the sight of him, Lysandridas got politely to his feet and waited at attention. Krantios smiled. "Welcome back, Lysandridas." His eyes seemed to linger on the scar on his forehead.

"I was knocked out, sir. I didn't come to until I was in a Tegean hospital."

"I can believe that. I was there, remember?" What Krantios didn't say was that when the news of Lysandridas' imminent return had reached the city, several divisional commanders had flatly refused to have "the coward" in their units. Krantios' own lochos commander, Epicydes, however, had spoken spiritedly in Lysandridas' defence and said he would "be proud" to have the young man in his lochos. But the process had been repeated when the officers of the lochos were told Lysandridas would be joining them. One of the battalion commanders had said Lysandridas belonged in jail, not the army—or should be sold "like the slave he is" to the barbarians. A second had expressed "concern" that Lysandridas would be out of condition and practice. Krantios had then volunteered to take him into his battalion. Although he had some qualms about a man who had been almost four years in slavery, he thought it was unfair to blame Lysandridas for his fate. He remembered, if the others preferred to forget, that it had been the counter-attack of the Guard that had enabled the bulk of the survivors to get home safely.

Krantios did not mention any of this, only the names of Lysandridas' company and platoon commanders respectively. Then he asked Lysandridas if he felt up to regular drill immediately.

"Yes, sir, but I have neither arms nor armour."

"That's not a problem. I'll have standard equipment waiting for you when you report in the morning."

"May I spend the night away from barracks?"

"I think you owe your father that much, yes."

"Thank you, sir."

Krantios considered him thoughtfully. He could see that Lysandridas was not entirely comfortable, but that was not surprising. He could see, too, that aside from the scar, he appeared in good health—better than he had expected, really. "Your attendant was killed, I presume."

"That or he too was sold into slavery or ran away," Lysandridas admitted. "I've never seen him again, and my father said he didn't make it back here."

"You'll need a man to serve you then. Will that be a problem?"

"I don't think so." Teleklos had told him that Thorax was anxious to join him in the army.

"All right. See you tomorrow then."

Lysandridas now had about an hour before it would be time to report to his syssitia. He therefore returned north of the city to the low hill on which the acropolis stood. There he gave the sword he had purchased in Tegea to Zeus and the dagger to the Dioskouroi. He thanked all three for his safe, uneventful return. He swore that he would serve his city loyally in the future, begging the deities to help him to do this without violating his vow not to harm Tegea. Last but not least, he purchased wine and offered this to Apollo, asking him to prevent hostilities between Lacedaemon and Tegea. Then he made his way to his syssitia.

The various syssitia were scattered across the city. Lysandridas' happened to have its andron on the western edge of the city. The building was only one-storied, with a red tiled roof over whitewashed stone. A simple propylaeum with four Doric columns fronted the rectangular hall, with its solid couches built right against the wall. Braziers, with coal to keep the chill off the air, and a huge krater took up the centre of the room, while twenty small, portable tables waited around the periphery before the couches.

When Lysandridas had left Sparta almost four years ago, they had had eighteen members, and two tables had gone unused. He wondered how many members they had now. Others of his comrades might have been killed, and new members accepted from the four age-cohorts that had come of age since his departure.

At the far end of the hall, square pilaster columns framed a door leading to the kitchen. The door was open and the smell of grilled hare, fried leeks, cooked carrots, and fresh barley bread escaped into the hall.

Although he was hungry and the food smelled good, Lysandridas briefly regretted the fact that he would never again enjoy the fine, well-spiced dishes of Antyllus' table.

From the kitchen came the high-pitched voices of small boys and then the gruff orders of the helot cook. A moment later, two little boys with shaved heads, short, plain chitons, and dirty bare feet came into the hall, each lugging a heavy amphora. An outsider could easily have mistaken them for slaves, but Lysandridas recognised them for what they were: sons of Spartiates attending the agoge. He too had served like these boys in the messes of the syssitia, learning his manners, the Spartan code of behaviour, and the values of his society, not to mention rhetoric—as Antyllus had been quick to note.

These two boys were very small, and they dropped their amphora and stared at the sight of him. "Who are you?" one of the boys blurted out.

"Who are you, *sir*," Lysandridas corrected the boy automatically.

"Sir? Are you Spartan then—sir?"

"Yes, I'm Lysandridas son of Teleklos son of Apollonides, and a member of this syssitia."

The boys looked at one another.

"Who are you?" Lysandridas asked them.

"Eurypon son of Diactorides, sir."

"Lichas son of Euxenos, sir." They answered obediently, still staring at him and his scar with wide eyes.

"How old are you?"

"Seven," they answered in chorus. So his suspicions had been right, and they were in their first year at the agoge. Lysandridas could remember that year vividly. He had been absolutely miserable. He hated living in the unheated barracks among a bunch of loud, silly classmates and away from his father, his home, and his horses, not to mention Zoë's good food and comforting arms. He remembered his first year at the agoge as the worst of his life—until he found himself a chained slave in Tegea. But the latter, he reflected with bemusement, had been easier for having gone through the former.

"How long have you been with this syssitia?" he asked. The boys in the agoge rotated among the syssitia so they could learn from as many citizens as possible, and also gain an impression of which mess they wanted to join when they came of age.

"We just started at the new moon," Eurypon declared.

From the kitchen the cook roared, "Where did you little buggers get to? Do I have—Oh! I'm sorry, sir. I didn't realise there was anyone here. Lysandridas?" The man slowly recognised him.

"Yes, it's me. I got back today."

The cook smiled hesitantly. "Congratulations, sir. Welcome back. I suppose this calls for some kind of celebration...." He didn't sound too sure of himself, and Lysandridas waved it aside. "No need. I didn't exactly return victorious, did I?" He was suddenly reminded of his lost shield, the infamy of having lost it to the enemy, and he felt naked and ashamed.

"So it is true," the voice came from behind him; and Lysandridas turned around to see Orsiphantas, the senior member of the syssitia, limping into the hall. Orsiphantas was well over sixty and used a cane to walk these days. He'd suffered some kind of leg injury during his prime, and with age it caused him increasing distress. He came and stood directly before Lysandridas. He looked him up and down, focused hard on the scar on his forehead, and with a wave of his hand and a snap of his fingers sent the boys back to the kitchen. The boys fled and the cook withdrew. "I never thought to see you again," Orsiphantas admitted; and Lysandridas still could not tell if he was hostile or just restrained. "Most people thought your father was mad to insist you might still be alive after all this time. You—don't look much worse for wear."

Lysandridas held up his hands to show the scars.

"You will find there are many here who think a Guardsman should not survive a defeat."

What was he supposed to say to that? Lysandridas felt guilt forming in the pit of his stomach again.

"Well, you're here. Take your place." Orsiphantas indicated a couch, and limped toward his own place near the kitchen.

The others arrived in ones and twos in quick succession. They all showed initial surprise and then more or less reluctantly welcomed Lysandridas back. Only one, Nicoles, refused to give him his hand. "You belong to this syssitia and I cannot prevent you from attending, but don't expect friendship from me!"

"Nicoles!" Orsiphantas called sternly. "You've sworn an oath to Lysandridas no less than to the others of this mess."

"I must be ready to give my life for him—as he did *not* for me!—but I don't have to like him!" Nicoles snarled back and stalked over to his couch.

Lysandridas had not completely recovered from this encounter when a young man who he was not expecting came through the door. It was Dorussos, who as a youth had belonged to the agoge unit that Lysandridas had commanded as an eirene. At the time, Dorussos had been only sixteen. Now he was a citizen, and had apparently become a member of this syssitia while Lysandridas was in captivity.

"Lysandridas!" Dorussos embraced him happily. "My father said you would be coming, but I hardly believed it! I'm so glad to see you! You must come for lunch with us one day. There's so much to tell you."

Lysandridas was flattered and grateful, but before he could even reply, the member of the mess he was most dreading came into the hall. It was Thessalos.

Thessalos, like the others, first looked surprised, and then he smiled broadly and came toward Lysandridas with open arms. "I can't believe it! I thought your father was fooling himself. I'm so glad. What a miracle! Hermione will be delighted. You have to meet our children. We have a little girl, Chrysie, and a son we named for my father-in-law."

Lysandridas could not reject the welcome—not in front of all the others. Everyone knew they had been best friends. He therefore found himself embracing Thessalos and muttering words of delight automatically, and all the time his insides were churning with agitation. Thessalos seemed hardly to have changed, except that his hair was longer now, and he seemed more self-confident than ever. Why shouldn't he be? Lysandridas thought bitterly as he smiled and said how glad he was to be home. Thessalos was in the Guard—and he had Hermione.

Lysandridas was glad that Orsiphantas called for the meal to be served, putting an end to the little reunion. Lysandridas scanned the company settled now on their couches and counted eighteen. With Dorussos new, this meant one of the old members was missing. "Where's Pleistonax?" he asked generally.

There was an awkward silence, and then Nicoles flung at him, "He was made of nobler stuff than you: he died rather than grovel at Tegean feet."

More than one of the others protested, telling Nicoles his remarks were out of order. Orsiphantas told him he would be expelled from dinner if he could not show more respect for a "brother." Thessalos was Lysandridas' most heated defender, saying loudly, "The Gods chose who was to die and who fell into enemy hands! Have you forgotten that Lysandridas counter-attacked while *you* withdrew, Nicoles? You *fled* the field—as did I and all of us here! Lysandridas, with the 2nd and 3rd companies of the Guard, advanced to enable our withdrawal. None of *us* have the right to criticise any of them."

"Oh, is that what they say in the Guard these days?" Nicoles sneered.

"It is," Thessalos insisted, staring the other man down.

It's so easy for him, Lysandridas thought bitterly. Thessalos had been chosen for the Guard because of his courage on the field—not for driving a chariot.

After dinner, Lysandridas tried to hurry away to meet his father, but Thessalos caught his arm and held him back. He looked Lysandridas straight in the eye and said earnestly, "I can't tell you how glad I am you're back, Lysandridas. I've missed you so much. You must come and see the new team my grandfather will enter at Olympia this summer. The best four horses you've ever seen—all Hector's brothers. You can help us prepare for the Games. What is it, Lysandridas?"

"What is it? Is the fact that you married *my* bride so unimportant to you that you can forget it? Well, I can't! I loved Hermione. All these four years in hell, I continued to love her. To mourn her."

"Surely you knew she would marry someone else."

"There *are* girls, you know, who wait until they are twenty-three or more before they marry," he pointed out sarcastically.

"You know Hermione well enough to know she's not that type," Thessalos retorted, a touch of anger in his own voice for the first time. "Besides, it wasn't a matter of waiting. We thought you were *dead!*"

"Did it have to be you? Did it have to be less than a season after I was presumed dead? Did you have to share her bed even before that?"

"Who says I did?" Thessalos' face was hard and his voice harsh.

"My father says he only had to take one look at her belly—"

"Your father is an old fool!"

"How dare you?!"

"No! How dare *you?* You heard what Nicoles said tonight. That's the way at least half this city feels. You have no right to pass judgement on any other citizen! You should be grateful for whatever friends you have!"

"I don't have to call a man my friend who stole my bride away from me behind my back!"

"If that's the way you want it." Thessalos turned on his heel and strode away with a quick, firm, military stride, his red himation swinging in time behind him.

Still inwardly upset, Lysandridas found his father and Dion waiting at his father's syssitia. "Is everything all right, Lysandridas?" his father asked at once, reading his son's face flawlessly.

"Fine," Lysandridas lied.

"Weren't you welcomed as you should have been?"

"Most men welcomed me. The rest don't matter."

Teleklos sighed, not because of what Lysandridas had said but because he was not being open. But he reminded himself that Lysandridas had always been like this. He could be stubbornly incommunicative when it suited him.

It was now getting dark. Lysandridas mounted and they set out on the road leading north, past the west flank of the acropolis. They wound their way along the valley floor and despite the confrontation with Thessalos, Lysandridas found himself rejoicing at each familiar landmark.

Just beyond the halfway point they came to the ancient monument reputedly erected by Ikarios at the spot where Penelope covered her head with her shawl to indicate to her pursuing father that she *wanted* to go away with Odysseus. Lysandridas insisted on stopping and showing Dion the temple. The simple Doric temple contained a bronze figure of a woman with her veils pulled up over her head and across her face. Her head was bowed so that the veils dripping off her forehead shielded them. Her hands, too, were lost in the folds of her peplos; only the toes of one foot emerged as she stood with one knee bent slightly, her weight on the other foot.

"It is a monument to Penelope?" Dion asked uncertainly. He had never heard of a man putting up a monument to his daughter.

"Well, not exactly. It is to modesty, humility, devotion to duty, and respect for the law—all those things we value almost as much as courage itself."

They were losing the light rapidly, however, and hurried on. As earlier in the day, the first glimpse of his kleros brought an exclamation of joy from Lysandridas. Again he used Dion as an excuse to stop and point. "There, the stables, and follow those steps to the top and you can see—well, you can't. But up there is the house itself. Do you want to ride up to the house, Teleklos—"

"Nonsense! I can walk the last stretch. I'll start walking while you see to your horse and the mule." Teleklos dismounted carefully and turned the mule over to Dion. He hoped that Leonis was in the stables and that Lysandridas would encounter her there.

When Lysandridas and Dion caught up with him a few minutes later, he asked, "Everything all right?"

"It feels empty without the team."

"Was no one there?"

"No, Thorax must be up at the house. I put Afra in Hector's old stall and the mule next to Taygetos."

"Fine," Teleklos said absently. Maybe Leonis was up at the house.

When they reached the terrace, a cry went up from inside the house, and in the next instant Zoë came flying out of the door. She was followed by what seemed like a dozen other people of both sexes, who all crowded around Lysandridas, congratulating him and welcoming him home. The men nodded or shook his hand. The younger women gave him hasty kisses on his cheek with a giggle or two of embarrassment. Zoë clung to him so possessively that Dion would have thought she was his mother, if Lysandridas hadn't explained that his mother had died long ago.

Only slowly did it dawn on Dion that these must be the helots that Lysandridas spoke about. Lysandridas had always insisted that the helots of Lacedaemon were different from slaves in the rest of Hellas, but Dion had not believed him—until now. Much as Antyllus' slaves liked and respected him, it was inconceivable that they would have crowded around like this, touching him and joking with him.

"Is that you, Lysandridas?" It was the voice of Apollonides from the balcony above.

Smiling, Lysandridas lifted his face and waved to his grandfather. "Yes, it's me, Grandpa. I'm home."

His grandfather seemed to snort and then made his way slowly and unsteadily down the steps to the terrace. Lysandridas went forward to meet him at the foot of the stairs, still smiling. But as he reached up to help his grandfather down the last steps, his smile froze.

Apollonides was looking at him with cold, narrowed eyes. "You came home?!" the old man croaked. "Without your shield? Without *my* shield? Why? Why do you disgrace me in my old age? Isn't it enough that you let them take it from your living hands? Did you also have to come back and shame me with the sight of you?!"

He was standing one step from the bottom of the stairs, and his head was level with Lysandridas. He lifted his right hand and slapped Lysandridas across the face four times, and then he spit at him. "I only waited here to say that to you! Now I'm leaving!" He turned on Teleklos, standing white and rigid in the middle of the terrace. "I won't stay a single night under the same roof as this *coward* you sired! If you had any honour, you wouldn't have brought him back here to disgrace us in front of all our peers. You should be ashamed of him—and yourself for breeding him!" Apollonides stepped down the last step, shoved past Lysandridas as if he didn't exist, and made his way to the front of the house.

"He has all his things in the donkey cart out front," Zoë whispered to Teleklos; but Teleklos didn't care about his father. He went to Lysandridas, who was still standing where his grandfather had left him, burning red from the blow and his inner agitation.

"Don't take it to heart, Lysandridas. He's old and bigoted and—"

"Don't say any more," Lysandridas warned, his face hot and rigid.

"Please! Don't let him spoil your welcome home, Lysandridas!"

But he already had.

CHAPTER 20

By mid-morning the agora was crowded with merchants from all over Lacedaemon and beyond. The trade routes had reopened a few weeks earlier, and the first shiploads of produce from more distant shores were being offered. These were sold by intrepid merchants who had braved the still uncertain spring weather to claim the higher profits of landing the first cargoes of the season for the markets of Hellas. There were Egyptians with papyrus, Syrians with dates, Persians with rugs, Thracians with amber jewellery, and Ethiopians with ivory. But the units on active duty had morning drill, and it was almost noon before Lysandridas had time to come to the agora.

He came in search of Hermione, and he did not bother to bathe or change. He was not entirely sure what he wanted to say to her, but he wanted to confront her. At the very least, he wanted to make her feel guilty for taking his best friend to her bed while he was wounded and enslaved.

By the time he reached the agora, however, many of the helots with farm produce were already packing up their stalls and preparing to return home. The sun was bright and hot from a cloudless sky, and sensible people—customers and merchants alike—were seeking the shade of the stoa or the cool interior of one building or another. There were hardly any shoppers left.

Lysandridas' eyes swept over the dispersing crowds anxiously, and suddenly his heart leapt. She was there! Plumper and noticeably more 'matronly' than he remembered her, but there could be no doubt that it was she—and still so beautiful that she turned every head. The remaining merchants were nearly falling over themselves in their efforts to attract her attention; and there, in that corner of the agora where Hermione lingered, no one was closing up or fleeing for the shadows.

Lysandridas started for her at once, noting that she was accompanied not only by a helot, who was carrying her purchases, but also a nanny with two small children.

He saw Hermione raise her hand and call out to another young woman, turning her back on him unconsciously as she did so. She stood with her back to him while conversing with an attractive, tall woman in a green striped peplos with cascades of chestnut hair. Lysandridas did not recognise the other woman, and she was not a beauty like Hermione, but Lysandridas noted with approval that her skin was a healthy bronze and the muscles of her arms were firm and shapely. The contrast to the maidens and young matrons of Tegea was sharp, and Lysandridas was reminded of how sickly his intended Tegean bride had looked. At least Sparta's *women* were a reason to come home, he told himself, slowing as he approached.

He could now hear what Hermione was saying, and stopped dead at the sound of his own name. "... he says Lysandridas is being very unreasonable and was angry at him—his best friend! You know how *few* friends Lysandridas has after what he did—"

"What do you mean, 'what he did'?" the other woman challenged belligerently—to Lysandridas' astonishment.

"Well. This whole thing. Being a slave for four years."

"He didn't exactly *choose* that, did he?" the other woman snapped back. Who on earth was she? She was familiar. Very familiar. And yet Lysandridas couldn't place her at all. "It could just as easily have been Thessalos. There were a 197 of them, remember?"

"Yes, but the others came home within months. Only Lysandridas was away *so long*."

"That was hardly his fault, either."

"No, I suppose not," Hermione admitted. "But that's not the point, is it? The fact is, many citizens think his behaviour was dishonourable. He ought to be thankful that Thessalos—a *Guardsman*—is still willing to be his friend."

"Lysandridas was in the Guard," the other woman reminded Hermione, and Lysandridas was grateful to her.

"Yes, but only for a couple of days," Hermione dismissed his status with a toss of her head, adding, "and all because of driving his father's chariot—not because he really *deserved* it. Not like Thessalos. But you won't believe what he said to Thessalos last night! He said he didn't *need* a friend who would steal his bride. Can you fathom that? Calling me his *bride* after all this time!"

"And weren't you?" the young woman croaked out. Lysandridas had the uncanny feeling that she had not only said what he was thinking, but in a tone of voice to match his own feelings.

"His bride? No! Of course not! We were betrothed a couple of days, that's all. There was nothing more to it than that. I was hardly betrothed to him, and already the news came that he was dead. Really, I don't know why people behave as if I should have torn myself apart with grief!" There was a defensive edge in her voice, Lysandridas noted. Apparently this wasn't the first person to criticise Hermione for the speed with which she had married Thessalos. But her answer hurt him all the same, particularly as she continued: "I hardly knew Lysandridas. My father chose him, after all, and it was all so sudden, and just because of his success at Olympia."

The other woman, in evident contempt, turned her back on Hermione without another word and walked away. It was only then—seeing her long, certain strides, flinging the peplos open to reveal her slender, shapely legs—that Lysandridas finally realised who it must be: Leonis.

Hermione, meanwhile, had recovered from her surprise, and with an air of injured pride told her helots and children it was time to go home for lunch. She too hurried away, leaving Lysandridas standing.

He did not consider going after her. Her words had hurt too much to make him feel strong enough to confront her just yet—or perhaps his need to follow Leonis in that moment was greater. She was headed straight for one of the fountain houses and disappeared inside. He hurried after her.

Inside the fountain house, it was cool and dark after the glaring sun. For a moment, Lysandridas was blinded. He sensed more than saw Leonis reach out her hands under the bronze water spout in the shape of a lion's head. She splashed water onto her face and stood for a moment with her face in her hands, as if trying to regain her composure. Then she sensed his presence and spun about in alarm.

For a moment they stared at each other, each absorbing the changes carefully. Lysandridas could feel her eyes upon the scar and dent in his forehead, but then she seemed to take in all the *other* changes as well. Lysandridas knew that he had changed in many ways. The lines in his face were deeper, which made it look more mature, older even than his twenty-six years. His body, by contrast, was still thin, more like a youth than a man. He was acutely aware of his mangled fingernails and scarred knuckles, and that he was sweated and dusty from the drill fields. He was still in leather training armour with leather greaves, and sweat was running down the side of his face from under his crestless training helmet, shoved onto the back of his neck.

Lysandridas soon forgot himself, however, as he took in the changes to his childhood playmate. Gone was the tomboy with cropped hair and skinny limbs. In her place was an attractive woman with bold, green eyes. "Leonis?" he asked, but just to be sure, although it was not really a question.

"Who else?" she quipped back, with a crooked smile.

"Thank you."

"What for?" Her tone was so defensive it was almost belligerent.

"For defending me like that to Hermione."

She sank onto the edge of the basin as she asked in horror, "You overheard us?"

"I came straight from drill to the agora hoping to see her. I rushed over to greet her. Fortunately, she didn't notice."

"I'm so sorry," Leonis whispered.

Lysandridas made an unconvincing gesture of shrugging it off, his eyes averted, and then he focused on Leonis again. "I didn't recognise you at first," he admitted. "I thought Hermione was speaking to a stranger." He paused before adding, "I owe you thanks for all you did for my father and the horses while I was away."

"You don't have to thank me," she remarked wearily. "I wanted to help."

Lysandridas was gazing at her so intently that Leonis started to feel self-conscious. She fussed with her shawl and then fingered her earrings to be sure they hung properly.

"I guess I'd better go get out of these things," Lysandridas remarked, becoming aware of the smell of his own sweat, which made him ashamed of himself—because Leonis was not just a neighbour girl any more, but a lady. So Lysandridas nodded goodbye and fled from Leonis.

That night, however, as he fell asleep, he found himself not only going over the insulting things Hermione had said, but thinking of Leonis as well. He couldn't get over how much she had changed. She had always been an awkward, annoying girl with freckles, a boy's figure, and hair cropped short. Now, when Lysandridas closed his eyes, he pictured the way Leonis had moved across the agora, with the lithe, energy of a racehorse. Even her face was much handsomer than he remembered it. And her eyes! They glittered green and gold under coppery eyebrows. Leonis had the temperament of a racehorse, too, Lysandridas thought smiling. He promised himself he would call on her during the next holiday, then drifted off to sleep and—for the first time in his life—dreamt of Leonis in an erotic way.

But at the next holiday he was assigned to the "watch". Ever since the Messenian rebel Aristomenes had raided the city and slaughtered hundreds of children in the agoge in his great-grandfather's day, the city was never left completely denuded of fighting men. In consequence, even on holidays, when the men on active service were released from duty and had leave to go to their families, a "watch" was always left behind in the city. This was made up of one member from each platoon, a total of 144 men.

When his platoon leader told Lysandridas that he had been selected, he added with a grin, "After all, you haven't been on watch for four years."

Lysandridas wanted to reply, "I haven't been on holiday for four years, either," but he caught himself just in time. He knew he had more to gain by graciously accepting the unpopular duty than by protesting.

The "watch" was always commanded by the man detailed from the 1st Platoon, 1st Company of the Guard. This young Guardsman, who had been selected at the last annual review, greeted Lysandridas with: "You? What am I supposed to do with the likes of *you?*"

"What you would do with any other peer," Lysandridas told him bluntly. The Guardsman made a sneering face and assigned Lysandridas to the sentry post at the back entrance to the Agiad royal stables. It was meant as an insult, and had the added sting of forcing Lysandridas to watch Thessalos as he prepared to drive King Anaxandridas through the city for the sacrifices at the Temple of Athena. Thessalos caught sight of him and lifted his hand in greeting. Lysandridas played sentry and refused to return the greeting.

As Thessalos drove out, however, he stopped the chariot. "These are two of the team we're going to enter at Olympia." He indicated the prancing black colts in the traces. One had a white blaze, but the other had only a star—like Hector. Without thinking, Lysandridas reached out a hand to stroke and calm the near-side horse, who was throwing his head up nervously.

"Why don't you come around one afternoon and look at the whole team?" Thessalos offered Lysandridas the olive branch of reconciliation.

Lysandridas didn't look at him. He patted the colt, and murmured to it. Even if part of him was beginning to realise that Hermione took a greater share of the blame for their "betrayal," he still couldn't forgive Thessalos for taking her away from him. Then again, his hands itched for the reins of a chariot. Thessalos might be a Guardsman, a hero, a husband—but by all the Gods, he was *not* the better driver!

"I'll think about it," Lysandridas told his one-time best friend with a hostile, hard glance that said he had no intention of doing what he said.

Thessalos sighed and retorted, "Suit yourself," before clicking to the horses and driving away.

In the days to follow, Thessalos talked more and more frequently at the syssitia about the team his grandfather would enter at the coming Olympic Games. He enthused about their stamina, strength, and speed. "But best of all," he explained in a tone of delight no one (except Lysandridas) could begrudge him, "is the way they seem to meld into a single animal with a single will when they are hitched together before the chariot." He turned to Lysandridas. "Was your father's team like that?"

"You know it was," Lysandridas snapped, earning a frown from Orsiphantas.

"Do you think they're still up to competition at the 56th Olympics? They lost at Delphi, after all."

"I don't know. I haven't seen them in four years." The bitterness in his voice was so raw that this time that Orsiphantas rapped his knuckles on his table to indicate that both young men should cool off and/or change the subject.

"And Antyllus' team?" Thessalos pressed him, ignoring the warning.

"What about it?" Lysandridas was as tense as a bowstring. He sensed that Thessalos had somehow learned that he had been training Antyllus' team, and he knew that if this information became public knowledge it would make it more difficult than ever for him to be reaccepted into Spartiate society.

"How do you rate it?"

"Good. It won at Delphi, didn't it?"

"It did, yes, but I hear that Antyllus has made some changes in it."

"Oh, really? Where did you hear that?"

"From my grandfather, who heard it from your father. Your father *was* Antyllus' guest this last month, wasn't he?"

"Yes."

"As were you, weren't you?"

"Yes."

They were all staring at him, astonished, suspicious, disbelieving—shocked.

Thessalos didn't take it any further. He waited just a moment and then said in a casual voice, "You must come see our team. You'll be able to judge best whether it has a chance of beating these other teams you know so well."

Nicoles, however, wasn't prepared to leave it at that. "You were Antyllus of Tegea's *guest*, Lysandridas? We were told you were a quarry slave."

Lysandridas realised that his father had been talking. If the story was out to Agis, it was out to his uncles and his brother-in-law, and the helots talked, too, of course. It had been foolish to think it wouldn't get out. There was nothing he could do now but tell the story as his father knew it and hope it satisfied his listeners. "I was—for three years. Then Antyllus bought me. I worked in his stables until my father brought my ransom."

"I see. Not such a bad life after all, it seems, so—"

"I'd be happy to sell you as a stable slave—" Lysandridas started, but Orsiphantas wrapped his knuckles loudly and was supported by the rest of the older members of the syssitia, drowning out Lysandridas' outburst.

"Gentlemen! That is enough!" Orsiphantas declared sternly. Turning to the wide-eyed boys gawking from their post by the kitchen door, he snapped his fingers at them and ordered them to fetch the next course. Unfortunately, he had also drawn attention to them. No sooner were they back with the meat than Nicoles, with a pseudo friendly smile, addressed one of them, "Lichas, tell us what the most important quality in a man is."

"Courage, sir." It was an easy question. Everyone knew the answer.

"And how do we demonstrate courage?"

"By not showing fear," Eurypon, the other little boy on mess duty, hastened to answer, anxious not to be outshone by Lichas.

"Very good," Nicoles smiled at Eurypon, but redirected his attention to Lichas. "Is a courageous man afraid of death?"

"No, sir."

"So what can we conclude about a man who prefers surrender to the enemy over death?"

"Nothing!" The answer was abrupt, rude, and furious. The little boy had gone bright red and his hands were clenched into fists. Too late, Lysandridas remembered that the boy Lichas was son of Euxenos—and Euxenos had not only been in his company in the Guard, but he too had survived to be ransomed.

Nicoles cuffed the boy for his impudence, and the other members of the syssitia were loudly admonishing the boy to remember his manners. If he didn't want to answer a question, he had the right to refuse—but only in a polite tone, and never without the all-important "sir" at the end.

"My father is *not* a coward!" the boy shouted at them all, stubbornly refusing to take their advice to stick to the rules of the syssitia.

"I'm warning you, Lichas!" Orsiphantas called out in his thin, aging voice. "If you don't behave, we will be forced to report you to your eirene."

"Leave the boy alone!" Lysandridas countered.

"Stay out of this! This is not your affair."

"Yes, it is! Nicoles was attacking *me*. Only *he* is such a *coward* that he was using a little boy—"

"After kissing Tegean ass for four years—"

A half-dozen other members raised a roar of protest; and when things had settled down enough for Orsiphantas to make himself heard, both Nicoles and Lysandridas were expelled from the mess for the remainder of the meal. They left together and stood out front in the early dusk, united by smouldering, mutual antipathy.

"You're not going to get away with this," Nicoles warned Lysandridas ominously. "You can't kiss Tegean ass for four years and then come back and pretend you're still a peer. We'll see to it that you pay the price for your treason."

"Who's 'we'?"

"The kryptea," Nicoles hissed with a smile and then walked away, leaving Lysandridas chilled by a cold sweat to the marrow of his bones.

CHAPTER 21

The next day, as soon as he'd washed off the sweat and dust of the drill fields, Lysandridas went in search of Chilon. He'd known his father's friend all his life, and always respected him as a kind, wise, and understanding companion to his father. However, he had never sought him out on his own before, much less in his official capacity of ephor. The five ephors were elected officials who served as administrators between meetings of the Assembly and Council, the former being composed of all adult citizens and the latter of twenty-eight men over sixty, elected for life, and the two kings. The ephors could be elected only once, and only for one year. Chilon had been elected at the last winter solstice.

When Lysandridas learned that Chilon was at the Agiad royal palace, he felt even less comfortable, but after lying awake all night thinking about his situation, Chilon was the only "answer" he had come up with. Rather than waiting for the ephor at his home, Lysandridas went to loiter before the Agiad royal palace.

Of course, he had a dual purpose. He found he couldn't entirely resist Thessalos' offer of looking over the Spartan racing team. After asking the sentries if Chilon was inside and receiving an affirmative answer, he went around to the stables and found, as was to be expected, Thessalos.

Thessalos smiled at him. "I thought you'd give in eventually. Come see them."

Lysandridas went along in stubborn silence, still refusing to be friendly. Thessalos led him to one stall after another, introducing the horses by name and describing their characters. Lysandridas petted them, inspected them, and nodded admiringly. They were a wonderfully matched team, all sons of the same sire, by three different dams. They were young but well filled out and all taller than Hector, who had been rejected by the royal stables as too small.

"I was just about to take them out for a little practice. Why don't you come along?" Thessalos invited.

"I've come to see Chilon, actually," Lysandridas begged off lamely.

"He'll be here for hours!" Thessalos dismissed the objection with a shake of his head and a wave of his hand. "Three of the lochagoi are in there with him, and half the Council. They're planning the campaign against Tegea—or against King Agesikles. I don't know which, but one or the other," Thessalos grinned.

Lysandridas was torn. He had to see Chilon today, before dinner. After all, the kryptea might strike at any time. Of course, it was more likely to do so in the dark or when he was out of the city. But if Chilon was advising King Anaxandridas along with the lochagoi and Council, then probably it would be hours before he came out. What was the point of just hanging about worrying?

Thessalos tossed him a hoof pick. "Get him ready, would you? I'll finish with the others."

Lysandridas couldn't resist, so he soon found himself west of the city at the hippodrome, watching from the stands as Thessalos drove his splendid young team around the track. They were beautiful to watch, in a way the mismatched teams he had raised with his father or trained with Antyllus were not. Thessalos was right, too, about them seeming to melt into a single beast. Yet, was it just jealousy? Lysandridas was convinced that Thessalos wasn't getting the most out of them. He flung his whole body around on the car and didn't really prepare the team for his commands. He was a strong man, more powerfully built than Lysandridas, and he was heavy-handed. He pulled the whole team to the right on the straight and then yanked them over to the left on the curves, rather than oozing them left and right.

At the end of the training session, Lysandridas was deeply depressed by the thought that Thessalos would go to Olympia. If he won, it would be because of the horses, and if he lost, because of his driving. Much depended on what driver Antyllus found. His team wasn't as strong as this one, but it was very willing, and all four of the horses would break their hearts trying—for the right driver. It depressed him that it wouldn't be him. It depressed him that he wouldn't be given a chance with *either* of these splendid teams. He would probably never drive a chariot in competition again, he told himself gloomily. If the kryptea had its way, he wouldn't live to even *see* another Olympics.

Thessalos pulled up, grinning and wiping sweat from his forehead with the back of his arm. "Well? What do you think of them?"

"They're the best team of horses I've ever seen," Lysandridas told him honestly.

"So why do you look so glum? You can't want Tegea or Corinth to win?"

"No. I just wish I were going to drive them at Olympia."

Thessalos laughed, taken aback by the honesty; but then he said seriously, "if something happens to me, you can be sure my granddad will give you the reins."

"Thanks. I'd better go find Chilon."

At the royal palace, Lysandridas was told that Chilon was already gone, so he went back to Chilon's house and at last caught up with him. Chilon greeted him warmly, holding out his hands and then giving him a firm hug. He looked much younger than Teleklos, younger than his sixty years. His hair was abundant, unlike Teleklos'. It was salted with grey like Antyllus', but on Chilon the grey hardly showed against the natural dark-blond hair. His shoulders might have lost much of their muscle over the years, but they were still firm and square. His face was lined, but the crevices gave it a permanently friendly expression. The grip of his hand was firm. "What a pleasure to see you again, young man! Frankly, I never really thought I would—not until the day your father sent word that he'd found you. I only pretended to hope for your father's sake. He was the only one who wouldn't give up hope."

"It was my own fault, sir. If I hadn't been so vain, my name would have been on the list."

Chilon was surprised by the insight and honesty, and he looked at Lysandridas more closely. He had known Lysandridas from the day he was born. Chilon had been the one to take the infant Lysandridas to the Council to show he was in perfect health and register him as a Spartiate citizen, because Teleklos had been in such grief over his wife that he had refused to perform this duty. "They can throw it off the cliff, for all I care," Teleklos had told his friend at the time.

Chilon had been the one to consult with Zoë about the boy's progress in his early years when his father insisted on ignoring him. Chilon had been pleased to see how he had grown into his father's greatest pride and joy as the years went on. But Chilon had sons and grandsons of his own, and he had served as Paidonomos, head master of the agoge. He was not as uncritical of Lysandridas as his father. He liked Lysandridas, but it had not escaped his notice that Lysandridas had been somewhat one-sided in his obsession with horses and too full of himself after driving his father's chariot to victory at Olympia.

Chilon didn't blame him for that. He didn't know a man alive who could win an Olympic victory without it going to his head, at least for a little while. At twenty-two, it was particularly heady stuff. No, he never held it against Lysandridas that he had been so convinced of his own superiority and invincibility after the last Games, but he had worried that the Gods would disapprove. And they had. They had punished him severely for his little burst of self-deification. More harshly than he really deserved. And now here he stood, and he didn't blame the Gods at all, but himself. That showed a degree of maturity and honesty that Chilon had not expected in the twenty-six-year-old. It was missing in many men of sixty, he reflected—not least in King Agesikles!

"Sir, I need your—help," Lysandridas admitted, uncomfortable under Chilon's scrutiny.

"Whatever I can do," Chilon answered with disarming simplicity.

"Sir, my father will have told you where he found me—and in what condition."

"Yes, you were very lucky. We were very lucky. If it weren't for Antyllus, you might never have come home, as I understand it."

"That's right, sir. I wanted to die, and eventually I would have succeeded, one way or another. But, the kryptea ..." Lysandridas started in a low, tight voice. "The kryptea considers my actions treasonous."

Chilon raised a hand to stop him from going any further. They were still standing out in the courtyard where Chilon had come to greet him. The cook was collecting rosemary for dinner from the blooming plants beside the kitchen, two maids were chattering while hanging up laundry, and one of Chilon's granddaughters was playing with a half-grown cat. He signalled for Lysandridas to come with him.

Chilon led Lysandridas not into the dim, cool, empty andron that would have echoed, but up the wooden stairs to his own chamber and out onto a small wooden balcony. The balcony was cramped with a mosaic table and two chairs, but was enclosed with window boxes overflowing with blooming flowers. Chilon indicated that Lysandridas should sit down, and then fetched watered wine, which he poured for them both from an unglazed pitcher. He sat down opposite Lysandridas and, giving the young man his full attention, nodded for him to speak.

Lysandridas told him everything. Not just that he'd been purchased by Antyllus, but that he had been freed, adopted, and betrothed. He admitted that despite refusing to fight for Tegea, he had been helping train their cavalry. Chilon listened attentively, only asking occasional questions. Lysandridas tried to explain himself as he narrated what had happened. He stressed that he had done everything on the assumption that his father had rejected him. He had given up all hope of returning home, of ever seeing Lacedaemon again. "I would never have done any of it, if I'd thought I had any chance of ever coming home—"

"Of course not," Chilon soothed him as he started to repeat himself. He paused and then asked cautiously, "Does your father know what you did?"

"How could I admit to him that I'd let another man adopt me while he lived!?" Lysandridas protested emotionally.

"It was just a question. Your father does not know about the adoption, the betrothal—or your services to the Tegean cavalry?"

"No, sir; only that I was driving Antyllus' racing team."

"Yes, that was mentioned." Chilon's eyes glinted with amusement. "I gather they are pretty good?"

"Yes, sir."

Chilon laughed out loud, remarking, "You never could resist a good team. But then, what young man with a gift at the reins can?" To himself, Chilon was registering that Lysandridas had for the last three months moved in the very heights of Tegean society—and he couldn't help thinking that this might prove to be a wonderful asset.

"My father isn't the problem, sir," Lysandridas said slowly and deliberately. "It's the kryptea...."

"The kryptea has no right or authority to pass judgment, much less sentence, on any citizen!" Chilon retorted quickly, instantly agitated. He was a vehement opponent of the kryptea precisely because it often acted as if it were above the law. He added in a calmer tone, "Only the Assembly can pass judgment on a citizen."

"I think their reasoning is that I sacrificed my citizenship at surrender, or at the latest when I started training Antyllus' team. If they learned the rest—that I allowed myself to be adopted and train the Tegean cavalry—they would have no doubt whatever. You know the kryptea acts without instructions, if it wants to. Once I'm dead, the protests of the Assembly—if there are any—won't matter much." This was said in a low, depressed voice.

"The protests of the Assembly matter a great deal," Chilon countered energetically. "Don't forget, the Assembly can take away the citizenship of any citizen—including the members of the kryptea. It can exile them or sentence them to death. Don't think the kryptea is not afraid of the consequences of their actions. If they had reason to believe the Assembly would censure them severely, it would stay their hand." Chilon paused to let this sink in, and Lysandridas started breathing a little easier—until Chilon continued soberly, "Your problem is that if the whole truth came out, it is unlikely you'd find the sympathy of the majority in the Assembly."

Lysandridas dropped his head for a moment in despair, but then he looked up and straight at Chilon. "Do *you* think I'm a traitor?"

"No. I don't think under the circumstances that your actions were treasonous. Maybe ill-advised, but not treasonous. Lysandridas, you were in an unprecedented, extremely difficult situation. None of us—much less any member of the kryptea—can know how we would have acted in the same situation. You responded as a healthy, intelligent man *should* to adversity: by trying to find the best way out. I've always said that what distinguishes a man of breeding and character from the common riff-raff is the ability to hope, even in a dismal situation. You demonstrated the quality of your upbringing by *not* losing hope, by continuing to struggle. The issue is: where do you go from here?"

Lysandridas gazed at the older man, uncomprehending. "What do you mean? Surely you know I will do everything I can to be a good citizen from this day forward. I will go to war against Tegea if I'm ordered to. What more can I do but be a good and loyal citizen?"

Chilon seemed to accept this question as rhetorical and smiled a little absently, nodding and gazing out over the flowers to the street below. Then he turned his attention back to Lysandridas, who sat tensely opposite him, and asked in a relaxed, casual tone, "Tell me something, Lysandridas. Did you by any chance meet the Tegean tyrant, Harmatides?"

Lysandridas answered without thinking. "Yes, sir, I knew him quite well. In fact …" He cut himself short.

Chilon cocked his head and raised his eyebrows, waiting for him to finish what he had started.

"I met him several times, sir."

"And what about the other men of influence and power in the Tegean government?"

Lysandridas couldn't hold out against Chilon's look of expectation, and admitted, "Antyllus sometimes included me in his symposia—but only those where no politics was discussed. Ambelos, however—"

"Who is Ambelos?

"Ambelos is Harmatides' son."

"And you knew him?"

"He asked Antyllus to teach him to ride, and Antyllus delegated me— while I was still a slave. But ..."

"Yes?"

"Ambelos is a youth, sir, just eighteen. He was thrilled to know an Olympic charioteer. He treated me more like an elder brother than anything else."

"Which means?" Chilon could not disguise his own interest. He had leaned forward, and was literally sitting on the edge of his chair.

Lysandridas was aware he was sinking deeper and deeper into a quagmire. He tried to shrug and make it sound innocent. "He liked showing me his city. He liked telling me about it. I learned a great deal from him."

"You're saying that you knew Harmatides and others in the Tegean government—at least indirectly." Chilon wanted to be absolutely sure he had the facts right.

Lysandridas nodded with a sense of gathering doom. Chilon clearly expected him to reveal military secrets—or at least information that could be used to Sparta's military advantage. He would soon be forced to choose between his life or his oath.

"That makes you an invaluable source of information." Chilon put his thoughts into words.

In a last desperate attempt to save himself, Lysandridas admitted, "Sir, I swore an oath not to betray Tegea's military secrets to Sparta. If I hadn't, Harmatides wouldn't have let me leave. He would have had me arrested or killed."

To Lysandridas utter amazement, Chilon wasn't the least bit shocked. On the contrary, he remarked reasonably, "That's understandable. We would have done the same, if the roles were reversed. Indeed, the kryptea would probably have just eliminated any Tegean who posed the same kind of threat as you undoubtedly do to Tegea. It was, when you think about it, incredibly naive of Harmatides to accept your oath and let you walk away."

They stared at one another.

236 The Olympic Charioteer

"I intend to keep my oath," Lysandridas said steadily and slowly.

Chilon stared back for a long time before saying in a low, deliberate voice, "Think carefully about the consequences."

"Do you mean that you want me to break an oath I took on the altar of Zeus?"

"Not exactly," Chilon demurred, not entirely displeased with Lysandridas' response. He was beginning to like the young man more and more. As for the oath, Chilon was a pious man. He did not think an oath was something to be taken lightly, but he believed that the Gods were with them constantly. "Zeus knows under what circumstances you made that oath. If you were under duress, he will forgive you for breaking it."

"I wasn't being tortured, if that's what you mean," Lysandridas snapped back bitterly.

"No." Chilon considered Lysandridas, and the young man gazed back at him resentfully. "But he knew it was the price you had to pay to come home."

Lysandridas looked down, his face flushed.

Chilon considered him for a moment and recognised an opportunity. "More to the point, we're talking about the meaning of an oath. You promised not to betray Tegean military secrets, but you just said to me you would take up arms against Tegea if we go to war."

"Of course."

"So you are not saying you swore to put Tegean interests first."

"No, of course not!"

"And what if there were a way to serve the interests of both Tegea and Lacedaemon?"

"I don't understand, sir."

Chilon replied in a leisurely, explanatory tone, "Spartiate society is much divided just now. We are in the midst of our most serious domestic crisis since the Second Messenian War. King Agesikles is doing his best to renew hostilities with Tegea. If he has his way, we will attack Tegea within the month. Fortunately, King Anaxandridas is not supporting him—at the moment. As long as the kings remain deadlocked, we can avoid war.

"But Anaxandridas is a young man, and the shame of his defeat four years ago sits deep. He'd like to expunge it with a victory. He was very close to supporting a new campaign. Fortunately, the kryptea got itself bloodied in its attempt—instigated by Agesikles—to provoke new hostilities. That unnerved Anaxandridas again, and made him back off from a quick, early campaign for fear of a second defeat. If, however, he had some reason to believe success is certain, or near certain, he would join Agesikles instantly.

In which case, we will only be able to prevent the war by deposing the kings altogether and introducing absolute democracy."

Lysandridas was shocked to hear Chilon talk so openly of a coup against the kings. He gazed at his father's friend with a mixture of awe and shock.

"For a man who has been less than 100% orthodox in his interpretation of the duties of citizenship, I expected more understanding," Chilon pointed out dryly.

Lysandridas caught his breath and swallowed hard. "Yes, sir." He looked down, embarrassed, and then back up at Chilon questioningly.

Chilon looked amused. Lysandridas relaxed a little.

"I don't want to do violence to Lycurgus' laws any more than you do," Chilon resumed the discussion in a relaxed tone, "which is why I and three of the five lochagoi—including your own—are trying to find a basis for a negotiated settlement. Surely peace would be in the interests of both cities?" Chilon suggested.

"Yes, sir! Very much so!" Lysandridas agreed eagerly; there was nothing he wanted more than to be freed of his conflicting loyalties.

"Well, to secure peace we have to find some solution that allows both kings to feel they have achieved something more than the status quo ante. But it has to be something that the Tegeans, too, can accept."

Lysandridas nodded. He understood the concept, but he couldn't picture any concrete solution that would meet these criteria.

Chilon continued, "Don't you see that the more information we have about the way Harmatides thinks, his motives and his weaknesses, the easier it will be to negotiate with him—or outmanoeuvre him? There is, as I understand it, a peace faction in Tegea as well. If we could establish contact to Onimastros, for example—"

"Onimastros? He's—" Lysandridas cut himself off, confused. Was it a military secret to admit that Onimastros was a more bitter opponent of Lacedaemon than Harmatides?

"What?" Chilon asked gently.

Lysandridas' feelings of loyalty were to Antyllus, Ambelos, and, indirectly, Ambelos' father—not to the cold-blooded, intrigue-loving Onimastros. "Onimastros hates Sparta, and he profits more than the rest of them from the war. He supplies the army and makes a huge profit from it. Harmatides, in contrast, admires us to a great extent. And he cares about his troops. He does not want excessive casualties. Onimastros doesn't care about the costs of war at all."

Chilon was silent for a long time, while Lysandridas sat opposite him feeling guilty for having said so much. At last Chilon said slowly, "That's very useful information, Lysandridas. It's the kind of information that could help me end this war. Furthermore, you have just prevented me from making a serious mistake. I had planned to send a secret embassy to Onimastros. He came to us last fall begging for assurances of peace and warning that if we couldn't give them to him, there was a risk of Harmatides seizing power and making himself tyrant. He seemed to sincerely want peace—and his prediction came true. I thought he was the leader of the peace faction in Tegea."

"No." Lysandridas was still feeling guilty for what he already said, and he couldn't bring himself to say any more.

"*Is* there a peace faction in Tegea?" Chilon pressed him.

"Yes."

"Who is the leader of it?"

Lysandridas clamed up. His lips were pressed together and his eyes were blank. It was an expression Antyllus would have recognised. Chilon took a deep breath and poured himself more wine, but didn't drink it. He respected Lysandridas for trying to keep his oath, but he was convinced of the utility of Lysandridas' information. It frightened him that he had come very close to making a fatal error: trusting the wrong faction. His approaches would have resulted in his own humiliation. He was grateful to the Gods for having sent Lysandridas home with this vital information about Onimastros at the right moment. There could be little doubt that Lysandridas had other information that would be of untold value. Chilon realised that he had to convince Lysandridas to reveal everything he knew about Tegea without feeling as if he were perjuring himself. Chilon sipped his wine and then laughed aloud.

Lysandridas looked at him uneasily and puzzled.

"I was just laughing at myself." This was true, he had been laughing at his own impatience, but he explained himself to Lysandridas differently. "You came here asking my help—and ended up helping me instead. Anything more you want to tell me, I'd be glad to hear. But I want it to be voluntary and in good conscience. With regard to the kryptea, I suggest you talk to your brother-in-law. He's an officer now, you know, and he may be able to prevent any action against you—provided he's convinced of your loyalty. For my part, I will mention to the Council that you have been threatened by the kryptea—I presume that's why you're here?"

"Yes, sir."

"I'll suggest that it would be wise to warn the officers of the kryptea that if anything happens to you they will be held responsible for a serious crime. I can't guarantee anything, of course, and you'd be wise to be cautious. Avoid moving around alone at night. Avoiding hunting. Sleep only in the barracks or at your kleros."

"Thank you, sir." Lysandridas got to his feet, suddenly aware of how late it was. The pipes would be calling the men to dinner any time.

Chilon also got to his feet and led his guest back downstairs to the courtyard of his house. There he paused and laid his hand on Lysandridas' arm. "Remember, you did not choose the situation you are in, but you can choose how you deal with it."

Lysandridas left feeling less frightened, but more unsettled, than when he arrived.

Chilon lost no time. On his way to dinner, he intercepted one of the Council members known to be closest to King Agesikles. He informed him that Lysandridas had invaluable information about Tegean politics and politicians. "If the kryptea—as I have reason to suspect—harms Lysandridas, we'll lose the best source of inside information we could want."

The man looked astonished and then greedy. "We must interrogate him at once!"

"Do you seriously think you'll be able to draw more information out of him than his father or I? Don't be a fool. But you can tell Alkemenes from me that if the kryptea lays a hand on Lysandridas, I will personally demand the death sentence and see that the Assembly votes it. I can deliver that, and you know it. And then—" he paused and said even more deliberately and confidentially, "I will see that the kryptea itself is disbanded and prohibited. It has done more than enough damage to this city already!"

He did not wait for an answer, but continued on to his syssitia. He was feeling not only confident that Lysandridas was safe in the short term, but that the prospects for peace had never been better—provided he could get Lysandridas to talk before King Agesikles or the kryptea decided they should try to *make* him talk.

CHAPTER 22

At the feast of Artemis Orthia, the matrons of Sparta baked little cheesecakes to be laid upon the altar of the Goddess. Then, while the sixteen-year-old youths from the agoge defended the temple armed only with sticks, the fifteen-year-olds had to try to steal as many cheeses as possible. The origins of this strange, uniquely Spartan ritual were vague, but it was generally agreed that the ritual represented the re-enactment of some ancient battle. How this re-enactment had evolved into a mock battle between the sixteen-year-olds and the fifteen-year-olds, no one seemed to know any more. Nor was it clear how, over the generations, the objective had shifted away from the defence of the cheeses to a contest among the raiding fifteen-year-olds for the honour of stealing the most. Nowadays, however, a boy who did not brave the gauntlet even once was disgraced, and the boy who ran the gauntlet most frequently to bring back the largest number of cheeses was honoured for the rest of his life. Because the youths were proving themselves before the Peers, it was more or less obligatory for the Peers to attend.

Lysandridas came directly from the barracks with the rest of his platoon; but when they arrived at the temple, they dispersed in the crowd, each man looking for family or sweetheart. Lysandridas found himself alone in the multitude, and then he caught sight of Thessalos with Hermione on his arm. The sight of them together reawakened all his jealousy and resentment. He tried to turn away, but Thessalos had already seen him. "Lysandridas!" he called out, waving.

Resentfully, Lysandridas walked stiffly over to stand before the happy couple, nodding a greeting and avoiding Hermione's eyes. Hermione clung to Thessalos' arm and stared up at Lysandridas' face with wide blue eyes. He felt her staring at his scar. "My brother-in-law is among the defenders today," Thessalos reminded Lysandridas; "that's why we want to be right up front. Could you hold my place while I go fetch my mother-in-law?" Thessalos was already disengaging from Hermione's arm and slipping back through the crowds.

"You're looking much better than I expected," Hermione ventured when they were alone. She smiled up at him from under her bright blue eyes, a smile that usually melted men's hearts and loins.

"Thanks." Lysandridas avoided looking at her, pretending to be completely fascinated by the preparations going on before the temple.

"You know I *am* very happy that you are home safe," Hermione insisted, the smile replaced by a wounded look.

"Really? One would never have guessed," Lysandridas snapped back.

"That's not fair!" Hermione cried out. "I've asked Thessalos to invite you over more than once—but you refuse to come."

This was true; but Lysandridas was not about to defend himself, and so just shrugged in answer.

"What did you expect me to do?!" Hermione was forced to ask. "If you'd been on the list, I would have waited, no matter how long it took to raise the money. My father would even have contributed to your ransom! But we thought you were dead! Should I have waited for a dead man to return?"

"No, I don't blame you for remarrying," Lysandridas was provoked into answering; "only for doing it so soon!"

Suddenly her voice was a low hissing, too low for the others to hear. "You didn't leave me any choice, did you?"

Lysandridas started and stared at her squarely for the first time.

She met his eyes, her own flashing with anger. "After what you did to me before you left, I couldn't risk waiting." She spoke so softly he wasn't even sure he heard her correctly. Lysandridas looked so stunned that Hermione mocked him bitterly, "Did you never think about it? Not even once?"

Lysandridas was still stunned. "Do you mean? Your daughter—"

"No! Of course not! Don't dare even think it! But it might have been, mightn't it? I couldn't risk it, not when you were presumed dead."

Lysandridas didn't have an answer. His brain was registering that not only had his extended slavery been his own fault, but the "betrayal" of his bride as well. If he hadn't—in his triumphal mood after his Olympic victory—insisted on that night together, Hermione would have been free to at least mourn him. There were widows and maidens who had mourned ever since the battle, but he had put Hermione in a situation where she *had* to take another man to her bed as soon as possible. The thought dizzied him.

Thessalos returned with his mother-in-law, and Lysandridas was forced to exchange pleasantries with this woman, who had nearly been his own mother-in-law. She was kindly and seemed genuinely pleased to see him. She took his hand in both of hers and looked up at him earnestly. "We were so delighted to hear you had been found. I don't understand why you weren't on the list with the others, but that doesn't matter now. You must stop around some afternoon."

Lysandridas assured her he would, and on the pretext of going to look for Teleklos, he slipped away. In fact, he had no particular desire to find his father just yet. He needed time to think and absorb the implications of what Hermione had just said. He worked his way toward the edge of the crowd near the riverbank.

Behind him the sixteen-year-olds took up their positions on the steps of the temple. Armed with thick, long sticks, they formed a single aisle through which the fifteen-year-olds had to run up the steps, into the temple, and back out again. The fifteen -year-olds were completely naked and bareheaded. Their lean, adolescent bodies were tanned, their feet dirty, their faces often marred by acne. They rushed forward in a group with a shout and surged up the steps, bowing their backs and protecting their heads with their arms from the wild, enthusiastic blows of their seniors.

The beginning was always like this: wild, loud, exuberant. All the boys got up into the temple and quickly surged out again, through the gauntlet of blows a second time. The cheeses they had retrieved were turned over to their eirenes, who kept count for each member of their respective units. The boys turned around and made a second attempt. In a short time, however, the group lost cohesion. The slower boys lagged behind; the less willing lingered longer in the safety of the Temple or "out of bounds" by the tables. One or another even stopped trying to compete altogether and hung back, trying not to draw attention to himself. The most ambitious, however, ran again and again through the gauntlet.

Lysandridas wasn't really watching the ritual. Instead he was seized by an oppressive sense of worthlessness. He was to blame for his situation, but he couldn't change what he had done in the past. Chilon said that the issue was what he made of his future. But what *could* he make of it? He did his best to be like the others. His muscles ached from the drill. But it would never change the minds of Nicoles or Derykleides—or his grandfather. To them he would always be a traitor and a slave. Suddenly he was homesick for Antyllus and Ambelos. He wished he could have a racing team in his hands again, and spend his days at leisure, his nights away from the perpetual noise and smells of the barracks. It was easy to forget that in Tegea he hadn't really been accepted, either. Today Tegea seemed gentle and beautiful and benign.

"How are you doing?" Chilon asked, and Lysandridas started. He had not noticed the older man come up beside him.

"Fine, sir." He could hardly confess his thoughts here in public. He changed the subject. "Your peace efforts seem to have been successful."

"Is that what you call it?" Chilon lifted the corners of his lips, but his eyes were very sober; for the first time, he looked old to Lysandridas. "You don't seem to realise how precarious things are," he added, his eyes focused on the river. "I honestly don't think we're going to prevent a new campaign...."

Lysandridas felt his stomach tighten. War against Tegea was the worst thing he could imagine. It meant a repeat of the nightmare that had ended in chains and humiliation—and it meant war against men he now knew, respected, and liked. There had to be some way to stop it. "Can I help?"

Chilon snapped his head back to look straight at Lysandridas. The young man held his gaze. Still, Chilon spoke cautiously. "It would be a great help if you would tell me who heads the Tegean peace faction. We have to establish some kind of communication with them. We have to know what kind of compromise we could make that could prevent all-out war."

"You can approach Antyllus. He may not be the leader of the peace faction, but he belongs to it. He knows the others, and he has influence. If he says they should listen to you, they will."

"Good." Chilon waited. He wanted Lysandridas to give his information voluntarily.

"You—could—also send a message to Ambelos."

Chilon raised his eyebrows.

"He was born with a club foot. His father is very protective of him. His father would do almost anything for him. Ambelos is very intelligent and observant and sensitive. He does not approve of everything his father has done, and—more important—he refuses to believe his father is evil or greedy or ambitious. He thinks his father does everything for the good of Tegea."

"Then surely any message we send to this Ambelos will get to his father," Chilon objected.

"Of course; but Harmatides is more likely to believe it if it goes via Ambelos. Send the following message from me: 'We can stop cavalry.'"

"What?" Chilon was so startled by the blatant betrayal of Spartan military capabilities to the enemy that he couldn't believe his ears.

"For the last four weeks—ever since I arrived back—we've trained every day for it. I don't know that we can *really* stop cavalry—but we're one hell of a lot better prepared than we were four years ago. I think we might well stop them."

"And you want to warn the Tegeans?" Chilon asked, still finding it hard to believe what he was hearing.

"You need to give them a reason to want peace. They beat us last time. They think they can win again—at least the rabble does, and Onimastros. Outside the peace faction, Harmatides is the only one who's not sure about it. This summer Ambelos will be in the cavalry—at risk."

Chilon thought very carefully about what Lysandridas had said, and he was impressed. He had not expected so much subtlety from Lysandridas. The Lysandridas he remembered from before would not have thought like this. He had underestimated the young man.

Chilon's dilemma up to now was that he knew that Lacedaemon had to re-establish its reputation at arms or it would be vulnerable to aggression from its enemies, particularly Argos. At the same time, he was afraid that military success would go to Anaxandridas' head and convince him they had nothing to fear by attacking Tegea again. He had become convinced that what they needed was another *indecisive* encounter—like that of this past winter—that would frighten both sides. His problem had been how to "organise" an indecisive skirmish without risking victory, defeat, or excessive casualties. At least Lysandridas' message offered an alternative. If his message—just possibly—gave the Tegeans pause without actually risking a bloody confrontation with uncertain outcome, and if the Tegeans made an overture, maybe …

The cheers behind them indicated a victor had been established. Chilon, as ephor, had a role to play in the ceremonies that followed. He had to return to the temple. He laid his hand on Lysandridas' shoulder. "Thank you."

Lysandridas shrugged in confusion and let Chilon return alone to the crowd. He stayed where he was, staring at the river, hoping he had done the right thing. If he couldn't return to Tegea, the least he could do, surely, was prevent a new war?

"Lysandridas! There you are!" Teleklos called from behind him. "What are you doing here? Come, the procession is forming!"

Lysandridas took a deep breath. "I'd rather just go home. Do you mind? For the first time since I've been here, I *don't* have the watch!" His tone was bitter and it was a good thing no one overheard them.

"Home?" Teleklos looked blank for a moment, but then he recovered. "Whatever you want. I'll just go find Leonis and see if she wants to stay or return with us. The donkey cart is over there. Can you get it ready?"

Lysandridas had everything ready by the time his father returned. To his relief, Leonis was with him. He smiled at her. "I was hoping you'd come. I was thinking, we could go for a ride up to the Horse Grave—if you like." He added the latter a little hesitantly—unsure if this new Leonis, the woman who was so elegant and feminine, would be willing to ride. Even in Sparta it was not considered proper for women to ride—only girls. But Lysandridas wanted to get away from the city, away from all the disapproving crowds, and the Horse Grave was one of his favourite places, high up on the road to Arcadia.

"I—I'd need to change," Leonis stammered, taken by surprise.

"That won't take long, will it?" Lysandridas replied, confused by a response that seemed so unimportant.

In the stables, Teleklos watched while Lysandridas finished grooming Afra. He had already groomed and tacked the mare Leonis liked best. Lysandridas had removed his bronze breastplate and greaves and was wearing only his scarlet chiton. The shadow in the door attracted their attention, and both men looked over as Leonis entered.

She was dressed for riding in a short chiton, like a youth, with sandals on her feet. Her slender legs were exposed from the knee down, and her hair was pulled back in a ponytail. The elegance was gone—and in its place, something more dangerously erotic. Lysandridas was startled and then embarrassed. He turned his back on Leonis to brush the last pieces of straw from Afra's tail, because he found Leonis so attractive that he could not control the quickening in his loins. For the first time in his life, he felt uncertain of her. Could she really still find him attractive with his emaciated body and scarred face?

Leonis led her mare out of the stables, and Teleklos gave her a leg up. "Zoë's packing a lunch for you," Teleklos informed them. "You can stop by the house and collect it."

Lysandridas emerged with Afra and flung himself nimbly onto her back. They set off together without further ado, stopped by the house where Zoë handed a leather satchel up to Lysandridas, and he slipped the strap over his head and carried it on his back like a shield. They continued.

The road wound along the first outposts of the Taygetos, which stretched like fingers into the valley. They were climbing almost imperceptibly but steadily. The two horses were eager and soon sweating. They met no one on the road. Even the villages seemed deserted. Apparently everyone was in town for the festival.

Beyond the second little village, they turned off the road and started up a steep, rocky path that zigzagged up the slope. They rode for some time through forests of oak and maple, yew and myrtle, with occasional flowering chestnut, wild fig, and almond trees. Abruptly they came to an open meadow, green with tall grass and littered with wildflowers blowing in the refreshing breeze.

At first glance the red of the poppies dominated, but at closer inspection the field was also growing blue larkspur, purple field gladiolus, two-toned globularia, and many other flowers Lysandridas could not identify. He jumped down and started leading Afra toward the sanctuary standing in a semicircle of cypress trees at the far side of the meadow. The flowers came up to his thigh and the bees hummed as he waded through the meadow.

Lysandridas glanced over at Leonis. Her face was flushed from the ride, and strands of hair that had escaped from her ponytail blew in the wind. The grasses came to her waist, obscuring her naked legs. It was strangely wonderful to have her beside him. Strange—because she was at once familiar and completely mysterious. He could remember at least a half-dozen times they had been here together as children and adolescents. More often than not, she had tagged along unwanted, and he and Thessalos had done their best to shake her off or ignore her. Lysandridas smiled at her now. "You can still ride as you used to."

"So can you," she quipped back with a toss of her head.

He laughed.

They continued in silence for a moment, both acutely aware that they were separated by a vast gorge although their bodies almost touched. To bridge that gorge they had to explore what separated them: the past four years of their lives. Lysandridas knew what the problem was, but he didn't know where to begin. It was Leonis who made the first tentative step to close the gap.

"Teleklos said you were living with the horse breeder Antyllus in Tegea. What was he like?"

"Antyllus?" Lysandridas was surprised by the question at first, and then realized it was as good a place to start as any other. "Antyllus is a refined, educated man. He is thoughtful—sometimes too thoughtful for his own good. Above all, he's kind. When he bought me, he had no idea who I was. All he saw was a slave who was being beaten for being sick. He bought me in a casual gesture of kindness—never thinking there would be any benefit for himself." And in the end there wasn't, Lysandridas reflected with a sense of guilt.

Leonis held her breath. It hurt her to hear Lysandridas talking about himself as property that could be bought and sold. She wasn't used to it. After all, even the helots couldn't be bought and sold. "And when he found out who you were, he exempted you from every other kind of work? Let you do nothing but train his racing team?"

Lysandridas hesitated for several minutes, unsure if he should tell Leonis the whole truth or leave the story the way his father knew it. They had reached the little creek that plunged down the mountainside, separating the meadow from the sanctuary of the Horse Grave. Both horses stretched out their necks and started slurping up the water with loud, sucking noises, their necks working visibly. Lysandridas stroked Afra. "Antyllus offered me my freedom at once—when he found out."

Leonis' intake of breath was audible, and she looked at him, astonished. He did not dare look at her. "When he offered it to me, I thought my father had refused to pay my ransom. I thought he knew I was alive and didn't want me. I couldn't imagine going home and facing him. Can you understand that?" At last he looked over at her.

Leonis gazed at him in utter disbelief. "How could you think *Teleklos* would reject you?"

"Because everyone had been ransomed but me, and I knew from Antyllus that Teleklos was still alive and even racing the team. What else was I to think?" His tone was defensive.

Leonis, who had been a witness to Teleklos' grief and then his desperation to ransom Lysandridas, at first couldn't understand; but the more she thought about it, she knew that Lysandridas was right. Even Teleklos had been most tortured by the thought that Lysandridas would *blame* him for not being clever enough to recognize his pseudonym. So she did not argue, but replied: "But you know the truth now. You're glad to be home, aren't you?"

"Most of the time," Lysandridas replied honestly, stroking Afra.

Leonis was horrified. "You mean, there are times when you aren't glad? When you would rather be back in Tegea?"

"Yes, when my grandfather crosses to the other side of the street to avoid greeting me; when I watch Thessalos mishandling that magnificent team of his grandfather's—or when Nicoles smirks at me and reminds me, 'They won't let me get away with it.' Then, I wish I were back in Tegea driving Antyllus' team."

Leonis was hurt. She looked down, and Lysandridas—glancing over— could see the sadness in her face. He reached out and touched her cheek with the back of his hand. It was the first time he had touched her since his return, and it was like an electric shock. She looked up sharply, flushing. "Don't be sad," he urged her. "Come on, let's make a sacrifice and then have something to eat."

He leapt over the little brook and only after taking a stride, thought that he ought to offer Leonis assistance. But she had not waited for it and had already jumped the little brook on her own. That pleased him, and he smiled at her.

They hobbled the horses and let them graze. Before the little Doric temple a limestone altar stood, naked and washed by the rains. Lysandridas took the satchel off his back, opened the drawstrings, and found the apples Zoë packed. He laid these on the altar and then, opening the wineskin, he poured wine into the scooped-out bowl in the altar as well. Then they entered the low temple together.

Inside it was very dark. There were no windows, and the walls had been painted generations ago. Still, there was a fine bronze of a horse that Lysandridas had always loved. The horse stood with his ears out straight and with one foot forward. His wide nostrils seemed to sense the presence of a visitor, and his mane stood up stiff and proud. "What a waste," Lysandridas remarked.

"What?"

"Sacrificing a horse to get Helen's suitors to swear to help one another. If they'd spared the horse, they could have saved themselves the whole Trojan War."

Leonis laughed. She'd been raised to see war as a good thing.

They left the sanctuary and sat down on the steps in the swaying, unsteady shade of the cypress tree. They sat facing the sunlit field of waving wildflowers. Leonis pulled her chiton down over her knees and wrapped her arms around her knees, holding it in place—evidently embarrassed with her own attire.

"Why didn't you marry, Leonis?"

"Marry?" Her heart stopped.

"Yes," he pressed her, looking at her hard, devouring the sight of her healthy, well-proportioned body and the well-shaped bones under the flushed skin.

"Don't you know?" She did not look at him as she spoke, but sat with her chin on her knees, gazing at the waving flowers. "When I was a young maiden, I told my father I would only marry the man who could beat me in a race."

Lysandridas laughed. "That was because you thought none of us ever could! Surely you've outgrown that phase?" He glanced at her sidelong, realizing that he hoped she had.

Her face was rigid, and she didn't dare look at him. She just stared at the field of flowers. "No; it's because I thought *you* were the only one who could beat me."

Lysandridas looked so astonished that she felt compelled to explain herself. "When I was a little girl, I never questioned that we would marry. It seemed so self-evident that I never gave it any thought at all. Only when I started to notice how you ogled and gawked at Hermione did I start to doubt. But even then I told myself that Hermione would never choose you out of all the young men pursuing her. After all, you *all* gawked and ogled her, and there were many youths of better family, greater wealth, more impressive beauty, and equal athletic ability who were just as keen to win Hermione. Why should it be you? When the betrothal was announced, I was devastated. There was never anyone else for me. Then, even before I fully comprehended what had happened to me, you failed to return from Tegea." She paused and glanced nervously at Lysandridas. He was only gazing at her wide-eyed, as if he'd truly never known—never even imagined—that she might love him.

"When you did not come home with the army, I learned that I loved you more than I wanted you. I made sacrifices to all the Gods—one after another—begging them to bring you home alive. To Persephone I gave all the trophies from the races I'd won as a girl. To Athena, the shawl my mother left on the banks of the stream when she jumped in to rescue my brother and was swept to her own death instead. To Artemis went the pressed flowers from a garland you once made for me. I promised the Gods that I would never be jealous of Hermione again. I swore that I would accept Hermione as your wife, if *only* they would bring you home. But instead, you were declared dead."

"Hermione married within a few months. You could have, too." Lysandridas pointed out softly.

"Who?!" Leonis flung back at him angrily. "For me there never *was* anyone but you. Never. I'm not beautiful like Hermione! No one wanted me—not even you. So you see, whether you were dead or alive with Hermione made no difference to my future, really. I lost my husband the day you promised yourself to Hermione." She did not dare look at him as she spoke.

Lysandridas did not answer immediately. He gazed across the field, feeling the wind blowing his dark curls and playing with the skirts of his chiton. He heard the cypress trees rustling overhead and the bees in the wild asparagus beside the steps. He realised to his own surprise that she was right: Leonis was the only wife he could picture for himself.

Hermione had been his bride—and the only place he could picture her was in bed. He could not honestly picture her spinning or weaving or bringing refreshments to the harvesters in the heat of the day. A life with the pale girl Antyllus had selected for him was even more difficult to imagine. Leonis, by contrast, fit in everywhere. She'd even help him with the horses, encourage him to keep breeding and training and competing—just as she had encouraged his father when he would have given them all away. She never seemed to see his scar when she looked at him. She'd defended him to Hermione. She was desirable. He desired her.

He turned to look at her, but she had turned her face away. He saw her chest heave as she gulped for breath. He reached over and turned her head back with his hand. She had her eyes pressed shut, and tears glistened on the lashes. The lashes were chestnut-coloured, he noted with surprise. That's why they didn't stand out, but they were long and beautiful. He bent and kissed her eyelids one after the other very gently.

Leonis couldn't hold her breath any longer, and sobbed once before biting down on her lips.

Lysandridas pulled her into his arms and kissed the top of her head. She smelled of lavender and thyme and sunshine. He bent his head deeper and nuzzled the back of her neck. "Will you marry me—even I can't beat you at a race?"

Leonis opened her arms and wound them around Lysandridas, too dizzy to even be ecstatic as she should have been. She had never in her whole life been held like this. Her father, as far as she could remember, had never held her in his arms. Teleklos had not done so since she was eight or nine, except that once in the stables—and that had been in comfort, not desire. Lysandridas was not comforting her—even if her tears had been his excuse to take her into his arms. Lysandridas was caressing her, kissing her, enclosing her in his strength and warmth. He had found her lips with his and he nibbled on them, played with them gently, and parted them.

The kiss lasted a long time, and then Lysandridas ended it and matter-of-factly took up the satchel and opened it. He removed the loaf of bread and tore it in two. Taking his knife from his belt, he cut slices of cheese and sausage for them, offering Leonis everything first. He set his own portion beside him, and dug into the satchel until he found the two chipped pottery mugs with a cream glaze of typical Laconian manufacture. He stood and carried these to the brook, filled them with water, and returned. Then he tossed out a little water and poured in a touch of wine. He handed one of the mugs to Leonis. "You haven't said yes," he pointed out.

Leonis took the mug and held it in both hands. She stared at Lysandridas. He had never looked so attractive to her, and that frightened her. The force of her own emotions frightened her. She had thought she was in love with him ever since she had learned that girls were supposed to fall in love and marry boys, but what she felt now was overpowering, oppressive—frightening. "Yes," she whispered, and had never sounded so uncertain of herself in her life.

Lysandridas leaned forward and kissed her again. As they drank and ate together, Lysandridas started talking about Tegea. He told about wanting to die until he saw the apple blossoms, and he talked about Dion and Ambelos and "the women of Tegea" and how they were never seen in public unless they were veiled. "They're weak and pale and timid."

"That makes it sound like you knew them better than you admit," Leonis teased, beginning to relax a little.

"Not as well as I would have liked to," Lysandridas quipped back, adding seriously, "The whole time I was a quarry slave I never saw a single woman—not one! After I was bought by Antyllus, I saw only the slaves of his household—mostly older women and a couple of younger, but distinctly unattractive, girls. They are different from our helots, Leonis; none of them have any brains. And I did not meet the mistress of the house until the day Antyllus introduced me to her as her adopted son."

"But how could she—I mean—if she didn't know you …?"

Lysandridas shrugged. "Apparently her consent wasn't required. Antyllus made the decision to adopt me and he informed her about it. It was very awkward for me, but she didn't seem to care. She was a heavy, listless woman, covered with thick make-up—white cream and red rouge and lips. Even her eyelids were painted. She held out her hand to me, welcomed me into her family, and then turned away.

"But the worst thing that happened to me with respect to women in Tegea was my betrothal. Antyllus told me when he adopted me that he wanted me to marry his niece. She had been intended for his natural son, and now she was getting 'old' and her father could not find a suitor. By then

I knew that in Tegea men never saw women or girls of good family except at religious and family festivals. Most men married either relatives, whom they might have glimpsed at family festivals, or utter strangers selected for them by the fathers. In short, as Antyllus' son I had no choice. He would choose a bride for me—or rather already had."

"But an older woman?" Leonis asked, puzzled.

"That's just it, Leonis. She was *seventeen*—a pale, frightened child, who had never set foot outside of her father's house. I felt so sorry for her—being given away to a former enemy, a former slave, with a hideous scar in the middle of his forehead." He touched it as he spoke. "She was terrified of me. At the betrothal, when they put her hand in mine, it was clammy and trembling. She barely managed to say three or four words to me the entire afternoon. It was terrible." He fell silent, remembering the embarrassing scene. Then, to change the subject, he asked Leonis with a smile, "Tell me about your suitors."

"What suitors?"

"All the men you turned away while waiting for a slave to come home."

"You were never a slave to me, Lysandridas."

He didn't answer, but looked down at his mangled hands.

Leonis reached over, took his hands in hers, and then bent and kissed his scarred knuckles. They smelled of leather and horse sweat, and she loved them.

Lysandridas kissed the back of her head. "Were there really no others?" he persisted.

"One."

"Who?"

"Your father."

Lysandridas drew back sharply. "That's disgusting! He's nearly forty years older than you! How dare he—"

"He was very lonely. He'd lost his only son. I was there, familiar—"

"It was an insult," Lysandridas insisted indignantly.

"No," Leonis told him simply, adding gently, "it was a very sweet gesture."

"So why did you turn him down?" he challenged, still sounding outraged.

"I didn't. He changed his mind when he realised I didn't love him—when he realized I loved you."

Lysandridas sat beside her for a few minutes, frowning, and then he seemed to come to terms with the thought. "More wine?"

She nodded and held out her mug. Again he fetched water and then poured the wine into it. "I want to keep breeding horses. I want to breed and train another winning team," he told her solemnly.

"Of course." She was smiling, amused by his intensity.

"It's expensive. More than we can afford. Taygetos was a stroke of luck—and he's past his prime. I'll breed Afra with him next year and hope, but really, I'll need a new stud stallion. Poseidon alone knows where I'm to get the funds to buy one," he admitted somewhat gloomily.

"We'll find the money. Do you think the Agiad team is better than your father's and Antyllus'?"

"Yes—but not with Thessalos driving them," he said bitterly, and Leonis knew he was jealous and didn't mind.

"Why don't you enter Afra in the horse race?" she suggested.

Lysandridas stopped in mid-drink. "Have you ridden her?"

"Your father said I should exercise her, since you didn't get home very often. So I did ride her once or twice. Mostly I drove her—"

"Drove her?! But she's never been trained to the traces!"

Leonis looked at him, uncomprehending. "But she was much calmer in the traces, I thought...."

Lysandridas laughed and then reached over and gave her a quick kiss. "You're wonderful!" he told her truthfully, adding, "She's fast, isn't she?"

"I never risked letting her have her head, but she seems very fast just watching her in the paddock. She leaves the others in her dust—but then they're lazy."

Lysandridas liked the thought of racing Afra, and decided to think about it, but first he refilled their mugs with wine. He was stiff from sitting on the stone steps and settled himself in the soft grass, stretching out on his side. He signaled for Leonis to join him. She stood but then hesitated, aware again of her near-nakedness. Lysandridas smiled up at her, blinking contentedly. "You remind me of Artemis standing there."

"Don't be ridiculous." She went onto her knees beside him and lay on her stomach, her head on her crossed arms, looking at him. He sipped his wine and considered her from half-closed eyes. He was remembering his dreams. In all of them Hermione had been naked and Leonis dressed like this, in a short chiton. He leaned over and kissed the back of Leonis' neck. His hand slipped inside the back of her chiton and caressed her warm, sweet-smelling skin. She did not give any sign of protest. He fumbled with the brooches at her shoulders. "Shields," he noted.

"Do you like them?"

"On you, yes." He undid one pin and then the other. He pulled the chiton off her back and laid his head upon it. Her skin was white and flawless. He stroked it gently, and she seemed to wince slightly under the touch of his fingers, but then she relaxed. She let him undo her ponytail so he could run his fingers through her long hair. The bees hovered around them and the flowers swayed in the wind.

Lysandridas slipped his hand under her side and gently but firmly rolled her over. She opened her eyes wide, alarmed. The touch of the wind and sun on her naked breasts was so unusual that she could hardly get her breath. Her lips parted, and her chest heaved as she felt him looking at her naked breasts. He bent and kissed her lips. "Don't be frightened."

It was not surprising that Leonis was dizzied and disoriented by what followed. It was her first sexual experience, and she had the great good fortune to love the man who deflowered her, gently yet with enough passion to kindle a fire in her. It was more surprising that Lysandridas was left dazed by the experience.

As he lay beside her in the aftermath, trying to regain his breath, waiting for his heart and pulse to find a more stable pace and letting the breeze dry his sweat, he felt as if the earth had shaken under him. He looked up at the puffs of clouds sliding down the sky from the Taygetos, and he wasn't sure where he was any more. The thought formed slowly that Hermione had been right after all: their night together had been meaningless compared to this. Leonis was all that mattered to him.

Now, he was embarrassed that Leonis was wearing only a short chiton. *Now,* he was ashamed he had brought her out here with no concern for her reputation. *Now* he wished he could wrap her in a long peplos and a himation and keep the eyes of others off her. Now she was his.

For the first time since he had returned to Lacedaemon, he was not only glad to be home, but looked forward to his future here. He was suddenly certain that he would be a good citizen and found a family, and that he *would* regain the respect of all of them. With Leonis to help him, he'd race again at Olympia. He'd win the right to be restored to the Guard. He'd make the others accept him.

They did not speak, but they held hands as they returned to the horses. Lysandridas gave Leonis a leg up, and then sprang onto Afra. They crossed the meadow in silence. As they entered the forest road, he said simply: "I will speak to your father at the first opportunity."

CHAPTER 23

Zeuxidamas did not come to his kleros for the holiday, so Lysandridas had to seek him out in the city. The day after the holiday ended, Lysandridas dressed in his best chiton, armour, greaves, and sandals and took his crested helmet under his arm. He waited for his future father-in-law outside the latter's syssitia.

When Zeuxidamas arrived for dinner, he was surprised to have anyone waiting for him, much less in so much ostentatious splendour. At first he assumed it was one of the men in his battalion come with a request for special leave or the like. When he recognised Lysandridas, his face clouded.

"Sir, if you could give me just a minute, I'd like a word with you," Lysandridas started, ignoring the hostile countenance of Leonis' father.

Zeuxidamas looked annoyed and impatient, but he adjusted his walking stick and waited, staring at Lysandridas grimly.

"I've come about your daughter Leonis."

Zeuxidamas had already made that deduction himself, and so he only nodded once and waited with his hard, uninviting face.

"I would like to marry her," Lysandridas declared, unable to think of any reason not to be direct.

Zeuxidamas nodded again.

"Was that your consent, sir?" Lysandridas asked uncertainly. He hadn't expected the meeting to be this cold.

"Yes."

"When may I—"

"Take her whenever you like. You know where to find her. Take her and be done with it." Zeuxidamas removed his walking stick from under his arm and disappeared inside his syssitia without a backward glance.

Lysandridas was left in his wake, feeling insulted and angry. Zeuxidamas' ill-concealed contempt angered Lysandridas-the-citizen, but Zeuxidamas' indifference to his daughter infuriated Lysandridas-the-lover. Zeuxidamas hadn't even mentioned a marriage contract—as if he were willing to let Leonis live like a concubine!

Lysandridas had to hurry to his own syssitia, however, as he was now late. Here, the others, particularly Thessalos, did much to restore Lysandridas' good mood when he told them his news. They congratulated him, toasted him and his bride, and one of the others at once ordered the cook to roast the pheasants he'd brought and serve them with chestnuts as a special course. Most of the members even stayed late, drinking a bit more than was usual, teasing and joking in a good-natured way.

Thessalos kept repeating, "But this is wonderful, Lysandridas. Hermione will be so pleased to hear." Adding, "You aren't angry with us any more, are you?"

"No," Lysandridas admitted with a sincere smile, and Thessalos laughed in delight.

The following day, Lysandridas spent his free afternoon looking for a town house where Leonis could live for the next four years while he was on active service. He wanted someplace close to his barracks, so he could visit her in the afternoons and at night.

Throughout the city there were small houses suitable for young, small families, built specially for the wives of men still on active service. Many of the perioikoi also made extra income renting out the rooms behind and above their shops and warehouses to young couples. Such houses and apartments were always becoming available when families got too large or the men went off active service, and so moved to their kleros.

The prettiest houses near the barracks were too expensive, however, and the cheapest apartments were unacceptable. Lysandridas was not going to have Leonis housing above a fishmonger, with the smell of his wares permeating every nook and cranny of their rooms. The apartment offered by a merchant of the coveted purple dye shells was too cramped and dark. The rooms rented out by a furrier were musky and run-down; and so it went.

It was not until the third day of looking that Lysandridas found something he considered suitable and could also afford. It was located beyond the old agora, convenient to shops and a fountain house. It was also on the west part of the city, near the "racecourse" for running, which would enable him to slip home on his way back from sport. Lysandridas even managed to convince himself that the nearness of the Sanctuary of the Horse-Breeding Poseidon was a good omen.

The owner, a Perioikoi trading in wool, said he only needed one room for storage and one to sleep in occasionally when he was in the city; the rest of the house Lysandridas and Leonis could use as they liked. This meant their quarters really started at the courtyard, accessed by a narrow outdoor corridor leading between the houses from the street. A small, very cramped andron opened off the courtyard on one side and a kitchen ran along the opposite side. Since Lysandridas did not want the house for entertaining, he considered the small andron an insubstantial defect. It bothered him more that the courtyard was not terribly attractive. It was naked and paved with cobblestones. A colonnade stretched across the north side with two Doric pillars that marked the beginning of a slightly raised terrace. Beyond the terrace was a large room with a central hearth, which gave access to a small bathroom tucked in the corner between this chamber and the kitchen. Wooden stairs led up to the second story, where there were three rooms under the eaves.

The entire house was empty of furnishings, and the walls were freshly whitewashed but devoid of decoration. Lysandridas thought wistfully of Antyllus' lovely manor with the frescoes and the delicate patterns painted on the door frames. He remembered the painted ceiling panels and marble or mosaic floors. He wished he could afford to improve these simple rooms, but he could not. He was lucky to be able to afford the house at all.

Meanwhile, Teleklos obtained from Zeuxidamas a signed marriage contract. One look at the lovers when they returned from their ride had sufficed for Teleklos to know what had happened. Furthermore, the young couple made no attempt to conceal their affections from the households of their respective kleros. The helots had been amused and indulgent, but they would also talk. Teleklos had therefore lectured Lysandridas severely about his careless treatment of Leonis' reputation; and when he learned of Zeuxidamas' response to Lysandridas' proposal, he had gone straight to his neighbour to make sure things were "put right" before another day went by.

Zeuxidamas had been as short-tempered to Teleklos as to Lysandridas. This made Teleklos angry, and he demanded to know what Zeuxidamas had against the marriage.

"Nothing!" Zeuxidamas retorted—although this was evidently not the truth—adding stubbornly, "I've given my consent."

"Without a marriage contract to make it legal, binding, and respectable?" Teleklos challenged.

"Oh is that what you want?" Zeuxidamas finally understood the drift of the conversation.

"Yes, it is. You should have at least that much respect for your own child!" Teleklos' anger came to the surface and his eyes glinted with real fury.

Zeuxidamas capitulated at once. He wrote out a marriage contract on the spot, then signed and sealed it. Teleklos also signed and sealed the contract in his son's name. He had proudly shown this document to Lysandridas and Leonis, and then filed it away in the family archive.

Lysandridas and Leonis agreed that as soon as she had furnished the house with the essentials, her maid would move in and take over the housekeeping. Leonis said she'd have everything fixed up in five to six days, since it was mostly just a matter of transporting beds, chests, tables, chairs, and rugs from her own kleros. She would bring her own loom and spinning things as well as the essential utensils and pottery for the kitchen. They agreed that Lysandridas would "abduct" her from her aunt's house in the city near Lysandridas' barracks at the new moon, ten days away.

On the day named, Leonis took her short chitons and her stuffed animals, the symbols of her childhood, to the Temple of Artemis of the Goats. This "sacrifice" left on the altar would find its way into the hands of poor children and orphans. She also made sacrifices at the Temple of the Horse-Breeding Poseidon, begging him to bless Lysandridas with success in breeding and training so he would always be a contented husband. She went to the Temple of Demeter to ask for protection over her new hearth, and she also prayed and sacrificed at the Temple of the Dioskouroi, because she knew Lysandridas believed the Twins were particularly protective of him. It was by then mid-afternoon, and the air was hot and heavy. The mountains on both sides of the valley were nearly lost in milky white haze, and she was sweating and footsore.

Returning to her aunt's home, Leonis found her friend Kyniska waiting happily to assist her. "I can't stay all night," Kyniska warned at once, "but I'll help you get through the next few hours. The waiting is the worst part!" She happily chattered about her own wedding day.

Kyniska and Leonis' aunt bathed the bride in water scented with crushed rosemary. They washed her hair and then cut and styled it with great care. Knowing how much Lysandridas liked her long hair, Leonis found it hard to part with it—and yet this was the symbol of her new status, which she was proud to show the rest of the city after so long.

It was late afternoon by now, and the streets and courtyards of the townhouses were in shadow. From the distance came the sound of pipes wailing. "I hadn't realised it was that late!" Kyniska exclaimed, surprised.

Leonis and her aunt stopped and listened, and Leonis knew even before her aunt exclaimed in shock: "That's not the call to dinner! That's alarm!"

The three women looked at one another in stunned amazement and then rushed down the stairs, across the courtyard, and out into the street. In every doorway women and small children clustered, while men in various states of dress clattered out and past them. The men ran, often pulling on their caps and helmets as they went. Their shields, over their backs, clacked against their swords with every stride. A unit of youths from the agoge plunged down the street in a pack, jabbering and shouting to one another. A senior commander, in the distinctive cross-crested helmet, galloped by with his scarlet cloak streaming out behind him.

"You don't think that the Tegeans could have attacked the city?" Kyniska asked in distress; and then without waiting for an answer, she declared: "I must get back to my babies!" Forgetting her shawl, she rushed down the street in the opposite direction to the last men still responding to the howling of the pipes.

Then the street was silent and still. The women returned inside to wait.

Lysandridas had been at the barracks, fretfully whiling away the time till dinner, impatient for darkness and curfew, when he could legally fetch Leonis home. At the sound of the alarm, he and all the others sitting around in the barracks atrium dicing or playing draughts started, stared at one another, and then dropped everything to grab their arms. The helot attendants helped whichever of the Spartiates needed it. Thorax got Lysandridas into his breastplate and greaves first but then gave others a hand, while Lysandridas himself pulled his baldric over his shoulder and drew his shield down off the wall. It was a new shield that he had himself commissioned, painted with his own device: a chariot driven by a helmeted and armoured man. His shield slung over his back, Lysandridas pulled his arming cap over his head before he put on his crested helmet. He wore the helmet cocked back onto his neck, the nosepiece on his forehead for now. At last, fully armoured, he grabbed one of the standard-issue eight-foot spears from where they were lined up neatly by the door, and ran out into the street.

He followed those who were faster than he along the street to the battalion's muster grounds before the Temple of Heracles north of the racecourse. The men from the barracks arrived in a ragged group, while others arrived breathless from across the city in various states of array. The Battalion Commander, Krantios, was already on the scene, although he was unarmed and bareheaded—a situation quickly remedied by his attendant, who galloped up with the missing equipment. Krantios was sorting the men as they arrived. All who were fully equipped, like Lysandridas, were quickly segregated and organised into a phalanx regardless of their designated company or platoon. Other officers were delegated to organise the incompletely armed men.

"What's happened?" Lysandridas heard his own company commander ask, as he arrived breathless and red-faced but fully armoured.

"The Tegean cavalry has penetrated the upper Eurotas valley. They burned one of the villages."

Lysandridas' heart was thundering in his chest. He could picture Harmatides leading the Tegean cavalry—the cavalry he'd trained—down the narrow defiles thought unsuitable for cavalry, and into the head of the valley. No matter what else one thought of him, Harmatides was a magnificent horseman and an audacious leader of men.

Already the signal was given to advance, and the improvised phalanx under Krantios' command marched out of Heracles' square, past the Temple to Asklepios, and started up the street leading north along the valley floor. They crossed the road leading up along the foothills to Lysandridas' kleros and remained on the road that paralleled the Eurotas River. Ahead of them lay "The Planes", a grove of planes trees planted around the moated ball field.

The games played here reached their climax in a match between the two best teams of eirenes shortly before the winter solstice, when the age-cohorts graduated. For the eirenes it was their last event before citizenship, and so the victors were particularly honoured. But throughout the year, teams of various ages held practice matches and contested here. It was therefore not surprising to hear shouts coming from the direction of the artificial island made by diverting water from the Eurotas.

But something was odd about the shouting, and after a moment Lysandridas realised that he could hear the clang of swords on shields above the shouting.

He was sweating now—and not just from the sun on his bronze armour. The sweat soaked his arming cap and ran down the back of his neck, and the sweat from his armpits soaked his chiton under the leather jack and heavy breastplate. His loins were soaked under the leather panels of the armour skirt. The sound of battle, nearing with each jogged stride, reminded him of the last battle he had fought—the battle that had ended in four years of slavery.

The high-pitched whinny of a horse reached him and he started to make out a line of horses, somewhat further down the valley; but the fighting was taking place nearer the city, at the foot of the ball field itself.

"The fools!" Krantios cursed.

Lysandridas was beginning to make sense of the apparent chaos. It appeared that youths—possibly the twenty-year-old eirenes or the nineteen-year-old meleirenes—had seen the approaching Tegeans and, not being content to bring word to the city of the approaching threat, had plunged down from the playing ground to attack the Tegeans. The ball game was traditionally played in the nude, and the youths had rushed into battle against the Tegean cavalry like the heroes painted on their pottery and embossed on their shields—nude except for the shields and spears they had hastily retrieved as they left the playing field.

The phalanx started to jog forward at a faster rate because of a collective will that required no order from their commander. At a shout, they dropped their helmets down to cover their faces, and their shields were brought from their backs to the ready. Krantios was calling for them to slow down. "Steady! Steady! Hold your ranks!"

That was hard. Before them, just a couple of hundred paces away, the gallant but foolish youths were being cut down in an orgy of blood. Lysandridas was furious. This wasn't what he'd trained the Tegean cavalry for—to slaughter youths not yet out of the agoge, naked but for their weapons! How dare they misuse his training for this! Guilt made him almost berserk.

The others had spontaneously, from years of training, struck up one of Tyrtaios' anthems. The words were challenging, threatening, calling on the Gods to stand by them in their just cause. Lysandridas joined in, the melody sweeping him up with it, helping him forward over the last dozen paces. Lysandridas thought he caught a glimpse of another phalanx approaching from the eastern edge of the city. That would be from one of the other lochos. Krantios, meanwhile, was furiously shouting at the eirenes to withdraw. His orders were desperate. It was impossible to tell if they were heeded. At last Lysandridas' unit came in contact with the enemy, and Lysandridas had no more time for the larger picture.

They flung themselves at the Tegean cavalry and with a touch of amazement, Lysandridas saw that the Tegeans were no match for them at all. The Tegean line broke at once. The horses reared and bolted. The riders flung away their javelins and sprinted back toward their fellows.

There was no way men in armour could hope to follow on foot. Krantios sharply called back the few men who seemed tempted. "FORMATION!" he screamed at them, his voice already hoarse from so much unnatural shouting. Usually they had a piper to give the orders, but Krantios had sensibly not waited for one to arrive.

The Tegeans were fleeing headlong up the valley, away from the Spartan phalanx, without a backward glance, and Lysandridas instantly knew they had never intended to fight. They had come to "tweak the lion's tail" by burning down a village and penetrating to the city itself. Maybe they had hoped to carry off some treasure from a temple—something to humiliate

Lacedaemon and revenge the theft of Orestes' bones. But they had not come to fight. The eirenes had forced the fight upon them by attacking.

Now one of the eirenes was there. Blood gushed from a head wound, drenching half his face in shimmering, brilliant red. He was screaming at them. "They've taken captives!"

All eyes went back to the fleeing horsemen. They were too far away to see.

"Who? How many of you?" Krantios demanded, as more and more of the eirenes limped over and crowded around, gasping, bleeding, and cursing.

"We don't know!"

"It wasn't us they took!"

"They took girls from the sanctuary of Helen by the Dorkian Spring!"

"That's why we attacked. We heard the girls screaming!"

So it wasn't just youthful bravado and glory-seeking after all.

It also explained why half the Tegeans had held back. They had held the hostages. Why hadn't they just fled? Mounted, they could have left the eirenes in their wake in an instant. But sweeping the battlefield with his eyes, Lysandridas saw corpses and wounded far out in the valley. The eirenes must have managed to nearly block off their retreat. Then the Tegeans had driven them back with half their force.

"How many casualties?" Krantios was asking.

"A dozen, maybe more."

The second phalanx, which Lysandridas had seen coming up from the east, arrived. It was the Guard. Krantios took one of the eirenes, who was less badly wounded than the others (albeit limping badly on a swelling knee), and explained the situation. The Guards Commander ordered a runner to return to the Agiad royal stables and bring up every available horse. "Thessalos?"

"Sir!"

"Get out of that armour and prepare to pursue."

"Sir!"

"Anyone else here good with horses?"

Lysandridas stepped forward with a dozen others.

"Pitch your armour," they were ordered, while another man was sent to get javelins to arm them.

Thessalos caught sight of Lysandridas and clapped him on the shoulder. When the horses were brought up—rearing, fretting and distressed by the smell of blood—Thessalos assigned them. There was no doubt he kept the best colt for himself, but he assigned a second member of the racing team to Lysandridas. He was a taller horse than Lysandridas was used to. It took him two tries before he managed to fling himself up onto the broad black back, and already Thessalos was beside him. "Let's go!"

He raised his arm in a signal, and suddenly they were galloping at breakneck pace across the plain. Their horses were fresh. They had not come forty miles from Tegea, down difficult gullies, cutting and bruising their fetlocks on the rock. They had not breathed smoke in the burned-down village and thirsted in the sun all day. They were fresh and strong and half-wild as they raced each other in rare, apparent freedom.

Even Lysandridas felt he was doing little more than hanging on, clinging to the mane, glancing every second stride at Thessalos. It was only Thessalos who mattered. The others were left behind them. It was just the two of them, and they were gaining, steadily gaining, on their quarry.

The Tegeans had turned sharply right, making for the steep slopes of the Parnon range. It was terrain where the freshness of the pursuing Spartan horses would be less advantageous once they reached it. Lysandridas thought he could make out the ostentatious gold-encrusted armour of Harmatides. Harmatides was holding back, sending the horses with the men holding the captives ahead but keeping half his troop back to fight.

Thessalos saw it, too. With an audible curse, he sat back and started pulling up his colt. He glanced at Lysandridas, but no command was necessary. They knew they had to wait for the others to catch up if there was to be a fight.

They did not stop, however—just slowed enough for the other dozen riders to join them, and then they rushed forward again to the attack. Harmatides had pulled away from them again. The last of the Tegeans were a good third of the way up the trail, while the captives were more than halfway up the slope.

The Spartans reached the slope. They had to slow to a tortured canter. The horses were drenched in sweat, breathing heavily. Stones loosened by the horses ahead of them rolled down towards them, unnerving them.

Halfway up the slope Harmatides stopped his little rearguard. He waited until the Spartans were in range, and then he loosed a barrage of arrows. Because his men were stationary, their aim was good. Lysandridas could hear the grunts, curses, and cries of what sounded like half a dozen men being knocked off their mounts. Horses squealed. The sounds of drumming, fleeing hooves, and stones and pebbles sliding and rolling came from behind him.

But Thessalos and Lysandridas were still unharmed and mounted. The Tegeans turned and started to flee again, but the terrain was rough. They could no longer flee at a canter, only trot and then walk.

The Spartan horses were starting to balk, too. Thessalos dug his heels into his colt to get it to overcome its fear, and Lysandridas kept close behind him. More than once the stones slipped out from under their horses' hooves. The colts lost their footing, slipped, and stumbled over rocks. Lysandridas, still in Thessalos' dust, felt a mounting sense of superiority. Thessalos was trying to force his colt to go where he wanted, forcing it to go where it felt uncertain. A battle of wills was ensuing between horse and rider that drained them both of strength.

Lysandridas gave his colt his head, urging it forward and upwards with his legs, while burying his hands in the mane. A horse always moves fastest and surest on ground it picks for itself. In only a few minutes Lysandridas had worked his way past Thessalos and was leading the pursuit.

But the Tegeans had reached the top of the slope and were over the nearest crest, lost temporarily from sight. Behind him, Thessalos was cursing violently. By the time the Spartan pursuers topped the crest of the hill, Harmatides had gained a half-mile on them again. The Tegeans with the captives were even farther away.

The fact that there were only five Spartan horsemen left by the time they crested the ridge did not bother the pursuers. They were not thinking, just hunting. On the more level ground here, Thessalos—furious to have been overtaken by Lysandridas—took the lead again. His colt was lathered on both sides of his neck and between the thighs and was foaming at the mouth, but he was no less mad with the desire to be first than his rider. Both horse and rider stretched out as they galloped forward, and Lysandridas and his colt followed—racing, not pursuing. The others were left strung out behind.

The Tegeans with the captives had disappeared again. Harmatides seemed to veer and take a different route. Lysandridas was conscious of it. He shouted ahead to Thessalos that they should ignore the decoy and follow the captives. But he was no longer exactly sure which of the several mountain paths the retreating Tegeans with the captives had actually taken. He was galloping far too fast to read any tracks. Besides, Thessalos had already veered to follow Harmatides. The latter was on the upper edge of another steep slope. Within minutes, Harmatides was lost from sight over the crest again.

Lysandridas could not resist proving his superiority again. As before, he gained steadily on Thessalos as they worked their way up the slope. Triumphantly, he was the first over the top of the crest—and instantly looked death in the face. Just beyond the crest, the mountain fell away into a crevice three hundred feet deep. It was as if Poseidon had simply torn the mountain apart. Lysandridas' colt reared up and nearly lost his balance.

When he crashed back down onto all fours, he was trembling from head to foot. And so was Lysandridas.

Thessalos came crashing up behind him, and Lysandridas shouted to him. His rival/friend drew up so harshly that his colt lost his footing and crashed down on his side with a loud squeal.

The next thing Lysandridas knew, he and Thessalos were dismounted and side by side, trying to calm the terrified colt and keep him from throwing himself over the precipice in his terrified attempts to regain his footing. Somehow they managed.

All blood seemed to have drained from Thessalos' face as he stroked his colt, still muttering soothing sounds. A moment later he started to feel for damage. Only then did it cross Lysandridas' mind that if either colt were injured, Thessalos could kiss his Olympic victory goodbye. Returning to the colt he'd ridden, Lysandridas, too, started to look for serious injuries. Both men and beasts were still trembling and breathing heavily when the last three riders finally topped the crest at a more decorous pace.

It was only when one of these asked about the Tegeans that Lysandridas and Thessalos looked at one another blankly. Neither had given the Tegeans a thought from the moment they crested the hill. Now they too looked everywhere, but there was not a trace of them.

CHAPTER 24

Although a widow, Leonis' aunt had the news from her neighbour before nightfall. The Tegean cavalry had seized seven women from the shrine of Helen by the Dorkean spring. An eighth girl had struggled so hard that she had managed to free herself from her captors, but had injured herself as she fell from the galloping horse. She was still unconscious and it was not certain she would recover. All seven captives were from the best Spartiate families, including King Anaxandridas' widowed elder sister and her young daughter. The city was in shock.

"I'm so sorry for you, my dear," her aunt ended. "It's a terrible thing to happen on your wedding day."

Although they waited for several hours into the night, Lysandridas did not come. Leonis' aunt sighed and patted Leonis on the shoulder. "You mustn't take this personally. I'm sure Lysandridas just wasn't able to get away from the barracks under the circumstances. Indeed it could be several days before he can risk it."

Leonis nodded numbly. She was sure that Lysandridas would come when he could. She had waited twenty-three years for him to want her; she could wait another night or two. But the raid itself frightened her. The fact that she had so recently lost her virginity made the images of rape more vivid. She could picture all too easily what it would mean to have an utter stranger tearing away her clothes and ramming himself into her. She thought of the women and girls, all of whom she knew at least by sight and name, being flung down onto the ground and cruelly, brutally ravished. They were slaves now. They had no rights, not even the right to identity or kindness. When their captor was tired of them, he could sell them or lend them out to guests or force them to sell their bodies for the benefit of his own purse.

And almost as chilling: it could so easily have been her. She had often gone to the Sanctuary of Helen. It was one of the nearer sanctuaries to her kleros. Because the temple was not directly in the city, it was quieter than those on the main streets and squares. It was an ideal place for contemplation and prayer, while the Dorkean spring beside it was particularly cool and refreshing on a sweltering day. Leonis had often sat by that spring, cooling her feet and listening to the gossip of the other women. In fact, she had been there just yesterday, in a kind of farewell to her past and her childhood....

"There will be consequences to this raid," her aunt said with a sigh as she got to her swollen feet. Then, patting Leonis on the shoulder again, she added, "Don't wait up too long, my dear. Tomorrow is another day—and you'll need your strength in the days to come." Then she made her way slowly up the creaking stairs to her chamber.

Leonis did not follow her. She sat by the hearth, staring at the slowly dying flames, and tried to think what the consequences would be. There seemed only one answer: war. Lacedaemon would invade Tegea again to take revenge for what had happened. Lysandridas would be at risk again. He might be killed, wounded, or captured again. And it wouldn't even help the captives, she reflected as she put more wood onto the fire. This very minute, she imagined, they were being mocked and abused, forced to serve their masters, forced to humble themselves before utter strangers.

The worst of it would be being made to feel that you were nothing but fresh meat—no one's daughter, no one's sister, not human at all. Nameless, soulless property, denied the right to individuality and emotion.... Just as Lysandridas had been until Antyllus rescued him.

A knocking at the door from the street startled her so much that she gasped in alarm. Then she realised it must be Lysandridas. She jumped up, overturning her stool and stubbing her toe on the base of the column leading out to the courtyard. "I'm coming!" she called out, so that he wouldn't get discouraged and go away angry. They should have left the door unlocked for him!

As she drew the latch back and Lysandridas half fell into the entry hall, he was already angry. "What kind of a reception is that? I thought I was welcome!"

"Of course you're welcome! We just were so sure it wouldn't be tonight after what's happened—"

"Leonis? What's going on down there?" The alarmed voice of her aunt came to them from the upstairs window.

"It's Lysandridas," Leonis called up.

"Oh!" The older woman at once withdrew into her chamber, pulling the wooden shutters closed.

"Aren't you ready?" Lysandridas asked, still unnerved at having found the door locked. He was taking a high risk leaving barracks after the alarm of the afternoon, and he was in a hurry to get Leonis settled into their joint home. His impatience to establish his possession of her legally and officially was irrational, but consuming. He was not prepared to wait another night, because he couldn't be sure they wouldn't march out tomorrow or the next day. He was not prepared to risk what had happened with Hermione. He wanted the entire city to recognise Leonis as his wife—or widow, whatever the case might be.

"Let me get a himation." Leonis had been so lost in her thoughts of the captives that she was somewhat disoriented. She went back into the hall and collected the himation, which she had woven for this occasion during the long winter of waiting before Teleklos went to Tegea. She had put all her love and longing into it, and she hoped he would notice that it had a border of racing chariots between iris and lavender. She arranged the himation carefully, regretting it was too dark to see the wonderful purple and blue tones that she had woven into it.

But Lysandridas took no notice of it. He was impatiently standing by the door, and he all but shooed her out when she emerged. Then he moved at such a pace through the darkened streets that Leonis almost had to run to keep up with him. They did not speak, and if they saw or heard anyone approaching, they ducked into the shadows of the doorways or into alleyways. Lysandridas hid particularly well whenever he heard the tramping and singing of the watch going by.

At last they reached their little rented house. Lysandridas had the key to the door that led down the narrow, roofless corridor between the neighbouring house and their landlord's chambers to the courtyard in the back. They felt more than saw their way through the dark. Inside the courtyard itself, however, they were greeted by the gentle light of oil lamps that had been lit by Leonis' maid in preparation for them. A glow of orange seeped from the hearth-room out onto the terrace as well, casting shadows from the two pillars onto the cobblestones. The smell of rosemary and thyme wafted from the kitchen window, soon overlaid as they moved toward the terrace by the sweet mixture of scents from the hanging flowerpots. Lysandridas had not been here since Leonis had fixed it up, and he was amazed by how the house had been transformed by such simple things.

Although a table with refreshments awaited them in the hearth-room, Lysandridas slipped his arm around Leonis' waist, and he whispered in her ear, "Let's go up to bed."

He was feeling invincible and victorious at this moment. It did not bother him that Harmatides had escaped. He had outridden Thessalos on one of Thessalos' own horses. The thrill of the chase was still in his blood, although he knew that if he stopped for a minute or drank any wine the exhaustion would obliterate the lingering excitement. He was relieved, too, that he had Leonis here. She was now, by Spartan law and custom, legally his. He wanted to make love to his *wife* and then get back for a good night's sleep in the barracks before he was confronted with tomorrow and the consequences of the raid.

Leonis did not protest. She had not expected anything different; and yet she could not share his triumphant mood. She was still depressed by the fate of the captives and distressed by the prospects of war again. Her experience of war was defeat and grief and the loss of Lysandridas. She couldn't bear the thought of going through it all over again.

Loose-woven rugs with geometric patterns bedecked the floor of the bedchamber, and the low bed had a striped curtain, tied back to reveal the fresh, white linens on the firm mattress and soft pillows. Lysandridas pulled Leonis into his arms and kissed her passionately, fumbling to unwind her from her himation.

Thinking of all the work that had gone into it, Leonis resented his rough hands. "Not so roughly; I spent months making this."

"What's the matter?" Lysandridas demanded, sensing her mood through the words.

"Nothing." She stepped away from him to remove the himation and fold it together carefully.

Lysandridas looked at her back, noting the short hair with displeasure. Although he knew that this, too, was traditional, it made her look less attractive than before, and he remarked in annoyance, "You looked better with long hair."

"Thanks!" Her tone was sarcastic and more resentful than ever. She knew she was no beauty, even if Lysandridas had made her feel pretty ever since they'd become lovers.

The exhaustion was beginning to get the better of Lysandridas. "Maybe tonight isn't the night to celebrate our wedding after all," he snapped, expecting her to protest and run into his arms to stop him from leaving.

"Maybe not," Leonis flung back at him, more hurt than angry now, all her self-doubts coming back. Did he regret marrying her already?

"All right, then. Good night." Lysandridas turned on his heel and was out the door. Leonis heard him pounding down the stairs and out into the courtyard. After another moment or two the door slammed shut. Leonis was still standing in their pristine, virgin bedchamber, her heart cringing inside her chest, too chilled by his rejection for tears.

Lysandridas paused in the corridor beside the house, trying to calm his anger. He was already regretting leaving, but by the time he was back out in the street he had found fuel for his own indignation. He reminded himself that during childhood, Leonis had insisted *she* was *never* going to marry. She was going to be a priestess to Artemis. She was going to have control of her *own* life. Maybe she really didn't want to marry, Lysandridas found himself thinking. Maybe it was all a terrible mistake....

He heard a noise behind him; but before he could even turn or stop to listen, something heavy, dank, and suffocating was thrown over his head. He felt powerful, crushing arms around his chest. He struggled until a rope replaced flesh and he was bound inside the blanket, his arms pinioned to his sides. He flung himself left and right, trying to break free, and he tried to run. They tripped him. With no way to catch himself, he fell face first onto the pavement with an audible thud. They were on top of him, pinning him down, grasping his head, and pulling the blanket tighter so that he was truly suffocating. Then they lifted his head and cracked it down on the pavement until he went limp. His last conscious thought was simply: the kryptea.

Torches lit up the Council Chamber. The smoke and flickering light added to the atmosphere of agitation as the members of the Council of Elders—the lochagoi and ephors—stood about in little groups, arguing and contradicting one another rather than taking their seats. No one had officially called a meeting of the Council; it hadn't seemed necessary. The Elders had come to the Council Chamber automatically. But the absence of King Anaxandridas made it impossible to convene a full session of the Council.

"Well, where the hell is he?" his co-regent demanded impatiently.

"He's at the Agiad royal palace."

"The palace?! If he were halfway to Tegea with the Guard, I could understand, but the palace? Hasn't anyone sent word to him?"

"Of course. Several times. He refuses to come."

"Why, in Zeus' name?" King Agesikles thundered, his voice echoing in the rafters of the chamber. "I know the boy's timid—but by Ares, surely this will at last have made a man of him? For the love of Aphrodite, he's got the blood of Heracles in his veins! He can't mean to let the bastards get away with this! We must pursue at once! In full force! The dithering has got to end!" He flung a furious look in Chilon's direction, but the ephor refused to be provoked. "Anaxandridas should be here demanding revenge!" Agesikles insisted, frustrated into rage because of the time they were wasting waiting for his co-regent.

"Chilon, won't you go and make another attempt to get Anaxandridas to join us?" One of the oldest of the Elders turned to Chilon in exasperation.

Chilon, who had been sitting some three rows up, a little apart from the rest of the unquiet crowd, nodded. He stood, flung the end of his himation over his shoulder, and clambered over the polished marble bench to mount the stairs leading up to the doors at the back of the chamber.

Outside it was dusk; the last rays of orange light lit up the bellies of clouds streaking across the sky. The dying light to the west transformed the Taygetos into ominous silhouettes, while the eastern sky was already a luminous blue in which the stars hung. Chilon found himself staring at the night sky. He was filled with a profound sense of humility mixed with guilt. He had not foreseen this turn of events, but he sensed vaguely that he had in some way provoked it with his messages to Ambelos and Antyllus.

With a deep breath he pulled his courage together and went to face the victim. The Guard let him into the formal front of the palace without question; but when he tried to pass through the propylaeum to the inner atrium, an elderly man stopped him. Chilon recognised him as King Leon's attendant of many years, an ageing but trusted helot who had served the Agiad royal family for years. "King Anaxandridas is not receiving guests."

"I'm not a guest," Chilon countered; "I'm an elected ephor acting on the instructions of the Council of Elders."

The helot could hardly maintain his resistance in face of this authority, but his loyalties clearly lay with his young master. "King Anaxandridas was very close to his sister, sir. This is not a matter of honour to him. It is a wound that will not heal."

"All wounds heal—or they kill us," Chilon reminded the helot. "Take me to him."

The helot led the way through the double columns and down the steps into a walled garden with two little temples, one on either side, and a larger, more imposing two-storied colonnade opposite. Chilon knew that the library and archives of the Agiads were housed in the upper story of the building opposite, but to his surprise, the helot led him to the little temple at the right. He asked Chilon to wait at the foot of the steps and went into the temple alone. After several minutes he returned and nodded to Chilon.

Chilon found the young king sitting on the floor at the base of a statue to Cassandra. Now he understood; Cassandra was the name of his captive sister. Anaxandridas was still in the armour he had pulled on at the sound of the alarm. Only his helmet was missing, tossed into the corner and lying there still. He gazed up at Chilon with large, wary eyes. "What do you want of me?" he challenged.

"The Council cannot convene without you, sir. We beg you to join us so we can decide what is to be done."

"Done?" Anaxandridas continued to stare at him, his arms on his bent knees, his hands dangling. "Did you know my sister?"

"Not well."

"No. No one but her family knew her well. She was not the type of woman to draw attention to herself." It struck Chilon that he was speaking of his sister as if she were dead. "She was widowed four years ago. My brother-in-law was taken wounded in the battle and died in captivity before the ransom money arrived. She was devastated—" Anaxandridas broke off. "She will not survive this. She is as delicate and fragile as a flower. The brutality of what they're doing to her will crush the life out of her. And if her heart does not give out from pain, it will stop from sheer shame. She will—" He stopped himself again, and turned his head away.

"We don't know what they've done with the captives."

"What!? You don't know!? *I* sure as hell know what is done with female captives!" Anaxandridas retorted furiously; and then he looked up into the face of the statue over him. The captive women of Troy surrounded them in the little temple, lamenting and accusing with deafening silence.

Chilon did not answer right away. Tradition and law were on Anaxandridas' side—and all he had was a very nebulous hope that he could not openly justify. If this raid was in some way a response to his overtures to Antyllus, then it might be something other than what it appeared to be.

But he couldn't know for sure. It might just be a raid. It might be what all the others thought it was—a challenge and an insult and an intentional provocation.

"You may well be right. Indeed, you probably are, but what if you're not?"

"What do you mean?" The young king snapped his head down and levelled an angry gaze at Chilon.

"I mean, if there is just one chance in 100 that your sister and the others have not been violated yet, wouldn't it be worth trying to ransom them?"

"I'd ransom anything but the Kingdom itself!"

The force of the emotions behind that surprised even Chilon, and he took a moment to absorb what it might mean. "Then come with me to the Council and stop the hotheads from turning this into an ill-conceived rampage of revenge."

Anaxandridas pulled himself to his feet. By his movements, it was clear that he was stiff and must have been sitting here for some time. Chilon bent and picked up the young king's helmet and handed it to him. Anaxandridas pulled it down onto his head so that his face was shielded, his eyes lost in the deep sockets flanking the nosepiece.

They walked together to the council house. It was now very nearly dark. They entered unnoticed by the door at the top of the seats. Below them the others were still arguing and planning. Only a few of the elder men had sunk, exhausted, onto the nearest seats.

"What do you propose to do?" Anaxandridas asked in a low voice, hesitating at the top of the steps.

"Do? I can't do anything on my own. The Council must decide."

"What do you *want* to do?"

"I want to send ambassadors to Tegea, offering substantial ransoms on the condition that the women are unharmed."

"But what if they've already been—harmed?" the helmet asked.

"Then we offer less of a ransom, but we bring them home. If we go to war—whether it's a full-scale invasion or just a raid—the captives will be the first to pay the price. If we ransom them, even if they have suffered much, we can put an end to that suffering. Our ambassadors can be in Tegea by tomorrow night. We could have them back safely in two days—if all goes well."

"They'll never be the same," the low voice came from the immobile mask of the helmet.

"Perhaps not. None of us are the same after going through a horrible experience; but we can go on living. We can become stronger. That's what all our training is about. Not dying gallantly, but being strong enough to go on living—even when it hurts. Would you really rather that your sister dies?"

The helmet moved slowly from side to side. Then the voice added, "Don't forget my niece. She's only eight. Even if the others have been—she's still a child. If the Tegeans have any decency, any honour, any mercy, they will leave her alone—surely?"

"I think you can count on that. Tegea is not a barbarian country. They're no less Greek than we are."

"What price do you think we should offer?"

"Twice what we paid for our men."

"700 drachma?"

"Yes."

"Even if they've been harmed?"

"If they *haven't* been harmed, that price is far too low." Chilon was gambling, but he had a gambling streak in him, and sometimes he couldn't resist.

He heard Anaxandridas catch his breath. "What then? A thousand? 7000 Drachma – the Council will never approve it. We don't have it."

Chilon refrained from pointing out that Anaxandridas alone could raise that sum, just by selling off some of his Messenian properties. "I wasn't thinking of any sum. You said back there that if your sister was not harmed, you'd be willing to pay anything but the Kingdom itself to have her back safe."

The helmet did not move, but Chilon could see Anaxandridas' eyes glinting in the sockets.

"Offer the Tegeans peace—a treaty of non-aggression. Put an end to this simmering war that has brought us nothing but grief."

The helmet looked away and started down the steps to the floor of the chamber. Chilon had no option but to follow him.

It took three hours, but in the end Chilon had what he wanted. He and two of the other ephors were appointed Ambassadors to Tegea, with the mandate to secure the release of the captured women—at almost any cost. In exchange, the war faction had secured the promise of both Anaxandridas and two of the lochagoi, who up to now had sided with Chilon, to vote for war if the mission failed. That meant that failure would inevitably result in war, because then both kings and the majority of the lochagoi would be in favour of it. Furthermore, Chilon was certain that as a result of the raid alone, sentiment in the Assembly would shift in favour of war. In short, he had to succeed, or his long fight to prevent new hostilities was at an end.

To help him succeed, he secured the approval of the kings and Council to take Lysandridas with him. After stopping by his home to inform his wife and give instructions to his helots to pack what he needed for the mission, he continued to Lysandridas' barracks. When he learned that Lysandridas was absent, he laughed. How could he have forgotten what it was to be young and in love? Still amused by Lysandridas' ardour, he made his way to the house Lysandridas had rented. He felt a little guilty disturbing an ardent bridegroom in his marriage bed, but he didn't have a choice. He knocked loudly and called out.

Leonis was still sitting stiffly on the bed, lost in gloom and self-hatred. At the sound of the knocking, she leapt up with relief and ran downstairs so fast she almost fell. She tore open the door calling out, "Lysandridas, I'm so—" She stared, bewildered, at a startled Chilon.

Chilon recovered first. "Isn't Lysandridas here?"

She shook her head, disappointment obliterating all other thoughts.

"He hasn't been here at all?"

"No. I mean he collected me from my aunt's and brought me here, but then he left again in a hurry...."

"How long ago was that?"

It was dark; it was hard to tell how long she'd sat there regretting all she'd done wrong and cursing herself and feeling sorry for herself. "An hour; maybe more." She still did not realise the significance of what she was saying.

Chilon, cursing, left her standing in the doorway. He ran to the nearest barracks, arriving out of breath, but still capable of shouting the entire battalion awake. "Where's your piper? You have to sound muster *immediately!*"

While most of the men fell out of their beds, reaching for their weapons instinctively, and one of the sentries went to rouse the piper specifically, the other sentry was asking, "Don't you mean "alarm", sir?"

"No! I don't want anyone wasting time with getting armed. Just muster! Blow muster!" he addressed the naked piper stumbling out of the darkness at him.

The wailing of the pipes seemed to come from very far away. At first the sound did not even penetrate to Lysandridas' consciousness at all, but the others heard it. Their voices changed—surprised, baffled, and alarmed. They fled, dousing the torches as they left.

Lysandridas was alone in the darkness. Alone with his pain and self-loathing. He'd vomited over himself when they'd punched his stomach. His bladder, too, had weakened at some point. He wanted to die. He felt that if he could just lie down, he would escape into oblivion before they came back to finish him off. But the chains held him upright, and when his head fell forward the iron at his throat choked off his breath. He tried to find a position that was halfway comfortable, but there was none. Everything hurt.

Then the voices came again. They opened a door, and the light that came in with it was not just torchlight. The men were silhouetted against the grey of a door at the end of a long corridor. The men advanced; the light from the torches revealed the neat stonework of the tomb. The torches lit up their faces, and for the first time this night Lysandridas was truly terrified. This was no longer the kryptea: it was at least half the Council, King Agesikles among them, and all five ephors; and several army officers were with them, including his battalion and divisional commanders, Krantios and Epicydes, respectively.

That could only mean the kryptea had been acting on orders, Lysandridas' brain told him. They were here to legalise his execution.

They seemed to stare at him for an inordinately long time, and their expressions were harsh and shocked. King Agesikles snapped out an order, and Nicoles wormed out from behind the dignitaries to unlock the irons. Chilon moved forward to catch Lysandridas. "Can you stand?" he asked in a low voice.

"I think so," Lysandridas pulled himself together.

"Can you walk?" Chilon asked next.

"How far?"

"Tegea."

"Have I been exiled?" Lysandridas could hardly believe it. Exile was life. He might even be allowed to take Leonis with him—if she wanted. But how could they let him go to Tegea now? It made no sense.

"No; of course not. We want you to assist us in persuading the Tegeans to release the captives." Chilon pulled Lysandridas' arm across his shoulders and was supporting him with an arm around his waist, ignoring the drying vomit on his chest and chiton.

Epicydes came up on his other side. "We must have a physician examine him for serious injuries," he said over Lysandridas' head to Chilon.

Krantios responded to the implicit order: "I'll fetch our surgeon, sir." He pushed his way through the crowd back out toward the light.

Another councilman ordered someone to fetch a cart or chariot; but Chilon was saying to Lysandridas, "Can you ride, do you think? We have to go to Tegea today. I *need* you to come with me. It's our last and only hope."

"Can I rest a little first, sir? And I need a bath."

Epicydes took Lysandridas from Chilon, because he was stronger, adding in a matter-of-fact tone, "We'll get you cleaned up and have the surgeon look you over. If he agrees, you can rest in the chariot on the way to Tegea. You can have use of my chariot, Chilon," he added. The lochagoi all had large, representational chariots for ceremonial purposes, and they were large enough to carry a driver and four men—or for a man to lie down in.

Outside it was dawning, but not yet sunrise. A crowd had collected, and people gasped and murmured at the sight of Lysandridas. He was ashamed; but from behind him came the vehement cursing of King Agesikles, and the cursing was directed at the kryptea. "You idiots! Don't you realise what you've done?! You'll lose your citizenship for this! Chilon won't let you get away with this. He'll use this incident to disband the kryptea altogether! How could you be so stupid?! Attacking a Spartiate!—An Olympic victor! Absolute idiots! You deserve what you'll get!"

And then Leonis was there. The crowd parted a little to let her through. Her face was ashen, her hair in disarray; she looked at Lysandridas with eyes that seemed not yet to have recovered from shock. Lysandridas wanted to take her in his arms and comfort her. He wanted to assure her that he was alive, and assure himself of the same thing. He wanted to tell her he loved her before something else came between them, but he was too aware of the vomit and blood. He reached out his hand instead, and she grabbed it fiercely. Their eyes met, and it was all right.

CHAPTER 25

By mid-morning Lysandridas had been cleaned up and dressed in his armour. None of the bruises or internal damage inflicted by the kryptea were visible. It had meanwhile been decided that the ambassadors would travel in two ceremonial chariots. Chilon and Lysandridas with their attendants were in the first, the other two ephors and their attendants in the second. A herald was sent ahead to the border to warn of the ambassadors' approach.

They passed the border without any difficulties. Diplomatic immunity was a sacred custom that no civilised people would dream of violating. As they started the final descent into Tegea, they were met by Tegean cavalry, sent to escort them in parade dress into the city.

By the time they reached the walls of the city, the sun had set, although the last light lit up the sky to the west. Normally, the gates to the city would have been closed, but they were opened and the streets lined with curious, excited crowds. It was easy to sense the triumphal mood of the spectators. Now and then someone called out some phrase to remind the Spartans they were here as supplicants. Others reminded them of their defeat nearly four years earlier. One or two went so far as to refer to the captives, making reference to how easy it had been to seize them: "Just like Helen!"

Lysandridas thought that the Tegeans should not be so quick and happy to put themselves into the role of Troy. Helen had been taken easily and retaken only after ten years of war; but in the end the Spartans had brought her home, and Troy had paid the higher price.

Nevertheless, all of the Spartans were relieved to arrive at Harmatides' walled house on the outskirts of the city and to leave the catcalling crowd behind the gates. The chariots were drawn up and turned inside the outer courtyard. "That's Harmatides waiting for you on the steps into the main house," Lysandridas murmured to Chilon. "He's flanked by Onimastros and Lampon," he added, and then let Chilon dismount first and go forward with the other ephors, while he hung back humbly as befitted a younger man.

Harmatides, Onimastros, and Lampon greeted the Lacedaemonian ambassadors with great dignity and formality. They were graciously invited into the house, which was alight with more lamps than for even the most luxurious political symposium. The guests were led to a wing of the house Lysandridas had never entered before, and four chambers were put at their disposal, all magnificently furnished. Fresh linens smelling of thyme and fresh air waited pressed and pristine on the beds. Fresh-cut lilacs were arranged in the vases. In the washing bowls, orchids floated. Bowls of fruit offered refreshment. Lysandridas was impressed by how quickly Harmatides had prepared such a magnificent reception. The guests were also shown the baths and invited to make use of them before the dinner, which would be served "whenever they were ready".

Lysandridas was stiff, aching, and tired. He wanted only to rest before dinner, but Ambelos found him almost at once. "It *is* you!" He stood in the doorway hesitantly, adding with evident dismay, "You look so Spartan in all that scarlet and bronze."

Lysandridas nodded solemnly, getting to his feet again. His own emotions were in turmoil at the sight of the youth who had befriended him when he was no one. "I am—but I've come to try to make peace between our cities."

"Truly?" Ambelos' eyes lit up with hope.

"That's what Chilon wants."

With the impulsiveness of youth, Ambelos left all his doubts behind him in the doorway as he closed the door and came into the room. He had never needed a friend so much as in these last two months since Lysandridas had left; and now he opened his heart with the familiar intimacy of the past, asking earnestly, "Do you think you have a chance?"

Before Lysandridas could answer, all his pent-up worries came tumbling out. "Oh, you don't know all that has been going on here! It's horrible! The mob—led by that horrid Phaeax and his slimy friend Polyphom—has turned against my father. They've started to demand either war or an end to the emergency powers. From day to day they grow more restless and destructive. First they disrupted performances at the theatre—throwing rotten vegetables and whistling so the actors couldn't be heard. Then they smashed up booths in the agora, stealing openly, and once they tried to break into our tile factory. He *had* to do something. The raid was the best thing he could think of, but—"

"What's happened to the captives? Much of our success depends on the state they're in."

Ambelos' eyes grew large. "It was horrible! To show what he had done, to win back the approval of the mob, my father paraded the captives through the streets in cages, thinking that would bring the mob back on his side; but they demanded an *auction*. They said it wasn't fair for him to keep the women for himself—as if he were going to keep them as his personal concubines!" Ambelos' outrage would have been amusing if the situation hadn't been so serious.

"My father called an Assembly. He went before them and argued that if he auctioned the women off, only seven men would be happy and the rest would go empty-handed. He reminded them that the rich would win any auction—which, of course, brought most of the rabble back onto his side. He said that to hold the women for ransom would be more democratic, because the ransom could be divided equally among the citizens." Ambelos seemed unaware of the irony of a tyrant arguing on the grounds that some course of action would be "more democratic". He continued breathlessly, "But then someone shouted out that even if Lacedaemon paid 1,000 drachma a head, that wouldn't amount to a drachma per citizen. So they started roaring that the women should be put in a public brothel so that all citizens could have their—forgive me—'piece of Spartan ass.'" Ambelos felt guilty for the vulgarity of his language.

Lysandridas' face was unreadable. "Go on."

"My father said that seven women would be hard pressed to service 12,000 citizens, but with Spartan ransom money he could build them a brothel with 1000 whores."

"But the crowd started chanting that they wanted—excuse me— 'Spartan ass', not worn-out whores. I honestly don't know how it would have ended if the news hadn't arrived that Lacedaemonian ambassadors had just crossed the border. My father managed to convince the majority to wait and at least hear your offer."

"So the captives haven't been touched yet?" Lysandridas pressed for confirmation.

Ambelos shook his head.

"Not even by the cavalrymen who captured them?"

"No. You can visit them if you like. They're all being kept here, in this house."

"I'm sure the ephors will want to see them and speak to them."

Ambelos nodded absently, "But you've got to offer something my father can sell to the mob, Lysandridas! They're so bloodthirsty—and ungrateful. They don't remember anything he's done for them in the past—not the extended franchise, nor the theatre, nor the games, nor the wine allotment—nothing! They want something new every day! Especially Kapaneos! He's insatiable and—I don't know—I can't help feeling he's just someone's puppet. But I don't know whose." Ambelos' agitation was evident in the way he kept playing with the knife in his belt.

A knock at the door was followed by Chilon asking Lysandridas if he was ready for dinner. "Yes, sir," Lysandridas answered, before turning to Ambelos and asking, "Can you get word to Antyllus that I'm here and would like to meet with him?"

"Of course—but my father and Antyllus don't speak to one another these days," Ambelos warned.

"Your father wouldn't stop him from seeing me, would he? I can't leave here. Antyllus must come to me."

"I'll see what I can do," Ambelos promised solemnly, and then flung his arms around Lysandridas. "I've missed you so much!"

Lysandridas was touched, and he could honestly admit, "And I you."

As was to be expected, the dinner was opulent and excessive. Lysandridas was given a couch farther down the hall, where he could only catch fragments of the discussion between the principals. More than once, however, he noticed Harmatides gazing at him. He was certain Ambelos had gone straight to his father after their talk—just as he himself had immediately informed Chilon and the other ephors of the content of it as well.

But Lysandridas was at the end of his strength. He hurt all over, he had been urinating blood all day, he was exhausted, and the doctor had warned him not to drink anything but water. He was relieved when dinner was over, and he retired immediately afterwards rather than joining the rest of the delegation in visiting the captives.

Lysandridas was wakened by Thorax when it was still very early morning. "Sorry to wake you, sir, but there's a man here—a Tegean—who says you sent for him."

"Antyllus! Let him in at once." Lysandridas flung back the covers and swung his legs down, reaching for his chiton.

But Antyllus was already in the room, striding towards him smiling. Abruptly his face dropped and he stopped in his tracks, staring at Lysandridas' battered torso. "Zeus! What happened to you?"

Lysandridas looked down at the bruises, which had darkened overnight, and smiled wanly. "The kryptea."

"What?"

"There are some people in Sparta who consider me a traitor. They— were trying to get information out of me. Fortunately, Chilon interceded on my behalf."

Antyllus sank onto the nearest chair, staring in horror. "Your own countrymen did that to you?" And then, with a sense of wonder, "You kept faith with us despite all that?"

"No one has yet succeeded in forcing me to say something I don't want to," Lysandridas reminded him with a crooked smile.

Antyllus laughed briefly at the memory of Philip's insolence, but then he looked down at his manicured hands with the signet ring and shook his head. "We don't deserve your loyalty, Lysandridas. This city is—" He searched for the right word, took a deep breath, and decided on: "corrupted, degenerate. I have never seen such a display of vulgarity as in the Assembly yesterday. Led by that wastrel Kapaneos! To think I once let that desolate, useless wretch sleep under my roof, that I seriously thought of adopting him once upon a time, that I—"

"*You* deserve my loyalty, Antyllus," Lysandridas interrupted him gently, and then signalled to Thorax to bring his clothes so he could cover the offending bruises. While Thorax helped Lysandridas to dress, Antyllus described the shocking events of the day before, nearly as upset by them as Ambelos had been.

Lysandridas came and stood opposite him, and Antyllus looked at him uneasily, searching his face for something. "Ambelos said you called yourself Spartan, but he didn't know—I mean, about what they did to you. Are you sure you made the right decision?"

Lysandridas did not answer instantly. He sat down opposite Antyllus and met his eyes. "There have been times when I wished I was back in Tegea with you. My own grandfather spat on me and moved out of our kleros rather than sleep under the same roof. My brother-in-law pretends I do not exist, and my sister's children run away from me. The Agiads have a splendid racing team which they will not let me drive—"

"Well *that's* something to be thankful for, at least," Antyllus quipped, and Lysandridas remembered too late that it would have meant driving against Antyllus. He opened his mouth, but Antyllus shook his head. "I know. You can't resist a good team. But with all these negative experiences, why *not* return here?"

Lysandridas was shaking his head. "It's not that simple. If I returned, I would prove all my enemies right, for a start; and," he shrugged—a little embarrassed—"I'm married, Antyllus."

Antyllus was astonished. "Your bride—but your father said—"

"No, another girl—woman." Lysandridas tried to explain. He spoke at some length, trying to give a picture of what he had found in Lacedaemon. There was the kryptea, yes, but there was still his father and also Leonis. There were Dorrusos, Euxenos and his son, Krantios and Epicydes—and Chilon. Lysandridas paused and said very solemnly, "Sir, I want you to meet Chilon."

Antyllus smiled at the young man before him, amused by his earnestness. "But of course; I assumed that was why I was here."

Lysandridas was reminded of the other's far greater political experience and annoyed with his own naivety, but all he could do was nod and ask Thorax to fetch Chilon.

Antyllus got to his feet as the Spartan ephor entered the chamber. Chilon smiled, and Antyllus started slightly. "Have we met before?"

"At Olympia, I believe," Chilon answered, "when this remarkable young man drove his father's chariot to victory against your better team." He gestured towards Lysandridas without taking his intelligent blue eyes off Antyllus' face.

"Before the last war," Antyllus reminded the Spartan more seriously.

"Indeed," Chilon agreed, adding, "Teleklos knew nothing of it at the time, nor did Lysandridas here."

"But you knew?"

"I knew—and was helpless to stop it. I want to stop it now. I think you can help me."

"I will try." They sat down simultaneously, Chilon taking Lysandridas' vacated place and his eyes still locked with Antyllus'.

"We were given a mandate to secure the freedom of the captive women at almost any price, provided they had not been violated," Chilon explained.

"And have they been?" Antyllus asked with raised eyebrows.

"No. We were able to visit them last night and speak to them in private. Harmatides surprises me. For a tyrant he seems remarkably—humane."

"Don't underestimate him. He is capable of cold-blooded murder. But he is losing control of the mob."

"What use is a tyrant who does not control the mob?"

"No use," Antyllus agreed.

There was a moment of silence. Then Chilon remarked, "Odd. Then why didn't he sacrifice the captives for his popularity? It would have been so easy."

Antyllus shrugged. "I agree. I expected him to. Maybe he would have— if the news of your imminent arrival hadn't stayed his hand."

"Does the mob want blood? War?"

"It thinks it does. No, that was worded imprecisely. The mob does not *think*. But it believes it will be victorious as it was in the past, and the prospect of loot and women is enticing—all the more so after yesterday's disgusting spectacle. You have the misfortune of having very attractive women in Lacedaemon."

Chilon hesitated briefly. Princess Cassandra had admitted to the ephors in their brief talk the night before that she had told Harmatides her identity, in the desperate hope that it would protect her and her daughter from rape. In retrospect, it had been unnecessary, she admitted, but no one could blame her for her panic. The captives might not have been physically abused and mishandled as yet, but they had been ruthlessly terrorised nevertheless. The threat of violence was ever present, and their slave status indisputable. The humiliation of being paraded through the streets in cages, mocked and subjected to lewd remarks and gestures, was reflected still in their faces when the ambassadors were admitted to visit them.

Chilon suspected that Harmatides might have given in to the mob far sooner if he hadn't known he held a Spartan princess captive—something he had apparently told no one else. This fact had made him confident of a ransom offer. But the discussions last night only reinforced what Antyllus was saying. The mob wanted blood and loot, and was not at all inclined to peace. A tyrant could ill afford to make peace under the circumstances. For the moment, Chilon could see little hope for his mission, and he was discouraged despite his naturally optimistic nature.

"One of the captives is the widowed sister of our Agiad King Anaxandridas," Chilon told Antyllus.

Antyllus caught his breath and then asked slowly, "And what is the Lacedaemonian government prepared to offer for her safe return?"

"A non-aggression pact." Even as Chilon said it, he knew it wasn't enough. "Is there anyone here who wants it?"

"Yes," the answer came without hesitation. "The responsible citizens want it. The landowners, the merchants. Surprisingly enough ..." Antyllus' voice trailed off and he glanced over at Lysandridas, who was standing politely to one side, not daring to partake in the delicate discussion. "Surprisingly enough, I think even Harmatides wants it—if he could have it without losing his popularity and power." Antyllus shook his head. "But I don't see how he can manage that trick."

After a long silence, Chilon's impatience got the better of him. "Do you see no hope at all?"

Antyllus looked again at Lysandridas. "I see only one hope: Ambelos."

"What do you mean?"

"I mean that Ambelos might be able to convince his father to choose peace—provided Lacedaemon is prepared to sweeten the package enough to satiate the greed of the poorer citizens." He paused, thinking through his idea again, looking for weaknesses. He did not sound confident, but he was hopeful as he continued, "I estimate that roughly forty per cent of the population wants peace. A non-aggression pact would bring them behind Harmatides, but he would lose precisely the most vocal and violent elements that have so far supported him. If those elements, however, could be bought off with a ransom large enough—when distributed to those elements alone—to excite their greed, then Harmatides might actually have a narrow majority behind him. At least for the short term."

"Long enough for the treaty to be signed and the captives returned?"

"Yes."

"And how large must the ransom be?"

"The faction that needs to be bribed is maybe 1,000 – 1,200 strong. They would need at least ten drachma apiece to be sated."

"Twelve thousand drachma," Chilon calculated. "Two thousand apiece for the citizens and double that for Cassandra and her daughter would make 18,000. I think we could manage that." He glanced over at Lysandridas as if he might know. In fact, the Spartan delegation carried 20,000 drachma with them, put at their disposal by the Agiad treasurer at Anaxandridas' orders. "Let me discuss this with my fellow ephors."

"When you present the proposal to Harmatides, be sure Ambelos—and if possible, Lysandridas—are present." Antyllus advised.

Chilon glanced briefly at the silent und immobile Lysandridas and nodded.

For more than a day, the emissaries and their hosts politely danced around the topic of a concrete offer. Finally, however, Chilon found the opportunity he was looking for. Harmatides had taken his guests—including Lysandridas, accompanied by Ambelos—to see his extensive library. Neither Onimastros nor Lampon was present, because it was assumed "real" discussions would take place at table later. Chilon addressed Ambelos in a casual tone, "Lysandridas tells me you are in cavalry training?"

Harmatides stiffened noticeably and seemed to want to intervene, to speak for his son—but he respected him too much for that.

"Yes, sir. Lysandridas helped me choose a suitable mount last winter."

"And how long is training in Tegea?" Chilon asked in a fatherly tone, as if he were just making casual conversation with the youth and had not already learned this, along with many other details of Tegean cavalry training, from Lysandridas.

"Six months, sir. I'll be on active service after the summer solstice."

Chilon managed to look astonished, even though Lysandridas had told him all this. "But" —and he glanced at Harmatides, who was looking stiff and hostile—"you're very young, aren't you? I thought Lysandridas said you were just eighteen?"

"Yes, sir. We serve from eighteen to twenty."

"In Lacedaemon we don't allow men onto active service until they are twenty-one," Chilon pointed out.

"A good practice," Harmatides agreed at once in a tight, gruff voice. "Unfortunately, if I changed the custom now, everyone would accuse me of doing it only to protect my son."

"And I don't want to be protected," Ambelos insisted with youthful indignation.

"Ah, you want to prove yourself, as all young men do," Chilon nodded knowingly. Then, smiling indulgently, he added, "Young men are hotheaded. No doubt you can hardly wait for the war to be renewed."

Lysandridas felt Chilon was being far too obvious and that Ambelos would see through him, but Ambelos took the bait without a thought. "Not at all, sir! I have no reason to hate Lacedaemon—my best friend is Lacedaemonian." He looked pointedly at Lysandridas, who was embarrassed and looked down. Harmatides was watching the exchange with narrowed eyes; *he* had seen through Chilon, and he waited for his next move.

"You would welcome peace between our cities?" Chilon asked Ambelos in a sceptical tone of voice, as if he could not believe it.

"Yes, sir—as would my father." Ambelos challenged his father with his words and his look, and Chilon thought how good it was that Antyllus had advised him in advance.

Harmatides raised his eyebrows and told his son, in a less indulgent tone than usual, "That depends on the terms—and you forget the mob that still thirsts for Lacedaemonian blood."

"Blood or loot?" Chilon questioned with a slight smile.

"That depends. There is a faction that wants revenge for the insult of the invasion and the theft of Orestes' bones. There is another faction that is only interested in enriching themselves—at others' expense." Harmatides' contempt for the latter was obvious.

"And among those elements there will be leaders with the skill to rile up others to their cause, to fire them up to action," Chilon seemed to reflect, and then raised his eyebrows at Harmatides.

"Of course—Phaeax and Kapaneos for a start! I know them all by name, believe me!"

"Then …" Chilon paused, and seemed to consider what he was going to say very carefully. The other ephors and Lysandridas held their breath, while Ambelos looked from the Spartans to his father and back, confused. Harmatides was leaning against a table, waiting expectantly. "Then you should be in a position to buy their silence."

"Perhaps," Harmatides admitted.

"With 18,000 drachma?"

Harmatides gave no indication that he was surprised by the sum, but Ambelos caught his breath audibly, and a touch of a frown indicated that Harmatides was annoyed by the youth's reaction. Harmatides spoke calmly and neutrally, "A non-aggression pact for the peace-loving and a bribe for the greedy."

Chilon nodded.

"And what do I give the rest?"

Chilon had no answer. He hadn't expected the question.

Harmatides crossed his arms and ankles as he leaned back against the table and considered the Spartan ambassadors for a long moment. Then he uncrossed his legs and arms and turned his back on them. The entire length of the library was open on one side to an upstairs colonnade. He walked onto the long balcony and leaned on the railing, looking down to the courtyard below. The breeze ruffled his hair, and his long chiton fluttered. Lysandridas looked at Ambelos questioningly, but the young man shook his head and licked his lips, waiting. Finally, Harmatides turned and strode back into the room. "And Orestes' bones," Harmatides told the Spartans.

Theopompos, one of the other ephors, scowled and said "no" at once, but Chilon waved him silent. "Chilon," he started in a warning voice, but Chilon shook his head again, and this time Theopompos held his tongue.

"You ask a great deal," Chilon pointed out to Harmatides.

"So do you," Harmatides countered, and then added for the others—not Chilon, he knew Chilon understood— "This isn't about seven captive women, even if one is the sister of your King Anaxandridas. This is about the future safety of our respective borders. What good is a non-aggression pact signed by a deposed or murdered *former* tyrant?"

"Father—" Ambelos was horrified, but his father waved him silent and continued. "If you want a non-aggression pact worth the paper it's written on, then you want it to be accepted not by me, but by the majority of Tegean citizens. Peace will appeal to a third, and the rowdies can be bribed, but the majority needs something to restore their pride and dignity—and a guarantee of your own good behaviour." Harmatides narrowed his eyes at the other two ephors, the ones he wasn't sure of. "Do you think we haven't heard the oracles you got? Give us back Orestes' bones, and we will sign your non-aggression pact."

It took Chilon two days to get the other ephors argued around, but in the end they accepted Harmatides' conditions. Now, at the dinner following the signing of the agreement, the mood was one of relief. Many men seemed to be talking at once, and even the Spartans were drinking wine in their water.

It took a few moments before Onimastros' penetrating voice could be heard declaring that "while there is no one who loves peace more than I, there is a problem with the proposed treaty."

The chatting silenced gradually in disbelief.

"Namely?" Theopompos demanded, harshly and suspiciously.

"Whereas Harmatides has the power to sign the proposed non-aggression pact for Tegea on the basis of the powers voted to him by the Assembly, you—" his eyes swept slowly from one ephor to the next—"do not have a similar authority. Only your entire Council can sign a treaty, and your Assembly must ratify it. I don't mean to imply," he added, smiling and bowing his head, "that any of you would intentionally deceive us. But what is to protect Tegea from returning the captives in exchange for a treaty that is subsequently not ratified—and so worthless?"

"We've already handed over the ransom, in the Name of Zeus!" Theopompos thundered at him, making Chilon reach out a hand to calm him instinctively.

"But that is only a small part of the price," Onimastros insisted. "The women must remain here until this treaty has been ratified by your Assembly."

Lysandridas tried to read Harmatides' face, wondering if he had planned this with Onimastros or was himself surprised, but he couldn't tell. What was obvious from the look on Chilon's and the other ephors' faces, however, was that *they* had not reckoned with this complication. Indeed, Chilon was so stunned by the unexpected obstacle that it was Theopompos who responded. "Either the women return with us, or you can forget everything! We did not come here to return empty-handed!"

The third ephor, usually content to let the others talk, remarked after a glance at Chilon, "You can't expect us to leave the captives and the ransom here! Do you think we are idiots? Why should the Spartan Assembly ever approve a treaty with such an unreliable partner?"

"The terms of their release are threefold: the ransom, the treaty, and the return of Orestes' bones. You cannot expect us to return the captives for a third payment!" Onimastros made it sound like it was a joke.

"Then let us take a third of the captives back," the third ephor started, but Theopompos waved him silent. "No! All or nothing!"

Onimastros shrugged, "Then it will be nothing."

Everyone looked at everyone else in sheer disbelief. The Spartans felt they had made huge concessions—from coming in peace in the first place to promising the restoration of Orestes' bones. It was hard to believe it was all for nothing. And the cost of failure was war. Theopompos knew that and he didn't care, but Chilon did. He was as white as marble, and as lifeless.

"Surely a small delay in the return of the captives cannot be more important than their return itself?" Harmatides asked with pseudo-reasonableness into the stunned silence. "If you have negotiated in good faith, then the ratification of the treaty can only be a formality. Why is it so important that the captives return with you today rather than in a few days' time?"

"Today they are still unharmed," Theopompos pointed out. "But who's to say what will happen to them after we leave?"

Harmatides looked shocked and insulted as he announced in a definitive voice, "You have my word on it!"

"And, of course, we would be prepared to give you hostages as a guarantee of our good intentions," Onimastros added, smiling graciously.

"Hostages of equal value?" Theopompos challenged. "Will you turn your sisters and your wives over to us tomorrow?!" He did not expect consent, while Lysandridas remembered that Onimastros was reputed to hold his wife in such low regard that he entertained hetaerae in his own house.

"I'll go," Ambelos announced suddenly.

"Don't be a fool—" Harmatides burst out at his son, and then cut himself off.

Ambelos stared at his father. "But what have I to fear? You intend to honour the terms of the treaty, so I know the captives will be returned unharmed."

"The captives are women. If we provide hostages, they too will be women—"

"No, Father, you can't ask Mother to go. She's not well," Ambelos told his father earnestly, and then turned and looked at the Spartan ephors expectantly. "Will that be enough for you? If I and six other Tegean hostages come with you as a guarantee of the welfare of the captive women?"

"We'd have to know who the other hostages are to be," Theopompos insisted, frowning; but Chilon was staring at Ambelos so hard that the youth blushed and looked nervously at Lysandridas.

"You will release the girl, of course," Lysandridas risked addressing Harmatides directly for the first time. "You wouldn't keep a child in captivity longer than necessary."

Harmatides shrugged. He was pale and distracted. "Of course not. Take the girl with you."

The Spartan ephors exchanged looks again. "I think we can agree to this," Chilon ventured slowly, looking first to Harmatides before focusing on Onimastros with narrowed eyes. "We will take the girl and six Tegean hostages, including Ambelos, back with us to Sparta tomorrow. When the Spartan Assembly approves the treaty, Orestes' bones will be brought here in exchange for the remaining six Spartan captives. Provided they are still unharmed, the Tegean hostages will be released the minute the women cross back into Lacedaemon."

"That sounds reasonable," Onimastros agreed, smiling. He was the only one in the room who was.

CHAPTER 26

Travel was slow with the heavy baggage wagon carrying the Tegean hostages' things, and it was already getting dark by the time they reached the border. They decided to spend the night in the little fortress, while a runner was sent ahead to the city with the news. The following morning, the little convoy continued down into the Eurotas valley, arriving in Sparta shortly after midday. Word, of course, had spread throughout the city, and many people—citizens, perioikoi and helots—turned out to catch a glimpse of the Tegean hostages. But there was no triumphant mocking or sneering. The crowds were silent and the mood sober.

Anaxandridas himself was waiting at the bridge. His niece, with a squeal of delight, flung herself off the back of the chariot and ran into his arms almost before Lysandridas could bring it to a stop. Anaxandridas caught his niece in his arms, swept her off the ground, and covered her face with kisses. "Uncle Anaxandridas! I have so much to tell you! Mama says I'm to tell you everything!"

"Indeed you must." The king looked up at Chilon reproachfully. "I had expected to hear it from her directly."

"Mama is all right. You mustn't worry," his niece assured him anxiously.

"Let us report in Council, sir. Not here in the middle of the street," Chilon responded wearily.

Anaxandridas nodded, holding his niece still, his mouth set and his eyes heavy with disappointment. His gaze shifted to Lysandridas. "You are exempt from service until your trial."

"Trial?" Chilon and Lysandridas asked in unison.

Anaxandridas shrugged. "Nicoles' relatives have brought charges of treason against Lysandridas. They claim to have evidence that he is a Tegean citizen, agent, and spy. He will have to answer before the Assembly."

The Extraordinary Assembly was called for three days later, giving those citizens living on more distant estates time to come into the city. The agenda was divided into three parts: the ratification of the non-aggression pact, including the return of Orestes' bones; the disbanding of the krypteia; and the exile of Nicoles and/or Lysandridas.

Leonis helped Lysandridas dress in the armour Thorax had spent half the night polishing. They did not speak until he stood ready with his helmet under his arm. "Will you come with me?" Lysandridas asked simply.

"Of course," Leonis answered, catching up her himation and slipping her feet into her sandals. Although Spartan women did not have a vote, they were not prohibited from attending Assembly as in other cities, and many wives did attend. In fact, men had been known to openly consult their wives before casting their own vote—to the incomprehension of the rest of the Greek world.

"I meant into exile," Lysandridas explained himself.

Leonis looked up from her feet and stared at him. She had never been beyond the Eurotas valley in her life. The thought of leaving her home and all the people she had grown up with—Zoë, Kyniska, and the helots of her kleros—was terrifying. She refused to believe it would be necessary. But in this moment, she also knew that there was only one answer: "Of course."

Together they walked along the seemingly abandoned streets toward the stoa on the agora where the Assembly met. The shops were closed, and so the perioikoi and helots had no business in the city. The citizens who came from throughout Lacedaemon, however, were already collecting in the agora. The narrow streets leading into the agora were congested, and the low rumbling of the crowd could be heard some distance away. In the agora itself, the exceptional number of citizens made it impossible for all to find a place under the roof of the stoa, and so the crowd spilled out onto the pavement. Lysandridas and Leonis found a place to stand in the shade of the council house, knowing that they would lose the comfort of the shade when the sun moved higher.

With a signal the Assembly was called to order, and the ephors presented the bills that were submitted by the Council for ratification. The debate on the treaty with Tegea was opened. Lysandridas tried to concentrate on what was being said, but he could not. His mind kept wandering to the speech he would have to make in his own defence. Chilon had advised him to tell the truth—all of it. This meant his father would hear the full truth for the first time. He was doubly ashamed: for having accepted Tegean citizenship and for having hidden it from his father. Leonis slipped her hand in his and gripped it wordlessly.

Around them, the debate raged. The ransom and even the non-aggression treaty were accepted without demur, but the outrage against the return of Orestes' bones was so great that it deafened reason. Lysandridas could not understand. He tried to, but he couldn't. The Assembly voted down the agreement because of this symbolic gesture, and Chilon stood grey and defeated at the front of the Assembly before they even moved to the second point on the agenda.

The proposal to disband the kryptea was based primarily on what it had done to Lysandridas. The ephors and Council testified to the way they'd found him. Tensely, Lysandridas noted that the kryptea found no defenders, and Leonis squeezed his hand and smiled, encouraged. But the Assembly, despite condemning the actions of the kryptea in this case, refused to disband it entirely. The need for some kind of "secret police" to keep the "unreliable helots" under control was argued eloquently. The Assembly wanted a new commander and new members for the kryptea, but not an end to the institution as such. The fear of rebellion sat too deep, particularly among the older citizens. The memories of Aristomenes and the Second Messenian War sat too deep. Again, Chilon was defeated.

"You'll like Tegea," Lysandridas whispered to Leonis, without daring to look at her. The debate opened on his own fate.

The evidence was brought by Nicoles' relatives. Although it was not clear where they had obtained the information, they reported accurately that Lysandridas had been freed and adopted by Antyllus, making him a Tegean citizen. They went on to argue, circumstantially, that he must be acting in Tegean interests, citing his failure to catch the fleeing captors of the women as evidence.

Thessalos opened Lysandridas' defence by retorting scornfully that he, too, had failed to catch the fleeing Tegean cavalry, and he dared any man to doubt his loyalty to Lacedaemon. Epicydes and Krantios both testified to Lysandridas' devotion to duty, how hard he'd worked to regain his fighting skills, his readiness to do extra duty, his unhesitating pursuit of the Tegean raiders.

Lysandridas was surprised that Euxenos and Dorrusos also risked speaking in his favour, as did others he hardly knew. When Derykleides took the floor, Lysandridas held his breath; but his brother-in-law only stated simply that, "Despite all the differences of opinion we have had over the years, I have never had reason to doubt Lysandridas' loyalty to Lacedaemon."

At last Chilon spoke. Lysandridas placed his greatest hopes in the respected statesman, but he could see that Chilon was exhausted and discouraged by his earlier defeats. He spoke eloquently in Lysandridas' favour, stressing that without Lysandridas' familiarity with the Tegean politicians and his willingness to share all he knew with the Lacedaemonian envoys, they would have returned empty-handed. This, however, aroused hissing from the crowd that was displeased with the terms of the negotiated treaty. "The clause you object to was not his work," Chilon tried to argue; "the fact that we have valuable hostages, however, was!" But Lysandridas could sense that Chilon's arguments had failed to win new supporters.

At last no one else had anything to say, and Lysandridas was asked what he had to say for himself. Leaving Leonis, he walked forward to the front of the stoa. He faced his fellow citizens, looking for his father in the crowd. He did not find him, but his eyes met those of Derykleides and Thessalos and Krantios, one after the other, before he spoke. "It is true that I was adopted by Antyllus." A murmur swept through the crowd. "But I accepted his offer only because I believed my father had chosen not to buy my freedom. I thought I had been abandoned and discarded. I believed I had already lost my Spartan citizenship. Only under those circumstances—thinking I was already stateless—did I accept Tegean citizenship." He paused; but there was only a tense stillness in the crowd, which he could not read.

He continued: "I was betrothed to a girl of good family and was heir to a wealthy man with a stable of racehorses. But as soon as my father came to Tegea and I learned that I had *not* lost my Spartiate status, I gave up everything to come home.

"Neither in Tegea nor since my return have I ever worked against the interests of Lacedaemon. I had no contact with my acquaintances in Tegea until I accompanied our ambassadors on the orders of the Council. I used my connections there to try to secure the release of the captives. The child, at least, was returned at my request...." Self-praise was difficult to speak, and he sensed it did not go down well with his audience. He fell silent, unable to remember the other things he had wanted to say. He swallowed, waited, and then shook his head. "That is all I can say. I am not a traitor nor a spy nor an agent. I want nothing more than to be accepted as one of you again."

The silence lasted until it was clear that no one else had anything to say. Lysandridas made his way back to Leonis. He still had not been able to locate his father in the crowd, and in a way he was grateful for that.

They called for the vote. Those in favour of exiling Lysandridas were asked to say "aye". From the ranks of the accusers came loud and aggressive shouts, supported by a low murmur from a large body of other citizens. Those opposed to the exile were asked to say "nay". Although none shouted with as much vehemence or conviction as the accusers, still there were many, and the vote was close. The ephors frowned and consulted. The vote was repeated. Both sides shouted louder this time, aware that the vote was close and that noise alone could decide it. Lysandridas himself could not decide if he had taken the vote or not.

The ephors consulted a second time. Chilon and one of the others clearly insisted that the "nays" had predominated, but the other three officials shook their heads. Shaken by a third defeat, Chilon wiped his face with his hands, his shoulders sagging. It was left to another ephor to announce that Lysandridas had one day to leave the city.

Lysandridas turned and started for the house he had been allowed to live in only three days. Leonis walked beside him, unable to believe what had happened or grasp what it meant. Behind them, the debate on Nicoles opened.

"You don't have to come with me," Lysandridas told Leonis, sensing her bewilderment.

"I'm your wife," Leonis replied. She was trying to picture leaving, wondering what she would be allowed to take with her. The helots couldn't leave Lacedaemon, she reminded herself; they belonged to the city. Lysandridas and she would be completely alone.

Behind them, the shouts of "aye" reverberated angrily. The "nays" were a frail, faltering whimper. They had exiled Nicoles, too, Lysandridas registered; but it gave him little comfort.

They reached their little house, and it had never looked more beautiful to him. The sun spilled into the courtyard, and the flowers in the hanging pots and the window boxes were bright against the fresh whitewash.

The shadows were crisp and dark. Sparrows tittered as they bathed and drank from the kitchen trough. The smoke rising from the hearth smelt of pine. "I'm so sorry," he told Leonis, ashamed of having brought her to disgrace.

Leonis wrapped her arms around him and held him tightly, her head on his armoured chest. She wanted to cry, but instead she said, "A house doesn't matter. We've only rented it, anyway. We'll take everything with us."

"We don't need to. Antyllus has a fine house filled with everything one needs and more. You'll have slaves to wait on you." Lysandridas' voice was dead, and it was this that made Leonis cry. For a long time they just clung to one another, until a knocking startled them apart.

Leonis drew back, trying to wipe her tears away. Lysandridas turned towards the door and called in a harsh, angry voice, "Who's there?"

"Your father—Teleklos."

Lysandridas cast Leonis a glance that said he wasn't sure he could face this; but he went to the door and opened it. Teleklos stumbled into the courtyard, blinded by his own tears. "It's all my fault," he sobbed. "It's all my fault," and he collapsed in Lysandridas' arms.

PART IV

❀

THE FINAL CONTEST

CHAPTER 27

On the surface, nothing had changed in Tegea. Antyllus was overjoyed to welcome Lysandridas back into his home and family, while Pheronike seemed pleased in her cool way to have another lady in the house. The horses recognised Lysandridas and responded eagerly to his hand. Although there were two new grooms who had never known Lysandridas as a slave and were subservient and distant, Cobon was gruffly friendly, willing to gossip in the shade after training.

Because the war was still prevented by the hostages (the Spartans insisted on renegotiating the treaty, and the Tegeans insisted on the fulfilment of terms), the strange illusion of peace continued. As spring ripened into summer, the routine of training for the Olympics continued as if it had never been interrupted by the unexpected arrival of Teleklos. On the surface, it was as if Lysandridas had never returned to Sparta—only to be exiled again.

But beneath the surface, everything had changed. Lysandridas was not content. Although he enjoyed the horses and training, after seeing the royal Spartan team he no longer believed Antyllus had a real chance of success at Olympia. Besides, how could one truly get enthusiastic about the Olympic Games when war between his two cities (as he had come to think of them) threatened? He missed Ambelos' company and feared for his safety; if the tedious and seemingly futile negotiations broke down, then none of the hostages had a future worth living. Worst of all, as soon as the horses were put away, Lysandridas was confronted by the emptiness of his life. He asked himself what he was living for. Was he nothing but a horse trainer? A charioteer? At home he had been a citizen with duties and responsibilities. Here he was a spoiled guest.

Things were worse for Leonis; she was miserable. She tried not to complain. She even tried to hide her loneliness and boredom from her husband, but he had only to glance over when she was unaware, and he could see the hopelessness etched onto her face. Of course, she admired the beauty of Antyllus' house and marvelled at the baths and fountains. She had been delighted by his gardens, amazed by the creativity of his cook, and even enjoyed Pheronike's lessons in scents and make-up and hairdressing. But the novelty had worn off within a week or two, replaced by a listless sadness. She was not herself here, Lysandridas realised uncomfortably. She had lost all her fire and temper and courage. She was not the woman he had grown up with, fallen in love with, and married in Lacedaemon. He did not even particularly *like* the woman she had become, but he knew the fault was his, not hers.

Only their nights were happy, filled with an almost frantic passion, after which Leonis would curl up in his arms, cuddling against him as if she could not get enough of his warmth and presence. It made him feel strong and protective—and determined to make something of their lives.

Lying awake at night with Leonis snuggled up beside him, he knew that Harmatides would be happy to give him a senior position in the Army. He could be an officer and commander in Tegea, as he was not at home. But despite what the Spartan Assembly had done to him, he could not bring himself to seek such a position. He was bitter about his exile, but he did not want the death and defeat of all those citizens who had voted *for* him in that fateful Assembly. He lived in dread of a summons from Harmatides that would confront him with the necessity of fighting against the city of his birth.

Instead, he wished that he could have had some kind of civic role—in the courts or administration, a role that would not bring him into direct conflict with his former city, yet make him feel like a full citizen again. But in a tyranny there was not even an Assembly at which he could vote, and Antyllus had made it very clear that he did not want to support Harmatides' tyranny by serving under him—or letting his adopted son serve under him.

So night after night, Lysandridas fell asleep no closer to a resolution of his dissatisfaction than before. And when at first light he roused himself to go to the horses, the sadness returned to Leonis' eyes.

One morning, when he had been back in Tegea a little more than a month, Leonis did not bother to get up with him. "Don't you want to come and watch?" he asked as he pulled his driving chiton over his head.

From the bed Leonis shrugged, her eyes closed and her face strained.

"You can't stay in bed all day," Lysandridas told her sharply, his dislike for her listlessness getting the better of him.

"Why not? There's nothing to do anyway."

"What did you do at home?" Lysandridas asked, buckling on his belt and frowning.

"At home?" Leonis' opened her eyes and glared at him hotly. He shied away from her look, concentrating on twisting a rag around his forehead to catch the sweat while he drove in the summer heat. "At home," Leonis told him in a proud tone, "I had my father's kleros to run! I had to decide what pasture to send the herds to, what work took priority, what we were to eat or store or sell. I had to keep the inventory and purchase those goods we could not produce ourselves, or send the men out to cut firewood before there was too little wood to keep the hearth going day and night. I had to decide what the women should weave—clothes or bed linens or rugs, whatever we needed most urgently. I had to settle disputes between the helots—or deal with crises like the fact that your helot Dion has been courting two girls at once. They had a horrible fight, clawing and biting, and one girl broke two fingers that I had to set!" She had worked herself up, and her eyes flashed with indignation.

Now she looked more like the Leonis he remembered, and Lysandridas abruptly realised that Leonis shouldn't be kept inactive any more than a racehorse. It didn't matter what the Tegean customs were; here on her own estate—and Antyllus' estate was hers now—Leonis had to be allowed to ride, or at least drive. "Come out with me to the stables," he urged. "We'll try an experiment today."

Leonis, ashamed of her little outburst, dressed herself hastily and followed him dutifully without another word.

By the time they reached the stables, Antyllus was waiting for them and looked a little worried; Lysandridas had never been late before.

"Is something wrong?" Antyllus asked, his eyes politely averted from Leonis, who was looking pale.

"I've been thinking," Lysandridas admitted. "You know I had the opportunity to watch the Spartan team train. In fact, Thessalos let me drive them once briefly."

Antyllus waited.

"They're very good."

Antyllus knew that, and it had not escaped his notice that Lysandridas trained with less enthusiasm than before. He had tried to put Lysandridas' mood down to the humiliation of exile, rather than doubts about the team itself, but Lysandridas' tone of voice now was pregnant with more bad news. Antyllus anticipated it. "Are you trying to tell me we don't have a chance?" Even as he put his worst fears into words, his heart lurched in disappointment. He had never believed in a victory as absolutely as he had since Lysandridas returned and he thought he had the perfect team and perfect driver. He did not want to—no—he *could* not give up his dreams of an Olympic victory so easily, much less casually. "You used to think the world of this team," he reminded his adopted son, in a tone that expressed his chagrin at Lysandridas' defeatism.

"Yes, sir, I still think you *could* have a winning team, but ..." He cut himself off, looking over at the four horses waiting impatiently in the traces, held by Cobon, who was listening very intently, a frown on his weathered face.

"But?" Antyllus prompted him, his face stiff with disappointment.

"Frankly, sir, I don't think Penny's up to it."

Antyllus sank onto the trough, his heart giving out on him as he stared at Lysandridas. Leonis, too, was gazing at her husband in disbelief. If he didn't believe he could even win, what *did* they have to live for and look forward to?

"I want to put Afra in Penny's place."

"Afra? She's never trained in the traces at all! She's too skittish! She'll make them all crazy! It's less than a month until we have to leave for Elis!" Antyllus threw up his hands in despair, and his tone of voice reflected his vexation and frustration.

"*We've* had her in the traces," Lysandridas said with a little, conspiratorial smile at Leonis. Leonis held her breath. She did not mind that he said "we". She knew that Antyllus would not believe she had driven Afra, and she looked down flattered that Lysandridas did not take all the credit for himself. Meanwhile, Lysandridas had gone on to explain to Antyllus, "She's calmed down a great deal this last year, and she's the fastest horse I've ever seen. She's faster than the entire Spartan team."

"But she's small and light."

"So am I, and Ajax has strength to spare."

Antyllus just looked at him. Part of him thought Lysandridas was crazy, and was not prepared to admit that a young man could know more about his horses than he did. On the other hand, Lysandridas had as good as said his present team didn't have a chance of winning. And Lysandridas wasn't just any young man.

"Afra and Zephyrus have the speed, Ajax and Titan the strength. Let me try."

With a deep, resigned sigh, Antyllus waved a hand in a gesture of unconvinced consent. Cobon, who had heard the entire exchange, shouted to one of the new slaves to fetch Afra, and unhitched Penny himself. Lysandridas joined him, and Cobon muttered, "I hope you know what you're doing."

"Penny isn't up to it any more."

"I know, but Afra? What if she acts up?"

"We could put blinders on her."

Cobon nodded and went back to the barn to fetch some.

Lysandridas went back to Antyllus. "If this works, we'll need to practice racing conditions—not just one other chariot, but two. I need to get all of them completely used to weaving in and out between other chariots."

"Two?"

"We can use the everyday chariot and your usual team on the inside, and Boreas and Penny before the two-horse racing chariot."

"But I don't have another driver!" Antyllus reminded him, irritated by his failure to consider this.

"Yes, you do," Lysandridas told him steadily.

Antyllus frowned at him, trying to think what he could mean.

"My wife is an excellent driver."

"Your wife?!" Antyllus gapped at Leonis, who had been watching Afra being backed into the traces and had not heard what Lysandridas had said. He was completely flustered and turned back to Lysandridas. "This is ridiculous! I know women are allowed to drive in Sparta, but you aren't in Sparta any more. Women do *not* drive here in Tegea!"

"I'm not suggesting she drive in public, not into the city. I'm only suggesting she help *you* to victory by driving on the training track here."

"But that's the most demanding kind of driving there is! And what horses could I give her?"

"She drove my father's team—two at a time. How else do you think he got them in shape for Delphi? My cousin Nikandros certainly didn't do it!" Lysandridas scoffed.

Antyllus raised his eyebrows. He looked back at the oblivious Leonis. She was not his type at all. He found her tanned skin "common"—like a slave's—and she was too tall and lanky to be appealing. Her face was too square and her mouth too wide. She was even old by Spartan standards! When he thought of poor Timosa, crying her heart out because she had been rejected and had no bridegroom, he felt guilty. Empedokles had rightly been offended; and how much more offended would he be if he actually saw the woman Lysandridas had preferred to his gentle daughter? Antyllus had no notion what Leonis' personality, education, or temperament were, because it was not polite to have any discourse with another man's wife—not even his son's.

But he could not change the fact that she was Lysandridas' wife, either. He sighed loudly and turned back to Lysandridas. Part of him felt that Lysandridas was taking advantage of him. He almost said, "Haven't I done enough for you already?" But he didn't dare. Lysandridas was very proud. He thought back with an unconscious smile to how proud he'd been even as a slave. He knew that if he in any way suggested he felt he was being exploited, Lysandridas would as likely as not move out. Instead he complained, "I think this is all too much at once!" He meant for the horses, but Lysandridas smiled, knowing that he was really speaking of himself.

"Just give her a chance."

Antyllus shook his head and made a face, but he raised his voice and ordered the two-horse racing chariot brought out and his driving team hitched to it. "If something happens to your wife—"

"Something will happen," Lysandridas assured him. "Watch!"

Lysandridas called Leonis over. "We have decided you should drive the two-horse chariot ahead of me to simulate racing conditions."

Leonis' eyes widened and her lips parted. "But I thought—" She looked quickly to Antyllus, could see disapproval written all over his face, and understood; she owed this chance entirely to Lysandridas. "Thank you!" She flung her arms around him, gave him a hasty kiss, and then nodded to Antyllus, whispering again, "Thank you," before rushing away to change.

Lysandridas was feeling pleased with himself. "I'll take the team out and do a few laps. Then we let Leonis out alone and do some laps. Then we try it together."

"We'll see," Antyllus answered sceptically. "You may find you have enough trouble with Afra alone."

Lysandridas chose not to contradict Antyllus. Instead, he went over to the mare where she was fretting in the traces. Petting her, he talked to her soothingly. Then he climbed onto the chariot and whistled to them. They were all excited by the change—especially Afra, who had never been hitched to a four-horse chariot before. She tried to rush ahead, and was irritated by the others lagging behind her. She put her ears back and kicked out. Ajax kicked back, but only half-heartedly. Zephyrus surged forward, incited by Afra's eagerness. Titan half reared up. Antyllus put his hand over his eyes and shook his head. This was going to be a disaster; but he was so discouraged by the thought that his old team didn't have a chance that he made no attempt to intervene.

Maybe the Spartan team would suffer some injury, he told himself, as he walked behind the chariot out to the training track. Then he would have a chance, surely—provided none of his own horses suffered an injury today with this mad experiment.

He was on the brink of calling to Lysandridas to come back and put Penny back in the traces, when they reached the track. Rather than sensibly trotting around in a warm-up round, Lysandridas did what he had never done before: he let the horses spring away in a gallop. Antyllus rushed forward and clutched the railing, his heart in his throat. Lysandridas had never been irresponsible with horses before, but his behaviour today was enough make Antyllus doubt he knew the young man at all.

Meanwhile, the team was racing down the track at an uncontrolled, foolish speed. Zephyrus and Afra were fighting each other for the lead and dragging the sensible pair, Ajax and Titan, along in their frenzy of competition. Lysandridas was easing them far to the outside edge of the track without them even noticing it, and as they came to the end of the stretch he bent into the curve, and Antyllus could see him reach forward and grab a fistful of reins halfway to Afra's bit. He pulled it, and Afra turned her head but kept galloping straight ahead. Antyllus closed his eyes, but when no crash, squeal, or shouting followed, he opened them again. Afra had now bent into the turn and the others, used to the track, followed around elegantly.

By the sixth lap, they were all so tired from having expended themselves too early that they were decorously galloping around the turns as if they were glad of the opportunity to slow down a bit. Lysandridas leaned back and brought them to a trot, trotted them one lap, and then came and drew up before Antyllus. He waited for Antyllus' judgement anxiously.

Antyllus gazed up at him and shook his head. He did not want to approve. He wanted to give Lysandridas a piece of his mind for taking the risks he had taken, but what could he say in the face of his success? He shook his head again. "You think *they* can beat the royal Spartan team?"

Lysandridas shrugged. "Not necessarily, but we have a chance. Did you see how she fired the others to greater effort?"

"I saw—and I also see that they're already spent after half the distance. That was enough for today." Only now did he remember Lysandridas' suggestion that his wife drive a second chariot. He glanced over his shoulder and saw Leonis waiting patiently on the cab of his two-horse. She had changed into a simple linen peplos with no sleeves, and the sun burned down on her face and arms. He shook his head at the sight of her. He did not understand why Lysandridas wanted his wife exposed to the elements like this—much less to the risks of driving.

Lysandridas followed his gaze, and he could read Antyllus' disapproval in his face, but he found Leonis beautiful with the breeze blowing her peplos against her supple, curved body. To Antyllus he only remarked, "Just watch."

Antyllus sighed in answer and leaned on the railing again. Lysandridas drove his chariot over to Leonis and then turned it around. They drove out onto the track side by side and did one lap like that, walking. Then Lysandridas took his chariot off the track, dismounted, and turned the chariot over to the waiting slaves. He went and joined Antyllus at the railing. Leonis was letting her team trot around the track. They fretted and fussed and tried to get away from her, but she had them in hand.

"Forget who's driving, sir. Forget it's a woman. Just watch the way the team responds."

Antyllus glanced over at Lysandridas, and then returned his attention to the track critically. Leonis had completed one lap and went into the next, still trotting. Only on the stretch did she let the horses canter for a few strides, but hauled them back for the next turn. Lysandridas could see that she was red and sweating, nervous to be watched so closely, feeling Antyllus' hostility—not to mention driving two horses she didn't know. The horses felt her nervousness and took advantage of it. They started rearing up to get away from her. Antyllus shook his head, his lips pressed together angrily. Lysandridas ducked under the railing and walked out onto the track. When Leonis saw him, she pulled up beside him. She was crying from frustration, and biting her lips.

"You're just nervous," Lysandridas told her calmly. "You were the one who put Afra in the traces, remember? Neither Antyllus nor I risked it. You can handle these old nags." He nodded toward the retired racehorses, and then went around in front of the chariot and spoke to each of them. He returned to the cart and looked up at Leonis. She was calmer. "You've handled much better horses than these. You had Agamemnon and Hector in your hands—and they hated each other."

She smiled hesitantly and nodded. He stepped back, and she set off again. He watched her from the track at first, only ducking under the rail after she'd taken the far turn. He said nothing to Antyllus, just rested his arms on the railing and his chin on his arms and waited. Finally Antyllus admitted, "All right. I admit it. She can drive."

Lysandridas turned his head and smiled at his adoptive father. "Yes, she *can* drive. *She* put Afra in the traces, not me."

Antyllus shook his head again, but then he clapped Lysandridas on the shoulder. "You win—as usual. But don't rush things. Train separately for a few more days. Let your wife get more familiar with my horses. Then you can start your manoeuvre practice."

Lysandridas smiled and stood up straight. "We can win with Afra—she's like my Hector."

"I certainly hope so." Antyllus turned to return to the house, waving to Leonis to bring her chariot in. Lysandridas wanted to wait for her and tell her Antyllus' decision, but one of the new slaves, Timodemos, was running toward them. "Master! There's a messenger here from Harmatides! He's sent for Master Lysandridas! He's to come at once. I've got Boreas tacked and waiting for him."

Antyllus glanced sidelong at Lysandridas. His face was impassive. He had been expecting this ever since Lysandridas arrived; he only wondered why it was suddenly so urgent. Now that he was an exile, Harmatides would naturally expect Lysandridas to fight for Tegea.

Lysandridas nodded, and told Tim he'd come at once.

"You know what he wants?" Antyllus asked cautiously.

"For me to join his cavalry," Lysandridas replied; and Antyllus nodded, glad that Lysandridas was prepared for what was coming.

The guards at Harmatides house were double what they had been three months ago. More tellingly, they were no longer Tegean. Like most tyrants, Lysandridas registered, Harmatides no longer trusted his own people. He had brought in hired mercenaries, in this case Syracusians. They did not recognise Lysandridas, and stopped him roughly. His story about a summons was checked before he was even admitted to the outer courtyard. Here his horse and weapons were taken from him. Then two guards escorted him into the house—where once he had been a welcome guest—as if he were a prisoner. He was taken to a windowless study and shoved inside, the door slammed shut behind him. Only a single oil lamp was lit. A man stood and came towards him with open arms. It was Chilon.

Lysandridas did not return the embrace, and Chilon drew back and studied his face sadly. "You blame me for the vote."

"No, not particularly. Not at all, really. You spoke for me." Lysandridas kept his eyes averted.

"But it wasn't enough," Chilon admitted with a sigh.

Lysandridas shrugged, but his entire body belied this gesture of indifference. He was bitter and angry and resentful, and it hurt Chilon so much that he leaned against a table, his strength giving way. "I'm so sorry."

Lysandridas relented a little. With a sidelong glance he noted, too, how tired and aged Chilon looked. "Why are you here?" he asked in a voice that was not overtly hostile.

Chilon shrugged. "We're still haggling. The Assembly offers more and more concessions—but not the symbolic ones Harmatides needs. They will not see reason on the subject of Orestes' bones, and Harmatides needs them." Chilon ran his hands over his greying braids and sighed unconsciously.

"How is Teleklos?" Lysandridas asked.

"He's recovered enough from the stroke to leave Dorothea's. He returned home at the new moon. Ambelos visits him daily."

"Ambelos is free to move about?"

Chilon lifted the corners of his lips. "Of course; all the hostages are. The women seem to have settled quite comfortably into the royal guest apartments and can be seen shopping in the agora now and then, accompanied by loyal helots, of course. Ambelos has an escort of six Guardsmen wherever he goes, but that doesn't seem to bother him. On the contrary, I think he's come to know them quite well and even like them. They've certainly come to respect him! He's travelled throughout Lacedaemon—to Gytheion and back. He has inspected our quarries and lumberyards, and has gone hunting in the Taygetos and fishing in the Gulf. He even asked to go to Messenia, but the Council drew the line at that."

Lysandridas did not answer at once. He was glad for Ambelos' sake that he was not being confined or treated like a prisoner. The Spartan captives, as far as he knew, were still locked in Harmatides' slaves' quarters. "Does Harmatides know?"

"I presume so. I've delivered letters to him from his son—unopened." Chilon was gazing at Lysandridas so intently that Lysandridas asked somewhat angrily, "What do you want of me?"

Chilon sighed. "Your father asked me to tell him how you were doing."

"Ah, so." Lysandridas was still refusing to look at him directly.

"What should I tell him?"

"He knows how rich Antyllus is. I lack for nothing. I even think I can beat the Agiad entry at Olympia." He tossed this last remark like a challenge.

"But are you happy?"

"What does that have to do with anything? The happiness of her citizens has never been the slightest concern of Sparta—much less the happiness of her non-citizens!"

"It wasn't Sparta that asked—it was your father," Chilon reproved him gently, and Lysandridas looked down, ashamed. He knew Teleklos was suffering, but he did not see what he could do about it. He was not going to lie and say he was happy. Maybe his father didn't even want him to be happy. His father had been jealous of Antyllus.

Chilon considered the young man looking sullenly at the floor and reminded him, "The Assembly can and has been known to reverse its decisions. If there were ever a solid peace between Lacedaemon and Tegea, I think you would have a good chance of being invited back."

"Why on earth should they do that—and why should I accept?" Lysandridas demanded angrily, lifting his head and glaring at Chilon.

"It was a very close vote. I think you had the majority on your side. And many who voted against you did it in the heat of the moment, shocked to have learned you'd accepted Tegean citizenship. They hadn't had time to think it through. I think they could be persuaded to forgive you with time."

"Forgive me," Lysandridas repeated sourly. "What is there to forgive? What *right* do they have to judge me at all? They have never known slavery and rejection or the temptation of a new beginning! They can all go to Hades! They will have to *beg* me to return! And even then I might not come!"

Chilon said nothing. It was better for Lysandridas to be angry than disheartened. After a long silence in which Lysandridas had time to become ashamed of his outburst, Chilon asked in a neutral tone, "And how is your wife?"

Lysandridas hesitated. He wanted to lie and say she was happier than ever, but he couldn't. "She is having a hard time adjusting to her status here. It will take time to—to win freedoms for her. But I am working on it. At least in her own home, I will not let her be imprisoned."

Chilon nodded knowingly. He felt sorry for Leonis. If ever there was a Spartan woman who needed more rather than less freedom, it was Leonis. He pulled himself upright again. "I must return with the rest of the delegation to Lacedaemon. We have yet another rejection to report. Only Anaxandridas' devotion to his sister has prevented a new outbreak of war.

He is convinced that any hostilities initiated from our side will instantly result in his sister's ravishment."

"But if something happened to Cassandra, Ambelos would be made to pay the price."

"Of course. The chances of him ever seeing Tegea again are not looking good at the moment. That's why we let him have so much freedom. Anaxandridas has already told me *how* he intends to kill him—if something happens to Cassandra. I'll spare you the gruesome details, but it is a slow and ugly death."

"We call ourselves civilised?"

"Is it civilised to ravish captives?"

"Is slavery civilised?"

Chilon laughed briefly, and his eyes were lighted with genuine pleasure for the first time since the interview began. With that light in his eyes still, he said soberly, "I want you back, young man."

"Don't count on it," Lysandridas shot back, but this time he returned Chilon's embrace. Then Chilon was gone, and Lysandridas was left in the dim chamber, still wondering who and what he was.

CHAPTER 28

It was only days before Antyllus and Lysandridas planned to leave for Elis and the final stage of training when one of Harmatides' mercenaries arrived at the estate. Lysandridas was on the track, racing against Leonis. The mercenary insisted that training be interrupted, and he was the kind of man who revelled in his strength and vicarious authority. He barked his orders to Antyllus as if he were a slave, and cut him off in mid-sentence when he protested that so close to the Games, every day of training counted double.

"Games? Is that all you care about?"

Antyllus did not allow himself to be riled by this rude behaviour, but rather let the mercenary feel his disdain as he signalled for Lysandridas to interrupt training.

Lysandridas drew up beside him with a frown, but the sight of the mercenary explained everything without words. Lysandridas knew from Antyllus that a Spartan delegation had again left Tegea empty-handed the night before. He presumed that Harmatides had a message for him from Chilon, or had decided to make active use of his knowledge of Lacedaemon.

At least the approaching Games would protect him from being asked to serve in the Tegean army in the short term, he reasoned. Since athletes had

314   The Olympic Charioteer

to be at Elis at least one month before the Games, Lysandridas felt relatively safe, since he believed Harmatides wanted him to drive for Tegea no less than Antyllus did. Indeed, there was hardly time for Sparta to launch an attack before the Olympic peace. So he dismounted from the chariot and returned with the mercenary to the city without undue concern.

The mercenary's colleagues did not stop them at the gate, but again Lysandridas was disarmed before he was allowed into the house. The mercenary led him beyond the formal atrium and down a long corridor, then knocked on a carved door and called out, "We've brought you the Spartan Lysandridas, sir."

"Let him in!" Harmatides replied.

The mercenary opened the door and stood back for Lysandridas to enter. The door closed behind him, and Lysandridas found himself in a large room with tall doors giving access to a private atrium. A fountain bubbled in the sunlight and the gauze curtains billowed inwards on the early morning breeze. Bees hummed around the roses in the garden. Light streamed across the marble tiles. It took a moment for Lysandridas to find Harmatides in the shadows.

The Tegean tyrant was dressed in only a light, long chiton, and he stood leaning on a desk as if he were in pain. The face Lysandridas remembered as ruddy and firm was pasty and sagging. He had puffy bags under his eyes as if he had not slept for some time. His hair was sticking up as if he'd come from his bed without combing it. Lysandridas started at the sight of him and drew his head back slightly. "You sent for me, sir?"

"Yes." Harmatides' eyes bored into him. "Yes. I sent for you."

"Sir?"

Harmatides continued to stare at him as he took a deep breath. "My son is very fond of you. He calls you his best friend."

"I'm honoured, sir."

"Really?

"Yes; he's an exceptional young man."

"You really care for him?"

"Yes, sir. Do you doubt it?"

Harmatides just stared at him without answering.

"Has something happened to him, sir?" Lysandridas was thinking of what Chilon had told him at their last meeting. For a moment he feared that the latest Spartan delegation had informed Harmatides that Ambelos was already dead; but then he told himself Harmatides was too calm. Or was he? How would this man show his grief?

Harmatides snorted, left the desk he had been leaning on, and went to stand in the doorway, shoving the curtain aside to stare unhindered through the elegant columns of the atrium at the sun-bathed garden. When he started speaking, he spoke so softly that Lysandridas had to strain to hear him, missing half of what he said. He was only certain that he caught the words, "… raped her."

"Who?" Lysandridas asked urgently, meaning which of the women.

"Onimastros," came the astonishing answer

"What?!" He couldn't believe it. "Onimastros raped one of the captives? But why should he?! Surely he knows what the consequences will be?"

Harmatides swung around on Lysandridas, and his lips smiled although his eyes did not. "I like you, young man. You remind me of myself when I was younger—but sometimes you are incredibly naive! Why do you *think* Onimastros would do something like this? To ruin me! To throw me to the wolves—and resume the war. He did this *because* he knows the consequences will be the murder of Ambelos and war—or my fall from power. Preferably both."

Lysandridas had no answer to such a scenario. It meant the execution of an innocent young man who had voluntarily put himself at risk for the sake of peace. It meant war between his two cities, and no matter what he'd said to Chilon, he did still love Lacedaemon. Even the fall of Harmatides was no comfort if another, even less scrupulous, tyrant were to take his place. After digesting all this, Lysandridas finally asked softly, "What do you want of me, sir?"

Harmatides drew a deep breath and looked out at the garden again. "Isn't it lovely?" he asked after a moment.

Lysandridas agreed with him, more puzzled than ever.

"You would never know anything had happened, would you?"

Lysandridas shook his head. "No, sir."

"How long do you think we can keep it that way?"

Now he understood. "Only until the next delegation comes with the next proposal from the Spartan Assembly."

"Half a month at most. By then we will be only ten to fifteen days away from the Olympic Peace. Sparta could hardly hope to invade in so short a time, could it?" He looked at Lysandridas with a small flicker of hope; but Lysandridas only looked down, thinking of what Chilon had said. Sparta might not risk an invasion just days before the Olympic peace, but Ambelos could be executed at any time.

Harmatides understood his silence and sighed. They stood for what seemed like a long time. Then Harmatides asked, "I know Antyllus hates me, but does he hate me so much that he would deny refuge to one or two of the captive women?"

"Refuge, sir?"

"I want to remove them from my house. I want them hidden where Onimastros would not think to look for them. I want them in safety—as much as any place in Tegea is safe. Would Antyllus do that—if not for me and Ambelos—for them?"

Lysandridas answered without thinking, "Of course, sir."

"Would he—" Harmatides finally turned and faced Lysandridas. They were standing close to one another now, and their eyes were not more than three feet apart. "Would he risk giving refuge to Princess Cassandra herself?"

Lysandridas was aware that he was committing Antyllus to something without even consulting him, but he could not (and Harmatides *knew* he could not) deny an Agiad princess refuge. "Yes, sir."

Harmatides' eyes bore into him for a long time, and then he nodded and looked away. "The women will have to be removed secretly. I will organise something and let you know what, if anything, you must do."

"Yes, sir."

Harmatides held out his hand. "Thank you."

By mid-afternoon, riots had broken out in the city. Antyllus' cook, who had gone to buy fish, spices, and various other items in the agora, returned in an agitated state. Red, sweating, and convinced he had barely escaped with his life, he reported that a mob of angry "ruffians" led by that unholy pair, Phaeax and Polyphom, had rampaged through the agora, overturning tables and loudly demanding war. "The Spartans again refused to return Orestes' bones!" he told his owner indignantly, wiping his near-bald brow with a wet rag. "The rioters kept shouting we should go and take the bones back!" The cook was in the kitchen and all the kitchen staff were gathered around anxiously.

Antyllus nodded grimly and ordered his chariot. Lysandridas went with him into the yard. "Where are you going, sir?"

"To consult my friends."

"Do you want me to come with you?"

"No, you better stay here and wait for word of our guests." Antyllus had backed Lysandridas without hesitation when he learned that Harmatides wanted to send Cassandra to them. Now, however, Lysandridas felt Cassandra was just a flimsy excuse to keep him here. He couldn't help feeling that Antyllus still did not trust him entirely. Antyllus had not once taken him along when he went to meet with the other aristocrats of the "peace faction".

"Are you sure you'll be safe?" Lysandridas tried to get his adopted father to reconsider.

"Safe? No, but I will be careful. I have no real enemies."

"A violent mob doesn't need enemies, just targets."

"True. I will try to avoid running into the mob."

"What do you think caused things to ignite this time?"

"Onimastros."

"I don't understand."

Antyllus was annoyed by Lysandridas' apparent lack of political acumen. "Onimastros wants war," he reminded his adopted son in a short-tempered voice. "First, he made sure that Ambelos' life was forfeit, and that Harmatides knew it. Then he riled up the mob to demand war. Harmatides either has to give in this time, knowing that his son is dead in any case, or—if he still resists—he will be overthrown. Either way, Onimastros gets his war. That's why my friends and I have to meet and decide on a course of action as soon as possible."

"Can I help?"

Put like this, Antyllus' annoyance vanished, and he reconsidered his adopted son. He saw with sudden clarity that Lysandridas was unhappy, and a part of his mind registered that the young man needed to be given a greater role than driving chariots. Lysandridas wasn't a slave or a professional driver—nor was he a youth like Phaedolos, content with pursuing his own pleasures. He had greater abilities and ambitions. But this, Antyllus rationalised, was not the time to start initiating him. The situation was too critical. There was no time for training and nurturing latent political abilities. This was an emergency. "Not now. Later," Antyllus retorted, taking up the reins.

Lysandridas had no choice but to step back and watch Antyllus drive away.

An hour or two later, when the heat of the day was over, a delivery wagon lumbered up the drive, drawn by oxen. The wagon itself was dusty and creaking; the two drivers were burly men, tanned dark by their daily work in the sun. Dirt was ingrained on their hands and faces. The wagon was loaded with roofing tiles.

They drove around to the yard, and one driver, dusty and sweating as if from a long drive, clambered down and loudly demanded Antyllus. Timodemos replied that Antyllus was away. The driver of the delivery wagon burst out in an angry, complaining voice, "Isn't there anyone here who can sign a fucking delivery receipt!? I've driven all the way out here in the fucking heat of the day, nearly got torn apart by a bunch of shit-head ruffians, and all for a wagon full of fucking tiles! I'm not going to just turn around and drive the shit back again! The streets are still full of fucking hooligans!"

Timodemos, deeply impressed by this display of masculinity, went in hasty search of the slave clerk who did the bookkeeping for the estate. This man, portly and short-sighted, came out of his office, already bewildered by Tim's report. He declared in a flustered voice before the driver could get a word out, "We didn't order any tiles. This all has to be some kind of mistake."

"Nonsense! I ain't moving that fucking wagon until someone signs a fucking receipt. And you better have some hands ready to offload the fucking crates, too. They weigh a fucking ton."

"But we don't need any tiles. Certainly not roofing tiles," the flustered clerk insisted.

"Well, then smash them up for all I care. I'm not budging from here until all the fucking crates have been offloaded and I have a fucking signed receipt for the delivery."

Although the bookkeeper did not entirely approve of Lysandridas' adoption, he was relieved to hand over responsibility to someone else in this situation, so he sent for Lysandridas.

To his surprise, Lysandridas hardly let him report before he ran out into the yard. He found the driver leaning against the water trough with his arms crossed over his massive chest and the front of his chiton drenched from having splashed himself cool. "Who sent you?" Lysandridas asked urgently.

"Harmatides," the driver answered with his eyes levelled on Lysandridas.

"Unload all the crates as quickly—and carefully!—as possible," Lysandridas ordered, and the driver grinned.

The bookkeeper gave Lysandridas a disapproving scowl, but he clapped his hands and ordered all the stable slaves to give the drivers a hand offloading. Lysandridas was already scanning the crates, looking for the one not carrying tiles. It was stowed well forward under a canvas. As soon as he spotted it, he clambered aboard the wagon and tried to open the lid. It was nailed shut. He shouted for a wedge, and finally wrenched it open, oblivious to the curious looks of the rest of the household.

Inside, bedded in straw, he found Cassandra clutching another of the captives in her arms. The other girl looked up at him and screamed. "Hush! Shhh!" Cassandra pressed the girl's face to her chest and looked up at Lysandridas questioningly. "You look—familiar."

"Lysandridas, son of Teleklos."

"Of course! Thank all the Gods!" She sat up straighter, straw clinging to her long, tangled hair, but hope and colour returning to her face

Lysandridas could not leave her in her false hopes longer than necessary. He cut her off before she could say any more. "I was exiled by the Assembly, ma'am. I'm no longer a Spartan citizen."

"I know. Chilon told me. But I know, too, that *you* would never harm us or let harm come to us—if you can help it!" She said it as if she meant it, and it shamed Lysandridas that he had failed to give his life for her brother as he should have done.

"I will defend you as I should have defended your brother, ma'am— with my life!" Lysandridas promised fervently.

Cassandra did the most beautiful thing possible: she held out her hand to him, for him to help her out of the crate, as if it was the most natural thing in the world. Lysandridas, still feeling completely unworthy, took her hand and then fastened onto her upper arm above the elbow to leverage her to her feet. She had clearly been cramped inside the crate for several hours and was very stiff. She was pale and thin, too, from two months of captivity.

Cassandra then bent to help the other young woman to her feet as well. This girl seemed to be in even worse shape than the princess. She was visibly trembling, and Cassandra seemed to have to hold her upright, her arm around the younger woman's waist.

"Can you at least tell us what is going on? Why has everything changed so suddenly?" She glanced at the girl cowering in her arms, and then looked up at Lysandridas with wide, confused eyes.

"Ma'am, let me get you off this wagon and inside the house first."

Pheronike emerged from the house with Leonis. While Pheronike importantly ordered beds and baths made up by the slaves, Leonis swept forward to embrace first Cassandra and then the younger captive. The latter recognised her and burst into inexplicable tears. Cassandra was confused until Leonis explained, "I am Lysandridas' wife; I followed him into exile."

"Ah, of course." Cassandra squeezed her hand and nodded. There was time for no more, as Pheronike herded her bewildered but relieved guests towards the women's quarters.

Lysandridas turned to sign the driver's receipt. "Nothing but tiles," he remarked as he signed.

"What else would I have aboard a delivery wagon?" the driver asked back.

Lysandridas reached into his purse and gave him two drachma for good measure.

The driver grinned. "Good luck repairing your roof!"

That evening, after Antyllus returned, Cassandra sat clutching one of Pheronike's broad, angora shawls around her shoulders and gazed into the fire as she explained what had happened to her and the others. It gradually turned dark; but none of her audience, Lysandridas, Antyllus or Pheronike, thought to disturb her narrative by fetching lamps. She was thus bathed in the gentle, unsteady light of the dancing hearth-fire as she approached the end of her story. Leonis was absent; she was looking after the younger of the two captives.

"Last night we were woken by a fat, balding man in a very fine, long chiton. It was the first time anyone but the Spartan ephors had ever entered our quarters, and he must have had a key or bribed someone who did, because he did not break in. He was just there, among us in the dark. He went among us, tearing back our blankets, peering at our faces and probing with his soft, sweating hands. Of course we protested, but he hissed us silent, saying: 'Your Assembly has rejected our peace offer categorically. You are less important to them than their pride. The negotiations have ended, and you remain slaves!' Gyrtias indignantly told him she could not believe him, and he slapped her hard three or four times. 'Shut your mouth!' he ordered, 'or I'll have you flogged properly!' We were stunned into silence. Then he took Polyxena by the wrist and yanked her to her feet. 'You come with me,' he ordered her.

"Polyxena resisted, begging him to let her be, begging us to help her, but again he slapped her roughly, and told her that he did not tolerate 'disobedient slaves'. If she made trouble for him, he said, he'd sell her to a brothel. Polyxena stumbled out after him, begging us to help her, but what could we do?"

"The negotiations have *not* collapsed," Antyllus pointed out, reaching out to help himself to wine. "Stalemated, yes; but neither side has risked breaking them off altogether."

"But how were we to know that?" Cassandra asked, raising her head with its damp, freshly washed mane of hair and focusing her deep-set, dark eyes on Antyllus. She was a delicate woman with very fragile bone structure. All skin and bones, she looked so weak that her audience was repeatedly surprised by the strength of her voice and will.

"You couldn't. I just wanted *you* to know the truth. What happened next?"

"Well, sometime later one of the mercenaries brought Polyxena back and flung her in among us with a rude remark." She hesitated, and then repeated it. "He said he'd never had a girl who was so little pleasure. 'If that's what you Spartan women are like, it's no wonder your men prefer to live in barracks and bugger each other.' That's how we learned that Polyxena hadn't just been raped by the first man, but by two others as well. She was in terrible shape—bloody, sore, bruised, and too shocked by what they had done to her to even cry...."

"But only her? You were untouched?" Antyllus asked urgently.

"Don't you understand?" Cassandra asked. "He chose the youngest of us, the only virgin, so there could be no doubt or denial of what had happened."

"But you're the only one your brother cares about—really." Antyllus pointed out.

"But I'm a widow. I've borne two children. They could have given me to the entire watch, and I would have denied it. Do you think I don't know what this means? That poor youth—not even out of the agoge—will pay the price as soon as my brother hears of this. All the rest of us are wives, if not mothers. To secure our freedom again, we would all have been willing to pay the price Polyxena paid. But Polyxena was still a virgin. She is the only one among us who cannot deny it, even if she had the heart and strength to want to...."

Her audience was stunned. Pheronike was scandalised and Antyllus shocked. Lysandridas was humbled with admiration. After a pause, Cassandra continued her narrative in a low, steady voice.

"When daylight came and the usual slave brought our breakfast, I demanded to speak to Harmatides. The slave looked frightened and fled. The next thing I knew, Harmatides himself was there demanding to know what I wanted. I pointed to Polyxena, who had finally recovered enough to be sobbing and trembling from her experience. I was unkind. I asked him if he loved his son so little, and he blanched." Cassandra sounded ashamed of herself.

"Harmatides demanded to know who had violated Polyxena. I could only describe what had happened the night before. He said, 'Omo—? Onomandros?'"

"Onimastros," Lysandridas and Antyllus supplied in chorus.

"Yes; and then he asked if I or any of the others had been touched. Then he disappeared—but he sent a woman with boiled water and some ointments, and later one of the kitchen slaves brought us sweets fresh from the oven. Then, without any warning or explanation, a dozen armed men arrived—not the foreign mercenaries, but Tegean cavalrymen. They herded us out of the house and into a wagon. We were told to lie down on the boards and they threw straw over us. In this state we were taken a short distance, then ordered out into the yard of some factory—a tile factory with huge ovens. There we were ordered to climb into crates—two to a crate—and they nailed the lids shut over our heads. At one stage, we seemed to go through a crowd of people shouting and screaming. People beat against the side of the wagon, and for a moment it seemed as if the wagon was going to be turned over. I heard the whip cracking, and then more shouting and screaming. We broke through the crowd and finally arrived here. We didn't know why or on whose orders we had been moved."

Antyllus rose and offered Cassandra wine. She accepted it, although she had refused it earlier. He explained, "Onimastros acted without Harmatides' knowledge or approval. Onimastros is trying to push him into war, and has also riled up the mob against him. When I was in the city this afternoon, they had laid siege to his house and factory. You were very lucky to get out in time."

"And what do you intend to do with me and the others?" she asked Antyllus, but with a short, hopeful glance in Lysandridas' direction.

"We are to keep you safe," Antyllus answered firmly, "and out of Onimastros' hands. I am known to oppose Harmatides, so we don't think Onimastros will look for you here."

"Will you send word to my brother?"

Antyllus licked his lips uncomfortably. The peace faction was convinced that Onimastros planned to depose Harmatides and take power for himself. Onimastros wanted war and had the mob behind him. He had no use for the hostages any more, and probably wouldn't even make much effort to find them. But the peace faction needed them as bargaining chips with Lacedaemon, and they also needed troops with which to control the rampaging mob, which even now was threatening all those who did not side with them. The mob was trashing the property of respectable citizens all across the city. Antyllus and his friends had spent the entire afternoon attempting to persuade Tegea's subordinate strategoi to take action against the mob, but the Tegean commanders were afraid to use their troops against their fellow citizens. The only hope of ending the riots seemed to be Harmatides' loyal cavalry and mercenaries. Or Lacedaemonians....

Antyllus wondered if he could "suggest" to Lacedaemon that they come to the "rescue" of their captives? But how long would they take? And wouldn't the arrival of Lacedaemonian troops bring all the Tegeans together again—in a common front against their hated enemy, Lacedaemon? And how would they ever convince the Lacedaemonians to withdraw, once they were in Tegea? It was too risky! He shook his head sharply. "No, we will not inform your brother at this stage. We must first restore order in the city."

Cassandra nodded with understanding, and her gaze returned to the fire as she said, "I'm very tired. Will you excuse me?"

"But of course!" Antyllus sprang to his feet again. "Please, make yourself at home here. Ask for whatever you like, and it will be our pleasure to give it to you."

"Except my freedom, of course," Cassandra reminded him with a weary, understanding smile.

CHAPTER 29

At dawn Lysandridas and Antyllus scanned the western horizon. It was smeared with smoke, and the glow of flames was still decipherable at isolated points. The smell of burning oil and wood hung faintly but recognisably in the still air. Antyllus shook his head. "I must go into the city and see the damage."

"May I come with you, sir?" Lysandridas requested yet again. He wanted Antyllus' full trust.

Antyllus looked over at his adopted son. Lysandridas was dressed only in a light chiton for driving, but Antyllus had not forgotten he was a Spartiate Guardsman. It would be a comfort to have a trained hoplite beside him today. "Yes. We should both get our armour and weapons. There's no way of knowing if the riots have ended or not."

They armed themselves and met again in the yard, where the driving chariot was waiting for them. Antyllus took the reins so that the younger, stronger and better-trained warrior could have his hands on his weapons.

As they approached the city, it was the unnatural stillness that struck them first. No farm carts were on the road bringing produce to market. No merchants were setting out with their caravans. Slaves were not running errands. Craftsmen were not on their way to work with their lunch satchels, and the shopkeepers were not setting up their wares on tables before their shops. There were not even any drunks making their way merrily or miserably home from an all-night symposium. The shutters of the shops and houses were closed tight. The doors to the courtyards were firmly shut and bolted. The streets were utterly abandoned.

As they approached the agora, they ran into the first signs of actual damage. Here, overturned wagons and shattered barrels, broken crates and crushed amphorae littered the streets. Smoke hung in the air from extinguished or distant fires.

The agora itself was filled with wreckage. The remnants of the stands and goods offered for sale lay about in disorder. Rotting vegetables, stinking fish, puddles of stale wine, pools of melted, rancid butter, and heaps of cheese littered the cobbles amidst the debris. Along one side, the shops had been set on fire and were blackened and gutted. The columns of the elegant stoa were smeared with smoke.

Continuing to the north in the direction of Harmatides' estate, the signs of destruction increased. There had been no wind, and the flames had never been out of control. In contrast to an accidental fire, the destruction did not come in sheets, but sporadically. The destruction reflected malicious intent and was clearly targeted. Antyllus' unease increased with every street they entered. The targets of the rampage had been the wealthier and politically moderate citizens: his friends and allies. In most cases, the stone houses had withstood the mob. Doors and shutters were battered and in some cases broken, but the heavy bolts had held. Filth had been thrown at the walls, rude or threatening phrases scratched or painted on the plaster facades. Here and there something had caught fire, but had been put out again before the damage could spread very far.

Greater damage had been done to the warehouses and factories to the west. Here the thatched roofs, wooden frames, and densely packed storage crates had caught fire quickly and burned until there was nothing left but charred architectural skeletons. Antyllus kept shaking his head in speechless horror at the senseless destruction of property and wealth. Didn't the fools realise that by destroying the factories, they destroyed their own economic well-being? He couldn't understand how they could be so short-sighted. Without goods to sell, how could Tegea retain her prosperity? Without her prosperity, who would pay for the wine allotment and the theatre, the monuments and the festivals for the mob?

In this part of town there were still scattered plunderers at work, but they took cover rapidly at the sight of a chariot carrying two armed and armoured men. Here Antyllus and Lysandridas also came upon the first casualties. It was impossible to tell if the victims were workers or slaves

326   The Olympic Charioteer

killed defending their master's goods, or plunderers, overpowered by stronger men. Most of the corpses lay naked in the gutters with bashed-in faces, crushed skulls, or slit throats.

Soon Antyllus and Lysandridas caught sight of the first patrol of mercenaries. The hoplites were in a small detachment of six men with their shields at ready. They seemed to be dragging two or three men in their middle in the direction of the courthouse and jail. Around the next corner, the street was blocked by another handful of mercenaries. Antyllus at once went to push his helmet off his face, but Lysandridas stayed him with a hand on his arm. "Don't reveal yourself," he urged in a low, tense voice.

Antyllus turned his head with the heavy, crested helmet still down over his face and gazed at Lysandridas. "Why not?"

"We don't know whose side these men are on."

"But they're Harmatides' mercenaries. He hired and pays them."

"And they did Onimastros' bidding, when they raped Polyxena. Can we be sure Onimastros didn't pay them more?"

Antyllus started inwardly, registering that Lysandridas was not so politically naive as he had thought. In any case, there was no time for further debate. One of the mercenaries had stepped forward and held up his hand to stop the chariot.

"Haven't you heard there is a curfew in effect? No one is allowed on the streets without the explicit permission of the King Archon."

"What in the Name of Zeus is that?" Antyllus answered in annoyance, the title being unknown to Tegea.

"He was appointed last night to deal with the emergency."

Lysandridas had his eyes on the street beyond the guards blocking their way. There had clearly been some kind of street skirmish here. Broken spears and swords, discarded shields, and ownerless cavalry hats, along with the corpses of several horses, were evidence of it. Further up the street, he could see what looked like human corpses, dragged to one side and lain side by side.

"Harmatides, no doubt." Antyllus scoffed at the new title Harmatides had apparently awarded himself.

"Harmatides is dead. Onimastros is King Archon." With a dismissive gesture, the mercenary told them, "Now, get off the streets before I'm compelled to arrest you."

Antyllus turned to stare at Lysandridas, who shook his head vigorously, making the crest shiver over his immobile bronze mask. Antyllus took this to mean they should not debate the issue, and decorously backed the chariot into a side street to turn it around.

As they drove away, Lysandridas stood facing backwards, with his spear at ready and the shield covering Antyllus' back. Only when they were out of javelin range did he say, "Did you see the bodies? Cavalry casualties."

Antyllus nodded, still stunned by the news that Harmatides was dead.

"We should try to get to Harmatides' house by a back street. Someone there will be able to give us more information."

Antyllus looked at his adopted son, but his expression was hidden behind his helmet, and he offered no verbal protest. They turned again and made their way back in the direction of Harmatides' estate. When two mercenaries tried to block their way, Lysandridas took the reins and whistled the team into a canter, while Antyllus ducked down and held his shield up over his head and Lysandridas' back. Shouts followed them, and one javelin bounced harmlessly off the side of the carriage. It clattered onto the cobblestones behind them as they broke through.

They met no further opposition, and regained the main street shortly before Harmatides' tile factory. Antyllus let out a cry of horror at the sight before them. The factory had been completely destroyed. The gates had been battered down and the various buildings set on fire, so that only two blackened brick kilns loomed up out of the piles of charred rubble. Worse still, dozens of charred corpses, presumably the slaves that had worked here, lay in grotesque poses amidst the ashes.

On the opposite side of the road, Harmatides' house stood like a wrecked ship, partially destroyed, partially intact. The outer gate had been battered down, and in the outer courtyard the trees were blackened and leafless. The kitchen was a roofless, gutted hall, with only one or two of the roof-beams still reaching out like claws against the pale sky of early morning. Beyond, however, the stables seemed to have escaped destruction. And although the whitewash of the house itself was grey-black from smoke, the colonnade still stood, and the great door was closed but intact.

The sight of the chariot in the outer yard brought men running from the stables, and Lysandridas shoved his helmet back. The man limping toward him was one of the grooms, and he recognised Lysandridas instantly. "Master Lysandridas! You're too late! It's all over! It's all over!" he cried out.

Antyllus also shoved back his helmet, revealing his face. "What's over?"

"They brought the Master back on a stretcher, but there was nothing more the doctor could do! He's dead. Killed by his own people! Killed trying to restore order!"

328 The Olympic Charioteer

"Who was with him? Who brought him back? We need to know more about what happened," Antyllus pressed the distressed slave.

"May I see the corpse," Lysandridas asked instead; and at once the man called over his shoulder for someone to come take the horses and then gestured for Lysandridas to follow him.

"This is no time to be paying respects to the dead," Antyllus hissed at Lysandridas. "We need to find out more about what Onimastros is—"

"Whoever brought Harmatides home will know what happened," Lysandridas countered, and Antyllus had to admit the logic of that. They went into the great, elegant house, and at once they could hear the lament of mourning women. The stablehand approached the inner sanctuary of his master's house with mincing steps and after passing through the formal atrium, he did no more than point toward a closed door and nod. "In there is where you'll find him."

"Thank you."

At the door they hesitated. From beyond came the keening of women. Not wanting to intrude on Harmatides' wife without warning, Lysandridas knocked vigorously.

The door was yanked away from under his fist almost before he had finished, and he was confronted by four angry and armoured men. For a moment, both parties were equally astonished, but then recognition set in on both sides. The four men facing Lysandridas and Antyllus were all cavalrymen, men Lysandridas had briefly trained. They looked from Lysandridas to Antyllus with surprise and then suspicion, but Lysandridas pushed past them firmly, saying: "We only just heard the news. How did it happen?"

They moved with him into the room. Harmatides lay lifeless on a low bed and his wife sobbed on the floor beside him, while other women keened as they washed and oiled the corpse.

The four cavalrymen talked disjointedly, now one, now another. "He tried to talk reason to the mob—"

"He went to the agora and tried to get them to stop, but they mocked him—"

"They threw things at him—"

"They attacked his factory—"

"He tried to call up the watch, but Phaeax refused, saying he would not ask his men to turn their weapons against Tegean citizens—"

"Then he summoned us—"

"It was hopeless trying to save the factory. The horses were terrified of the fire!"

"The mercenaries held the house, and we tried to drive the mob back and apart—"

"We chased them partway back toward town—"

"But the mercenaries refused to follow—"

"Suddenly we were attacked from the side streets—"

"They rushed among us and stabbed the horses in their chests or bellies—"

"Who?" Antyllus demanded urgently.

"Phaeax and his men!"

"They surrounded Harmatides and dragged him down, stabbing and clubbing him—"

"Phaeax?"

"Yes—with the men he'd refused to call up for restoring order!"

"We finally managed to fight them off and get him on a riderless horse—"

"He was probably already dead—"

"He was certainly dead by the time we got him here."

"And Phaeax?"

"After he was sure Harmatides was dead, he turned on the mob!"

"He and the mercenaries!"

"They hung back watching until Harmatides was dead!" The speaker, one of Harmatides' most dashing commanders, was livid with outrage and shaking with indignation. "They didn't make any attempt to assist us against Phaeax!"

"But they let us into the house and then advanced against the mob."

"They showed no mercy then!"

"They made mincemeat of the men they could lay their hands on!"

Lysandridas had advanced to the bed and was looking at the corpse. The women looked up at him and drew back, their keening instinctively stilled. Harmatides' widow lifted her wet, swollen face and stared at him. Her eyes widened as she recognised him. "What is to become of my boy now? Who will see that the Lacedaemonians release him?" She caught her breath as if she wanted to say more, and then she shook her head and looked away, leaning her face on the edge of the bed.

Antyllus came up behind Lysandridas, and the four loyal cavalrymen stood in a little circle behind them. "I did not always agree with him politically," Antyllus remarked in a solemn, statesmanlike voice, "but he was a brave man and a good commander."

"He was indeed," one of the cavalrymen intoned with a hostile look at Antyllus. "You worked against him—"

Antyllus spun about sharply, and Lysandridas was surprised by the intensity in his voice and the fire in his eyes. "No! I did not work against *him*, I worked against *tyranny*—and that is what we have now, worse than ever. Have you heard that Onimastros named himself 'King Archon'?"

The cavalrymen looked at one another, stunned. One ventured to ask, "What kind of animal is that?"

"A tyrant!" Antyllus answered without hesitation. "The title may be one borrowed from democratic Athens, but in this instance, there can be no question of what it *means*. It means the rule of one man. The rule of a man, to be precise, who is utterly without scruples. This tyrant is a man who raped a captive maiden to ensure war with Lacedaemon, a man who intentionally incited riots that have destroyed the wealth and prosperity of Tegea's most loyal citizens, a man who cold-bloodedly arranged for the death of our best strategos."

There was a low grumble of assent from the other Tegeans at the latter, and Lysandridas noted mentally that Antyllus was a powerful speaker when he was moved.

"We must get word to the subordinate strategos of what has happened. We must pull together a force to oppose these mercenaries—and traitorous Phaeax. Onimastros has no popular support as Harmatides did. He can only hold on to power with terror and force. If we move quickly to eliminate his force, we can make his terror toothless. Will you assist me in this?"

Lysandridas was impressed by how rapidly Antyllus grasped and summarised the situation—and no less by how eagerly Harmatides' followers accepted Antyllus' leadership now. They were all nodding and vowing to help him. He sent one each after the three remaining Tegean strategos, summoning them to Harmatides' house. "Onimastros will expect no further resistance from here," he explained himself, "and if questioned, they can always say they are coming to pay their respects to the dead and give their condolences to the widow. Tell no one I am here."

The young men again nodded agreement, and then they sprang from the room in an eager, purposeful group. As soon as they were gone, Antyllus took Lysandridas by the arm and led him to the far side of the room. He lowered his voice and glanced several times toward the women around the corpse as he spoke, "I must also get word to my friends. Most took their families and movable valuables to their country estates to avoid the mob yesterday afternoon. We must come up with a clear plan of action that will make Onimastros helpless. You knew Harmatides' household; are there any men here we can trust?"

"The driver of the wagon who brought Cassandra yesterday—if I can find him."

"Do your best. I'll give you the names of the men he must get word to. Offer him a rich reward."

Antyllus had written down on a wax tablet the names of the men who were to be summoned by the time Lysandridas returned with the driver. The driver shifted uncomfortably from one bare foot to the other, and kept glancing in horrified fascination at Harmatides' corpse. When Antyllus offered him a five-drachma coin, however, he turned it away. "Pay me when I get back," the man said in his gruff, unfriendly voice.

Lysandridas walked back to the front of the house with him in silence, but at the steps down into the half-ruined outer court, Lysandridas asked, "Why did you reject the pay?"

"Because I want you fucking aristos to understand that I'm doing this out of respect for Harmatides, and not for your damned coin! You think I'm a slave, don't you?"

Lysandridas laughed mirthlessly. "And what if I did? I was a slave—"

"You were a captive, not a born slave. Well, I was born in slavery, sired by a poor Tegean on a slave girl owned by one of you fucking aristos. My father had to pay a fortune to a richer man just to buy me and my mother. But that wasn't good enough for citizenship—not until Harmatides changed the franchise laws. Harmatides gave *me* —an illiterate, freed slave—the right to vote in Assembly. Now all I can do is help avenge him. You'll see that the fucking bastard that set him up gets it, won't you?"

"That is what Antyllus intends to do."

"Antyllus and his crowd of simpering aristos?! Don't bet on them! Send for your fucking Lacedaemonian friends! There's no one to stop them—now that Harmatides is dead. And they'll know how to deal with the likes of Onimastros and his pissing puppets." There were tears in his eyes as he said this, and out of embarrassment he turned sharply away and strode across the courtyard toward the stables.

Antyllus and Lysandridas waited impatiently as the sun climbed up the sky. In the house, the slaves slunk about their tasks in subdued silence, casting nervous glances at the uninvited guests. Harmatides' widow had been taken to another chamber to rest. The clean, oiled corpse waited peacefully under a freshly pressed linen sheet.

Antyllus paced about the interior atrium with increasing nervousness. He could not understand why none of the strategos had responded to his summons. "You don't think they support Onimastros, do you? Is that the real reason they refused to help us yesterday?" he asked in an agitated voice; but he did not wait for an answer, and Lysandridas had none. Antyllus had not included him in enough of his meetings for Lysandridas to venture even a guess about the motives of men he knew too little.

Finally, when the sun was at its height, the first of Antyllus' friends arrived. It was Pisirodos, a stocky, muscular man of middle years. He shook Lysandridas' hand firmly and gave him a long, penetrating look before embracing Antyllus. "What a horrible hour! Have you heard? The mobs managed to break into Sarapion's house and completely trashed it, carrying away his slave girls and murdering his ancient bath attendant. Completely lawless!"

Empedokles arrived next. He was notably cool toward Lysandridas, as he had been ever since the betrothal had been broken off, but he embraced Antyllus and Pisirodos.

By mid-afternoon, two other men had joined them as well: the ageing but quick-witted Melankomos and a dour-looking Endios. Two of their numbers were still missing when the sound of galloping hooves and shouting alarmed them. Lysandridas, who had been standing nearest the door, was the first out of the chamber, and following his ears and his instinct, he ran to the outer court.

Falling off a lathered horse, blood smeared across one arm and up onto his shoulder, was one of the four cavalrymen who had left in the early morning to fetch the strategos. He stumbled up the steps, calling for Antyllus as Lysandridas caught him. "What is it?"

"The strategos—all of them—have been arrested! Phaeax has thrown them all in jail. I was arrested for breaking the curfew! They put me in a wagon with everyone else they were picking up on the streets. I saw the others when they took us to the jail—but I got away. They grazed me with an arrow as I stole a horse," he was looking at the wound on his arm as he spoke, "but I kept going—the wrong way, of course. I rode as if for home. I—I think I shook them off. But you can't imagine it! They have all the strategos together in the jail—and other important citizens as well!"

The others were clustered behind Lysandridas listening to the cavalryman's breathless report, and their expressions ranged from astonishment to grim determination.

"Who are *they*?" Melankomos demanded.

"Phaeax seemed to be in command. He has made himself chief strategos, and the mercenaries obey his orders. Polyphom and Kapaneos were with him, of course."

"And we thought Harmatides was an unscrupulous tyrant," Pisirodos summarised succinctly.

Antyllus was the first to draw the necessary conclusion, perhaps because the thought had already occurred to him the night before. He voiced it for the first time: "We will have to ask Lacedaemon for help."

The others had been talking excitedly among themselves or asking the cavalryman questions. They went abruptly silent and stared at Antyllus, and then their eyes shifted to Lysandridas.

Finally Endios asked with raised eyebrows, "Invite Lacedaemon in?"

"Give up our freedom and independence?" Melankomos asked, frowning.

"I don't think that will be necessary. We have the captives, don't we? At least, the most important one. And, correct me if I'm wrong, Lysandridas, but most of the Spartans do *not* want to annex Tegea. They would be content with a return of the hostages, peace, and some kind of mutual non-aggression pact. If we ask them to help us restore the legitimate government in exchange for a non-aggression pact and the return of the hostages, I think we could eliminate both Onimastros and the mob at the same time."

The others did not look entirely convinced, and their glances kept shifting to Lysandridas. Finally Pisirodos asked him directly, "What do you think, Lysandridas? Do you think your countrymen would help us eliminate Onimastros and his mercenary army—and then peacefully walk away again?" He sounded extremely sceptical.

"They might." Lysandridas remembered the debate in Assembly about the treaty Chilon had negotiated. There could be no doubt that the majority of Sparta's citizens understood Chilon's arguments against annexation. Almost as important, Spartans were proud of their traditions, and this was the key. Lysandridas tried to explain. "Spartiates founded the first democracy in Greece, and they have always abhorred tyrants. A campaign to destroy a tyrant would win popular support. By restoring democratic government in Tegea, the vast majority would feel they had restored their pride and honour and image throughout Hellas after the humiliation of the defeat four years ago. If the majority feels they have restored their honour and their image in the world, they should be willing to withdraw. But you would have to let them keep Orestes' bones," Lysandridas added practically, remembering why the treaty so far had failed to win ratification.

Melankomos laughed shortly. "I think that would be a small price for the elimination of Onimastros and a restoration of democracy—on the basis of a more limited franchise, of course."

The others nodded agreement.

"Then we should draft a proposal we can send to Lacedaemon—" Antyllus suggested, and was slightly annoyed that Lysandridas lifted his hand to interrupt him. "Yes?"

"If you value Ambelos and the other hostages, you should send a messenger to Chilon immediately. You must make it clear that we—not

Onimastros—have Cassandra and will be sending a proposal later. Every hour lost puts Ambelos more at risk. Hermes alone knows if Onimastros has not already sent a message to Sparta saying the captives have been violated."

Antyllus felt guilty for not having thought of this himself, and he agreed at once. "Yes, of course. Who can we send?"

All eyes turned automatically to the wounded cavalryman. He looked up, and then pulled himself to his feet. "Yes, I'll go—but I must have ambassador status. I must have some protection against arrest and enslavement. We're still at war with Lacedaemon."

The others only looked at one another. They were not the government of Tegea—not yet. They had no means or right to appoint an ambassador.

"We can send Leonis. She's Spartan, and no one can forbid her return." Lysandridas suggested.

"Your wife?" Antyllus was horrified. "Alone? In this unsettled situation? And how would she get there?"

"She can ride well and fast. She won't be stopped at the border, and she will have Chilon's ear instantly. She can also report personally on Cassandra to Anaxandridas."

No one had any rebuttal to this catalogue of advantages, and so Lysandridas wrote a hasty message to Leonis and sealed it with his personal ring, so she would not doubt he sent it. This was given to the young cavalryman with instructions to ride outside of the city—since the curfew did not apply to the surrounding countryside—and take it to Antyllus' estate, where he was to ask to see Lysandridas' wife. "Tell her she must leave at once. Ambelos' life depends on it."

With the messenger gone, the conspirators settled down to discuss the details of the offer they should make to Lacedaemon, as well as how they should act in the meantime. Harmatides' widow sent word that they could go to the andron, where a meal would be brought to them. Antyllus and Lysandridas, who had set out even before breakfast, were grateful for the widow's consideration. They retired as a group to the andron, and removing their weapons and sandals settled on the various couches. Slaves soon arrived with water and wine, which they mixed in the krater, and then food.

The mood was one of excited urgency. Lysandridas told himself he had no right to criticise them for their apparent indifference to Harmatides' death. They had been his opponents for nearly a year. They had been seeking his downfall for at least half that time. Should he expect them to cry hypocritical tears? And yet he found himself remembering all Harmatides' good qualities—above all, the love he had always shown his handicapped son. He remembered, too, that Harmatides had never treated him with disdain, and had never demanded that he take up arms against his former city—not even after Lacedaemon had rejected him.

The arrival of a late guest almost went unnoticed in the lively discussion among the politicians. Lysandridas, less engaged in the conversation, was the first to notice the man standing in the doorway, smiling faintly. Then he started and wanted to call out a warning, but it was too late. Onimastros stepped deeper into the room, and now Lysandridas saw that behind him were Phaeax, Polyphom, and Kapaneos—and they were backed by at least a dozen mercenaries in full armour.

"What good luck to find you all collected here together," Onimastros opened, and only then did the discussion die on the lips of the conspirators. "So considerate of you to spare me the trouble of rounding you up individually."

"What do you mean, rounding us up?!" Pisirodos started indignantly. "What right have you to— " At a gesture from Onimastros, the mercenaries moved into the room. Pisirodos blanched.

Onimastros smiled, "You were saying, my dear Pisirodos?"

"What do you intend to do with us?"

"I don't know yet—keep you where I have my eye on you, for a start— chained to the wall of the jail, for example."

The protest was loud but short. The mercenaries had their swords out. Lysandridas felt naked. His own sword lay just out of reach on the floor below his couch. To reach for it, he would have to roll over onto his belly. Such a motion would attract attention, and the mercenaries would instantly know what he was trying to do.

"Take them," Onimastros ordered in his soft, rather high voice, which seemed so out of context in the situation. But then, Lysandridas thought as he watched the mercenaries roughly haul the elegant aristocrats from their couches and pinion their arms behind their backs, that was why he was enjoying this so much. He had never had so much power before in all his life. Before, he had had to let Harmatides give the orders; he had been forced to "suggest" and manipulate from behind the scenes.

Abruptly, Polyphom was standing in front of Lysandridas' couch, smiling vindictively. "My, but I am looking forward to *playing* with you," he told him, and reached out his hand to run it up Lysandridas' leg—just as he had that day so long ago when Lysandridas had been a slave. As then, Lysandridas' reaction was both instinctive and schooled. He swung his leg forward, kicked out at Polyphom's groin, and brought himself upright in a single, sharp motion that took his opponent by surprise. But he got no further.

Two mercenaries pounced on him from behind and wrenched his arms roughly behind his back.

"Not so brutal with that one!" Onimastros called out in alarm, waving Polyphom's outraged protest aside with a gesture of his beringed hand. "I need him to drive *my* chariot to victory at Olympia in just over a month!"

As he spoke, Onimastros came to stand directly before Lysandridas. He was a short, fat, balding man, but he looked Lysandridas directly in the eye. "You *are* going to drive the Tegean team to victory, aren't you?"

"That is for the Gods to decide," Lysandridas countered.

"The Gods? You better do all you can to be sure they feel well disposed to you, young man; because if you *fail* to bring me the crown of olives, I'm going to give you to my dear friend Polyphom here for his admittedly perverse pleasures. And as for your friends"—he gestured toward Antyllus and the other stunned aristocrats—"they will feed the vultures."

"Why should they pay a price for my ineptitude?" Lysandridas protested.

"Because I want you to be—shall we say—motivated?"

"The threat of servicing Polyphom is motivation enough," Lysandridas retorted, red with hatred.

"Really?" Onimastros seemed to consider this assertion, looking from his protégé to Lysandridas, but then he pursed his lips and shook his head. "I think not. I think you need to be *particularly* well motivated, given your confused—not to say fickle—loyalties."

Onimastros turned away from him and ordered the mercenaries to take the others out. Then turning back to Lysandridas, he added, "You will have an escort, of course: six men to watch you day and night."

Lysandridas shrugged, "What good will they do? A driver without a team can't win a victory for you."

"But you have a team, Antyllus' team—which I just expropriated to the Tegean treasury."

Lysandridas only shrugged again. "Even you must know enough about sport to know that without a trainer, no driver can succeed. If you really want the victory at Olympia, then you'll send Antyllus with me to Elis. Surely you can spare another six mercenaries?" His tone was so close to mocking that Antyllus felt he was listening to a stranger. The dutiful Spartiate he adopted had never used such a rude tone to any older man. But the slave had, he reminded himself, and suddenly he understood. Lysandridas didn't think he had anything to lose by his impudence. He was looking death in the face again.

Antyllus held his breath, his arms pinioned painfully behind his back by an unwashed, muscular mercenary. He watched Onimastros' face as his eyes narrowed and he stepped closer to Lysandridas.

But Lysandridas stared him down, and his entire body seemed to say: "Go ahead. Kill me. That won't bring you an Olympic victory."

"All right." Onimastros spat it out into his face. "Antyllus will accompany you, but you will be guarded day and night. And my men will have orders to kill you rather than let you escape."

Lysandridas only shrugged.

CHAPTER 30

Leonis had never ridden so long, so far, or so hard in her life. She had been honoured and excited that Lysandridas would entrust her with this mission. She had felt self-important when she ordered the astonished stable slaves to tack up Boreas. Indeed, Cobon had refused. She had had to fetch Pheronike and show her the message from Lysandridas. Pheronike, frowning and moving her lips as she deciphered the letters one by one, had to admit that Lysandridas had *indeed* ordered his wife to ride to Lacedaemon. But she looked up in horror without finishing the rest of the message and asked, "Surely you don't intend to follow such ridiculous instructions?"

Leonis had insisted that she would, and Pheronike declared her mad, but waved to Cobon to do as her adopted daughter-in-law asked. The young cavalryman was sent in to Hypathea to have his wound dressed, and then gallantly offered to escort Leonis as far as the border. For this she was grateful. She had only once made the journey and was not sure she would find her way alone. The cavalryman was loaned one of Antyllus' other riding horses, and together they set out as the sun started to sink down towards the mountains of Arcadia.

Avoiding the city, taking the back roads, or cutting across fields and through orchards, they made it to the edge of the Tegean plain without incident, but Leonis was already sore from riding hard. The ride up the winding road was particularly difficult. Boreas was sweating profusely, and she slid about on his back, almost losing her seat more than once as he lurched and slipped on the uneven, steep incline of the road. His bony withers bruised her crotch and the inside of her thighs. Her fingers were sore and blistered from trying to cling onto his mane and direct him with the reins. Her legs cramped from clinging to his belly. Her head ached from the scorching sun, and her escort, looking more and more worried, offered her his own broad-brimmed hat when he saw the sweat running in rivulets from her face and neck. Once or twice he asked if she was sure she could make it. But she *had* to make it. There was no one else.

The Tegean border post was manned by mercenaries who apparently had no orders to stop anyone wishing to leave Tegea—not in the direction of Lacedaemon, anyway—and they passed without incident. When the Lacedaemonian border post at last came into view, the Tegean cavalryman drew up. "I'll wait here and watch what happens. If you need help, scream, and I'll do what I can."

Leonis thanked him and urged Boreas into a last canter. The spoiled racehorse had never had to climb up mountain roads before and he too was tired, drenched in sweat, and nearly finished. They crossed the open stretch of no-man's-land at a lumbering, painful canter; and when the Lacedaemonian sentries moved out into the road to prevent someone trying to bolt across the border, Boreas just drew up of his own accord and sank his head down in exhaustion. Leonis half-fell, half-slid off his back into waiting arms.

She was recognised at once. "Look what we've got here!" the young Spartiate who had caught her called out jovially. "A runaway bride!"

Around him, the other sentries were laughing and leering. Leonis was dressed in a short chiton, her knees were exposed, and the front of the chiton was soaked with her own and Boreas' sweat so that it clung alluringly to her breasts. Her buttocks were all too evident from the dirt and sweat of riding astride.

"No!" Leonis struggled free of her unwelcome "rescuer." "I'm not running away! I must get a message to Chilon!"

"From whom? That traitor you married?" someone sneered.

"He's not a traitor!" Leonis flung back furiously, her face bright red from the ride and the summer sun and her fury.

"The Assembly ruled otherwise," one of the others pointed out dryly.

"You can't stop *me!*" Leonis retorted, suddenly afraid that they were going to prevent her from entering Lacedaemon and getting her message to Chilon. "*I'm* not a traitor!" she reminded them, and then, because she could hardly stand on her shaking and exhausted legs, she stopped being defiant. Almost against her own will, tears were in her eyes as she begged, "Please help me."

The mood shifted instantly. The mockery and amusement fled. Another of the men stepped forward and offered her his arm. Someone reached out and took Boreas. "Of course. We'll get you a fresh horse and an escort."

Leonis shook her head as she tried to hobble forward, all the pain of her bruised thighs laming her. "I—I can't ride any more. Don't you have a chariot?"

The company commander was suddenly standing in front of her. He flung his cloak over her to shield her exposed body from the leers of his ogling men. She was a married woman, after all, the daughter of a respected citizen and officer. It was improper for her to be seen like this by bachelors. "My personal chariot will take you into the city, ma'am. Are you leaving your husband?"

"NO!" Leonis all but screamed it as she stopped dead in her tracks and looked at him with outraged, glinting eyes. "No! I'm not abandoning Lysandridas! Why should I? No wife could have a better husband—but," the sense of urgency that had driven her to ride so hard overflowed and she spit it out, "there are riots in Tegea. Harmatides has been killed. If we invade now, there is hardly anyone to stop us! I must get word to Chilon!"

The commander could not leave his post, but he sent his deputy with Leonis. It was dusk and the dinner hour was almost over by the time Leonis reached Sparta. Indeed, some men were already departing their syssitia, making their way home or back to the barracks. The young officer driving Leonis knew the location of Chilon's syssitia, and drove directly there. Leaving Leonis in the chariot, he went straight in to fetch the ephor. A moment later Chilon came rushing out, his face wrinkled with concern even before he caught sight of her. "Child! What's happened?"

"I *haven't* left Lysandridas!" she greeted him, pulling herself together, tears shimmering in her eyes again.

Chilon laughed from surprise. "Of course not—but something terrible has happened, or you wouldn't be here." He clambered onto the chariot, took hold of both her hands, and looked down into her eyes intently.

His warm, dry hands steadied her. She took a deep breath. "Onimastros has seized power in Tegea. Harmatides was killed trying to put down the rioters that Onimastros had riled up—and then Onimastros seized power for himself with the help of 2000 mercenaries. He had all the subordinate strategos arrested. And—" Leonis looked angrily at the Spartiate officer who had escorted her here. She did not know him personally, and what she had to say now was not for his ears.

Chilon gently laid his arm over her shoulders and helped her off the chariot. Then he led her to the far side of the street. The younger man took the hint and stayed where he was, out of hearing.

"Oh, Chilon, it's horrible! Onimastros raped Polyxena—personally— and then let two of the mercenaries rape her as well."

"Cassandra—"

"She and the others weren't touched. When Harmatides found out what had happened—"

"I thought he was dead?"

"That was afterwards! First Onimastros raped Polyxena so that Ambelos' life was forfeit, and then he demanded war, and when Harmatides didn't agree, he incited the riots. Meanwhile Harmatides secretly sent Cassandra and Polyxena to us—to Lysandridas and Antyllus—with instructions to keep her safe from Onimastros. But that was before Onimastros let them kill Harmatides and seized power for himself. I—I'm so afraid something will happen to her now. We couldn't stop the mercenaries if they came. Antyllus' house is defenceless—but that's not why I'm here. Lysandridas," she had to pause for breath and now she clung to Chilon as she continued, "Lysandridas told me to tell you that if Lacedaemon attacks now, we will face only the resistance of the mercenaries. With Harmatides dead and his subordinate strategos arrested, there is no one to lead the Tegean army. The citizens are in shock, and Onimastros has no popular support. If we invade now, Lysandridas says, we would face no real opposition and would be viewed as liberators by most Tegeans. But he begs you to spare Ambelos if there is any way...." She'd run out of breath again, and words. She looked up at Chilon, pleading with her eyes.

Chilon nodded reassuringly. "Did you ride all the way from Tegea today?"

Leonis nodded. "We didn't get word from Lysandridas until mid-afternoon, and I took one of the old racehorses."

"I want you to come and report to the entire Council, just as you have to me."

Leonis looked indecisive. She bit her lower lip and tried to shove a strand of loose hair out of her face with the back of her hand—because her palms were black and sticky with dirt and sweat. She was conscious of what a wreck she looked, even with the garrison commander's cloak covering her indecent clothes.

"You want Lysandridas to be able to come home, don't you?" Chilon asked her gently.

"Yes of course!"

"Then come with me, just as you are."

The arrival of Antyllus and Lysandridas at Elis with an armed escort raised eyebrows and comment. No athletes had ever come to Elis with a military escort before, they were told with open disapproval. Antyllus eagerly suggested to the Olympic officials, the Hellanodikai, that they ban the mercenaries from Elis; but the mercenary commander countered that both Antyllus and Lysandridas were accused of "heinous crimes" and were awaiting trial. The Tegean government had only reluctantly allowed them to travel to Elis to participate in the Games, but had sent the mercenaries to assure that they return to face trial. The officials expressed their astonishment and inquired into the nature of the crimes. The mercenaries replied that they were not Tegean citizens and did not know the laws of Tegea. They were simply here to do the job they were paid to do. The Hellanodikai chose not to interfere any further, and Lysandridas and Antyllus were thereafter treated like pariahs by the other athletes and trainers.

Furthermore, the mercenaries made sure they rented lodgings in a part of Elis far from the other competitors. It was thus only on the hippodrome itself or in the stables that they saw the others. Even here, the mercenaries were never far away, and they were alert. Apparently Onimastros paid them extra for anything they could report back to him.

Thessalos and Agis arrived with their splendid team only three days after Antyllus and Lysandridas. Thessalos smiled and waved, starting toward Lysandridas at the first opportunity, but two of the mercenaries imposed themselves and stopped him. They "explained" the situation and asked him to leave their "prisoner" alone. Thessalos withdrew with a knowing—almost smug—look.

Damoxenos of Athens was the other participant who made a determined attempt to establish contact with Antyllus. He, too, was turned away firmly by their escort, and departed looking worried and concerned.

Not long afterwards, Lysandridas overheard Polycritus telling anyone who would listen that he knew about Antyllus' crimes. Polycritus claimed that Antyllus had been accused of embezzlement and the misuse of public funds. He waved a fat, contemptuous hand in the direction of his rival, who was on the other side of the stableyard. "Antyllus was Minister of Mines, you know, and there were rumours more than a year ago that he was siphoning off *huge* sums allocated for public works to his own pocket. The Tegean theatre almost didn't get *built* because he was embezzling so much silver. It's perfectly obvious his estates couldn't afford to support the horses he breeds. Antyllus only *pretends* to be such a *scrupulous*, honest man. Underneath he's as corrupt as that ex-slave he's adopted!"

"Lysandridas corrupt? He rejected your bribe, didn't he?" the Theban contestant reminded him in a sharp, disgusted tone.

Polycritus laughed. "I guess that taught him his lesson! He wouldn't make that mistake again!"

"Oh, are you going to make him another offer?" the young Milesian participant asked in a mocking voice.

"Why should I? I've got the better team this time."

Lysandridas had seen Polycritus' team. It was his father's winning team except for one change: Hector had been replaced by a strange grey colt. "Not without Hector," he called out from the box stall where he was grooming Afra, unnoticed the entire time by the others.

Polycritus spun around, surprised only for an instant. Peering into the relative darkness of the barn, he called in a sneering tone, "Hector? Oh, you mean that little runt you called a race horse? I fed him to my hunting dogs and bought a horse that will shit in your face!"

There was a murmur of disapproval at such language—or maybe at the thought of a horse that had belonged to a winning team being turned into dog food. The news shook Lysandridas so much that he could find no reply.

That night he drank too much, and the Hellanodikai fined him for breaking the strict rules against excessive drinking. He was warned that a second incident would result in his being disqualified from participation in the games.

Antyllus was furious with him. "How could you be so careless?! I've never known you to drink too much! Not even when you were first freed! You always prided yourself on not drinking too much!"

Lysandridas had no answer. A part of him knew that Antyllus had every right to be angry with him, because he was more distressed by news of what happened to the colt he'd trained and raced than by the fact that Antyllus' friends were being held in chains by a tyrant. He even felt a little guilty for his reaction. But Antyllus' co-conspirators were men he hardly knew, and he'd raised Hector from when he was a newborn foal.

Antyllus was clearly at the end of his nerves. It wasn't just the fact that so much depended on a victory, but seeing the royal Spartan team. When he watched the four nearly identical black colts sweep out of the start and stretch out to fly around the hippodrome, he knew everything had been in vain. The years of breeding and training, even the purchase and then adoption of Lysandridas. His poor, mismatched, mixed team looked like provincial patchwork compared to professional mastery. Even Polycritus' modified team seemed a match for his own. Not to mention Damoxenos, with his seasoned team and professional Egyptian driver.

With every day, Antyllus became more convinced that he didn't stand a chance of victory ,and he lost himself more and more in thoughts of the consequences. He tried to convince himself that Onimastros did not really intend to murder his co-conspirators just because he and Lysandridas lost a race. He had only said that to ensure Lysandridas' loyalty for the race in which he was to drive the team Onimastros had "expropriated" from Antyllus. He would attend the games and sit in the owner's box, and he wanted very much to be crowned with the olive wreath. Onimastros, Antyllus imagined, had probably already commissioned a large and impressive monument with his name and titles prominently carved upon it to commemorate his victory. He wanted to be remembered eternally as a powerful, successful man—when no one was left alive who remembered how he got there or what a miserable little figure he actually cut.

But if they lost, Antyllus knew, Onimastros would be bitter and vindictive. Onimastros would not forgive Lysandridas—or Antyllus—for losing. He would kill them both—or more probably, sell them into slavery. But what was the point of murdering all the rich and influential men Onimastros held in prison? If the tyrant killed them all, he would only ensure that their families would oppose him more bitterly. He would only make more enemies. Onimastros was an intelligent man. He must see that he had little to gain from the murder of the others—didn't he?

As the Games approached, Antyllus looked more and more haggard. Dark circles developed under his eyes. The lines of his face became more prominent. The skin around his mouth and chin grew slack. His colour was unhealthy. He often dozed off in the middle of the day or at meals. He helped Lysandridas with the horses mechanically and listlessly. More often than not, he simply sat about on the edge of a trough or leaned on a railing and watched as the two slaves helped Lysandridas groom, tack, water, or hot-walk the team. And when the team was on the improvised hippodrome, he sat watching glumly. He offered Lysandridas hardly a word of advice.

Lysandridas understood what Antyllus was going through, but he was hurt that Antyllus did not confide in him. Rather than drawing them closer together, their shared danger seemed to be driving them apart. Lysandridas blamed himself for not showing more concern for Antyllus' arrested friends, but what could he say? He had begged more than once to be included in the conspiracy, but Antyllus had kept him away until it was too late. It wasn't his fault the prisoners were nearly strangers to him.

Two days before the start of the games, the official procession of athletes from Elis to Olympia began. Abruptly, the Hellanodikai announced that the mercenaries could not take part in the procession. They were neither athletes nor trainers nor officials. Henceforth, they were informed, they were no more than spectators. Antyllus and Lysandridas, the Hellanodikai pointed out sternly, would soon be under oath to Zeus to participate in the games fairly and honestly. It was unthinkable that they would now try to run away.

The mercenaries might have had a different opinion. In the face of so much dignity and tradition, however, they capitulated. The great procession was formed as always, led by the Hellanodikai dressed in their deep purple robes. They were followed by the athletes and trainers for the boys' and youth events. Then came the adult athletes and trainers by sport, starting with the runners, the jumpers, the discus and javelin throwers, the wrestlers and boxers, and finally jockeys, drivers, and owners of the equestrian events. The tail of the procession was made up of all the lesser officials. First came the Mastigophoroi, who kept order among athletes and spectators with long whips, then the referees, masseurs, and doctors, and lastly the bath and gymnasium slaves from Elis, who would serve the athletes during their stay on the sacred premises at Olympia.

As soon as he was freed of the shadow of the mercenaries, Thessalos was beside Lysandridas, grinning. "Not bad!"

"What?" Lysandridas asked warily.

"You've brought sentiment back to your side completely!" Thessalos' voice was openly admiring. "And of course I sent word back that you were under arrest. I'm sure that will have helped."

"What do you mean?"

"If the vote was today, you'd never have been exiled! You stand a good chance of having your citizenship restored!"

"Why's that?" Lysandridas asked sceptically and defensively.

"The message you sent—and, of course, your wife! She covered the distance from Tegea to the border in just over four hours! Hermione may have mocked her for the way she looked, but you can be sure that half the bachelors of Sparta saw it quite differently! When I left, she couldn't go anywhere without young men approaching and congratulating her or just trying to start up a conversation. If Zoë weren't in attendance, she'd probably get even more attention!"

Lysandridas wasn't sure how he felt about this news, so he changed the subject. "And Ambelos?"

"What about him?"

"Is he alive?"

"Why shouldn't he be? Leonis said Cassandra is safe." Thessalos looked over sharply, as if he suddenly questioned Leonis' account.

"Cassandra was safe when I left Tegea. I have no way of knowing what's happened since. But Polyxena—"

Thessalos waved it aside. "Her father will demand extra compensation from Tegea when the time comes. I admit, Anaxandridas made some speech demanding we use Ambelos for archery practice or some such thing, but I don't think even he meant it seriously. He simply felt it was expected of him. In any case, the rest of the Council indignantly refused. Ambelos has made friends everywhere, and no one has forgotten that he came voluntarily. He is admired for that—especially given his foot."

The chill and apparent suspicion which had surrounded them for almost a month had shattered. The other owners and drivers also crowded closer. Damoxenos grabbed Antyllus' hand and remarked loudly, "Whatever happens, remember you are always welcome in Athens."

Antyllus started. "You know what happened in Tegea?"

"Not really, but rumours have been filtering in as more and more spectators and delegations arrive. It's being said that there was a civil war in which Harmatides was killed and many others arrested. A certain Onimastros has set himself up as 'King Archon' and rules with the help of Syracusian mercenaries—of which we saw a dozen."

"That's essentially correct—although calling it a civil war is exaggerating. It was riots and nothing more."

"The rumours say," Damoxenos continued, "that Onimastros had a score of men publicly executed in the agora—a bloody, barbaric spectacle that—"

"Who? Who did they kill?" Antyllus asked desperately, grabbing hold of Damoxenos' arm in horror.

"I'm sorry," the Athenian responded, taken aback by Antyllus' desperation and at once concerned. "I don't believe I heard the names; or if I did, they meant nothing to me."

"Traitors!" Polycritus spat out from behind. "Your *son* is making a regular career of treason, it would seem. No sooner does he get citizenship someplace, than he betrays the city that gives it to him."

The remark elicited grumbles of disapproval from the other owners. Treason in the highly volatile politics of Greek city-states was always a subjective and fluid notion. An assembly that voted one way today could vote the opposite way tomorrow. Majorities came and went for politicians and citizens alike. There was hardly a man among them who had not seen public mood shift suddenly and violently against formerly popular figures. Men who had won fame and fortune for their cities could be exiled and disgraced for some minor misstep. Besides, most of the men had heard the same rumours about the new Tegean tyrant that Damoxenos had heard. They looked toward Lysandridas to see what his reaction would be.

Lysandridas declined to take any note of the insult. Although his expulsion from Lacedaemon still burned him like a festering wound, he was utterly indifferent to the crimes Polycritus accused him of.

It was Antyllus who turned to the others and asked generally, "Have you heard of no opposition to Onimastros? Is no one in Tegea fighting back?"

Embarrassed silence was the only answer. Everyone looked at everyone else. Finally Damoxenos ventured, "I heard that even the playwrights dare not criticise or mock Onimastros. The only plays they perform now, it is said, praise Onimastros to the skies."

"He has promised every citizen an estate, cattle and—" the speaker cut himself off and glanced a little nervously at Thessalos and Lysandridas before continuing, "Spartan slaves and bedmates."

"He has certainly broken off all negotiations with Lacedaemon," Damoxenos reported, with a disapproving scowl at the young Rhodian who had spoken first. "He sent the last delegation back, it is said, with the message that he had no time to waste. He gave the Spartans an ultimatum to return Orestes' bones or watch them taken from the new temple by force of arms. The Lacedaemonian Council naturally replied that the Tegeans were 'welcome to try'."

Thessalos, who had already left Sparta by the time this exchange occurred, hooted with approval at the retort.

"What of the hostages?" Antyllus asked anxiously, not having listened attentively to Thessalos' conversation with Lysandridas.

"We are not barbarians!" Thessalos told him indignantly. "You cannot think we would really murder innocent women or youths!"

Damoxenos nodded, "That's true. The Lacedaemonian government released the hostages at once and even provided an escort for them to return to Tegea. One, the son of the former tyrant Harmatides—"

"Ambelos?"

"Yes, that's right. He refused to return and was granted asylum in Lacedaemon."

This too was news to Thessalos, since it had occurred after his own departure for Elis, but he turned triumphantly to Lysandridas and declared, "There, you see?"

The conversation around them moved on to other topics, other news and gossip. Antyllus had no ear for what was said. He was preoccupied with the image of a dozen men being publicly executed and no one even raising a voice in protest. What had Tegea come to?

Late in the afternoon of the second day, the athletes and officials arrived at the sacred enclosure. For weeks special crews had been working on cleaning and repairing the buildings and grounds, none of which had been used since the last Games. Now everything glittered. The walkways were strewn with crushed marble, and the facades were freshly painted. As yet, no one but the repair and cleaning crews had been allowed to set foot on the premises, and there was no rubbish, no excrement, no trampled grass or chipped plaster to be seen anywhere. Instead, the open areas were blooming with a variety of orchids and asphodels, bowing and dancing in the gentle breeze.

Around the sacred enclosure itself, however, a tent city had sprung up, and here thousands of men and beasts had already turned the countryside into a dirty, smelly shanty town. In addition to the spectators, there were herds of beasts brought along for sacrifice and food. There were merchants selling everything from perfume to good-luck charms. Smiths, leatherworkers, carpenters, and tinkers offered their services. Moneylenders charged exorbitant interest to those unlucky enough to have lost at gambling or been robbed.

Although women were strictly forbidden from setting foot in Olympia, whores openly plied their trade among the masses of men far from home and out for an "adventure". The women from the outlying farms also brought the work of their looms or produce from their kitchen gardens to sell to the men camped out for a week far from their own kitchens.

The arrival of the official procession interrupted the cacophonic buzz of activity, and a shout went up that soon brought the crowds to line the road. Individual athletes were cheered by their supporters, and whole choruses took up chants of support or sang patriotic ditties to encourage athletes from the different cities.

Lysandridas was distracted by the exceptionally large Spartan contingent. Because the Spartans placed so much emphasis on sport in the agoge and had over the years claimed a disproportionate number of victories, there were always a relatively large number of Spartan spectators. This year, however, there were so many that Lysandridas thought it looked like an entire lochos. The Spartans cheered all the Spartan entries and sang snatches of Tyrtaios' battle paeans between shouts to their competing citizens: "Nika! Nika! Nika! Win! Win! Win!"

Lysandridas was so distracted by this spectacle—comparing it to his own far less enthusiastic reception four years ago—that it was Antyllus who saw Onimastros first. He grabbed Lysandridas' arm and hissed into his ear, "There he is!"

Lysandridas followed Antyllus' gaze and saw the fat, balding man surrounded by a half-dozen men from Tegea and a large contingent of mercenaries. The latter were, however, disarmed. The risk of rivalry leading to brawling and murder or armed skirmishes was so great that the carrying of weapons was strictly forbidden, even in the improvised camps. It shocked Lysandridas to see not only Phaeax, Polyphom, and Kapaneos beside the tyrant, but Casambrus and Lampon as well. He had always thought of them as Harmatides' friends. Now he realised his mistake. Onimastros was smiling to them smugly.

"Since he pretends to be the owner of my team, he ought to be in the procession, not watching it!" Antyllus hissed. "Why is he there?"

Lysandridas could not know; but watching the way the mercenaries kept him isolated in the crowd, he speculated, "Perhaps he does not feel safe without his mercenaries and, as we know, they have not been allowed onto the sacred premises."

Polyphom shouted out gleefully, "I've sacrificed an ox to ensure you *lose*, my little Spartiate slave!"

Someone else was shouting "Lysandridas!" and that drew his attention away from the Tegean tyrant and his supporters. On the other side of the road, surrounded by the scarlet-cloaked Spartiates, was Ambelos. "Lysandridas!" he shouted again, waving vigorously to draw attention to himself, although he stood out in bright blue among the red of his companions. "Antyllus!" he called next, when he saw he had Lysandridas' attention.

Lysandridas nudged Antyllus and drew his attention to Ambelos. Antyllus nodded to him, still too benumbed by the sight of the Tegeans to even smile.

The arriving athletes and their attendants witnessed the sacrifice of a hundred head of cattle to Zeus before being allowed to disperse to their assigned quarters. Because of the ever-increasing number of athletes participating in the Games, the original athletes' dormitory built around two interior courtyards had been expanded by two further atriums, then supplemented by a new dormitory and, more recently, a series of long, low, thatched "barracks". The athletes were assigned to quarters on the basis of the sport in which they competed. The owners of the horses in the equestrian events were given rooms in the newer of the two dormitories, because they were usually wealthy and important men accustomed to luxury. The drivers and jockeys were assigned to the improvised huts, since many of them were mere slaves or freedmen. This had been the case four years earlier, but Teleklos had objected and insisted that Lysandridas be given accommodation with himself. Because he was known to the officials now, Lysandridas was again housed in the simple but elegant dormitory with the owners, as was Antyllus. Onimastros was still nowhere in evidence, but Damoxenos was in the next chamber, and Thessalos and his grandfather Agis, the owner of the Spartan entry, were housed two doors down the other way.

By now it was completely dark, and most of the athletes were anxiously crowding into the large, echoing prytaneion, where the braised meat from the sacrificial cattle was being distributed by harassed-looking, sweating slaves. Other athletes, however, were lining the fence or the rivers, which marked the boundaries of the sacred enclosure, to exchange news with relatives and well-wishers.

A slave brought a message to Lysandridas and Antyllus, asking them to come to the Alpheios to meet with "someone". Antyllus at once suspected Onimastros and shook his head. "I couldn't bear facing him."

Lysandridas went alone. It was dark, but lamps lit up the inside of hundreds of tents on the far side of the river, and men carrying torches criss-crossed between the tents, laughing, talking, singing, and quarrelling. Compared to the frenzy of activity beyond the river, the sacred enclosure seemed still and dark. Nevertheless, here too many men were moving around in the dark looking for old acquaintances, going to the temples to make personal sacrifices, or returning from the meal. Lysandridas' guide seemed to have some trouble finding the exact place he was looking for, but at last he pointed. "There! See that man up to his knees in water! He sent for you."

Although Lysandridas could only see a shadow against the uneven light of the torches and tents beyond, it was clearly not Onimastros. The figure was slight and youthful. "Hello! This is Lysandridas!"

"Lysandridas!" Ambelos called back, and at once splashed deeper into the river. He stumbled, fell into the water, got up dripping wet, but still came on. He slipped again and started swimming until he staggered ashore on the near side of the river, dripping water. Then he flung his wet arms around Lysandridas.

Lysandridas embraced Ambelos and then remembered to say, "I'm sorry about your father. Really I am. At least he died fighting and relatively quickly."

Ambelos pulled back sharply, and there was no youthful exuberance left in his face. He looked hard, and in the dim light Lysandridas saw a hint of how he would look as an old man. Ambelos replied in a voice that was sharper and harsher than Lysandridas remembered it: "Killed by his own countrymen, while the men he'd hired watched! I will not forget, and I will not forgive. I will see that those mercenaries pay the supreme price! They will pay with blood for their betrayal!"

Although Lysandridas had no sympathy for the mercenaries, he could not see how Ambelos was going to get the better of 2000 trained hoplites. He could only murmur, "Antyllus tried to eliminate them, but he was too late. Onimastros had already arrested the subordinate strategoi, and the cavalry had been decimated fighting with your father."

"Where *is* Antyllus?" Ambelos asked, looking around.

"We didn't know who had sent for us. He feared it was Onimastros and refused to come."

"But I must talk to him!" Ambelos insisted, lowering his voice and gripping Lysandridas by the arm. "The Spartan Council is prepared to invade Tegea following the Games, but they are willing to do so only if there are reliable Tegeans prepared to set up a new, democratic government—and then sign a peace treaty with Lacedaemon. They will eliminate Onimastros and his bloodhounds, but they do not want to be stuck with a civil war or even a power vacuum. They want Antyllus to form a government."

Lysandridas nodded, recognising Chilon in everything Ambelos said. He was surprised that he did not feel any triumph, even though this was what he and Antyllus had hoped for. Anticipating Antyllus' questions, he asked, "Do you have any information about the welfare of Antyllus' friends—Pisirodos, Melankomos, Endios …? Antyllus will not want to act alone."

"No reliable information. We sent spies into Tegea as soon as your wife brought the news. We could confirm most of what she reported, including the arrest of all the strategoi except Phaeax—although they have been released since and nominally restored to their commands. Tegea is openly preparing for war."

"We heard a dozen men had been executed publicly. Were—"

Ambelos was already shaking his head. "No, those were all rioters and looters, men of no importance. Onimastros wanted to set an example to make sure the mob didn't think it could threaten him as it had Harmatides. No one of substance has been executed—at least not publicly."

Lysandridas nodded, relieved. That was good news that might encourage Antyllus to come out of his depression. "I saw Lampon and Casambrus with Onimastros when we arrived this afternoon."

"Yes, they openly support him, but he's not popular," Ambelos insisted, although he could hardly know this for sure.

The sound of angry voices not far away suggested that a patrol of Mastigophoroi was approaching. "I've got to get back to the dormitory. I'll give Antyllus your message. Come tomorrow during the official visiting hours."

"Chilon is here," Ambelos told him, embracing again hastily. "He will want to speak with you."

Lysandridas nodded, started to withdraw, and then stopped. "And Leonis? How is she?"

Ambelos was already wading back into the river, but he stopped, and his grin was visible even in the darkness. "She's a heroine! Everyone admires her! I'm sure Chilon will bring you a message from her!" He waved and plunged into the water to swim back to the other shore.

CHAPTER 31

The solemn swearing-in ceremony for competitors and judges took place early the next morning in the Bouleuterion. Immediately following this ceremony, the herald and trumpeter contests began in the stadium, while the athletes for the youth competitions warmed up in preparation for their events in the afternoon. Lysandridas, like most of the drivers, took his team to the hippodrome immediately after the swearing-in ceremony. He was anxious for them to become familiar with the track. The chariot races were set for dawn the next day, and this was the only opportunity he had to familiarise his horses with their new surroundings.

It was particularly important to get Afra used to the elaborate starting gate, the aphesis, with its mechanical eagle soaring over the altar at the head of the starting "arrow" and the bronze dolphins that marked each starting position step for step behind the point. As was to be expected, Afra went half crazy when Lysandridas tried to position her in the starting gate beside one of the bronze dolphins. She infected Zephyrus first, and then all four horses started to rear up and dance sideways. Lysandridas circled again and again, but the team absolutely refused to go into position. While the other owners shook their heads or looked bemused as their own drivers successfully brought their horses onto the track, Antyllus just dropped his head in his hands. He had said from the start that Afra was too nervous for racing.

When all the other teams had started their practice laps, Lysandridas dismounted from the chariot and led the team up on foot. Afra reared up and flung herself sideways so violently that she pulled him off the ground briefly and the whole team leapt to the right, almost overturning the chariot. Antyllus stood to tell Lysandridas to give up. It was pointless, but he stayed rooted to his spot, unable to really call it all off at this stage. And what would Onimastros do if he tried? He sat down again.

Lysandridas unhitched Afra and led her alone towards the dolphins. Out on the track, the other teams were already into their third and fourth laps. Still Afra balked, reversed, and skittered left and right. By the time he put her back in the traces, the other teams were on their seventh, eighth, or ninth lap already. The sun was getting hotter by the minute. The team went into the starting gate with Afra still shying away to the right, but the others now impatient for a gallop. At last Lysandridas was on the track, but there was no way he could give them a complete practice run in this heat and after so much nervous fretting. He took them up to speed for two laps, and then slowed them down and let them lope for another four after the other teams departed. When he finally returned to the start, Antyllus alone was waiting for him.

"If that happens tomorrow, we won't even be allowed to start," he told Lysandridas unnecessarily.

"I'll bring them out here again this evening."

Antyllus scowled.

"Not to run, just to have them go through the start a couple more times."

Antyllus took a deep breath. "Do as you think best; but frankly, we don't have a chance—" He cut himself off. Onimastros was blocking their way.

Sweat dripped off the red, peeling skin of his balding scalp, and he glared at them over lips twisted into an unfriendly smile. "Not exactly an encouraging display of skill."

"No; I guess I'm no good. Why don't you get yourself another driver?"

Onimastros smacked Lysandridas across the face with his fleshy, sweaty hand, and Lysandridas was more disgusted than hurt. "Don't forget Polyphom! Your friends won't pay the price of your failure alone!"

Lysandridas laughed.

Antyllus could have kicked him for his impudence. Didn't he realise he was only provoking Onimastros and increasing his animosity? Even if the news from Ambelos was good and Antyllus anxiously awaited an official approach from Chilon, still he did not see the sense in feeding Onimastros' hostility. Nothing had been resolved yet, and in any case Lacedaemon could not move before the Olympic Peace was over.

"If you lose this race, you won't have anything to laugh about!" Onimastros told Lysandridas tightly.

"Tell me something I don't know," Lysandridas retorted.

"I hear your wife abandoned you and fled back to Sparta."

"She did that the day of the riots," Lysandridas answered evenly, but inwardly he tensed.

"She's been sleeping around, you know. I overheard some of the Spartiates comparing notes on her."

Antyllus looked horrified—as if he believed it. Lysandridas shook his head slowly at Onimastros. "You don't know Sparta very well, do you?"

"As well as I have to," Onimastros retorted, and without a word of farewell he turned on his heel and waddled away indignantly.

The youth races had started in the stadium, and roars of excitement and/or disappointment wafted into the atrium of the dormitory on the afternoon breeze. Antyllus paced back and forth in the shade of the peristyle, ignoring the gurgling and splashing of the fountain and the well-tended rose garden. Lysandridas had gone swimming, but Antyllus neither needed to exercise nor wanted to be amidst high-spirited young athletes at the baths. He was preoccupied with a single thought: how fast could and would Onimastros take action against them? Would he really risk arresting or even selling them into slavery before the Olympic Games—and so the Peace—were over? In short, before Lacedaemon could invade Tegea?

The other residents of the dormitory were either watching the youth races, training in the palaestra or gymnasium, or sleeping. Visitors were not allowed in the dormitory, and were kept away by the watchful Mastigophoren. The atrium was empty except for Antyllus himself. But then another man slipped into the shadows of the peristyle. Antyllus paused in his pacing and waited. It took him a moment to recognise the blond man with the long Laconian braids starting at his receding hairline and hanging down his back to his waist. When Antyllus was sure it was Chilon, however, he went forward, offering his hand. Somehow it did not surprise him that Chilon had convinced the Mastigophoren to make an exception for him.

"Lysandridas is at the baths," Antyllus announced as soon as the initial pleasantries were past.

"I came to talk to you," Chilon countered, and they sat down together on a marble bench. "Ambelos will have told you the gist of what we propose," he opened, leaning back and smiling faintly.

"Yes."

"And?"

"I'm a prisoner here. Onimastros has confiscated my team and will claim the olives if it wins. If it loses—which is almost certain—Lysandridas and I will be 'tried' for treason and condemned to slavery by noon. We could be in Alexandria, Sardis, or Babylon by the time the Olympic Peace ends." This, Antyllus had decided in the course of his contemplation, was the worst-case scenario, and his tone was bitter.

Chilon was surprised, but he tried not to show it. He had not expected Antyllus to be defeated before the competition even began. He took his time answering. "It should be possible to prevent such a development. We need only warn the Mastigophoren that you fear for your freedom. As long as you are on the sacred premises, it would be an insult to Zeus to allow you to be taken by force."

"And when the games are over? When I set foot on the other side of the Alpheios?"

"You can ask asylum in Sparta—and receive a Spartiate escort there, if you like. We will invade Tegea when the Peace is over. I have little doubt that we will be able to defeat the demoralised Tegean army. In fact, I expect the most difficult fighting to come from Onimastros' mercenaries. It's your choice if we help to re-establish a democratic but independent government in Tegea, or simply annex the territory, as King Agesikles has wanted from the start. The majority of us would prefer to have a 'friendly' but independent Tegea over a rich but unruly province in which we need to station troops. Only you can know whether your fellow citizens would prefer Onimastros or a government friendly to Lacedaemon."

"There are others—all arrested—who would help me build a new government. How do we prevent them from being murdered while you invade?"

Chilon took a deep breath, and then spread his hands in a gesture of helplessness. "Antyllus, we can eliminate Onimastros and his friends for you, but we are only soldiers. We cannot promise that the only blood spilled is that of your enemies."

Antyllus nodded wearily.

"If, however, you agree to cooperate, then the treaty we sign with you before withdrawing will state that both parties are bound by oath to come to the assistance of the other if ever a third party tries to invade *or* a revolt threatens the legitimate government of one of the signatories. That should discourage any new would-be dictators from trying to seize power in Tegea."

"And commits us to helping you keep the Messenians down," Antyllus countered with a cynical smile.

Chilon laughed shortly and agreed. "Yes, of course; but I'll have to put something into the treaty that wasn't there before. Otherwise, it will be difficult to get the Assembly to agree to withdrawal once we're in control of Tegea. The combination of letting the militarists have a victory, giving the democrats the role of 'liberators', and promising the old men a new ally against the Messenians is almost certain to give me the majority I need. But I need your help."

"You never really doubted it, did you?" Antyllus pointed out with raised eyebrows and a sad smile. Antyllus was feeling like a puppet, and he hated himself for it.

Chilon tread very carefully, sensitive to Antyllus' mood. "Your advice about Ambelos was invaluable. If not for you, we would never have been able to draw out the negotiations as long as we did. Since then, I have viewed you as an ally in finding a peaceful resolution to the conflict between our cities. I would like to think that in the future you will represent an allied city."

Antyllus nodded. That was diplomatically put, and what more could he ask? His only hope for freedom and restoring democracy to Tegea was Lacedaemon. Beggars, as the saying goes, cannot be choosers.

Chilon was waiting for Lysandridas when he left the baths. The sun was low and golden. The last of the youth events, wrestling, was being held in the stadium before the crowds of excited spectators. "I have to take my team to the hippodrome before it gets dark," Lysandridas told him, not meeting his eyes. Chilon knew this meeting was going to be more difficult than the one with Antyllus.

"I'll come with you," Chilon volunteered, and fell in beside him. They did not speak. Chilon, sensing Lysandridas' hostility, chose to wait, and Lysandridas' emotions were in such turmoil that they tied his tongue.

On the whole way to the stables and as he got the horses ready, Lysandridas tried to get his emotions in hand. He knew Chilon was a friend. He wanted to ask about Teleklos and Leonis. But how could he chat as if there were no borders between them? Chilon's very good humour angered Lysandridas. Didn't he realise that Lysandridas' freedom and good men's lives depended on how well Lysandridas drove tomorrow? Didn't he realise that Antyllus and he stood with one foot in chains—or in his own case, the grave—already?

When he had laughed at Onimastros this morning, Lysandridas reflected, he had done so because he had found the threat of slavery stupid. He would never let anyone put chains on him again—much less let Polyphom lay a hand on him. Although he had no weapons with him, his dagger would do the job well enough. No Spartiate grew up without knowing exactly where a dagger could be used most effectively. But he did not honestly think it would come to that. He felt certain that Onimastros would not try to seize him until the Games were over. It should then be possible to disappear in the crowds of departing spectators, or to seek sanctuary at a temple or even defend himself vigorously enough to arouse sympathy and support from others. He did not expect death or slavery tomorrow; but he resented intensely facing a stateless, uncertain future alone—without his wife.

He realised, too, that he was furious that he had been forced to send his wife back to Sparta. He was jealous of the admiration she had won. He did not for an instant doubt her loyalty and virtue, but he hated his former countrymen for making him look like an abandoned husband. More to the point, if he hadn't been exiled, he wouldn't be a Tegean citizen, and wouldn't be subject to the Tegean tyrant—nor driving the Tegean team.

Chilon walked beside him amiably as he drove to the empty hippodrome. The turf had been neatly raked and everything made ready for the race set for first thing the next morning. Just before they reached the gate, Chilon hit his forehead with the heel of his hand and announced, "I almost forgot!"

He had Lysandridas' attention. "Your wife asked me to give you this." He drew something out of his purse and held it out to Lysandridas. It was a bronze lion with a small chain through the loop of its tail so it could be worn as a pendant. On the side of the lion she had scratched: Leonis loves Lysandridas.

Lysandridas put it over his head and tucked it inside the front of his chiton. Getting a message like that from the hands of someone other than Leonis herself reignited his resentment, and he asked tightly, "How is she?"

"You know she's pregnant?"

"What!?" Lysandridas spun about on Chilon, shocked.

Chilon considered the charioteer beside him critically. "That ride you sent her on could have cost her the baby or her own life."

Lysandridas stared at him.

Chilon read the horror on his face correctly. "You were lucky," was all Chilon said, adding, "Antyllus has agreed to help us."

"Don't you think it's the other way around?" Lysandridas challenged. "*You* have agreed to help Antyllus."

Chilon looked up. "Is that *really* the way you see it?"

"Does it matter?"

"It does if you ever want to come home."

"Where's that?"

"Leonis thinks it is with your father—with Teleklos."

"Has she decided to stay?"

"No; she will come to you wherever you are and whenever you send for her." Chilon watched Lysandridas' face very carefully. The younger man was flushed and his jaw was set. The scar in the middle of his forehead stood out like an incisive gash, but Lysandridas did not answer.

"There's something I didn't tell Antyllus, but I want you to know."

Lysandridas held an impatient team and stared expectantly at Chilon.

"We aren't going to go back to Sparta to march from there. We've brought an entire lochos with us—"

"I thought you had," Lysandridas could not resist telling him.

Chilon nodded. "We will invade from the west and south the day the Olympic Peace ends. In fact, we'll shadow Onimastros all the way to the border, and be ready to follow him into the city."

They stared at one another. "Why are you telling me this?"

"So you can use the information to our mutual benefit."

Lysandridas seemed to think about this, but without another word he clicked to his horses and they sprang eagerly into motion again.

Chilon sighed and watched him take the chariot into the starting gate. Afra again made a fuss. Nothing Lysandridas did could get her into the starting position until he dismounted and led her on foot. Even so, she sidled and fretted so much that it was impossible to keep the chariot motionless, as the rules required at the start. Unconsciously, Chilon shook his head. Even a layman could see that this team was no match for the royal Spartan team, and that meant that Lysandridas was going to need Spartan protection tomorrow. He hoped he would have the sense to curb his resentment when he came to ask it of King Anaxandridas and the Guard.

CHAPTER 32

The drivers of the competing chariots were woken before dawn; they crept out of their quarters in the dark and dew of the predawn chill. A heavy mist shrouded the valley, clinging particularly to the rivers. The drivers had a light breakfast and then went down to the stables to oversee the final preparations. Some owners/trainers were also there: Agis because he was used to rising early, and the Theban and Milesian owners because it was their first Olympics and they were obviously nervous. Damoxenos, Polycritus, and Antyllus were conspicuous by their absence.

Lysandridas gave the horses hay and a small portion of oats. Many owners raced their horses on empty stomachs rather than risk colic; but it was almost two hours before the actual race began, and Lysandridas wanted his team both in good spirits and as calm as possible.

As the dawn crept up on them, more and more of the owners found their way to the stables. Altogether there were eight teams competing in these Games: from Tegea, Sparta, Athens, Corinth, Thebes, Miletos, Plataea, and Andros. The Plataean team had competed at Delphi and had been soundly defeated, but had a new driver. The Theban, Milesian, and Androsian teams were newcomers, like Agis' Spartan entry.

Antyllus finally arrived, looking more rested than he had in weeks. He came over to Lysandridas and smiled with a warmth that had been absent ever since Onimastros' coup. He clapped Lysandridas on the back and then offered to help him with the bandages for his hands while the slaves did the final grooming and clipped the fetlock hair. He chatted about this and that, but seemed to be avoiding giving any final instructions. Lysandridas sensed that he had already written off the prospect of victory. There was, he seemed to say by his failure to talk about the race before them, nothing Lysandridas could do to win, so there was no point debating one strategy or another. This attitude discouraged him more than any admonishments or even stupid advice would have done.

Polycritus arrived in a glittering chiton with gold thread woven into the bright orange. His sandals had coral beads on them and he wore a wreath of red carnations on his head. Lysandridas saw him whispering to the other owners, with his hand before his mouth but his eyes fixed on Lysandridas. It was not long before the Rhodian who was driving the Plataean team came over and asked casually, "Do you know what Polycritus of Corinth is saying about you?"

"I'm sure it's insulting, whatever it is," Lysandridas snapped back, backing Ajax into the traces without looking over.

"He says he saw you talking to one of the Spartan officials last night, and that he's sure you took a bribe to let the Spartans win."

"That's almost flattering," Lysandridas pointed out harshly, raising his voice, "to suggest the Spartans considered me a threat to their team. There's only one small flaw to the theory." Lysandridas was speaking so loudly that heads were turning, and Antyllus gripped the side of the chariot. He could see that Lysandridas was livid with fury and staring at Polycritus. The Corinthian felt his eyes and noticed that everyone else was looking over at Lysandridas.

Lysandridas raised his voice even more, so that everyone in the stableyard could hear. "If the Spartans considered me a good driver, they would have given me their own team!" Lysandridas told the hushed crowd, and his scar stood out so vividly now that it seemed to dominate his whole face.

Agis and Thessalos denied this vigorously, and Antyllus begged Lysandridas to calm down. The incident passed. The two Hellanodikai arrived in their flowing purple robes, accompanied by an entourage of lesser officials and a youth wearing a wreath of asphodels and holding the urn from which the starting positions were to be drawn. The owners were called over, and suddenly Onimastros appeared out of nowhere. Antyllus hung back and Onimastros—to the evident surprise of the others—drew from the urn. He then brought it over to Lysandridas, hissing as he pressed it into his hand, "if what Polycritus says is true, I will see you never drive a chariot again—that you aren't *capable* of it." With a gesture he indicated the amputation of both hands. "And *then* I'll turn you over to Polyphom."

Lysandridas turned away without answering and looked at the position scratched onto the shard of pottery. He had drawn the far outside position, normally a bad lot, but it put Afra as far away from the bronze dolphins as possible. That was something to be thankful for.

It was time to mount and line up for the procession. From the hippodrome came the low din of voices as the crowd gathered. The mist was burning off rapidly, promising a hot day. The trumpets blared in the hippodrome, and a cheer went up for the Hellanodikai.

The processional order was determined by the starting positions. The drivers who had drawn the two positions flanking the altar at the point of the gate led, followed by each successive pair at the receding steps of the gate. Lysandridas was last, beside the Plataean team. Leading were Polycritus' team and the Thebans. Thessalos had drawn the left-hand side in the second slot, with Damoxenos at the same level on the right—perfect for both of them. The third positions were held by the Androsian and Milesian teams.

All the teams were in place when Lysandridas headed for his slot. While the others danced and flung their heads about, Afra went decorously into her slot as if she had been doing it all her life. Almost immediately the eagle went soaring up to signal the start of the race; and the first of the dolphins, for the slots farthest back, fell simultaneously. Lysandridas was caught by surprise, and the Plataean team was off before him. As they came abreast of the third slot, the second dolphin fell and the next two teams sprang into motion, then the third and finally the last two teams at the head of the arrow.

By now, however, the Plataean team was already a good three lengths ahead of the pack, and flying toward the curve as if their hooves were on fire. The Plataean spectators were standing up and cheering as if this were the last lap rather than the first.

The Plateans were hotly pursued by the Theban team, whose driver pulled them hard to the left onto the rail. In doing so, they cut Thessalos off dangerously. The Spartan horses, unused to having a chariot cut in front of them, reared up and Thessalos lost momentum, while to his left the Athenian, and to his right the Androsians, surged past him. The Milesian team intentionally held back and then pulled onto the inside rail at the back of the field, while Polycritus' driver made no attempt to gain the rail but plunged down the centre of the broad track.

Lysandridas slipped in behind his former team, keeping a good two positions out from the rail. Here he could set his own pace, rather than being penned in by the others.

Lysandridas had the satisfaction of seeing Polycritus' new colt fail at the very first turn. The new colt was stiff and unresponsive as he came into the curve. He fought against the efforts of his driver to rein him in and although he turned his head, he flung his haunches out the other way. The chariot continued in too straight a trajectory and came dangerously close to smashing into the outer edge of the track; but just then the sun cleared the mountains, shattering the shadow that until then had clothed the hippodrome. Suddenly blinded by the bright rays of sunlight, all the horses responded with various degrees of panic. Veering now sharply left, Polycritus' team was saved from disaster, but the Milesian team flung themselves so violently to the left that the entire chariot was turned over and dragged along on its side for several hundred yards. The driver was thrown out and quickly carried off in a stretcher, while the race continued uninterrupted.

The Plataeans, the only team already around the curve when the sun hit the track, had increased their lead by another three to four lengths, and the Thebans were a good three lengths ahead of the next two chariots, the Spartan on the inside and the Athenian on the outside. Lysandridas was second to the last, with just the Androsian trailing him slightly on the rail.

Lysandridas ignored the others, concentrating only on his own team. They were excited and eager, Zephyrus and Afra racing each other again. He was having some trouble keeping them in hand, and Afra had her ears flat back on her head in frustration and protest. Lysandridas was smiling in pure pleasure now—feeling the power he held in his hands, the wind in his hair, the excitement of the chariots flying over the sand, and subconsciously hearing the cheers of the crowd, indifferent to the fact that the cheers were for someone else.

If he won today, Onimastros would wear a crown of olives he did not deserve and go down in history as an Olympic victor without ever having done anything to earn it. Better that the crown went to Agis, who had spent a lifetime carefully breeding and training horses until he had a team as near to perfect as they came.

If only they had given it to him, Lysandridas thought for a second; but at once he felt guilty for being disloyal to the four horses he drove, who were straining in his hands and thundering through the second turn to race again into the sunlight. Squinting into the sun, he could see far ahead of him the Theban team start to weave right and left, driven mad by the blinding light. The chariot started to swing more and more violently from side to side. The driver had lost control of his team, and Lysandridas winced and instinctively pulled his own team more to the right as he saw the Theban chariot careen against the inside rail and then tumble over itself, tearing the inside horses to the ground. Thessalos just barely managed to veer away from the accident in time. The Egyptian driver of Damoxenos' chariot was keeping well clear of the crowded rail just as Lysandridas was, and sailed past the accident site without trouble.

The Corinthian team also avoided the accident as such, but now the driver had lost control of his inside colt entirely. He bolted straight ahead and failed to bend into the turn. The Corinthian chariot hit the outside barrier and reared up on the inside wheel; the driver leapt out, expecting it to turn over. It didn't, but it was too late for the driver to recover, and the cart rattled away driverless. The Corinthian driver—the professional who had driven Antyllus' team at Delphi—limped off the track to the hoots and hisses of the crowd.

They were now into the third lap, and the Plataean team was already beginning to tire. Lysandridas suspected that the spectators hadn't noticed yet. They saw only that the Plataean chariot was more than half a lap ahead of the others, but Lysandridas noted that the horses' heads were starting to bob and their ears were drooping. Thessalos had noticed it, too, and he started to make his move. The Egyptian driving the Athenian entry kept pace with him a length behind, clearly determined not to let the strong Spartan team get so much of a lead that he might not be able to close it later. Lysandridas glanced back, but the Androsian team was lagging even more, completely outclassed. He eased up on the reins and let his team close some of the distance to the three leaders.

They kept these positions for the next four laps, the following horses gradually creeping up on the Plataeans as the team tired more and more. Going into the eighth lap, Thessalos finally made his bid to overtake the lead. Because the Plataean clung to the rail with such perfection that he was never offered a yard of daylight—let alone room for a chariot to get through—Thessalos had to overtake on the straight and hope to cut in front of his rival at the next turn. The Plataean horses still had enough strength under the whip to beat him off at his first attempt; but on the back stretch Thessalos finally overtook them, and so had the lead going into the ninth lap.

Now, Lysandridas calculated contentedly, Thessalos had a problem. The Egyptian driver of Damoxenos' team was just a length behind, waiting for him to make the slightest mistake. And Thessalos was too heavy-handed to ease his team around the curves. He always swung wide first and then hauled them around a good ten feet from the rail. Room enough for a good driver to get through. Obviously, this was what the Egyptian was planning to do.

Lysandridas, however, now eased his own team over to the rail, effectively blocking the Egyptian out. He saw the Egyptian glance back over his shoulder, and that raised his spirits. For the first time this race, he started to believe he just might pull off another victory after all.

Four years ago he had been obsessed with victory, ready and willing to take any risk. Now he was cooler and more calculating, but he also felt no exhaustion, no heat, and no sweat—only the wind and the strength of the four horses plunging forward, still eager, still racing with a will.

They came into the turn. Thessalos, as always, swung out. The Egyptian lashed his horses up, shouting audibly, and plunged into the gap so fast that Lysandridas had to haul back to avoid a collision. It had been a daring move, and the crowd went wild. But the crowd couldn't see that the move had been too sudden; that the inside trace horse had taken some injury in the too-abrupt motion; that his head was bobbing, his stride faltering. He broke gait. The Egyptian driver was cracking the whip, shouting to his Gods or merely cursing, but the injured horse was holding the others back. Thessalos and Lysandridas both overtook the faltering chariot on the outside as it gradually slowed on the rail. They had a lap and a half to go, and they were side by side—Lysandridas already on the rail.

But the Spartan team was stronger, and Thessalos could drive in his usual fashion with no additional risks or interference. All he had to do was tire the Tegean team. And they were tiring. It crossed Lysandridas' mind that if the Spartans won, Onimastros would never believe he hadn't done it intentionally. Anyone who was a judge of horseflesh knew that he had pulled off the almost impossible to be challenging the Spartans this late, but Onimastros was no judge of horseflesh.

The next turn was approaching and Lysandridas concentrated on a gentle, controlled turn—not so tight that he had to slow the team, but not so wide that he offered Thessalos a chance to cut him off. Afra was showing her mettle now, bending in the curve with her neck arched and her stride shortened, as Titan gallantly stretched out again, and the trace-horses tucked in their noses to counter the centrifugal forces swinging the chariot off the rail.

Thessalos swung wide and came roaring back close on Lysandridas' right—dangerously close. He was fighting for every inch, as if it mattered. Couldn't he see that Ajax was beginning to shorten his stride, his head was bobbing?

They had a whole lap and just one more turn. Lysandridas considered the whip waiting in the wicker pocket on the inside of the cart, but he couldn't bring himself to draw it. A whip had never once induced him to greater efforts when as a slave they had cracked it over his back. Nor did he see his team as slaves that needed to be threatened. If they didn't have the heart to race, then it was all over anyway. But they did have the heart. Afra and Zephyrus were furious to find another team pacing them. Afra had her ears flat again—not because he was holding her back, but because she was incensed by the strange colts threatening to overtake her.

Thessalos had his whip out and was firing up his team with it. He never touched them. He was too good a driver for that, but he was not above using everything he had. This victory was too important to him—as important, perhaps, as it had been to Lysandridas last time. It crossed Lysandridas' mind that he particularly wanted to beat Lysandridas himself.

The Spartan team started to draw ahead. They gained a head, a half length, and a length. The first bit of daylight showed between the Spartan chariot and Titan's nose as they went into the final turn. Lysandridas concentrated only on the railing and the turn; he could not spare a glance even out of the corner of his eye for Thessalos. He heard only the screaming of the crowd: hysterical, mad screaming. He came out of the turn with his team steady as a rock, but as soon as they entered the back stretch Zephyrus lifted his head up and lurched a bit. Titan was starting to slacken his pace noticeably, irritating the younger Zephyrus, who still had strength to spare. Preoccupied with getting them back in unison, Lysandridas did not register that Thessalos was not back on his right until they had gone another half-dozen strides. He couldn't believe what he sensed. He glanced to the right. Thessalos was still there, but he was a good two lengths behind and almost in the middle of the track. He was leaning forward over the front of the chariot, screaming and thrashing the whip over the heads of the team. They had no more turns. It didn't matter how far away from the rail he was, but he still had to make up two whole lengths, and they had only half a lap to the finish.

He *was* closing. Lysandridas could hear the huffing and puffing of the Spartan horses, and the whip seemed to be threatening his own scarred back. But Zephyrus and Afra were dragging their teammates toward the finish line as if it were their honour and their friends who were at stake. And then they were over the finish and going dutifully into the next turn, not yet aware that the race was over.

The crowds were going wild—with the notable exception of the Spartan section. Here the men sat in gloomy silence, some still standing from having sprung to their feet at the last turn. Others sat—as if turned to stone. They stared at the track as their magnificent all-black team gradually slowed to a canter. They couldn't believe it. Anaxandridas was gripping the railing in front of him so that his knuckles were white, his face a mask. Not one of them doubted that the last turn had cost them their victory. Thessalos, afraid of giving up too much of his lead, had tried to cut the corner tighter than he usually did. He had only succeeded in bringing his team too close to Lysandridas' chariot. The team had shied sharply away from it and veered out into the middle of the track, costing him both momentum and precious distance at exactly the wrong moment. The team hadn't been beaten; the driver had.

Chilon broke the silence with a heartfelt laugh. The other Spartans turned on him, angry and outraged. But he shrugged and reminded them: "It's your own fault. You threw him out."

That night Onimastros wore the olive crown and strutted about with his palm of victory. He did not once draw attention to Lysandridas' role in his victory. He did not draw him into the winners' circle. He did not even send him a note of thanks. Like a slave, Lysandridas was ignored; and like a slave, he helped hot-walk, wash down, and groom the horses; but it didn't bother him as much as Antyllus. The charioteer was never officially awarded the crown. It was Antyllus who had been robbed of his victory, while Lysandridas had had the pleasure of it.

They celebrated unofficially among a small circle of well-wishers—Ambelos and Chilon, of course, and even Thessalos and Agis and Damoxenos stopped by to congratulate them. But the defeated owners and drivers could hardly be expected to celebrate with much enthusiasm, and soon excused themselves. A mood of triumph never developed. Antyllus felt relief that the threat was past, but the events ahead of him were too important and the outcome too uncertain for him to even fully relax. After six years of training for this—Antyllus reflected as he laid himself to rest that night—his victory was a complete anticlimax. And officially, it wasn't even his.

CHAPTER 33

Antyllus felt as if he had barely drifted off to sleep, and already someone was shaking him awake. He grunted and tried to see who it was in the darkness.

"What—"

A hand was clapped over his mouth. By all the Gods, he thought, Onimastros was going to kill or sell them even though they'd won! Of course! Why hadn't he anticipated this earlier? Onimastros didn't need them anymore! They'd served their purpose, and now they were to be disposed of like unwanted baggage! They reminded everyone that the victory was stolen. Or had Onimastros learned they were plotting with the Spartans?

Rough hands were winding him in a cloak. He could feel, more than see, a man in armour, with the crested helm pulled down over his face assuring his anonymity. The man was tall, young, and strong, with hardened muscles. One of Onimastros' mercenaries! Antyllus was pushed off his couch. The mercenary shoved his feet into his sandals and buckled them on his feet. Antyllus' hands were bound behind his back, and a gag replaced the hand. He was then shuffled out into the darkness. There was the faintest hit of dawn behind the rustling trees, and a cool breeze on the night air. From beyond the Alpheios came the dull sounds of partying and drinking among the spectators—something that went all night, every night of the Games.

Other figures emerged out of the darkness and surrounded Antyllus. They marched him down and into the cold, swirling shallows of the stream. Where were the Mastigophoren when one needed them? Antyllus stumbled on the slippery stones, and was dragged to the far bank more than he propelled himself there. Here a wagon was waiting. Antyllus was grabbed by two men and heaved up onto the wagon like a sack of grain. He was made to lie down, and a canvas was pulled over him and tied down. The wagon rolled away, creaking and groaning as if under a great weight.

When they pulled open the canvas it was mid-morning, and the sun beat down bright and hot from a clear sky. Antyllus blinked and squinted up into it. To his astonishment, the face looking down at him was Lysandridas. Lysandridas frowned, and then reached down and started releasing the gag and the ropes around his arms. "I'm sorry. I didn't realise you were gagged and bound." He spoke with every appearance of sincerity. A moment later he was also offering Antyllus cool water from a wineskin.

"What in the name of Zeus is going on?!" Antyllus demanded.

"It was Ambelos' idea." Lysandridas indicated the frail youth who emerged from behind him. Antyllus was taken aback. He had been too preoccupied before to notice that the youth, although still thin, was tanned and seemed to exude a new strength and maturity.

"We can't return to Tegea in the wake of a Lacedaemonian army," Ambelos declared, stepping forward and helping to straighten Antyllus' still deranged clothes. "We have to get there first—while Onimastros is still here and feels safe because of the peace."

That made sense, of course; and Antyllus looked at the youth he had always dismissed as a "poor boy" in a new light.

"So why didn't you just come to me—"

"We were afraid Onimastros might—once he'd woken up from his victory hangover—decide to get rid of us on his own. He has no need for us any more, after all, and we had to forestall him. This way we were kidnapped—and no one knows by whom or why, but the suspicion will fall on Onimastros himself," Lysandridas explained.

"Everyone heard him threaten you and saw the way he treated you despite your victory yesterday," Ambelos continued.

"And who are these—gentlemen?" Antyllus indicated the young men—who by the light of day obviously wore Spartan scarlet—who had done the actual kidnapping.

"Members of the kryptea," Lysandridas explained.

"Ah. Your old friends, up to their old tricks," Antyllus observed unkindly, still shaken by what had happened.

Lysandridas flinched inwardly. Friends? Members of the kryptea had nearly killed him—and Antyllus had seen the state he'd been in. But he didn't have time to think about the implications of Antyllus' word choice. The kryptea had been purged of all the members who had abused him three months earlier; and these young men, mostly strangers, were clearly taking their orders from Chilon. Lysandridas chose not to respond to Antyllus' remark. Instead he said practically, "If we are to reach Tegea before Onimastros gets word to his minions that we have fled and orders our immediate arrest, we had best hurry."

Antyllus drew a deep breath and nodded. One of the Spartans led over a powerful stallion for him. Lysandridas and Ambelos were similarly mounted. "You aren't planning to come with us, are you?" Antyllus addressed the handicapped youth.

"Of course," Ambelos answered.

"But why? This is a highly dangerous undertaking, to say the least!"

"They killed my father," Ambelos answered grimly. "Revenge is my right."

"Revenge is a poor counsellor," Antyllus countered.

"Revenge is my motive, not my counsellor," Ambelos retorted, adding with a disarming smile, "*You* are my counsellor, Antyllus."

The situation in Tegea was more confused than they had anticipated. Although there was no outright rioting or unrest, there was an atmosphere of unease and tension everywhere. Many merchants and manufacturers were evidently reluctant to display their wares in a city with inadequate law and order, so many of the market stalls remained locked and bare. Most of the houses were barred and guarded, too. The shops that remained open were visibly protected by their owners and any able-bodied young relatives or slaves that they could muster. People moved about in groups, seeking safety in numbers. Some of the bands of young men roaming the streets seemed to exude a sense of general threat. There were virtually no women on the streets except prostitutes—and these seemed to have multiplied in number dramatically. The courts and public buildings were all closed and guarded by mercenaries—as was the public prison in which, passers-by assured them, the "conspirators" were still being held.

The little party arriving from Olympia made first for Empedokles' estate, where they were challenged at the locked and barred gate. Antyllus recognised the still high-pitched voice of one of his great-nephews, and identified himself. A moment later they were welcomed into the courtyard like saviours. Ever since Empedokles' arrest, his family had lived in fear. Apparently, bands of thieves had twice assaulted the house. Now Antyllus' great-nephews and nieces, his nephew's wife, and his household slaves crowded around the travellers, begging for news. They had been too afraid to leave the house, and could provide Antyllus with no specific information about what was happening in the city.

Mentally Antyllus noted, however, that at least his nephew's house could be locked and barred against bandits. His own could not. It was, therefore, with considerable trepidation that they continued on to Antyllus' estate, fearing what they might find.

Amazingly, the estate appeared to be an oasis of peace and normalcy in the desert of increasing lawlessness. Their horses were taken from them in the stables by Melissos with dull surprise. "Where did you come from, Master? Where's the team?"

"They won the crown—and Onimastros claimed it!" Antyllus answered irritably. "Is everything all right here?" He couldn't believe his eyes, but the mares and foals were out in the paddocks, while the stallions and geldings contentedly chewed at their hay nets as if there had never been an uprising, arrests, or a threat of war.

"Of course, master. What should be wrong? Where's Cobon?"

"He's still in Olympia with the team," Antyllus answered, and they went on into the house. Antyllus led the two younger men straight into the formal atrium, sending a slave woman to fetch Pheronike. She came to them in her languid, unhurried way, a mild smile on her face. "I wasn't expecting you back so soon," she declared, as if they had only been shopping in town, offering her powdered cheek to her husband.

"We came back immediately after winning the race," he told her briskly. "The whole city seems tense, and Empedokles' estate has been attacked twice. Has nothing happened here? You've not been molested in any way?" Antyllus still found it hard to believe.

"Oh." Pheronike pulled away from her husband and made an ambiguous gesture. "Kapaneos has been looking after us."

"Kapaneos?!" Antyllus asked, incredulous. Ambelos glanced in alarm toward Lysandridas.

Pheronike looked at her husband with narrowed eyes. "What's so strange about that? He loved Phaedolos, you know. Don't you remember that? Don't you remember your *real* son at all and how he died? Don't you remember how Kapaneos brought us Phaedolos' corpse? Or how he used to visit us in the months after Phaedolos' burial? I missed him when he stopped coming, but he says *you* stopped him from coming." Her tone was accusing. "He *could* have been a second son to us," she told her husband now, with an almost hateful glance at Lysandridas. "A good Tegean son."

"Has he been in this house while I was away?" Antyllus wanted to know, hardly daring to breathe for inner agitation.

"Yes; why not? He has looked after me as if I were his own mother. Things were so unsettled—just as you said. But he has influence, you know, with Phaeax and the King Archon. His word was enough, and no one dared trouble us here. He's been so attentive—more so than you've been in years—"

"But what about the hostages?" Antyllus interrupted in horror.

"Oh, he knows about them. I mean, I had to tell him—"

"By all the Gods! You fool! You stupid, brainless fool!" Antyllus grabbed her by the shoulders and shook her furiously. "Did he turn them over to Onimastros?"

"Let go! You're hurting me! Do you care more for some Spartan slave than for your own wife?!"

"Princess," Lysandridas corrected, unable to control himself any longer. "Where is she—"

"I'm right here, Lysandridas." Cassandra entered from behind them, looking very regal despite the simplicity of her peplos. She was barefoot and thin and tiny, as if she never got enough to eat. But that was by nature, and she looked unharmed. Antyllus let go of Pheronike in sheer relief and gazed from one woman to the other, more bewildered than ever.

Lysandridas went toward Cassandra with Ambelos limping behind him. "Do you come from my brother?" she asked, looking up at him hopefully.

"Yes, I do," he answered (to Antyllus' surprise), "but first tell me: are you all right?"

"Yes."

"And Polyxena?"

"No *new* misfortune has befallen either of us. What happened at Olympia?"

"I'm sorry; Thessalos made a bad mistake at the wrong moment."

"You beat him?" she asked with surprise.

"I did, yes—although your uncle had the better team."

She smiled and reached out her hand to touch his arm. "Congratulations. I'm glad. You deserved it. Besides, I was worried." She glanced over at Pheronike and then turned to Ambelos, her face serious again. "Ambelos, I'm sorry about your father. He was"—she hesitated, choosing her words carefully—"a man worthy of respect. I think in other circumstances, with better friends, he might have been a great man."

"I am here to avenge him, Madam," Ambelos said solemnly; and although Lysandridas thought the thin youth with the deformed foot looked somewhat pathetic in the role of avenger, Cassandra was enough of a lady not to belittle him.

"I wish you success."

"Madam, I have a personal message from your brother; if we could be alone a moment?" Lysandridas drew her attention back to himself.

Antyllus was frowning and Ambelos looked slightly hurt, but Cassandra at once laid her hand on Lysandridas' arm and let him lead her back outside. He took her down the narrow lane between the paddocks, and they did not speak until they were a long way from the house with only the wind and the mares as witnesses. "Madam, I hope you will not be angry with me for lying to you. I did not speak to your brother personally. My message is from Chilon."

"That is good enough for now."

"Your children are both well. Your son had to be flogged for trying to stow away with the men going to Olympia, but you know what that is like."

She smiled and nodded, but then paused to be sure, "He didn't disgrace the Agiads?"

"Of course not. Nor his father."

She squeezed his arm for that reference to a husband she had loved well.

"What Chilon asked me to tell you is that the Spartan army will invade from the south and west simultaneously as soon as the Olympic Peace ends. Chilon thought you would be safest here, but of course he couldn't know—as none of us knew—that Pheronike had betrayed you to Onimastros. Can you, in the name of the Twins, tell me what is going on here?"

Cassandra started walking again, gazing down at the grass under their feet with a slight frown on her face. "I'm not sure. From what I have heard—either from Pheronike herself or from the slaves—this young man Kapaneos was a lover of the son of the house. When the young man was killed, Kapaneos tried to talk Antyllus into adopting him and when that didn't work, he—apparently—sided with Antyllus' enemies, seemingly in the expectation that the estate would be expropriated and he would receive it. Whether his motives are purely venial or if he really hates Antyllus, I have not been able to decide. In any case, he has flattered and charmed Pheronike."

Lysandridas, remembering Dion, asked outright, "Has he seduced her?"

Cassandra cast him a sidelong glance and then nodded. "Yes. She seems a very lonely and weak-willed woman. Obviously, she is bored and her life is very empty. Antyllus has hired all these able clerks and overseers, so she has nothing to do all day but feel sorry for herself. Still, she seems singularly lacking in intellect and backbone." Although she spoke softly and carefully, the scorn of the Spartan princess shimmered through nevertheless.

"And how do you explain that no harm was done to you after she betrayed you to Onimastros?"

"I don't think Onimastros knows. I think Kapaneos kept the information about us to himself."

"Why would he do that?"

She shrugged and looked down at the long grass beneath their feet. "I'm not sure he knows himself. It is all gambling to him. He likes to have an 'ace up his sleeve'—something that no one knows about. He wants to be able to change sides when it suits him or to up the ante at will. I don't entirely see through the young man. While he seemed very pleased to discover that Polyxena and I were here, nothing seems to have changed. I believe he is still trying to decide what to do with us."

"What do you want to do now? There's a chariot here and two good former racehorses that could get you to the border in a day. If Ambelos and I escort you, we might be able to—"

"The risk is far too great. The best of the mercenaries are holding the border to Lacedaemon. Even if they didn't recognise me, they would recognise Ambelos. I think we must take the chance of waiting it out here. After all, the Olympic Peace will end shortly, and Ambelos is not the only one who wants revenge on Onimastros."

Lysandridas nodded in agreement and respect, and they returned to the house.

By nightfall, Antyllus had removed Pheronike and both Spartan hostages to his nephew's house, and from here he sent messages to various respectable citizens—not to the "aristocratic", landowning faction he had belonged to before, but to men of modest but honest means and sober temperament whom he thought might be won over to his cause. He carefully noted which shops were closed and which houses were barricaded and it was to these men, frightened of what was happening, that he appealed now for support.

Meanwhile, Ambelos and Lysandridas called upon the young men of Harmatides' cavalry. Lysandridas noted that Ambelos' tanned and energetic appearance impressed his father's former subordinates. They remembered him as a sickly, pale, and sheltered youth—as a boy raised more like a girl. Previously, he had been of no consequence. He had returned a young man. To be sure, his gait was still lurching and awkward, but he did not let that stop him. And on horseback he was remarkably normal. Ambelos appealed to their own frustrations and longings for revenge. Although the young men inclined to support them, they were also afraid.

"You have no idea what Onimastros is really like!" they insisted, the fear in their faces.

"He turned the agora into a slaughterhouse!"

"He had the men condemned of armed robbery crucified! They were there for days!"

"He sold the wives and daughters of the condemned traitors in public auction!"

"The daughters of Kleisthenes! Exposed to the jeering and howling of the mob!" The name meant nothing to Lysandridas, but Ambelos caught his breath.

"It was a near thing," another of the young men took up the story. "They nearly ended in the hands of a notorious brothel owner! My father and uncles had to pool their resources to buy them free!"

"We can't risk that happening to our mothers and sisters."

"And these Syracusians are barbarians! They'd as soon kill you as look at you!"

"We are short many horses, too," one of the others admitted.

"How many mercenaries are there?" Lysandridas entered the discussion for the first time. "1,500? 2,000?"

"More! They must number 2,500, 2,700 by now."

"And where are they deployed?"

The young men exchanged glances, and then started adding it up. "Well, he has a personal bodyguard of about thirty—say, fifty. Then a "palace guard" of another fifty protecting his various properties. There are about 100 men guarding the public buildings and temples. Five hundred men on the border to Lacedaemon, a hundred on the border to Argolis, and covering the other passes altogether another couple hundred."

"How many on the border to Elis?"

"Elis?" They shrugged. "A token guard—fifty, I should guess."

"But they'll move 100 men or more forward to meet Onimastros when he returns from Olympia, of course."

"He'll want more than that, since he returns a victor," one of the other young men suggested. "He'll want to make a triumphal entry. He'll want the troops lining the road to cheer and protect him from any impudent citizen." His voice was full of bitterness as he spoke.

"And an escort as well, to march before and after his chariot," another added, equally resentful.

"Altogether 1,000 men?" Lysandridas pressed them neutrally.

"More. He'll want almost that amount in the procession, and that amount again lining the road."

"Yes, he'll have them all turn out to impress and intimidate. Why leave anyone in barracks?"

"Why do you want to know?" one of the more perceptive young men asked Lysandridas.

"What if a Lacedaemonian army came out of Parnos on the day Onimastros makes his triumphal entry into Tegea from Elis?"

"So much the better! The troops would be assembled and in battle dress. They'd swing south and confront the Lacedaemonians at once."

Lysandridas nodded. "And what would you do?"

"Support them, of course."

"Why?"

"Better slaves of a Tegean master than a Spartan one!" someone said hotly.

"They aren't coming as conquerors," Ambelos re-entered the debate. "If a democratically elected Tegean government signs a non-aggression pact with them, they will withdraw."

There was a moment of silence. Lysandridas scanned the faces. They were doubtful, thoughtful, sceptical, but not hostile.

"Democratically elected?"

"What if, while the mercenaries and Tegean hoplites under Phaeax advance to meet the Lacedaemonians, you seized control of the government buildings and released the 'conspirators'?" Lysandridas asked.

"Antyllus is winning over more support every day," Ambelos told them enthusiastically.

They looked from one to the other. Finally someone asked Lysandridas, "And where will you be?"

"Where do you want me to be?"

There was a slight pause, and then after an exchanged glance, one of the young men said: "With us. Taking the same risks, facing the same odds—and ready to face the Spartans—if they should break through Onimastros' forces and reach the city."

"I'll be there."

Lysandridas felt far less happy in the role assigned him than he dared show. He had never fought on horseback in his life. He had never even ridden in armour. He felt naked without his hoplon, and although he had learned to use a javelin, he was acutely aware of his own inadequacies with it. He could only hope it would not come to an actual engagement.

Onimastros' triumphal return to Tegea, driving "his" winning team and wearing the olive wreath, was everything the others had predicted it would be. And the mercenaries turned out to ensure that no dissatisfied citizen would tarnish the event with unfriendly missiles or catcalls. An unexpected difficulty developed, however, when Onimastros sent word that he expected a cavalry contingent in his parade; but it was quickly decided to send half their number and keep the remainder with Lysandridas, hidden behind the walls of Harmatides' house and factory ruins.

Lysandridas noticed that some of the young men were very nervous, but he could not be sure if it was fear of the coming conflict—or fear that it would *not* come and that their less than loyal attitudes would be discovered.

In the event, things happened even faster than Lysandridas had expected. Somehow, word arrived in the city of both Spartan forces almost simultaneously. While Lysandridas knew that the Spartans had hoped to pin the whole Tegean army down in the south while the western pincer took the city unopposed, the premature discovery of the Spartan lochos advancing from the west did not affect the outcome negatively.

In fact, the news that Spartan troops were advancing from two directions produced such widespread panic that complete chaos ensued. The Tegean hoplites could be seen flinging their shields aside and running for any kind of shelter before the Spartans were even in sight. The mercenaries, in contrast, at once pulled together and formed a strong phalanx—and then marched determinedly in the direction of Argos, abandoning Onimastros to his fate.

Lysandridas with the reserve Tegean cavalry was able to seize control of all public buildings without opposition. They released the political prisoners, who were in very poor shape. Ambelos and the remainder of the cavalry meanwhile tried to capture Phaeax and the handful of men who rallied around him. By the time Antyllus arrived at the council house, it was surrounded by a company of the Spartan Guard, while other Spartan units were combing the streets for remnants of the Tegean army and summarily executing anyone who seemed likely to resist the new regime. Onimastros was tracked down trying to flee to the north, dressed as an Armenian peddler; he was killed before Ambelos could stop the cavalrymen who caught him. Kapaneos was found dead in Polyphom's home, apparently at his own hand, but the latter appeared to have escaped. At least, his corpse was never found.

CHAPTER 34

Antyllus organised a parade to celebrate the Treaty of Mutual Defence signed (and ratified) between Lacedaemon and the newly constituted Tegean Assembly. Lacedaemonian light auxiliaries and Spartiate heavy infantry marched alongside Tegean cavalry and hoplites through the streets of Tegea, while King Anaxandridas rode in the same chariot with the newly elected speaker of the Tegean Assembly, Antyllus. After the parade, a play by a Tegean playwright honouring the new alliance was performed in the theatre, followed by a dance performance and choral singing by the Lacedaemonians. The last event of the day was a reception for the official delegation at Antyllus' estate.

Escorted by torch-bearing cavalry, the guests drove to Antyllus' estate as the sky gradually darkened and the stars came out. The long drive up to the house was lined with lanterns strung between the cypress trees. The house itself stood out white, almost glowing, in the dark of the surrounding countryside, lit by torches anchored in the ground around it. The relief of the pediment stood out sharply in the light and elicited admiring comment from the visitors.

In the hall, the lamps were lit and a dozen slaves waited anxiously to relieve the guests of their arms and help them out of their himations and sandals. The mosaics of the floor glinted and the frescoes came to life in the soft shadows. The scent of broiled beef, onions fried with coriander, baked apples, and roasted chestnuts filled the hall. Wine waited in the large kraters in various mixtures to meet the wishes and tastes of the individual guests.

Everyone was in good spirits to have finally brought four years of tension and hostility to such a satisfactory conclusion. For the Tegeans, there was the added benefit of an end to the civil unrest that had led to tyranny. The men collected here were confident that henceforth Tegea would be more governable. For Antyllus, there was an added, personal reason for celebration. Word had reached him that the Hellanodikai had retroactively annulled Onimastros' Olympic victory and recognised Antyllus as the real owner of the winning chariot at the 56th Games.

Lysandridas ensured that the escort and their horses were properly provided for in the stables and kitchens, before entering the formal hall. He saw the Lacedaemonian and Tegean guests mingling easily. Throughout the elegant hall, little groups were engaged in lively discussions. Laughter frequently punctuated the low rumble of conversation. Antyllus' musicians could hardly be heard in the background.

Chilon had been watching for him, and at once excused himself to cross the room and greet him. They had not spoken since Chilon had returned the previous day with the ratified treaty. Chilon smiled at Lysandridas now, and taking his arm, drew him a little aside. "I have something for you," he told him excitedly, and then brought, out of a leather pouch that he wore attached to his belt, a papyrus with the seals of the Spartan Assembly.

Lysandridas took the roll slowly, almost hesitantly. He could guess the content, and he wasn't at all sure how to respond. Chilon urged him to read the document, however, so he unravelled it and read what he had expected: the Spartan Assembly had voted to restore his citizenship and invited him to return to Lacedaemon "in full honours". Lysandridas nodded noncommittally.

Chilon had hoped for a more positive reaction, but he was not entirely surprised by Lysandridas' reticence. He knew how deeply Lysandridas had been hurt by the rejection five months ago, and he was not blind to the honours Lysandridas enjoyed in Tegea. Here, where the army was composed entirely of young men between the ages of eighteen and twenty, he commanded the entire cavalry at twenty-six. In Sparta, where all citizens were required to remain on active duty to the age of thirty, he could not hope for more than a platoon. Here, he was already eligible for elective office. In Sparta he could not stand for office until he was thirty-one. Here he was the son and heir of Tegea's leading citizen and most

382 The Olympic Charioteer

powerful statesman. In Sparta, he was the son of a broken, dying man of no importance.

Chilon took a deep breath, aware that promises of being accepted into the Guard again would sound childish. The youthful Olympic charioteer, who had once wanted nothing more than the Guard and a pretty wife, had been transformed into a man with far greater expectations. So all he asked was: "Will you think about it?"

"Of course," Lysandridas said with a shrug. "I'll let you know tomorrow." He sounded disinterested, and for a moment he did not seem to know what to do with the roll of papyrus. Then he signalled to a slave boy and handed it over to him, telling him to bring it to his chamber. He turned and took a kylix from a passing tray—the perfect Tegean aristocrat rather than the respectful young Spartiate, Chilon noted with a twinge of discouragement.

"Keep in mind," Chilon found himself saying, unable to give up so easily, "that much of your present status results from the fact that Tegea was negotiating with Lacedaemon. You have been a useful go-between. Under normal circumstances, your influence would not be so great."

Lysandridas considered Chilon for a moment and answered carefully, "No doubt you're right, but at least I *am* respected."

"Are you so sure of that? Are you respected for yourself, or because you are Antyllus' son? What happens when Antyllus falls from favour with the Tegean Assembly?"

"I don't need any lectures on the fickleness of Assemblies," Lysandridas told him coldly.

"Then you know the day will come when it remembers you were born abroad and came here as an invader. Your years of slavery will be remembered."

"No more than in Sparta. Here or there, it is the same."

"I don't deny you have enemies at home—but you should have heard the debate. Hardly anyone dared raise his voice against you, and those who did were shouted down and hissed to silence."

"Ah, what an Olympic triumph will do," Lysandridas remarked with a cynical smile.

"Do you really think that's all it was?"

"What else?"

"The fact that you sent Leonis with a message about Tegea's vulnerability, for example. Many saw that as an indication of your true loyalty."

Lysandridas smiled cynically, knowing that he had sent the message to help Antyllus and Tegea as much as Lacedaemon.

"And then Cassandra spoke for you," Chilon continued. "She came to the Assembly especially to do it."

That, at last, took Lysandridas by surprise. "But I did nothing for her."

"You underestimate her. Cassandra is an Agiad princess. She was suckled on political intrigue with her mother's milk. She understands diplomacy at least as well as if not better than her brother. Cassandra insisted that you influenced not only Ambelos but Harmatides himself to moderation."

"She thinks I did that?!" Lysandridas asked incredulously. "I had no influence on him at all!" he protested.

"When Harmatides took Cassandra and the others captive, he was already looking for some means of bargaining for peace. He did not want to provoke; he wanted leverage. Cassandra argued that Harmatides was looking for a compromise because he had been convinced by you that not all Spartans were militant aggressors.

"And then she reminded the Assembly that she, too, had been a slave— exactly like you had been, a captive at the mercy of the victor. 'Would you now rob me of my citizenship and throw me back onto the mercy of the men who humiliated and insulted me?' When someone shouted out that you had accepted freedom and adoption, Cassandra had asked with just the right touch of pathos, 'Do you think I would have turned them down?' She paused and let her words sink in before continuing: 'If I had believed— as Lysandridas believed—that my city *and my family*'—and she looked significantly at her brother as she said this— 'had abandoned me, then I would have *gratefully* taken freedom and marriage to any Tegean nobleman kind enough to offer it to me!' She was brilliant," Chilon declared, his voice and face reflecting his unmitigated admiration of the woman. He added, "She is fragile, and her voice was so frail that the men at the back could hardly hear her. They had to stand particularly still and strain their ears, which made the silence and tension all the greater. 'You claim to love freedom,' she challenged the liberators of Tegea, 'but think so little of it that you expect a young man to scorn it? You claim to be peers, but you would look down on one of your fellows who did only what you would have done yourselves? You claim to honour courage, but you fled from Tegea like a pack of jackals while Lysandridas and the Guard tried to prevent the Tegean cavalry from pursuing you. And you dare to *blame* him for accepting Tegean citizenship when he thought you left him in chains?' Believe me, she did not need to continue. The shouts for your rehabilitation started immediately."

Lysandridas was still shaking his head, confused. "But she hardly knows me."

Chilon shrugged. "You impressed her deeply in the few encounters you had. Remember, after the rape of Polyxena, she knew that negotiations had broken down, and you were the first shimmer of hope. And again, after your victory at Olympia, you represented hope for rapid release. But do not underestimate your wife, either. Cassandra thinks highly of Leonis. When she heard that Leonis was trying to run your kleros and look after your father and maintain the town house, she sent a trained medic to look after your father."

"Is he that ill?" Lysandridas asked sharply, and Chilon was taken aback.

"Lysandridas," he said softly and intently, looking him straight in the eye, "didn't Leonis tell you? He's had a second stroke. He's paralysed on the right side. He can't go anywhere without assistance. He can't even cut his meat or braid his hair."

Lysandridas blanched and murmured, "I didn't know. Truly, I didn't know. I—but surely my sister—"

"Your father refuses to have anything to do with her or Derykleides."

"But he spoke *for* me, even at that first Assembly."

"Too weakly, according to your father. It doesn't matter now. Cassandra has organised things so that Zoë can again concentrate on running the kleros, as she always did."

Zoë was nearing fifty, Lysandridas calculated. She was getting old and tired. She wouldn't be able to manage for much longer. But his father wouldn't live much longer, by the sound of things.

Chilon was watching him closely, and inwardly he cursed himself for a fool. Lysandridas was not a young man to be moved by threats of lost prestige and power or by promises of honours. Lysandridas had moved beyond that. "When you make your decision," Chilon said gently, laying his hand only briefly and lightly on Lysandridas' shoulder, "consider two things: first, who you *really* are, and second, where you will be *needed* most." Then with a smile he left Lysandridas.

Lysandridas stood sipping from his kylix, making no effort to join the others. Ambelos came over and touched his elbow. "Is everything all right?"

"Fine."

"You look upset," Ambelos insisted, not willing to be put off.

"I just learned that—but you knew it. Why didn't *you* tell me?"

"What?"

"That Teleklos is partially paralysed, that he is an invalid who needs constant care?"

Ambelos gazed at him innocently. "I thought you knew."

"How could I?!" Lysandridas responded defensively. "I haven't been in Lacedaemon since I was driven out five months ago!"

"But he *is* alive," Ambelos pointed out solemnly. "You can visit him, talk to him, and *tell* him what you feel for him, what he's meant to you." He was speaking of his own grief, and Lysandridas knew it, so he held his tongue.

Ambelos got hold of himself. "Come, let's join the others. We have much to celebrate."

Lysandridas followed Ambelos, but he did not join in the conversation. Instead he watched Ambelos joking with the Spartans as easily as the Tegeans, and for the first time he saw his resemblance to his father. He had Harmatides' charm, despite lacking his physical stature and strength. Indeed, Ambelos' charm was greater than his father's precisely *because* it was effective despite the disadvantages of his handicap. In another year or two, he would be handsome in his own way. With his father's wealth and the guilty feelings of the entire city favouring him, he would quickly make a political career, Lysandridas guessed.

He let his imagination run ahead of him. He imagined working together with Ambelos in the Tegean government. But no sooner did the thought form, than he imagined the Assembly calling him traitor and slave and hounding him from office or out of the city altogether. It didn't matter what he did; there would always be malcontents who felt he had not done enough, or had done the wrong thing, or had enriched himself, or whatever. There was nothing as ungrateful as "the people". Politics was a thankless profession.

But Antyllus loved it, he reflected, letting his eyes wander across the room to where Antyllus was discussing something earnestly with Anaxandridas, Chilon, and Pisirodos. Antyllus was a different man from the one who had travelled with him to Elis. He walked with new vigour, stood straighter, and spoke with elegant and yet dynamic gestures. His face was alive now as he explained something to the others, who nodded in apparent agreement.

Antyllus had discovered that he had dozens of things he wanted to do for Tegea, including the reconstruction of the main temple to Athena. To distract attention from the stolen bones of Orestes (which the Spartans stubbornly refused to return), he proposed a much grander, more elegant, and more modern temple in which the chains once worn by the Spartan captives could be displayed in remembrance of Tegea's great victory. When he made this suggestion at a small symposium, the Tegeans had looked nervously at Lysandridas, but Lysandridas had shrugged. "As long as they're hanging in a temple and not on my ankles, I can live with it." The proposal had met with enthusiasm in the Tegean Assembly, and the funds were appropriated immediately. Antyllus had announced an architectural contest, and architects from all over Hellas were expected to participate. Despite this and other civic projects, Antyllus had not neglected the commissioning of a monument to be erected at Olympia.

Lysandridas' gaze returned to his young friend, thinking how Ambelos now turned to Antyllus for advice in almost everything. Whether he was unsure of how to pursue Phaeax and Polyphom (who had both escaped death and capture), or whether he should rebuild his father's factory, or repair or sell his house, he asked Antyllus for guidance. He had even gone so far as to ask Antyllus if he might marry Timosa.

Antyllus had been astonished. "But you're not yet nineteen!"

"I know, but I want to found a family."

"Lacedaemonian customs have turned your head!" Antyllus had insisted with a glance toward Lysandridas. But then he had laughed, shaken his head in bemusement, and agreed to talk to Empedokles about it.

Lysandridas recognised Ambelos' desire to be bound to Antyllus and Lysandridas by bonds of kinship. Ambelos was an orphan in a city where the mob had murdered his father. He needed ties of kinship to protect him, no matter how great his charm or his wealth. A bond with Antyllus' family, particularly with the solid and respected Empedokles, was a shrewd move.

Suddenly Lysandridas felt naive and provincial. Here was Ambelos at eighteen marrying for political advantage, while at twenty-two he himself had been interested only in a pretty face and an eager bedmate.

Chilon's question came back to him: where was he needed most?

Nowhere, came the brutally honest answer. Antyllus had his Olympic victory, and he certainly didn't need the advice of a younger, politically inexperienced man now that the negotiations with Lacedaemon were successfully concluded. He remembered how Antyllus had tried to exclude him from politics before the crisis.

But in Lacedaemon they would never entrust him with an elective office, not after calling him traitor and exiling him. Would they?

He looked questioning at the other ephor, Epicydes, then at King Anaxandridas and finally the new Guard Commander, Callicrates. Anaxandridas caught his eye and came over smiling. "Agis asked me to tell you that the team is awaiting you."

"Too late."

"What do you mean? They're young. They stand a chance at the 57th Games. Meanwhile, Nemea is only a year away, and Delphi two."

"Thank him for me," Lysandridas answered ambiguously, and Anaxandridas withdrew, puzzled.

In the course of the evening, the other members of the Spartan delegation sought him out one by one. Each tried in his own way to convince him to return to Lacedaemon. Lysandridas wondered if Chilon had put them up to it, or merely reported that Lysandridas was undecided.

Last came the Guard commander. "Chilon tells us you are reluctant to return to Lacedaemon."

Lysandridas nodded.

"Why?"

"I wonder if it is wise to trust an invitation from a body that can change its mind so rapidly. What do you think?"

"In Sparta it is not family or wealth that determines who rules, but character. I have the impression yours has been tempered like iron— hot and cold and with the blows of the anvil. I would rather trust my future to an iron sword than a bronze one. I don't think I'm alone in that opinion."

"Thank you."

Callicrates nodded and withdrew again.

Lysandridas slipped away from the symposium. As he crossed the formal courtyard, the sound of voices spilling from the hall gradually grew dim. The fountain spluttered in the cool night air, and at last he could hear the crickets cheeping in the surrounding orchards. The torches around the house had been extinguished or gone out, and he could see the stars against the night sky over the atrium.

The sound of someone behind him made him turn sharply. Leonis separated herself from the columns of the peristyle to come and stand beside him. She was very obviously pregnant now, and walked with an alien hesitancy. Her hair was free and she was barefoot. "Can't you sleep?" he asked, concerned.

Leonis had returned with Chilon and the other delegates the day before. She had come here at once, and so Lysandridas found her waiting for him when he came back from the city yesterday evening. They had been up all night exchanging news. Why hadn't she told him about his father? He opened his mouth to ask, but she laid her head on his arm and entwined her fingers in his. "I couldn't sleep knowing you were so near. I kept hoping you'd come early. I've missed you so much."

Lysandridas put his arm around her. "I thought you had lots of other admirers in Sparta."

Leonis frowned and stiffened. "What do I want with men who scorned me when I was a maiden!? Why do most men only take note of a woman when she makes a display of herself?"

Lysandridas couldn't help laughing, but he held her tighter and kissed the top of her head to conciliate her at the same time. "I'm glad they never took any note of you before. Think what it would have meant for me to return and find I had lost not only the bride of my bedtime fantasies, but the wife of my heart as well."

"Hermione made a terrible scene when Thessalos got home," Leonis couldn't resist reporting. "She said in front of dozens of witnesses that she regretted giving you up for him."

"The bitch! She never cared for anything but the reflected glory of Olympic ribbons!" Lysandridas was angry for his friend's sake. He sincerely felt sorry for Thessalos. Thessalos deserved better than Hermione. But then he noted that Leonis was shivering, and remarking on it, he turned and took her back into their chamber.

Leonis climbed onto the bed but remained sitting, the covers around her shoulders, while Lysandridas undressed. She watched Lysandridas' every move, full of awe at the sight of him in the moonlight and the thought that he belonged to her. "Lysandridas?" she ventured timidly. "We will go home now, won't we?"

He came and climbed into the bed beside her, gently pushing her onto her back and lying on his side to look down into her face. Her eyes were large and glittering, and he could see the fear in them. She was afraid he wouldn't return. "You would be very unhappy if I decided to stay here, wouldn't you?"

She swallowed and her eyes searched his face. "Yes—but I want *you* to be happy, too, Lysandridas. I couldn't be happy if you weren't. But Agis says he'll give you the team—"

Lysandridas hushed her with a finger to her lips. "I know; but if I ever drive at Olympia again, it will be with my own team. I'm not just a charioteer, Leonis."

"Of course not. I didn't mean that. I—"

He kissed her gently. "I know. You don't have to explain." He stroked the hair from her forehead and the side of her cheeks with the back of his hand. He thought of the way she'd told Hermione off in the agora, and the way she'd ridden in a short chiton to the Horse Temple. He imagined how she must have looked after galloping headlong for the Lacedaemonian border. Her timidity now was a sharp, disturbing contrast. It reminded him of her first weeks here, before he talked Antyllus into letting her drive. Whatever else he was, he was Leonis' husband, he reminded himself; and what kind of husband would he be if he condemned her knowingly and willingly to a lifetime of unhappiness?

He would also soon be a father. His hand went to Leonis' swollen belly. "I'm sorry I put you and our child at risk with that ride to Lacedaemon."

"But I'm not!" She sat up sharply. "Besides, you didn't know yet. I hadn't told you, but I knew, and I knew it was a risk worth taking."

"Why?"

"I—I thought it would enable us to go home," she admitted, dropping her lids over her eyes in embarrassment.

"Why didn't you tell me about Teleklos?"

She opened her eyes again and gazed at him earnestly. "He didn't want me to. He—he thinks the Gods are punishing him for what he did to you."

Lysandridas sighed. How often did he have to tell his father it was his *own* fault that he had not been ransomed?

"You look tired," he told his wife as he pulled her back down beside him. "Try to sleep, and we can talk again in the morning." She snuggled down in his arms, her head on his chest, and she kissed his naked breast. "I love you, Lysandridas."

He kissed her hair and squeezed her, and then closed his own eyes. He lay listening to her breathing, feeling her breath on his chest and the warmth of her soft body next to him. He shifted his free hand to lay it on her belly, and she smiled and moved his hand to a different spot.

A terrible thought came to him. What if she carried a girl child in her belly? How could he raise a daughter in Tegea? How could he confine Leonis' child to live a life alien to the sun and the wind and the strength or fleetness of her own body? And did he want to raise a son to privilege and wealth rather than self-reliance and self-discipline? Did he want a son who had never known the discipline of the agoge? The thrills of the "wild time"—or, yes, the bitter lesson of "the pits"? Did he want to one day have a son like Kapaneos?

He would be proud to have a son like Ambelos, he countered. And there were many fine young Tegeans in the cavalry.

But did he want a daughter like Timosa? Or worse, a daughter like Leonis, who was caged by Tegean custom? Chained not by iron, but by prejudice and convention?

In his imagination, he felt again the chains they had put on him before he even left the hospital. He felt them biting into his ankles and rubbing the skin raw as he tried to hobble forward, still half-crippled from the wound to his thigh and both dizzy and nauseous from the blow to his head. He remembered the laughter and the mocking of the strangers around him.

"Come to measure out the Tegean plain, are you?" they jeered. "Come to dance, did you? Go on! Dance!" they had ordered cruelly. "Show us your dancing feet!"

He remembered the sense of nakedness, so different from the nakedness of the gymnasium or the ball games or the running fields. He had worn a loincloth, after all, and his head had been bandaged. But he had stood with his ankles and wrists in chains, and they had surrounded him with their sneering, leering faces, and he had been utterly defenceless. He had been forced to stumble about in his chains to their clapping hands.

Lysandridas was not a fool. He knew that Spartans had never been gentle to their prisoners. Such rituals of cruelty had nothing to do with nationality. But was he going to raise his children in the city where the very chains they had put upon his legs were displayed as trophies? Was he supposed to sacrifice to Athena in thanks for those chains? He understood Antyllus' motivation. He recognised the political expediency of distracting attention from Orestes' bones. But did he have to live with it? Did he want his sons to gloat over the heroism of their "forefathers" in chaining Spartiate guardsmen? Did he want sons who thought it was more desirable to drive a chariot to victory at Olympia than to belong to the Guard? Did he want sons who didn't even know what it meant to *be* a Guardsman?

And wouldn't the day come when someone remembered—not silently in his mind or privately in his home, but publicly and officially—that Lysandridas had no right to enjoy Tegean citizenship? Either he was a freeborn Greek, but of Spartiate parents, or he was a freedman of Tegea. Either way, the reforms just passed excluded him from Tegean citizenship. Everyone was politely ignoring that fact at the moment, because it was expedient to ignore it for now. But as Chilon predicted, the day would certainly come when Antyllus' popularity waned, for whatever reason. When that happened and Antyllus' enemies started looking for ways to discredit and attack him, what could be simpler than pointing out that his "son" was not even a citizen?

Lysandridas' loyalty had always been to Antyllus, not Tegea, he realised. And Antyllus didn't need him. Antyllus had his Olympic victory, and a reason for living. He hardly had time for his horses or Lysandridas any more. When he wasn't busy with public affairs, he was helping Ambelos. Eventually, Antyllus would notice that his adopted son was only a political liability.

As he realised this, Lysandridas knew he would return to Sparta. He felt no joy—rather, trepidation—but he was glad for Leonis' sake. He stroked her sleeping body, and she stirred and nuzzled closer. He was no longer free to do what suited him, he reminded himself, feeling her belly. But then he had never really been free—except when he had been a quarry slave who welcomed death. Wasn't life worth more than that kind of freedom?

And perhaps Chilon was right when he said that a self-disciplined man could find hope even in a dismal situation. If he was half the man Chilon thought he was, then he had to hope that he could be of some use to his father, his comrades, and his city.

Knowing who he was, Lysandridas took a deep breath and sank into a deep, comfortable sleep.

Historical Note

Chilon and the Spartan kings are the only historical figures in this novel. Chilon, who lived in the mid-6th century BC, was one of the "seven wise men" of the Ancient Greeks. He was generally counted among the "philosophers", although he was also a poet, statesman, and ephor. In fact, he is credited with having turned the previously ceremonial office of "ephor" into a politically powerful instrument to check the power of the Spartan kings. He was respected throughout the Greek world for his opposition to tyranny and his support for democracy and the "common man". He was also—whether typical for Sparta or not—an advocate of education for women. His daughter Chilonis was one of the recorded disciples of the philosopher Pythagoras. The degree to which he was respected in Sparta can be measured by the fact that two of his granddaughters married Spartan kings, one from each of the two royal families, and by the fact that a monument was erected to him after his death where he appears by the side of his wife.

King Anaxandridas was known to have been Chilon's protégé, and his second wife was one of Chilon's granddaughters.

The history of Tegea is mostly blank; even the known "facts" are of dubious certainty. The timing of events is particularly difficult to determine, and the Tegean constitution and laws are unrecorded. The oracles cited are, however, quoted in ancient sources, and the chains of the Spartan captives could still be seen hanging in the Temple of the Alean Athena in the 2nd century AD. The removal of Orestes' bones to Sparta is also part of the ancient history of both Tegea and Sparta. A temple to house the bones was built on the agora in Sparta.

The dating of the attempted Spartan invasion of Tegea, which ended instead in the enslavement of many Spartiates, is uncertain. On the other hand, it is certain that in the mid-6th century King Anaxandridas, Chilon's young protégé, won a decisive victory over Tegea. Sparta—because of the influence of Chilon, historians believe—in contrast to previous practice, chose not to annex Tegean territory and reduce the population to helot status, but signed instead a mutual defence treaty. Ancient sources say that this treaty followed a "long" period of hostility and "indecisive" warfare. It is therefore logical to assume that the Spartan defeat and Spartan victory occurred during the same conflict. The bilateral treaty with Tegea became the prototype for future treaties that Lacedaemon signed with nearly all the city-states of the Peloponnese, and so became the basis of what was later known as the Peloponnesian League.

Although there is no recorded Tegean tyrant, neither Harmatides nor Onimastros, the second half of the 6th century BC is the period in which Sparta was credited with eliminating a series of tyrants. Given the many gaps and uncertainties in Tegean history, the invention of a Tegean tyrant seemed reasonable.

Spartan successes at the Olympic Games are well recorded, and in later centuries they were particularly strong in equestrian events. It was a Spartan, Kyniska, who became the first woman ever to win an Olympic event – by owning the winning chariot.

Glossary of Greek Terms

Agoge
: The Spartan public school attended by all boys from the ages of seven through twenty, and by girls for a shorter period—probably from seven until they had their first period. It was infamous throughout Greece for its harshness, discipline, and austerity. The children lived in barracks and were organised into "herds" or "packs" with elected leaders. Their instructors were the twenty-year-old youths on the brink of citizenship, the eirenes.

Andron
: The chamber in a private house where symposia were held. It was often provided with permanent benches or shelves built against the walls for the guests to recline upon.

Chiton
: The basic undergarment worn by both men and women. It could be long or short, belted or unbelted, and bound at one or both shoulders, whereas slaves seem more likely to have worn it clasped only on one shoulder.

Eirene
: A Spartan youth aged twenty, on the brink of citizenship.

Ephors
: Executives of the Spartan government elected from among the citizen body. Any citizen could be elected ephor, but no citizen could serve in this

	capacity for longer than one term. The ephors served for just one year each.
Gerousia	Council of Elders in Sparta. This body consisted of 28 elected members and the two kings. The elected members had to have attained the age of sixty, and were then elected for life. Although this institution was highly praised by commentators from other part of Greece, who saw in the Council of Elders a check upon the fickleness of the Assembly, the senility of some Council members and the "notorious" timidity of the Council were a source of frustration for younger Spartans.
Helots	The rural population of Lacedaemon, who were descendants of the original settlers of the area. Helots were not slaves. They could not be bought and sold. They were, however, similar to serfs in medieval Europe, as they were not free to leave Lacedaemon. Furthermore, they were required to give fifty per cent of what they produced to the Spartiate estate owners. (This was much less than for the slaves of other Greek city-states, who had to give up 100% of all they produced!) Much has been made of the fact that the Spartans—in at least one recorded incident, but by no means 'regularly', as some commentators assume—rounded up and killed the 'best' helots. The recorded incident dates to a period when increasing unrest among the population made rebellion a real threat, and the outrage of the commentators seems to ignore the fact that slaves in other Greek cities could be killed by their masters with impunity as well.
Himation	The long, rectangular wrap used by both men and women as an outer garment.
Hoplite	Greek heavy infantryman.
Hoplon	The round shield carried by a Greek heavy infantryman.
Lacedaemon	The correct designation of the Ancient Greek city-state of which Sparta was the capital. Lacedaemon consisted originally of only the Eurotas valley in

the Peloponnese, Laconia. In the late 8th century BC, the valley to the west, Messenia, was captured and remained part of Lacedaemon until the 4th century BC.

Lochos	The main unit of the Spartan army, variously compared to a regiment or a division.
Kryptea	The Spartan "secret police", made up of young citizens who were tasked with keeping rebellious helots under control.
Kylix	Drinking vessel with a low, shallow bowl on a short stem; these could be quite large, requiring two hands to hold, and were often passed around at a symposium.
Mastigophoroi	1) The assistants to the headmaster of the Spartan agoge, responsible for maintaining discipline among the boys attending the agoge. 2) Officials that helped keep order among the crowds at the Olympic Games.
Meleirene	A Spartan youth aged nineteen, two years from citizenship.
Perioikoi	Non-citizen residents of Lacedaemon. Like the helots, the perioikoi were descendants of the non-Greek native population of the area prior to the Dorian invasion of roughly 900 BC. The perioikoi enjoyed free status and ran their own affairs in their own towns and cities, but had no independent state, military, or foreign policy. The perioikoi—like the metics in other Greek cities—were required to pay taxes to the Lacedaemonian authorities. They also provided auxiliary troops to the Spartan army. Since Spartiates were prohibited from pursuing any profession or trade other than arms, the perioikoi had a (very lucrative) monopoly on all trade and manufacturing in Lacedaemon.
Spartiate	Full Spartan citizen; i.e., the legitimate son of a Spartan citizen, who has successfully completed

the agoge, served as an eirene, and been admitted
to the citizen body at the age of twenty-one.

Symposium

A dinner party among friends that often included
entertainment such as musicians, dancing girls, or
philosophical debate. Symposia were for men only;
the only women who attended were courtesans or
whores. Symposia were an aristocratic tradition,
and the costs of wine, food, and entertainment
were very high.

Syssitia

Spartan "messes" or "dinner clubs". Adult
Spartiates were all required to join one of the
syssitia at attaining citizenship at twenty-one, and
thereafter to dine at these messes. The existing
members of each syssitia had to vote unanimously
to admit an applicant. Recent research suggests
that membership in the various syssitia was based
more or less on family ties and clan relationships,
but this is not certain. They were not, however,
merely military messes based on military units,
and they were explicitly designed to encourage
men of different age cohorts to interact. Each
member was required to make set contributions
in kind (grain, wine, oil, etc.) and was expected to
make other gifts, particularly game, in accordance
with their means. Failure to pay the fees was
grounds for the loss of citizenship, and failure to
attend the meals without a "valid" excuse (such as
being out hunting) could result in fines or other
sanctions.

Paidonomos

Headmaster of the Spartan agoge.

Made in the USA
Lexington, KY
28 June 2012